ONE LAST THING

What Reviewers Say About
The Elite Operatives Series

"It has been a honey of a ride going from book one to book six [in the Elite Operatives Series]. The elaborately intricate, tense storylines, the extraordinary primary characters with their heart wrenching yet elevating love connections, and the pulsating multiple cliffhangers combine to produce a top of the line reading experience. Please, someone make a movie out of one or all of these books!"—*Rainbow Book Reviews*

"Okay, I admit it: I am a fan of adventure/spy/thriller mysteries and always have been. So of course I have been lured into the web of the Elite Operatives series because as a kid, I was always imagining myself in the male leads of the spy thrillers I read. Baldwin and Alexiou clearly had the same fantasy. [They] have established a formula for this series that works: short, staccato chapters set in different locales that unfurl the plot layer by layer and then they develop into solid chapters where the main characters…begin to reveal themselves. The authors manage to take two plot themes that have been done and done again, meld them, and turn them into a solid, convincing, compelling page-turner that is quite satisfying."—*Lambda Literary*

"Totally tense from nearly word one. [*The Gemini Deception*] has a good deal of twists and turns and one of the scariest villains I have ever come across. Hang on to your seat, it is not only going to be a totally bumpy ride, but the wildest and most engaging thriller I have ever read."—*Rainbow Book Reviews*

"Baldwin and Alexiou have written a barn burner of a thriller [in *Dying to Live*]. The reader is taken in from the first page to the last. The tension is maintained throughout the book with rare exception. Baldwin and Alexiou are defining the genre of romantic suspense within the lesbian genre with this series. You'll find yourself rushing to purchase the first three books in the series if you haven't already read them, or, if you have read them, wishing the authors would write the fifth in the series faster."—*Lambda Literary*

"Baldwin and Alexiou have given their fans a gripping read that's difficult to put down! *Dying to Live* has a complex plot with a pandemic created by an arch villain, and a rescue from Colombian guerrillas. This is a thoroughly enjoyable read, and I can't wait for their next adventure!"—*Just About Write*

"*Missing Lynx* puts the thrill in thriller. In true thriller style, Baldwin and Alexiou take their women around the globe…from Vienna, all around the U.S. Southwest, on to New York, down to some of the most dangerous parts of Mexico, on to China and Vietnam and back to the Southwest. Quite the wild ride. But that's what lends verisimilitude to this tale of the traffic in human beings. Lynx hooks up with a mercenary during her journey and that relationship sends a sizzle through the story that is palpable. Heroine and anti-heroine. Quite the chemistry. A dark, edgy, often grisly tale, *Missing Lynx* has the grit and pacing of a Bourne saga, but with highly engaging and thoroughly challenging female characters. Not for the faint hearted."—*Lambda Literary*

"Kim Baldwin & Xenia Alexiou just get better and better at coming up with tightly written thrillers with plenty of 'seat of the pants' action. *Missing Lynx* is a roller coaster ride into the seamier side of life and the bonds which bind humans into trying to better the world. This is a book which grips the reader until the final page!"—*Just About Write*

"Unexpected twists and turns, deadly action, complex characters and multiple subplots converge to make this book a gripping page turner. *Lethal Affairs* mixes political intrigue with romance, giving the reader an easy flowing and fast-moving story that never lets up. A must-read, even though it has been out for a while. *Thief of Always*, the duo's second, and equally good book in the Elite Operatives series, came out earlier this year."—*Curve Magazine*

Praise for *Dubbel Doelwit*,
the Dutch translation of *Lethal Affairs*:

"[*Lethal Affairs*] is a smoothly written action thriller which draws the reader into the life of special agent Domino. The plot surrounding Domino's secret mission is well constructed…the tension and emotional charge is built up to great heights, which makes it hard to put the book down. Equally admirable is the way in which the characters are given dimension. In most action-oriented (intrigue) fiction you won't find in-depth psychological portraits, but because of striking details, the characters become very real. As a cherry on top, the authors gift you a few sensual scenes which will leave you breathless. It's nice to know that [*Lethal Affairs*] is but the first entry in the Elite Operative Series."—The Flemish Magazine *ZIZO*

By the Authors: The Elite Operatives Series

Lethal Affairs

Thief of Always

Missing Lynx

Dying to Live

Demons are Forever

The Gemini Deception

One Last Thing

By Kim Baldwin

Hunter's Pursuit

Force of Nature

Whitewater Rendezvous

Flight Risk

Focus of Desire

Breaking the Ice

High Impact

Taken by Storm

ONE LAST THING

by
Kim Baldwin &
Xenia Alexiou

2015

ONE LAST THING

© 2015 By Kim Baldwin & Xenia Alexiou. All Rights Reserved.

ISBN 13: 978-1-62639-230-4

This Trade Paperback Original Is Published By
Bold Strokes Books, Inc.
P.O. Box 249
Valley Falls, NY 12185

First Edition: January 2015

Credits
Editor: Shelley Thrasher
Production Design: Stacia Seaman
Cover Design by Sheri (graphicartist2020@hotmail.com)

Acknowledgments

The authors wish to thank all the talented women at Bold Strokes Books for making this book and the entire Elite Operatives Series possible. Radclyffe, for her vision, faith in us, and example. Editor Shelley Thrasher, your insightful editing of this book is deeply appreciated. Jennifer Knight, for invaluable insights into how to craft a series. Graphic artist Sheri for another amazing cover. Connie Ward, BSB publicist and first-reader extraordinaire, and all of the other support staff who work behind the scenes to make each BSB book an exceptional read.

We'd also like to thank our dear friend and first-reader Jenny Harmon for your invaluable feedback and insights. And finally, to the readers who encourage us by buying our books, showing up for personal appearances and for taking the time to email us. Thank you so much.

My dear friend Xenia: working with you on the Elite Operatives Series—helping to bring these wonderful stories of yours to readers—has been one of the most fun and rewarding endeavors I've ever undertaken, and I'll long cherish the countless happy memories of writing, laughing, reading, and signing together. Here's hoping we do many more projects together.

For Marty, my family for more than forty years, my deep appreciation for taking such good care of my home and cats while I'm away. And thanks to my brother Tom, for always saying yes when I need a ride to the airport.

Kim Baldwin 2015

Now that all is said and done, I can conclude that there are too many people to thank and too many circumstances to mention that inspired me to write this series.

For all those who stood by me, supported me and believed in me, whether relatives, friends, the BSB family, I thank you all.

But most of all I thank the readers. If these books were able to take you away from your troubles, give you a few hours of entertainment and make your mind travel, then I am proud to say that it's because of you that I can consider myself an author.

Xenia Alexiou 2015

To Kim
Your faith in me has given me the chance to do
what I truly love and to truly love what I do.
You are a friend, confidante, solid shoulder, motivator,
and my inspiration.
S'up?

Xenia

"A man travels the world over in search of what he needs and returns home to find it."

—George Moore

PROLOGUE

Nazareth, Galilee,
A.D. 15

"Where do you go, my son?" the woman asked the youth, who was making a habit in recent days of disappearing for hours after lunch into the hills above the city. Not that he ever shirked his chores, which were considerable now that he'd grown into manhood and stood a full hand taller than she. But though he remained ever diligent about his duties, tending to their animals, fetching water from the well, and honing his carpentry skills as apprentice to his father, this newfound reticence was worrying.

"I will tell you all, and soon," he promised her, "perhaps even this evening." As though sensing her concern, he kissed her on the cheek and gave her a reassuring smile before he departed with a heavy goatskin of water slung over one shoulder.

She waited several seconds, then rose from her chair by the hearth and crept to the doorway, more curious than ever to know what he was up to. Rarely had she seen such mischief in his dark eyes. Perhaps she would follow him and watch him from a distance. Could it be that he was meeting a girl, away from her parents' prying eyes? He was of that age, to be sure; most in their village were expected to take a wife by eighteen, though he'd as yet shown little interest in such things.

He was not in sight, either on the pitted road to the village or the hillside opposite, which had to mean he was in the rear outbuilding that served a dual purpose as his father's workshop and the family stable. She reached the corner of their one-room home just in time to see him emerge from the doorway with something in his hands—fairly large and rectangular in shape and concealed in a dirty scrap of linen. Whatever it was, he'd taken great care to hide it from her and take advantage of the fact that his father was away in Tiberias on business. This deliberate secrecy only increased her sense of alarm. He'd always been such an open, guileless young man, devoted to her and a rapt pupil of the Torah and tenets of their Jewish traditions. And he had a maturity that few his age could match.

Should she confront him now? Demand to see what he was hiding from her? She watched him stride purposefully toward the rolling hills that towered over the city, his sandals kicking up a wake of fine dust. One more day, she decided. She would keep the faith a while longer.

Throughout the rest of the afternoon, as she baked bread for the week ahead, she returned to the doorway time and again to see if she could catch a glimpse of his return. Finally, his lean figure materialized on the distant slope, hurrying toward her. He was much later than usual—it was nearly dinnertime and dusk was fast approaching—and by the time he reached the house, he was out of breath.

"Forgive me, Mother. I wanted so to finish that I lost track of the time." When he set the empty goatskin flask and canvas bag on the table, she received her first clue about what he'd been up to. The distinctive sound of metal against metal from the bag told her he'd taken along his woodworking tools.

"Finish?"

He held out the linen parcel, watching her expectantly. "I made you something. I hope you like it."

"I am certain I will, my son." Over the years, he'd crafted a myriad of gifts for her: small pottery jars and clay animal figurines, mostly. But the weight of this offering was much more substantial. She smoothed one hand lightly over the linen covering, fingers tracing the curves and depressions in the object beneath. A carving of some kind. Until now, he'd confined his carpentry skills to the usual furniture and building materials. She began to unwrap it.

"Wait! Not yet!" He ignited a thin reed from the fireplace and lit one of the oil lamps to help her see better in the fading twilight.

She folded back the linen and tilted the tablet of wood toward the light, gasping in delight when she saw what it was. "Oh, my!"

"Do you like it?"

He'd carved a portrait of her in quiet repose, capturing well the nuances of her high cheekbones, thin nose, oval chin. Even the unusual arch of her eyebrows. Though somewhat crudely done, it clearly revealed the affection of the artist for his subject. And he'd painstakingly sanded the hardwood until it was as smooth as pebbles on a beach.

"It is wonderful, my son. A gift that I will treasure always." She clasped it to her heart. "You are an artist with your chisels."

He laughed. "I think you would not have said the same about my first try. Or second. But I am very happy you like it."

❖

Halkidiki, Greece
June 15, 2014

Konstantinos "Kostas" Lykourgos was grateful that his guest, Theodora Rothschild, wasn't an early riser. He didn't dare offend the woman—he needed her help, and he'd heard stories of how ruthless she could be over the most minor perceived infractions—but he cherished the opportunity for a quiet breakfast alone with Ariadne. He'd missed his daughter terribly while she was away at Oxford, then soon gone again for several more weeks island-hopping with her friends. The time they had together recently was too often scheduled time, devoted to business, but being on the yacht was helping to change that.

His family loved the sleek, long Fincantiere superyacht, the largest ever built in Italy, nearly as much as he did. A floating palace, the *Pegasus* had seven decks, two helicopter landing pads, a fifty-foot indoor seawater swimming pool, and storage for a large submarine, not to mention the latest state-of-the-art technological advancements.

And the yacht's huge ultra-luxurious interior was more impressive than any five-star hotel. Twelve elite cabins could accommodate twenty-four guests in extreme comfort, while additional living space below housed the ship's fifty-two-person crew. A theater, spa, wine cellar, and other specialty areas were all housed within a ship larger than a football field.

Not that such luxury could easily impress his current visitor. Kostas might have billions from his shipping empire, but Rothschild was a powerful businesswoman in her own right, accruing many millions annually from her legal and illegal enterprises. And he'd heard that TQ, or The Broker, as she was more commonly known, had an impressive and priceless collection of stolen artifacts and treasures from around the world.

"When are your friends coming?" he asked his daughter as a pair of stewards poured them more fresh-squeezed orange juice and strong Greek coffee. Around them, side tables with freshly pressed linen tablecloths held the type of fare the family enjoyed: fresh fruit, cheeses, croissants, and honeyed yogurt. His guest preferred a more American-style breakfast, so sterling-silver warming trays had also been set up nearby, awaiting the eggs Benedict, Florentine crepes, and other dishes she'd requested.

The other members of his family were also aboard the yacht, but both were sleeping in this morning. His wife Christine had been up late again playing *biriba* with her friends, and his son Nikolaos had partied with his twenty or so young guests until the wee hours. Kostas was grateful that the lounge and onboard casino were so far from the guest quarters there was no chance the noise would disturb Rothschild.

"Don't worry. I plan to leave you entirely on your own today, as you requested," Ariadne replied as she reached for another croissant. "Though I still wish you'd tell me what possible business you could have with that woman and why you wish to take this meeting alone."

He sought an answer that would satisfy her. Ariadne was exceptionally bright and perceptive, and he had been including her in all major business decisions since her recent graduation. "It's not necessary, that's all. A minor affair. I know you haven't warmed up to her, and it's too splendid a day not to take advantage of it with your friends."

In that respect, he wished that he, too, could do nothing more today than enjoy the perfect weather and splendid panoramic views as they cruised the rich blue waters of the Aegean. But if he wished to spend many more years with his loved ones, he had to strike a deal with the devil.

As though on cue, his guest headed toward them, dressed in a flowing printed kaftan and with a broad sun hat concealing most of her perfectly coiffed white hair. Rothschild was not unattractive for a middle-aged woman. In fact, many men would consider her beautiful, but Kostas found her coal-black eyes disconcerting.

"*Kalimera*, Theodora." He stood and pulled out a chair for her. "I hope you slept well."

"Good morning." Rothschild looked from Kostas to Ariadne.

"I was just leaving," his daughter replied as she got up. Her English was as perfect as his, but she spoke it with a very slight British accent from her years at Oxford. "Enjoy your morning. My friends will be picking me up shortly." She kissed her father's head and disappeared inside.

"May I assume the promised land isn't far off?" Rothschild asked as a steward poured her coffee.

When he'd invited The Broker aboard his yacht, Kostas had told her only that he wished to discuss an important business proposition. And so far, he'd continued to sidestep her urgings for particulars with the promise that all would be revealed by today's destination. "Agio Oros," he replied. "Mount Athos. The most splendid view in Halkidiki, and home to some of the world's most magnificent ancient treasures." The description received her rapt attention, as he knew it would.

"What kind of treasures?" she asked.

"There are twenty monasteries on the Holy Mountain," he said, "the oldest dating back more than a thousand years. They contain an abundance of medieval art, richly drawn icons, ancient manuscripts, and religious objects such as chalices, holy relics, and elaborate codices. Some of the icons are believed to work miracles. An effort to catalogue and preserve the treasures has been under way for some thirty years or more, but the sheer magnitude of the collection is so vast that it will take many more decades to complete."

"I can't wait to see some of them," Rothschild replied.

"That will be impossible, I'm afraid." Kostas frowned apologetically. "Women are prohibited from entering the mountain. Even for men, it is difficult and requires a special visa, signed by four of the secretaries of the leading monasteries. Although part of the Greek state, Agio Oros is self-governed, with its own rules."

"Surely an exception can be made." Rothschild sipped her coffee. "We merely need to provide the good monks with the proper incentive."

Kostas laughed. "I have heard that you do not take no for an answer, Theodora. But I assure you, even my money can't get you in."

"I doubt there's anything money can't do, but that aside, why are you taking me to a place I'm not allowed to enter?" She was clearly irritated. Kostas suspected she was not able to immediately obtain whatever she desired on very few occasions.

"Come." He extended his hand. "We're getting close now. Let me show you."

They started forward but were momentarily distracted by the approach of a much smaller but also luxurious yacht.

"Ariadne, your friends are here," he called out.

His daughter reemerged from below, wearing a new turquoise bikini that matched her eyes. Not for the first time, he marveled at what a beautiful young woman she'd become.

"Watch yourself, Father. I don't trust her," Ariadne told him in Greek. She paused momentarily to give their guest an icy glare before making her way to the lower-deck stairs. From there, she jumped into the water and swam to the waiting yacht, where a group of young women waited for her.

"She is my most precious achievement," Kostas said. A coughing fit came on, and he did his best to stifle it with his napkin.

"She looks very much like you," Rothschild replied.

"Only on the outside. She's sharper and tougher than I'll ever be. She's already thriving in the company."

"Good for her." Rothschild shrugged. "Now, back to what interests me."

He led her forward, six levels up via elevator, to the sundeck. There they had a 360-degree view, but the sight ahead demanded their full attention.

Mount Athos rose dramatically from the sea, a mammoth, sharp-peaked pinnacle that appeared a deep, dark blue against the azure Aegean. A magnificent spectacle all on its own, it made the sight of a lifetime with the addition of the sprawling monastery perched atop an enormous stone cliff just ahead. It towered over them, more than a thousand feet in the air.

"Once, three hundred monasteries existed on the Holy Mountain," he told her. "This is the Simonopetra Monastery, or Simon's Rock. It was founded in the thirteenth century by Simon the Athonite and is still in use. Its choir is world renowned."

"Breathtaking."

"Indeed."

He could have spent the entire day absorbed by the grandeur of the sight, but even the magnificence of the monastery was not enough to keep Rothschild's mind off business for very long.

"Tell me why we're here," she said, not bothering to hide her growing impatience.

"This sacred and very secretive monastery possesses some of the world's most priceless antiquities."

"You mentioned."

"Everyone knows, or at least suspects, that the monastery hides and protects artifacts the world has never heard of nor considers missing."

"Yes, yes," Rothschild replied eagerly. "I own similar relics."

"A high-ranking monk of another monastery is a close friend who has had the honor of acquainting himself with some of these missing relics."

She turned her full attention to him, her black eyes boring into his with interest and excitement. "Which? I'm sure I've heard of them."

"A solid-gold icon that dates back to the twelfth century," he replied, "and depicts—"

"The *Theotokos!*" She nearly yelped. "The mother of Christ."

He nodded and tried not to show his surprise. "Not many are aware of the existence of this icon."

"I'm not many."

"Are you a religious woman, Theodora?"

"Don't be ridiculous," she replied. "Such asinine beliefs are for the simple masses."

"I happen to have such asinine beliefs," he said quietly, "but that's another matter."

"One I'm sure will bore me."

"It is said that, aside from being priceless, the icon possesses the power to heal."

"Pish posh. But if the idea thrills you…" She shrugged.

"I want that icon," he said.

"May I ask why? I'm sure you have plenty of priceless goods already decorating your walls or in a safety-deposit box."

"I'm ill," he replied. "And the best doctors in the world can't do anything more than they already have."

"And you think the icon will heal you."

"I do, Theodora."

"How quaint."

"I'm willing to pay five hundred million euros."

Rothschild laughed. "I hardly think money will convince these God-fearing pathological worshippers."

"No one, Theodora, is immune to money, as you know. These people, however, cover their greed very convincingly."

"If you think you can bribe the robes, I'm sure the amount you mentioned will do the trick, especially since this country's economy is beyond repair."

He had thought the same. Money had always paved the way for whatever he sought, and these days in Greece you could get virtually anything for a few euros. Bribery had enabled him to bypass the usual red tape and visit the Holy Mountain on several occasions to pray before another miraculous icon, but no monk he'd chatted with would even acknowledge the existence of the *Theotokos*. Legend had it that the icon's healing properties would work only if one of pure faith touched the relic. "The monks will never feel the economic or social hit Greece has taken. They are a country of their own, and a very wealthy one at that, very much like the Vatican. The amount I mentioned is for you."

Rothschild pulled at the brim of her sun hat to shield her eyes from the glare. "Do explain," she said coquettishly.

"Your track record of acquisitions speaks for itself. If anyone can…get it, it's you." Kostas didn't dare resort to violence to obtain the icon. He feared such a move would prevent any chance that the Virgin Mother would bless and heal him. But Rothschild's methods of persuasion had no boundaries.

"I'm flattered that you estimate me accordingly, but my reputation is based on the fact I have always known the precise location of the object I'm after."

"I know where they hide it," he said.

"You what?"

"You have a renowned reputation in very private circles for trading in appropriated, priceless artifacts. I can lead you to it. In return, I will give you—"

But Rothschild had apparently heard enough. "We have a deal," she said, staring up at the monastery with an almost feral smile of anticipation.

CHAPTER ONE

Agio Oros, Halkidiki
Twelve days later

Father Antonis paced along the rocky shore beneath the monastery, peering out into the darkness. Despite the cooling breeze, his heavy black cassock clung to his upper torso, drenched in the sweat of his growing anxiety. Would he go to hell for this? In his panic to save his parents and sister from bankruptcy, poverty, and the threat of death, Antonis had somehow found the courage to turn his back on the church that had been his home and refuge for more than two decades. But that courage had since abandoned him, and he wasn't at all certain he could go through with this.

A week ago, Antonis had gathered with other monks as the daily visitor ferry from Ouranoupolis landed at Dafni, the first stop on its journey southward along the peninsula. When one of the men getting off approached Antonis and asked him to act as guide through the Holy Mountain, he readily agreed. One of the duties his abbot had assigned to him was to share the history of Agio Oros with the one hundred Orthodox and ten non-Orthodox pilgrims permitted to visit each day. When he learned that the man was most interested in seeing the very monastery Antonis called home—Simonopetra—he considered their companionship for the day especially fortuitous, perhaps even of holy design. As one of the most senior members of the cliff-side monastic enclave, he could provide the best possible experience for the man.

But as they made their way south through the thick chestnut forest that dominated the peninsula, it quickly became apparent that the stranger was no ordinary pilgrim in search of religious enlightenment, nor a tourist interested in the mountain's history and wild beauty. The man asked none of the usual questions as they explored the first three monasteries they reached and appeared bored with the insights Antonis shared at each stop. Instead, he seemed oddly more preoccupied with the other visitors, secular laborers, and monks that they frequently encountered on their trek.

Antonis discovered the man's true motivation during their visit to Xenofontos, the fourth monastery on the march south. The monks living there were in vespers when they arrived and no other visitors were about, so it was as though they had the place to themselves.

As they strolled the grounds, the man started to talk to Antonis about family. *His* family. He casually offered more details about Antonis's life than even his brethren monks knew: particulars about his parents and sister, his past, and even the dire financial straits his family was battling that threatened to leave them homeless. Surprised, Antonis initially thought the man had been sent by a friend or family member, or was perhaps an old school chum he didn't recognize.

The truth was revealed when they reached a secluded shed by the gardens and the stranger pulled him roughly behind it, out of view of the monastery. He planned to give Antonis the generous sum of one hundred thousand euros to save his family, he informed the monk, and in return, Antonis would help him obtain the *Theotokos*.

Antonis couldn't hide his shock. Few outside the Holy Mountain even knew of the icon's existence, let alone that he was one of the five elder monks charged with its safekeeping. He pulled away and stammered that he had no knowledge of any such icon.

But the man clearly wasn't buying his denials. He reached into his coat and pulled out two photos of Antonis's family: an old Christmas picture taken when he was about five and another from an Easter gathering a few years later. "If I can get into your house while your mother is cooking, find the family albums, and leave unnoticed, can you fathom what else I can do in there and go unnoticed?" The stranger's menacing smirk was chilling. "Give me what I want, I'll give you money in return, and it's a win-win for all."

"But the icon, it's…" Antonis looked around in desperation, praying in vain for divine intervention. "I can't. Even if I wanted to."

"I'm sure you can find out where it's kept."

Antonis shook his head. "It's too well protected. You need both a code and a key, and there are cameras everywhere."

"You get me the key," the stranger replied, "and a map to the easiest way in, and I'll take care of the security system."

"You don't understand. Even then, it's...it's just impossible."

"What the hell does that even mean?"

"The icon can't leave the Holy Mountain. Bad things will come to whoever tries."

The man laughed. "You let me worry about that. The only bad thing you need to worry about is what I can do to your parents and sister." He held up the family pictures. "And besides," he shrugged, "think of what they'll be able to do with all that cash."

"I don't—"

"Listen, man, I don't care what choice you make." He tore the pictures into pieces and they fluttered to the ground. "I get paid either way. Murder, map. It's all the same to me." He reached into his pocket and pulled out a cell phone. "Here." He pressed it to Antonis's chest. "You're going to get a phone call in about..." He checked his watch. "Five minutes. Give your final answer to that person. Meanwhile, I'll be waiting for instructions, you know? Which direction to drive in— toward your family's home or mine."

"What person?"

"Just make sure you answer, 'cause if you don't, then..." He looked at the torn photos scattered on the cobblestones. "You get the picture."

The man walked away without looking back, and Antonis stood staring at the phone in his hand. "I can't do this..." he whispered to himself when it rang. It took two more rings before he could muster the courage to answer. "Hello?"

"Good morning, Father Antonis," a woman said. He'd never before heard such an undercurrent of menace in a simple greeting. "Do you speak English?"

"A little."

"Have you made your decision?"

The voice was so cold and ominous Antonis made the sign of the cross. "I...I don't know."

"Hmm." Silence. "*I don't know* is not an answer, or at least not one I can deal with," the woman said. "So, that leaves me with no other choice other than to—"

"Yes," Antonis blurted out, afraid to hear the rest.

"Yes, what?"

"I'll…I'll do it."

"Excellent. Now, here's what's going to happen."

Her instructions had been brief and to the point. Someone would rendezvous with Antonis in one week on the rocky shoreline beneath his monastery, and he would provide the contact with whatever was necessary to obtain the icon. So now, here he was in the middle of the night, looking out over the dark sea. He himself had determined the timing of the rendezvous: one a.m. worldly time, which would get the thief into the monastery during the brief three hours that the monks were sleeping. The Athonite monks remained the only entity in the world to live on Byzantine time. Their clocks began a new day every evening at sunset.

From somewhere up on the Holy Mountain, a wolf howled, and the mule behind him brayed in alarm. He set a calming hand on the beast's neck as a dark figure came into view, slowly rowing a small boat toward shore.

As soon as the figure—a tall man—stepped out onto the rocks, Antonis silently handed over a clean black robe and pillar-box hat. Despite the circumstances, it suddenly struck him as almost amusing that he'd thought it necessary to wash his already clean cassock before lending it to the thief. It's what his mother had taught him, and even after so many years of monastic life, Antonis often felt her presence, telling him what to do.

He missed his family and especially his sister, though twenty years had passed since he'd left them for the Holy Mountain. They'd always been poor, but very close and religious. When he'd announced his decision at the age of twenty to join the monastic life, his parents fell on their knees and thanked God for choosing their son, but Antonis had done it because he knew they couldn't afford to further school and provide for him.

Without an advanced degree, he had limited options. He wasn't cut out to be a waiter, cab driver, or construction worker. If sacrificing sex meant he could at least have a place to eat, sleep, and live without burdening his family, then that was fine with him. Here, all that was expected of him was to do some gardening work, help with visitors, and dedicate the rest of his day to prayer. The prayer part was easy—he'd perfected that even before he ever left home. But now, although he had enough to eat, a roof over his head, and was no longer a financial drain, his family was eating out of trash cans.

Monks were supposed to cut all ties with family once they were ordained, and he'd managed to comply with that rule until a few months ago. When he'd heard about how the deteriorating economy had driven thousands to ruin and utter paucity, he'd called home to learn the worst. He had to do something to save them, and desperation mixed with fear had brought him to this unfathomable decision. Would he be damned for it? Maybe, but at least he'd go knowing that he had saved his family.

The man finished buttoning the robe and placed the hat on his head. "Map and key," the stranger said in English.

Reluctantly, Antonis handed both over. He'd spent hours on the map. The first version was a detailed layout of the entire tunnel maze beneath the monastery, but he'd scaled that down significantly in the version he gave the man, which contained just enough information to lead the thief to the secret underground chapel that held the icon.

"He take you." Antonis pointed to the donkey.

The man pocketed the map and key and jumped on the donkey. He looked up at the stony, steep incline for several seconds but didn't seem at all concerned, or at least didn't show it if he was. "You get your money when I get back," he said in a low voice, still staring up at his destination, then kicked the donkey forward.

Antonis understood he'd have to wait there until the man returned with the promised treasure.

What would happen to his family if the man got caught or couldn't find it?

The cool night breeze off the sea brought a chill to his sweat-soaked torso, and he hugged himself to keep warm. Forty-five minutes passed and still the stranger did not return. The monks would be up in another hour or so to gather for the eight-hour liturgical service that began their day. "I should give myself up," Antonis mumbled to himself. "So wrong. What have I done? God would have protected and eventually provided for my family." He grasped his hair in frustration with one hand. "What have I done?" There had to be a way to stop this. He paced some more, then stood and stared out at the sea, mesmerized by the sound of the waves against the rocks.

"Your key," the man whispered in his ear.

Father Antonis had never heard the mule or the thief's approach. He closed his eyes. "Did you find it?" he asked without turning around.

The man dangled a satchel at the monk's side. "Let's go."

"Go where?"

"To get you your money. It's in the boat."

"No…I…I don't want it," he stuttered. "I don't want the money. I don't want any part in this. I need you to give me the *Theotokos*."

The man laughed. "Yeah, that's gonna happen." He poked something hard between the monk's shoulder blades. "Move."

"No. I said, I—"

"In case you hadn't noticed, this is a gun in your back, stupid."

Antonis froze. "I…no…" He was pushed forward so roughly he stumbled on the rocks.

"Move, for fuck's sake." The thief grabbed Antonis by the back of his robe and dragged him to the boat. "Get in."

"But why?"

The thief sighed loudly. "Just get the fuck in." He pushed Antonis so hard he practically landed headfirst in the boat. "I hope that hurt, black-robe motherfucker." He untied the small craft and pushed it away from the rocks before he jumped in.

Antonis rubbed his head as he sat up. "What are you doing?"

"Taking you for a ride."

"This wasn't the deal."

The man shrugged. "So?" He grabbed the oars and pulled them away from shore, the boat rocking unsteadily in the choppy waves.

Father Antonis tried to stand up. "I—"

The last thing he saw was the oar coming at his head.

He didn't know how long he'd been out, but when he woke, his hands and feet were tied and the Holy Mountain was a mere dark outline in the far distance. He wanted to struggle but knew there was no point. Death was near and he deserved it. Antonis looked up at the stars. "Bad will come to those who try to move the *Theotokos*, and…" He looked at the satchel. "And all this is my fault, so I must die."

"Them's the breaks, Father." The man grabbed Antonis and pulled him over to the side of the boat.

The monk lifted his head to the sky. "I'm sorry. Please, forgive me."

"Don't worry about it. I'm sure there's a special hell for priests and shit."

Chapter Two

Southwestern Colorado
Next day

Montgomery "Monty" Pierce knocked twice on Joanne Grant's office door before entering, though no one was around and the entire campus by now knew they lived together. Old habits and all that, he supposed.

Joanne sat behind her desk chatting on the phone, but she smiled and waved him in. From her side of the conversation, he quickly surmised that she was counseling one of this year's recent graduates about what specialty they should choose. In addition to the usual subjects taught at all American high schools, EOO students gained skills they would need as agents in the field: hand-to-hand combat, proficiency in all types of weapons, lock-picking, and much more.

Monty closed the door behind him and kissed Joanne on the top of her head before taking a seat in one of the chairs opposite. While he waited, he plucked a framed photo off her desk and studied the faces of the 1968 graduating class of the Elite Operatives Organization. The three honor students who would go on to lead the EOO as its Governing Trio were scattered among the faces. He was the strapping young man in the front row, his blond hair still thick and lush then and much longer than he remembered. But they had to fit in everywhere, and those were the days of Haight-Ashbury and the Rolling Stones.

David Arthur, the EOO's Director of Training, was even more unrecognizable with his long hair, since he'd sported his copper-colored crew cut for at least the last thirty years. He'd kept his same athletic build, however, though now in his sixties, while Monty's had deteriorated as soon as he left the field for his administrative desk job.

He could pick out Joanne with ease since he'd had a crush on her even then, though she had undergone the greatest transformation of any of them. She'd fleshed out even more than he had over the years, and the long, ebony hair of her youth was now a short white pixie cut. But in his mind, she grew more beautiful by the day.

He skimmed over the other faces in the photograph. Three of their classmates had been killed in action on the job, and two others were still teaching at the campus. The rest had long ago retired and moved away, and Monty wondered what had become of them. Had they kept their secrets even as they married and had children? Did they ever miss the extreme challenges and adrenaline rushes that came with being an ETF—a member of their Elite Tactical Force? And most of all, he wondered, had their unorthodox upbringing impacted how well they could adjust to a normal life outside?

He, like every other EOO op but one, had been adopted by the organization when he was just a child. Monty was the brightest six-year-old at the Oslo orphanage. They'd found David in Belfast and Joanne in Sydney the same year.

"Reminiscing again?" Joanne asked.

He'd been so absorbed by the photo he hadn't heard her hang up the call. "You know, we should expand the anniversary dinner this year. Put out a call to all former ops. Might be fun to see who shows up." They always celebrated the founding of the ultra-secretive organization with a big feast and celebration for the current staff and student body, but they'd never before included those who'd retired from their service.

"What's gotten into you, Monty?" Joanne asked in a teasing voice. "Ever since your big field trip you've been one big sentimental mushball."

He smiled. "That'll be the day." But that assessment had a lot of truth. Maybe he was getting too soft for the job. He couldn't let personal feelings and attachments influence the choices he made, since most involved putting their agents into life-and-death situations.

Before Joanne could argue the point, his cell phone went off. The caller ID said *Private Number*, a rare occurrence. To most of the world, the EOO didn't exist. Though it took jobs for numerous governments and organizations, to handle issues that couldn't be addressed by normal law enforcement, most of their contacts had only the main switchboard number, which was answered with a generic, "How may I assist you?" He'd given his private cell only to their senior ETFs and a few others at very high levels of influence and power.

"Yes?"

"Mr. Pierce, this is Archbishop Giorgos Manousis. I am Protepistate of the Holy Mountain of Athos in Greece."

"How did you get this number?"

"From Cardinal Angelo Bertone."

Monty sat back in the leather chair. Bertone, his contact at the Vatican, wouldn't have readily shared his number without an important reason. "How can I help you?"

"I'm calling in regard to the *Theotokos*."

"I'm sorry, but I have no idea what that might be."

"Of course you don't," Manousis answered. "No one does. It is a very holy and clandestine icon."

"I see. I take it it's gone missing."

"How do you—?"

"You wouldn't be on the phone with me otherwise."

"Yes, of course." The archbishop hesitated. "It was stolen yesterday."

"Are you sure it wasn't misplaced?"

"Quite. The secure chapel where it was held was broken into. And Father Antonis, one of our monks who was apparently involved, was discovered dead. A fisherman found his body this morning off the coast, a gunshot wound to his head."

"How do you know he was involved?" Monty asked.

"We found an unregistered cell phone among his things and drawings of the tunnels that lead to the icon."

"Led to the icon."

Manousis hesitated. "Yes, of course."

"And you have no idea who else might be involved?"

"All we know is that Father Antonis had something to do with it."

"And dead men don't talk." Monty grabbed a pen and notepad off Joanne's desk. "My guess is the monk was either blackmailed, threatened, or bribed."

"And whoever did any or all of the above killed him to make sure he didn't eventually get a bout of guilt and confess," the archbishop replied.

"Sounds about right. Either way, the monk was their insider. The cell phone, drawings of tunnels in his quarters." Monty jotted down the particulars.

"Father Antonis was one of only five monks who had a key that led to the icon. A key that is now missing," the archbishop said. "But knowing all that still does not help us find who is behind this or where the icon is."

Monty cleared his throat. "You do realize that relics, artifacts, and the like are not our business. You should contact ICAR, the International Centre for Asset Recovery."

"And therein lies the problem," Manousis replied. "The icon is a hidden treasure, unknown to practically anyone. It was never insured because that would mean having to register it."

"You're not going to get a dime back."

"It's not about the money, because it's literally priceless. The *Theotokos* is…" There was silence on the other end. "Priceless," he repeated. "Hundreds of years old and…"

"And?"

"Miraculous, Mr. Pierce."

"Hmm." Monty was skeptical of any religion or mumbo jumbo that came with it, so he didn't ask for further explanation. "So, it was never registered, it has magical powers, and for that reason it was kept a guarded secret. But now that it's gone you can't report it stolen to the authorities but desperately want it back."

"Exactly. And aside from that, we do not want to advertise that it's possible to enter the Holy Mountain and steal the—"

"Icon."

"It is so much more than just an icon, Mr. Pierce."

"I'm sure you think so, Mr. Manousis."

"Consider, we're talking about a country that at this point has nothing to lose," the archbishop explained. "They're three generations in debt and overtaxed to the extreme. Thirty percent are unemployed, and scores are bankrupt or have lost their homes and are starving. The suicide rate is climbing by the day. Not four years ago, Greeks lived like kings, so we're talking angry, desperate people who lost everything overnight. Desperation and anger will make people do crazy things."

"You're saying you're afraid that mobs will show up demanding artifacts to help pay their bills," Monty said.

"If threatening a monk is all it takes to get in and steal priceless items, then yes."

"Are you sure he was threatened?"

"No, but…he was found dead. If he had been bought, he'd probably still be alive and wealthy."

"I see." Monty was skeptical. "This icon can't be such a secret if someone outside the Holy Mountain knew enough about it to have it stolen."

"Its existence is top secret and virtually unheard of outside the mountain, with the exception of the Vatican and a select few."

"Select few?"

"We've had inquiries from private collectors whose money could buy them anything."

"Even a devout monk."

"Perhaps, but I don't think Father Antonis would—"

"I think you overestimate him. He was human, after all, and if you do a background check, I'm sure you'll find dire financial issues. Maybe his own or his family's, but either way, you can bet they used that to bribe him. I don't think they killed him because they couldn't pay up. I think they killed him so he wouldn't talk."

The archbishop was silent for a long while.

"Are you still there?" Monty had felt tired all day and was growing impatient with this story of stolen icons and miraculous relics. "Father—"

"I am willing to pay you whatever you ask if you find the *Theotokos*."

Monty rubbed his temple. This was such a dead-end case. Stolen artifacts hardly ever showed up, and if they did, it was decades later during a sales transaction. "I don't think we can—"

"I don't think there is anything your company can't do, Mr. Pierce. Your reputation precedes you, and if the Vatican trusts you to get a job done, then nothing you can say will make me doubt you can and will do everything in your power to recover the icon."

He looked over at Joanne, who'd been listening to his end of the conversation with interest. All he wanted was to call it a day and go home with her for a nice, relaxing evening. "Fine. Okay. I'll put someone on it."

"Thank you so—"

"I cannot and will not promise we will find it. As a matter of fact, I can tell you now you're wasting your money. But I'll assign someone to take a look and ask around."

"Wonderful," the archbishop replied. "When will I meet him?"

"Him?" Monty already had someone in mind for the job, an op who lived a short boat ride away. He considered there to be so little chance of success in finding this icon, he wasn't about to fly someone halfway around the world just to ask a few questions.

"I imagine your agent will have to examine the premises and see pictures of the *Theotokos.*"

"Of course."

"I don't mean to sound sexist. I am a modern man, after all, Mr. Pierce, but you must realize the Holy Mountain is forbidden to women."

❖

Skiathos Island, Greece
Same day

Alex Jefferson blinked hard against the glare as she stepped onto the deck of the *Nostos* with a coffee in one hand and today's *Makedonia* in the other. The bright morning sun was already warm. "Another scorcher," she mumbled as she set down the mug and paper and stood staring out over the turquoise harbor. And this was only June, which didn't bode well for the rest of the summer.

Her Moody 54 was her floating home, equipped with luxury amenities and the latest high-tech navigation system. The main level of the fifty-six-foot sailboat contained a comfortable enclosed cockpit with plenty of storage and a large living space with oversized couches, a flat-screen TV, and teak dining area, all surrounded by windows for a panoramic view. Below, she had a master cabin equipped with a king-sized bed and full bathroom, two small guest quarters, and a full galley with the latest stainless-steel appliances.

Through frequently cruising, she maintained a slip in Skiathos

Town, to anchor the boat while she was away and to keep tabs on her art gallery there. The Jefferson Collection did a brisk business with the tourists who came to visit the island's seventy beaches, and her long-time employees needed little guidance to keep things running smoothly.

She settled under the canvas shade that covered one of the twin-engine control stations aft, but had barely unfolded the newspaper when a familiar voice hailed her from the pier.

"Don't bother, just the same ole depressing crap." Pavlos, a local fisherman, had the slip next to hers.

"I'm a glutton for bad news."

"The fuckers are killing us. They're going to slice the country up and sell it off piece by piece to the highest bidder."

Alex dropped the paper on her lap. "You spoiled the surprise." She smiled.

"You were gone for a while this time."

"Five weeks." Alex sipped her strong Greek coffee.

"And two days."

"Keeping tabs?"

"It's a small village." He shrugged. "Not much else to do other than mind everyone else's business."

Alex knew village life was all about people sticking their nose where it didn't belong. While most meant well and were honestly interested in each other's well-being, she sometimes found the curiosity and endless questions tiring, especially when she'd just gotten back from a trying job. "Too damn small, if you ask me."

"You should appreciate the fact that people care. A woman your age has no business being alone."

Alex stood and rested her elbows on the railing. "Haven't found Mrs. Right yet."

Pavlos quickly scanned the pier and surrounding boats with an expression of dismay. "Hush. You want everyone to know your business?"

Alex laughed. "They already do."

He frowned disapprovingly. "Because you won't even try to hide it."

"Why should I?"

"Because…well, because…it's unchristian," Pavlos stuttered.

"Nobody cares."

"Father George does."

"Tell Father George I don't give a rat's ass about his opinion."

The older man blushed. "Alex!"

"Also, tell him I said sex with a woman is as heavenly as it gets."

The blush deepened as Pavlos covered his ears and started to hum.

"See you around five for the game," Alex said. They were among a handful of soccer enthusiasts who regularly convened at the local café to watch games on its large-screen TV.

Ears still covered, he replied, "I'll be there. The wife wants to drag me to a christening, but I'll be there." He continued to hum as he walked away.

Alex sat back on her cushioned bench and after a sip of coffee was finally ready to get to her paper. The country's economic woes dominated the banner headline every day, but another story merited a place this morning on the bottom of the front page. FLEMISH MASTERPIECE RECOVERED AFTER 80 YEARS.

She smiled. Locating *The Just Judges* by Jan van Eyck hadn't been easy, but she'd singlehandedly managed to find the illegitimate owner of the fourteenth-century painting and return it to the Saint Bavo Cathedral in Ghent, Belgium. She'd just turned to page four for the rest of the article when she heard the distant ringing of her cell phone.

"You'd think reading the paper would be simple enough," she said aloud, not bothering to hide her aggravation. She went below to her bedroom to get her cell and frowned at the number on the display. "Give me a break. There's a game on tonight." She sighed before she answered. "140369."

"Meet our contact tomorrow at fourteen hundred hours in Neos Marmaras," Montgomery Pierce said.

She knew the area well. Neos Marmaras was a port in Halkidiki, the three-fingered peninsula that served as northern Greece's premier vacation destination for locals and tourists alike. Though her home island was also renowned for its gold sand resorts, tavernas, and diverse nightlife, she'd sailed to Halkidiki on numerous occasions to enjoy the natural beauty of its rocky coastline and secluded beaches. "What else?"

"You're going to talk with the archbishop of Mount Athos."

"I see." It was a well-known fact that the archbishop didn't move his ass off the mountain for anyone.

Pierce cleared his throat. "In his private quarters."

Alex sat on the foot of her bed. "I figured." She checked her reflection in the mirror opposite, more concerned with her hair than why the big cheese of the Holy Mountain wanted the EOO's assistance. Besides, asking Pierce wouldn't help, since jobs were never discussed on the phone even if the line was secure.

"You know what that means," Pierce said.

Alex ran her hand through her short hair, wondering if she needed a trim before she set sail. "I do."

CHAPTER THREE

Toroneos Kolpos, Halkidiki
Next day

Ariadne felt most at home in this clear azure sea, under the water and as far below the surface as pressure would allow. Not that she didn't enjoy a good party or socializing within the elite circles that had been part of her birthright. She could even say she found some satisfaction in the endless business meetings her father had started to insist she attend.

But here, within the vast expanse of blue silence, the lack of gravity unburdened her from the weight of her life, a life where she diligently performed as expected every hour of every day. From birth, she had been raised to be always in control of everything she did and said, forever mindful of whom she befriended, dated, or was even casually associated with.

Ariadne's life so far had been comprised of expensive schools, supplemented by private tutelage in a number of other areas. She had impeccable manners and knew how to respond appropriately to any situation. On the rare occasion when she deliberately strayed from the norm, her missteps had to be calculated ones, because even her mistakes had to be within the acceptable boundaries. In other words, she was being groomed to be as respected, feared, and dedicated to business as her father, the billionaire tycoon.

Yet, although she loved her father and was willing to be whoever he wanted her to be, a part of her had begun to feel she was missing out. She had everything she desired and had become exactly the person her father wanted her to be, but it was never more obvious than when she was with her friends that she hadn't developed her own unique identity. Even simple questions like her favorite color or dish were difficult to answer without taking her father's preferences into consideration.

Her mother had been saying for years that father and daughter were too dependent on each other, and she constantly accused her husband of neglecting their son. Ariadne figured her brother Nikolaos was already receiving more coddling than was necessary or normal for a grown man from their mother. Sure, Ariadne was close to her father, but at least he pushed her to achieve and improve, whereas her brother had rarely finished anything he'd ever started. He'd managed to get his master's in philosophy only because their father had bribed the chancellor with a new library. Their mother was undeniably the major reason for Nikolaos's laziness and indifference to everything but girls.

But Ariadne loved her brother, despite his faults. When their parents were gone and she took ownership of the family business, she'd be expected to be his provider and benefactor. It was the Greek way, and she readily accepted the responsibility.

Ariadne looked at her watch. She had only five minutes of oxygen left, so it was time to start her reluctant ascent.

"Good morning, sweetheart." Her father called out the greeting as soon as Ariadne broke the surface, as though he'd been watching for her.

She swam to the yacht's steps and peeled off her mask, then shaded her eyes with her hand to look up at him. She smiled. "You look rested today."

He hadn't looked healthy for a while. At Christmas, during her last bi-annual trip home from Oxford, she'd insisted that he go for a checkup. He'd reported back that the doctors said he was in excellent condition for his age, but he still looked gaunt and pale when she came home for good in the spring.

This morning, however, her father looked vibrant, his color good and with an unusual buoyancy of spirit.

"Today…" He looked up at the sky and extended his arms. "Today is a good day."

He remained in that position, unmoving, as if praying.

The behavior was completely out of character. "What's up, Dad? Everything all right?"

Her father clapped his hands. "Everything is perfect." He laughed loud and long, as though all of his dreams had just come true. "Just perfect."

"Uh-huh." *Is he having a stroke?* "Care to share?" Ariadne eyed him suspiciously.

He leaned over the stern and extended his hand, still smiling broadly, but didn't reply.

"Are you sure you're all right?" she asked again while he pulled her out.

"It's the third happiest day of my life." He squeezed her shoulders, then helped her out of her tanks and set them on the deck.

"Okaaay."

"First your mother, then you…and now this." He extended his arms to the sky again, as if referring to the perfect day.

"I have a brother, Dad." She unzipped her wetsuit and peeled it off.

"Of course. I meant you both."

"Good. So what's so special about today?"

"I can't go into details," he replied, his eyes shining with glee, "but I bought a priceless artifact."

"I hate it when words lose their meaning."

"A synonym for priceless is costly."

"My point. So they kinda cheated you."

Her father laughed.

"When can I see it?"

He looked away evasively. "Oh…I don't have it, yet."

"Well, when does the priceless artifact arrive?"

He cupped her face in his hands. "The only truly priceless things in my life are you and health." Still smiling, he let her go. "I'll see you at the meeting." He turned to go back inside.

"Twelve sharp," she called after him.

Ariadne hadn't seen her father this vivacious and enthusiastic in years. Why did this painting, or whatever it was, have such an impact on his…everything? Kostas had rooms full of treasures—artifacts, artwork, rare manuscripts, you name it—but they hadn't made him stare at the sky like a religious fanatic, or clap and laugh like a lunatic. And why was he being so evasive about his latest acquisition?

This whole voyage, in fact, was out of character, she realized. Her father rarely spent more than a few days at a time on the *Pegasus*, and he always kept close to the southern islands nearer their home in Glyfada: Ikaria and Samos, mostly. But this time, they'd come all the way north to Halkidiki for the first time in memory, and after three weeks at sea he still seemed in no hurry to return home.

❖

Agio Oros, Halkidiki

As the pilgrim ferry neared the port of Ierissos, where the archbishop's emissary would be waiting, Switch ducked into the onboard WC for a final quick assessment. The barber had taken a little more off than expected, but it was still within the range of what most men her age considered stylish these days: an inch or so long, and combed back from her face. She had naturally thick eyebrows and never trimmed them, but she'd enhanced them more with a little pencil.

No further makeup was required for her even, androgynous features, which was why her specialty within the EOO and her code name had both been easy to choose. With the right wardrobe, haircut, mannerisms, and speech, she could transition convincingly between a boyishly attractive man and a woman more readily called handsome than beautiful.

For her meeting with the archbishop, she'd dressed in men's black high-top sneakers, khaki trousers, and a black polo. Narrow-hipped and long-legged, with an athletic build she rigorously maintained at her home gym, she could easily shop in the men's department for pants, but she had to tightly bind her breasts to get form-fitting summer shirts to fit appropriately.

Their contact in Neos Marmaras, a bespectacled nerd they'd nicknamed Dilbert, had filled her in on what little Pierce knew about the case. He'd also provided Switch with detailed information about the Holy Mountain, including its history and customs, and how to get around the 130-square-mile peninsula.

She'd then called the archbishop's office to arrange their appointment, introducing herself under the pseudonym Alex Ramos.

Switch was on the same page with Pierce on this one. It was going to be a cold case. Stolen artifacts rarely resurfaced, and if they did, usually only decades later. He'd asked her to see the archbishop only because she was a couple hours away and spoke the language fluently, and of course, out of courtesy to the Roman Catholic cardinal who'd referred him. The EOO had knocked on the Vatican's door plenty in the past and wanted to ensure continued cooperation with the Holy See.

A short monk with a black-and-gray beard waved her over when she got off the ferry. "Good morning, Mr. Ramos." He extended his hand as she neared.

"Call me Alex."

"The archbishop is waiting for you." He gestured for Switch to follow him to the Jeep. Twenty minutes later, they were at the Athonite administrative offices at Karyes, a small settlement nestled amidst walnut and hazel trees in the middle of the peninsula. "I'll take you to him."

"I appreciate that."

The archbishop looked up from his desk when Switch entered his office.

"You're younger than I expected," he said in English and extended his hand.

Switch shook the offered hand with a firm grip. "Don't let my boyish looks fool you," she replied in Greek.

The archbishop examined her closely, as if trying to look past her. "Nothing fools me at eighty." He sat back down. "You're Greek." He sounded almost disappointed.

Switch sat without being asked, opposite the archbishop. "Is that a problem?"

"I did not know the EOO had people in Greece."

"They have people everywhere."

He crossed his hands on the desk. "Hmm. I hope you do better than our fellow countrymen. I'm sorry, but I refuse to hide my disappointment in our police, government, and politicians."

"There's nothing to be sorry about. The corruption in Greece is no big secret."

"I need to trust that whoever finds the *Theotokos* will return it to its home and not take it to the highest bidder."

"I understand your concerns, but you don't need to worry about that with me. Frankly..." She searched for a diplomatic way to lessen his expectations.

"Yes?"

"I have to be honest. The chances of the icon showing up are next to zero."

"I cannot accept that."

"With all due respect, if you are as God-fearing and God-trusting as is expected for your position—"

"Of course."

"Then why not wait for it to return? The story has it that the *Theotokos* cannot be moved. It will always return to its home on the Holy Mountain."

"It's not a story."

Talking to these people about religion was like stomping on eggshells and expecting not to break them. "No, of course not." What was she supposed to say? That it's all a heap of dung, but hey, if it floats your boat, then by all means? "I'm sure there's merit to what is said about the icon."

"We can't simply wait for it to return by itself, for reasons I can't explain."

Try "it's an inanimate object," she thought. Switch sat back in the huge leather armchair. "Start from the beginning, Father. When did you realize the *Theotokos* was missing?"

The archbishop talked nonstop for nearly a half hour, filling her in on what they knew about the theft and on specifics about the Simonopetra monastery.

"So, Father Antonis, one of only five monks to have a key, turned up dead."

"Yes."

"Have you considered the possibility of Father Antonis being behind the theft? You know, a deal gone wrong?"

"Unfortunately, yes."

"Okay, then." She got to her feet. "Let's start with Father Antonis's quarters."

Switch had never been religious, spiritual, or anything but pragmatic. She'd heard about the icon purely because of the circles she moved in. Her job was to retrieve and return stolen artifacts, paintings, and so on, so aside from her EOO training, her extensive studies had included everything from art history to archeology, and she was also a licensed authentication expert.

"I'll take you there myself, though I've already had the room searched."

"I'm sure, but it can't hurt to look again."

Father Antonis's quarters at the Simonopetra Monastery were Spartan, to say the least. A bed, a night table, a sink, a shelf for his cassocks and linens, and one bookshelf with various Holy Scriptures. The walls, ceiling, and floor were stone, leaving no place to hide anything. It didn't take longer than a few minutes to verify that nothing of interest was left behind. "You said you found maps?"

"Indeed. Hand-drawn maps were scattered on his bed. Various versions of how to get up through the tunnel system into the underground chapel that held the icon."

"If he had to make a map, then he obviously didn't tag along for the theft."

The archbishop touched his beard. "I suppose."

"Did Father Antonis have any visitors…guests, prior to the theft?"

"None that he was familiar with. Monastics leave behind family and friends when they are ordained. But he regularly gave tours to pilgrims."

"Do you keep a record of visitors?"

"We do. They must show their passports and apply for a special permit to gain access to the Holy Mountain."

"I'd like a list of all visitors from the past couple of weeks."

"Easily done. I have those records back in my office and will send someone to get them at once."

They left the annex that contained the monk's rooms and emerged into one of the narrow cobbled walkways that snaked through the massive monastery. Switch studied the building's seven-story exterior. "Security cameras?"

The archbishop hesitated before he answered. "As far as the outside world knows, we have none. To advertise such measures, especially in these turbulent times, would merely call attention that the fact that we have many priceless icons, artifacts, and manuscripts housed within the monasteries: some known, and some—like the *Theotokos*—forever a secret to all but a few. But a couple of years ago, we recognized the need to take whatever steps possible to safeguard our Holy Treasures. So we have discreetly installed cameras at all of the monasteries, including this one."

"And?"

"Two cameras—one inside the chapel where the icon is kept and one in the exterior hallway—caught brief images of a man in monk's garb. We could tell he was not one of us, but I don't think the footage is clear or long enough to help you. The icon was taken during the hours the monks are asleep and the lights are dimmed throughout the monastery."

"I'll review the footage regardless, if you don't mind. And whatever you have from the exterior cams during that time period." It was going to be a long, useless day.

"Please do."

"I'm also going to have to take a look at where the icon was kept."

The archbishop hesitated before he answered. "No one is allowed there but a select few of us."

"I'm sorry, but—"

He held up one hand. "Yes. I will make that exception." He led her to the abbot's office, where she spent the next couple of hours scanning the security-cam footage. Like the archbishop had said, the brief images of the thief weren't much help, and there were no images of him from any of the exterior cams. Reno, the EOO's crack computer op, might get something more with his enhancement software, so she asked the abbot's secretary for a copy of the footage.

When she finished, a waiting elder monk led Switch on a twenty-minute walk through a maze of courtyards, passageways, and winding corridors, down into the underbelly of the monastery. They passed countless frescos, murals, and spectacular icons dating back hundreds of years, and she was tempted on several occasions to pause a moment to study one or another. Not for any religious reason, but the art historian within her had rarely before seen such an impressive collection.

Finally, they reached a long, underground hallway lined with large painted panels, where the archbishop was waiting for her. She recognized the place from the surveillance-cam footage.

"I trust that everything you are about to see will remain in strictest confidence?" he asked.

"Of course."

He turned to the massive panel he was standing next to, which depicted Christ with outstretched hands, and ran his hand beneath the right side of the frame. A loud *click* opened the panel like a door, revealing another door, this one made of steel. "This is the way the thief got in," he said, then nodded to the elder monk.

The monk took a key out of his pocket, unlocked the door, and swung it open.

Switch stepped inside. The steel door hid the tunnel system, which had been carved out of rock and earth and reinforced by wooden beams. A string of dim lights every twenty feet or so illuminated the interior enough for her to see that this main passageway had several branches leading away on either side.

When she stepped back into the hallway, the elder monk locked the door again and returned the covering panel to its original position.

"Thank you, Father," the archbishop said, dismissing the monk. The man nodded to his superior reverently and retreated silently back down the hallway. Once he'd disappeared from view, the archbishop went to another panel farther down, this one depicting the Holy Mother and Child. He felt along the frame again until he released its hidden latch and swung the panel open.

Behind this painting was another solid steel panel, devoid of knobs or locks. The only way to gain entrance was to punch a code into the high-tech security panel beside it. "The thief must have great knowledge with such things," the archbishop said, pointing to the access panel. "He cut wires to disable it without setting off the alarm. We had a technician in immediately to fix it. I am the only one to know the current code." He started to reach for the panel but hesitated. "Would you mind?"

She turned her face away while he punched in the numbers, though the security system was one she could have cracked in her sophomore year at the EOO.

A *whoosh* of the door sliding open, then the archbishop's voice. "After you."

She stepped inside and scanned the room, dimly illuminated by a trio of tall candles. The security-cam footage had been too narrow to give her a real picture of the chapel, which was unlike any other she'd seen in Greece.

Orthodox chapels, even small ones like this, were usually highly decorative places, the walls replete with numerous gilded icons and other relics and with kneeling benches and rows of votive candles for the faithful. But this one had plain stone walls and flooring and contained nothing but a small wooden altar. Though not remotely religious, she felt strange, almost oddly awestruck, and couldn't explain why. "It was placed over here." She approached the altar.

The archbishop cleared his throat. "Yes," he whispered.

Atop the altar was a thick piece of wood. As she pulled out a pair of latex gloves and put them on, she asked, "Have the police dusted this for fingerprints?"

"No," he replied. "We could not afford the publicity it would involve. That is why we called you."

"That's all right. I'll do it now, though I expect the thief was smart enough to wear gloves." She removed the fingerprint kit from her daypack and carefully dusted the surface of the wood with powder, then used her lifting tape to preserve the half dozen prints she found. She also dusted the top of the altar and came away with several more good examples, probably all from monks. The archbishop remained silent while she worked, though he didn't look pleased with the mess she was creating with the powder.

When she was done, she picked up the piece of wood for a better look, handling it with care by its edges. A bit larger than a typical piece of printer paper, it was heavier than she expected and very old, with a rough groove carved across the middle. She turned toward the archbishop. "The stand for the icon?"

His eyes were wide with distress. "Please…p…put that down. It is very old."

Switch carefully set it back in place on the altar and took off her gloves. "I can see that. When was the icon last seen?"

"I personally visit it every afternoon around five, after the last visitor ferry departs the Holy Mountain."

"So no cars can come in or out after that?"

He shook his head. "There are few cars on the mountain. Only ours and a few service vehicles, which come in by ferry."

"How about by boat?"

"It's possible, but we have regular coast-guard patrols along the coast and video surveillance."

"CCTV cams there as well?"

"Yes."

"Do you have recordings for last week and this week?"

"We keep them for two weeks. They get erased today."

Switch turned around so fast the archbishop stepped back. "Tell them not to touch the recordings. I have an idea."

He took her back to the abbot's office for more hours of watching mind-numbing security-cam footage. Shortly after midnight, she stood and stretched. "Dead end," she said out loud and to no one. She was tired, and no amount of coffee could help keep her eyes open. More pressing than sleep, however, was the urge to take the restricting bandage off her chest and take a long, hot ba… She lost her train of thought when she spotted the enormous yacht. "I know you."

Switch paused the video. On and off the job, she'd had cause to socialize among the most affluent in Greece, and a life aboard her sailboat, endlessly touring the Aegean, meant she knew virtually every big boat. "What was your name again, beauty?" She couldn't readily decipher the lettering on the bow of the floating monster so she zoomed in as much as the computer would allow. The pixels blurred the name but she could still make it out.

"Of course. The *Pegasus*." The superyacht belonged to a multibillionaire shipping magnate, Konstantinos Lykourgos. "Since when do you sail these waters?" It was common knowledge that the man preferred the southern Greek isles, with occasional trips to Italy and Turkey. To her knowledge, his superyacht had never been spotted in Halkidiki before. "Worth looking into." She got a copy of that footage as well.

CHAPTER FOUR

Thessaloniki, Greece

TQ waited impatiently as the hotel waiter laid out her lunch on the terrace. From the seventh floor, the view of the Thermaikos Gulf and distant Mount Olympus was breathtaking. She could have chosen to stay at the even more luxurious Met or Excelsior hotels, but neither had the ambience of the Electra Palace. The five-star arch-shaped hotel, ideally situated in the very heart of Thessaloniki, featured a rooftop terrace garden and historic Byzantine architectural details.

She checked her watch. Her man would arrive any moment with the *Theotokos*, and so would her personal authentication expert. It wasn't part of the deal to have the icon validated, and had she not been interested in it for herself, she wouldn't have bothered. But no way was she going to let the Greek have one of the world's most priceless treasures.

Like Lykourgos, she wasn't interested in selling the icon, nor the satisfaction of bragging about her coup to other collectors, because both could land her in jail. Greece had gotten very strict about illicit trading in antiquities, and penalties could be extreme. She simply wanted it because she could have it; she wasn't buying the billionaire's crap about it being the cure for his cancer.

At this point in her life, very little mattered to TQ but money and her priceless collection. She used to care about her idiot brother Dario, but now that he was dead, she had no further obligation to anyone, which left more time for matters of significance.

Her one-eyed Asian servant came to stand mutely beside her. The girl had certainly become much more meticulous and obedient, TQ thought, since she'd stabbed her in the eye for announcing two minutes early that her bath was ready. "Talk."

"Your appointment is here."

TQ rolled her eyes, irritated that the girl wasn't being more specific. A blind servant, however, was completely useless, and they took such a long time to train. "Which?"

"He wouldn't give a name, just that he has what you asked for."

"Why is it so difficult for you to be specific right away?" TQ stood. "Must I pull everything out of you?"

The woman cowered in fear, her whole body trembling. "I'm sorry, Madam. I didn't know you had more appointments."

"Why would you, you brainless weasel?" TQ pushed her aside. "Now get out of my way and go make yourself useful."

The girl bowed and stepped back. "Yes, Madam."

"Start with ironing everything in my closet," she said, though the servant had been ironing her whole wardrobe for the past five days and had only finished that very morning.

"I've already ironed everything, Madam."

TQ stopped and turned to look at her. "What did you say?"

The girl bowed deeply from the waist, the shaking of her body even more pronounced. "Right away, Madam." Looking panicked, she ran off in the direction of the master bedroom.

"Is your intellect the result of incest?" TQ yelled. "Let my guest in, first." She followed her into the suite and went to sit at the antique desk.

The man came in and stood in front of her, holding a satchel to his chest. He waited there patiently, not speaking.

"Get on with it," she said. "I despise faux dramatic tension."

He smiled. "My money."

She opened the top drawer and pulled out a stack of euro bills. "Five hundred thousand."

He nodded and placed the satchel on the desk. "The *Theotokos*."

"Well, let's see it, then."

He carefully pulled the icon out of the case and placed it on the desk, facing her.

The icon was even more spectacular than she imagined. Solid gold and quite thick, it depicted the Virgin Mother with a beatific smile, her face ringed by a massive halo. "My, my. What an amazing piece." She smiled. "You did good," she remarked, looking up at him.

He was staring at her mouth with a look of dismay on his face.

She'd seen that expression before. "Yes, I don't smile very often," she said, "So it may seem—"

"Reptilian."

"I was going to say awkward."

"Unnaturally reptilian." He averted his eyes.

TQ stood. "Leave."

The man grabbed the brick of bills. "My pleasure."

Once alone, TQ marveled anew at the artistry of the icon, obviously many centuries old but very well preserved. She already had a spot picked out for it in the private museum that was her penthouse apartment in Houston. The *Theotokos* would be displayed in its own custom glass case in her office, next to the gold burial mask she'd had smuggled out of Luxor, Egypt.

She was so intent on the icon she didn't immediately notice that her servant had stepped back into the room. "What?"

"Mr. Collins is here, Madam," the woman meekly replied.

Her trusted authentication expert. "What are you waiting for? Show him in, and bring us some refreshments."

❖

Near Colorado Springs, Colorado

Jack Harding folded the last of the laundry, happy to see no trace of the bloodstains on Cass's favorite black jeans. She'd been alarmed when Cass had returned from her latest mission as Agent Lynx, until she learned the blood wasn't hers. "Okay, my share's done," she called out. She didn't mind folding, but placing the clothes back in drawers and closets was worse than being back in Israel having her teeth pulled out with pliers.

"You know what would make my life a whole lot easier?" Cassady Monroe, her partner of nearly five years, joined her in the utility room off the kitchen.

Jack frowned. "Is this about the laundry? Because you know I hate putting clothes back."

"No, this is about your father."

"Here we go." Jack rolled her eyes. Cass had been harping on the same subject since Montgomery Pierce had admitted to being Jack's dad in the aftermath of Operation Guardian, when that bitch, Theodora Rothschild, had kidnapped the president and planted a double in the White House. Granted, he'd orchestrated and participated in Jack's rescue from TQ's torture chamber, and had even insisted she recover from her injuries at the home he shared with Joanne Grant. But she still couldn't forgive him for abandoning her in Israel all those years ago, or for lying to her about her parentage all of her life. Not to mention how many times he'd put Cass's life in danger.

"So, it would help simplify my life if you'd answer the phone when he calls you," Cass said.

"Nah, I don't see that happening."

"I love you, Jack, but I'm not going to play family counselor."

"Didn't ask you to."

"No, but your father thinks I should."

"Then stop answering his calls."

"I can't do that. The man is trying very hard to reach out."

"Yeah, heartbreaking." Jack turned back to the table full of folded clothes. "So, anyway, everything's in neat piles like you requested," she said proudly. "See, I can learn."

"Jack." Cassady sighed. "Just talk to him. He wants to get to know you, that's all."

Jack loved her so much it hurt, but the constant talk about Pierce was getting on her nerves lately. "Let it go, Cass."

"I can't let it go when he calls three times a day, because if you don't pick up he calls me on my cell."

Jack shrugged. "Get a new number."

"Get a new attitude," Cass shot back.

Jack took a deep breath to calm her nerves. "Just because the guy feels guilty for being an asshole and has some fucked-up, misplaced need to be my father, I'm not required to play the part of his daughter. As far as I'm concerned, the guy is nothing more than a sperm donor. I was…am a mistake, the consequence of a ten-minute unsafe-sex session that resulted in unwanted offspring and nothing more. I therefore feel absolutely no obligation to humor his geriatric need for father-daughter bonding."

"I'm not asking you to bond or even treat him as a father. All I'm saying is that my life would be a whole lot easier if you spent five minutes on the phone so I wouldn't have to mediate and pass on information between and about the two of you."

"I never asked you to."

"No, but you imply it when you ask me what he was going on about and if he mentioned you, every single time he calls." Cass was getting angry, which didn't bode well for what Jack had in mind for the evening.

"I guess I'll have to stop doing that, then. I just ask because I feel you want me to."

"That's bull and you know it, Harding."

When Cass reverted to calling her by her EOO-given surname, Jack knew she was fast approaching implementation of the silent treatment. "Fine. Next time he calls, I'll take it."

"Next time, and every other time, because I'm done playing matchmaker."

"Good." Jack felt defeated and scolded and hated it.

"Great." Cassady turned to leave. "And try to sound somewhat civil, because the guy isn't well." She left the laundry room.

"What does that mean?" Jack yelled after her.

"It means, I think he's sick," she called back, and Jack heard a door slam.

❖

Halkidiki, Greece
Next day

Switch carried her Greek coffee topside for better cell reception. She'd anchored the *Nostos* off Neos Marmaras, some distance from the scattering of fishing boats that were plying the blue water for the anchovy, mackerel, blue fish, bogue, and dozens of other species they would sell to markets and tavernas along the coast.

"As expected, my visit to the Holy Mountain proved useless and time consuming," Switch said to Montgomery Pierce.

"Of course it did."

"The icon will show up in twenty to thirty years, and by then, whoever's taken my place can return it to whoever has taken the archbishop's."

"Can't say we didn't try," Pierce replied. "Anything else?"

"Yeah, just one more thing I want to look into. It's a shot in the dark, but let's just say it's tickled my curiosity."

"Oh?"

"The monastery's security cameras showed the *Pegasus* anchored in front of the Holy Mountain."

"*Pegasus?*"

"One of the biggest yachts in the Med, owned by Konstantinos Lykourgos."

"Who is?"

"A Greek shipping magnate. Worth billions."

"Go on."

"If anyone can afford to have it stolen, it's him."

"A bit of a long shot," Pierce said. "I can't see why a renowned man such as he would risk getting involved in theft."

"Well, aside from the fact that he can afford it, there's also the well-known fact that he owns one of the largest antiquity collections worldwide."

"Interesting."

"To say the least. I want to look into it, if that's okay."

"You're on the payroll, so let's say I give you a week to find out if he's a suspect. If it turns out he is, then we can figure out your next move."

"I'm going to need Reno." The EOO's computer op could break into nearly any database worldwide and was an invaluable asset to almost every mission.

"You know where to reach him."

"Talk to you in a week."

"You're enjoying this, aren't you?" Pierce asked.

"You know I like to stay busy, especially when it concerns stolen artifacts."

Pierce laughed. "And that's what makes you so good at tracking them."

"Ah…yeah." Switch wasn't used to the EOO chief being chummy or complimentary, on the phone or otherwise. He was always strictly professional and to the point and never exchanged pleasantries with anyone. Then she remembered the scuttlebutt she'd heard through the EOO grapevine—that he'd admitted fathering ex-op Phantom, aka Jaclyn Harding. Maybe his newfound daughter had something to do with his mellowing out, or maybe it was just age. "So, later."

"Good luck."

Switch disconnected and dialed Reno's number.

"Hey, Switcheroo," he said.

"Hey, dude."

"Are you working as you or your alter?"

"Alter."

"Then, *hey dude* to you, too."

Switch chuckled.

"Still in Greece?"

"Always."

"Things are messy over there."

"Yeah, but it's home."

"I know what you mean. Same here."

"I need you to check on someone," she said.

"That's what I do. Name?"

"Konstantinos Lykourgos."

She heard Reno typing away.

"Massively rich shipping magnate worth roughly five billion. Born in 1950, lives in Glyfada, Athens with his spouse Christine, daughter Ariadne, and son Nikolaos."

Switch tried not to laugh at his pathetic pronunciation but failed.

"Snicker again and I'll start slurping this soda so hard it'll give you permanent audio impairment."

"It's charming."

"That's more like it."

"Anything on his collections?" she asked.

"Says here he's got one of the largest private collections in the world. Art, artifacts, antiques, manuscripts, you name it. I'd say the guy has enough to start his own museum."

"Where does he keep it all?"

"Insurance forms indicate most are at a building he owns in downtown Athens, though I'm sure he keeps some in his house as well."

"They all do. What's the point if they can't flash it in front of guests," Switch said. "And then there are the illicit items that never see the light of day."

"I can understand flashing what you've got," Reno replied. "But why buy something you're never going to be able to display or talk about?"

"Because they can, or because it makes them feel superior to have an expensive secret."

"So, what did this Greek dude do to have you on his ass?"

"I suspect he may be behind a stolen icon."

"As in celebrity?"

"As in religious icon. The *Theotokos*. Its existence is one of the world's best-kept secrets, and its location even more so."

"Inside job," he offered.

"Help from an insider. I'm sure the dead monk involved was either bought or threatened, in order to reveal its location."

"But if no one knows about it—"

"Except for a handful of hardcore collectors who consider it the holy grail of antiquities. Some of them may even believe in its healing powers."

"And Lykourgos is in that handful?" Reno asked.

"I don't know, but he's on my list of suspects."

"With who else?"

"It's all I got."

"So, where to from here?" he asked.

"Can you locate him?"

"I can locate anyone who owns a cell. Give me sec." Reno typed away while Switch sipped her Greek coffee and gazed at her sailboat.

"She's gonna need a fresh coat soon," she mumbled to herself.

"You lost me," Reno replied.

"Nothing. Talking about *Nostos*."

"The homecoming as a literary theme, especially as it pertains to Homer's *Odyssey*," he replied, obviously pleased that he recognized the word.

"Also my sailboat." She sighed. "What's taking you so long?"

"I can't get a signal for Lykourgos. Hold on."

"GPS turned off, like most billionaires."

"I don't know if it's any help, but his daughter is…hang on."

"I don't care where his dau—"

"In the middle of the Aegean Sea."

"You don't say."

More clicking. "The son is there, too. That help any?"

"I'll let you know. Also, I'm emailing you a list of visitors to the Holy Mountain of Athos for background checks. See if any of them have criminal histories for theft or expertise in security systems."

"Will do. Easy peasy."

"And I need you to work your magic on some surveillance tape. There are a few grainy shots of the thief and some footage of Lykourgos's boat." As she spoke, she went below to her computer to send him the material.

"That'll take a bit longer, but I'll get right on it."

"Thanks, Reno. Gotta run." Switch hung up.

Chapter Five

Aegean Sea

Kostas Lykourgos waved at Theodora Rothschild as his helicopter touched down on the landing pad atop the yacht. Her faint smile told him she'd seen him. The copter messed up his hair, so he ran his hands through it before he walked up to greet his guest. "You look wonderful this beautiful afternoon," he said loudly over the noise of the dying rotors as he offered his hand to help her out. With her cold smile and red kaftan wafting in the wind, she looked malefic.

Rothschild frowned. "As opposed to?" She stepped out onto the yacht.

Kostas chose to ignore the question. Today was a grand day and he wasn't going to let anything stand in the way of his exuberance. He put his arm around her waist. "I have a lovely dinner prepared for us." When he saw Rothschild wasn't holding his last hope and imminent cure, he looked back to see who else would get out of the copter.

"The cyclopic Asian has it." Rothschild turned to the helicopter. "Move it!" She shouted so loud that both Kostas and the young woman currently disembarking jumped. "So hard to find decent help."

The diminutive servant—probably still in her late teens and with a black eye patch over one eye—hurried to her side, and Kostas let go of Rothschild.

"Hello and welcome," he said to the girl. "My name is Konstantinos Lykou—"

"Don't bother. She's just the help," Rothschild said. "Give me that." She grabbed the hard case the girl was holding.

Kostas had had plenty of maids, butlers, and domestics since birth, but he'd never treated any of them with anything other than appreciation and respect. "Theodora." He smiled. "Why so moody? It's a wonderful day today for both of us."

Rothschild gave him one of her cold smiles, devoid of any genuine emotion. "Indeed, Konstantinos. Please, forgive my testiness. Helicopters always aggravate me. They…move too much."

"Of course." He offered his arm and she took it. "Off to my quarters for wine, seafood, and the unveiling?"

"Lead the way." Rothschild walked a few steps with him before apparently realizing her servant was trailing them. "Have someone show her where she can iron my clothes."

"Of course." Kostas summoned the nearest steward to take charge of the girl and retrieve his guest's luggage from the helicopter, before he led Rothschild below to his quarters.

The master stateroom covered more real estate than many private homes, with a large bedroom, two enormous closets, Italian-marbled bathroom, dining area, and an expansive sitting area with his desk, custom couches, a bar, and an eighty-inch flat-screen TV. Many of his favorite artifacts and paintings were displayed here, so the room had museum-quality controls of temperature and humidity variations.

The dining table had been set with the ship's finest china and linens, monogramed with his company's logo, and the cutlery was solid gold. A trio of uniformed stewards stood by in one corner, waiting for Kostas to give them the go-ahead to serve.

"I've chosen a marvelous 1996 Domaine Leflaive Montrachet Grand Cru for dinner, but what can I offer you while we marvel at the icon?"

"Dom Pérignon." Rothschild took a seat on one of the plush white couches and placed the case next to her.

"Americans have a fondness for beverages I don't relate to." Kostas turned to one of the stewards and smiled. "You heard the lady," he said in English for her benefit.

Seconds later, the man returned with a bottle. He filled a crystal flute, set it before her, and bowed before he returned to the corner of the room.

"We need to be alone, guys," Kostas said in Greek. Once the

staff had left, he clapped so loudly his guest almost choked on her champagne. "I'm sorry but…I'm excited."

Clearly irritated, Rothschild placed her flute on the table in front of her and looked at the case on the couch. "Have at it," she choked out, then coughed.

Kostas was barely able to contain his excitement and practically ran to the couch to pick up the case. He took it to his desk and gently set it down. Though he still needed to have the icon authenticated, he knew immediately it was the real deal. He could feel it as he placed his hands reverently on the cool case.

Soon, his faith—together with this divine assistance—would help him return to the man he used to be. A man full of life, optimism, and love for his family and friends. A father who would be there for his daughter: to teach her all she needed to know about the future of their company, to love her, support her, and defend her choices, regardless of what anyone in his pretentious circles thought.

He released the two latches and took a deep breath before opening the satchel. The icon was wrapped in a piece of fine, white linen. He gently pulled it aside. "My God," he whispered. Before him lay the most striking depiction of the Virgin Mary he'd ever seen: the gold so vibrant, the Virgin's expression one of complete harmony, the detail astonishing.

"Breathtaking, isn't it?"

Kostas was so absorbed in the sight before him he barely heard or saw her approach his side. "It's magnificent," he replied quietly, never taking his gaze from the icon. He itched to touch it, to feel its powers, but he needed to be alone for that.

"So, now what?" Rothschild asked.

"Hmm?" He turned to look at her and hoped the irritation of her presence wasn't obvious on his face. His appetite had vanished.

"How do you intend to protect this gem?"

He frowned. "Why do you ask?"

"Because you need to be careful with something this precious."

"Of course I do, but why would you ask me something of such a personal nature?" Was he already becoming paranoid about the safekeeping of this treasure? "I'm sorry." He waved his hand. "I didn't mean to sound rude."

"Not to worry. I would be paranoid, too, if it were mine." Kostas fought back a cough and cleared his throat. "I'm going to keep it close."

"So that it cures you?" she asked.

"Yes. And once that's happened, I will have it returned to the Holy Mountain."

"What?" Her reaction came out as something between a shriek and a squeal of shock.

"I don't want to keep it," he explained. "That would be stealing."

She looked at him as though he was deranged. "It's already called stealing."

"Hardly." What didn't this woman understand? "I have simply borrowed it for the purpose of salvation."

"But—"

"I'm not a thief," he insisted. "Nor do I think it decent to add this marvel to my private collection. That would be selfish when it can also save so many others." He covered the icon again with the protective cloth.

"Kostas, be reasonable. You have the holy grail of icons in your possession."

"Like I said, Theodora." He was getting impatient with the woman's ignorance. "I need a miracle, not a relic." He placed the *Theotokos* back in the hard case and snapped it shut. "I already have more than any man should. I don't need anything. Not another artifact, not money, nor possessions. I can buy anything I want but my life." He shouted the last sentence.

Rothschild shrank back a half step. "Of course." She returned to the couch.

Kostas wanted to pay this shark with her cold smile and ask her to leave forever, but proper manners prohibited such rudeness. He walked to his bedroom and placed the case on his bed. "So." He clapped his hands loudly when he stepped back into the living room. "Shall we dine?"

"Let's." Rothschild walked over to the dining table.

He summoned his stewards back with the touch of a button and was about to take the seat opposite his guest when a knock on the door stopped him. "Yes?"

The security guard positioned outside his suite opened the door. "Ms. Lykourgos to see you."

"Wonderful! Let her in." He hadn't expected to see Ariadne, who'd arranged to have dinner with her friends on the aft deck. His wife and son had gone ashore for the evening.

"Hi, Da—" She froze when she saw who was with him.

Kostas noticed the deep frown lines between her brows. Ariadne only did that when he entertained a new client she didn't trust. It didn't happen often, but occasionally his daughter would insist he not make a deal with someone. It had taken him a few years and a handful of regrets to discover his little girl had been right. She had a sixth sense when it came to people, or was it just business?

"Theodora, you've met my daughter, Ariadne."

Rothschild's cold eyes appraised his daughter at length. "I certainly have." She looked away before she added, "Good evening, Ariadne. Nice to see you again."

"Uh-huh" was all Ariadne said before she turned to her father. "I saw the heli landing earlier."

He settled into his chair. "That was Mrs. Rothschild."

"Yes, I can see that." Ariadne looked at the other woman coldly. "May I assume Mrs. Rothschild brought the new acquisition you mentioned earlier?"

"That's correct." Rothschild smiled at Ariadne in a way that reminded Kostas of an animal baring its teeth.

Ariadne never took her eyes off her father. "I'm as surprised now as I was when she first appeared here."

Kostas was getting uncomfortable with the power struggle and obvious antagonism between the two women. "Ariadne." He smiled to mellow her out.

Ariadne shrugged. "I'm just surprised, that's all."

"Oh?" Rothschild ran a long fingernail across the smooth surface of the table.

Ariadne stepped closer and crossed her arms defiantly. "What with her being arrested for trading in black-market organs, illegal weapons, and who knows what else."

"False accusations, dear," Rothschild replied insouciantly. "I wouldn't be here if I were guilty."

Ariadne's smile was equally devoid of any warmth. "So it was innocence that got you off and not extortion." She laughed. "I find that hard to believe."

"Ariadne." Kostas scarcely recognized his daughter. Ariadne had never been this ill-mannered and blunt before. "Theodora is my guest." Ariadne slowly turned to him. "I'm sorry, Dad." But it was clear from her tone she didn't mean it.

"It's Theodora you need to apologize to."

"Oh, pish posh." Rothschild waved Ariadne off. "Kids will be kids."

"And criminals will be criminals," Ariadne replied.

This was getting out of hand. Kostas stood. "Ariadne, I'll see you later." His tone left no room for argument or discussion.

"Very well, Father." Ariadne pivoted and headed for the door.

"Don't believe everything you read," Rothschild called after her.

Ariadne opened the door and stopped, but didn't look back. "I don't have to read anything to see what you are."

❖

Late that night

"Darling? Are you sure you're all right? Should I summon a doctor?"

Kostas tried valiantly to stifle his wracking cough with a towel, but this episode was a particularly bad one and he could scarcely catch his breath, let alone answer his wife with any convincing reassurances. He could hear her trying the door to the bathroom, which he rarely locked.

"Kostas? You're scaring me. Please open the door or I'm going for help."

He coughed again into the towel and glanced at himself in the mirror. The toll of his illness and too many sleep-deprived nights was etched in the gaunt hollows of his cheeks and the expanding dark circles beneath his eyes. There was no way he would have been able to hide the truth from Christine and the rest of his family much longer.

But now he wouldn't have to, because the *Theotokos* would cure him. He was certain of it. He just had to spend every moment he could with it. He'd hoped to be instantly cured when he first touched it this afternoon, but though he'd felt the Holy Mother's presence during his two hours of prayer, she apparently wanted to test his faith.

That was no problem. His faith was strong and resolute. Tossing the towel into the hamper, he cleared his throat and opened the door. "I'm fine, dear," he told his wife, embracing her tightly to calm her. "I told you, the doctor said it's only a bit of lingering irritation in my lungs from that flu that was going around last winter. It's not uncommon, and nothing to worry about." He kissed her on the forehead. "I'm just sorry I woke you again. Come on. Let's try to get back to sleep."

CHAPTER SIX

Off Neos Marmaras, Halkidiki
Next morning

Switch surfaced with an octopus, its tentacles wrapped around her arm. Although she stayed clear of meat, she would eat anything that came out of the sea. After chucking her mask on the transom, she climbed the short ladder and sat. She'd started to peel the cephalopod mollusk off her arm when her phone rang.

She hurried up to the cockpit and grabbed her cell. "Whatcha got?"

"A headache," Reno said. "How about you?"

"An octopus wrapped around my arm."

"Gross. Yours is worse," Reno replied. "Why would you do that?"

"I just caught it."

"Oh, I see. You have me slaving away for you, while you go fishing."

"Uh-huh."

"In beautiful, warm Greece."

"Yup."

"In those Photoshopped waters."

"Yeah, that about sums it up." She chuckled.

"'Kay. Just checking." Reno sighed. "So, anyway, while you've been lounging on your luxurious yet understated Moody 54DS—"

"Is there nothing sacred about our personal lives?" She feigned surprise.

"Plato was suspicious of rhetorical questions, because, ethically speaking, they could be used for both good and bad. I personally like 'em 'cause they save me the trouble."

"So, what's new, smart-ass?"

"'Kay. Here's the deal." He paused to slurp something. Loudly. "I checked the list of names you sent me against the passports they used to get visitors' visas, and, big surprise, our guy's face doesn't match his name."

"Fake ID." Not unexpected. "At least you have a mug shot to go on."

"Sure do," he replied. "The face belongs to Gregoris Hatzis, a hired muscle convicted and sentenced for twelve months for his involvement in a national money-laundering and extortion ring. He got out seven months ago. He lives in Thessaloniki."

Not a lot to go on, but if she could talk to him, press him, maybe she could get the name of whoever hired him. "It's not much, but maybe—"

"I've got more."

"Okay."

"I wanted to see if he'd visited the mountain more than once, so I hacked into the database of the Mount Athos visa agency in Thessaloniki and got the visitors' list for the last twelve months." Reno stopped to slurp and gulp again.

"Really?" She wanted to reach through the phone and destroy whatever he was sucking on. "Did you just swallow a poodle?"

"Huh?"

"Never mind, Anaconda. And?"

"Although his name or face didn't show up, someone else's did. Matter of fact, this person visited four times in the past six months."

"Lykourgos?" she asked.

"Aw, crap." Reno sounded sincerely disappointed. "How did you guess?"

"Because he's my suspect, and it's the only other name in the sea of Greek names you've been swimming in that would draw your attention." She gazed across the expanse of blue toward Porto Carras, less than two miles away, where the *Pegasus* was anchored. Reno's GPS fix from the cell phones had pinpointed the ship, but it couldn't be seen from her position because of the rocky peninsula between them.

"Blah blah blah. I bet you feel all cool and smart right about now."

"I kinda do." Switch snickered. "Did you check if he'd visited prior to the past six months, like annually or something?"

"Of course I checked. And no, I went as far back as the electronic records would allow—which is twenty years—and no mention of him."

"Why the hell would Lykourgos want to visit the Holy Mountain all of a sudden and that often?"

"Scope out the area, find the right monk?"

"Yeah, maybe. Although he could have had someone do that for him. Why risk being seen repeatedly and go on the record, if you intend to steal?"

"And that's why you do what you do," Reno replied, "And I do what I do."

"I need to call Father Giorgos. Later, and thanks." Switch hung up and untangled the tentacles from her arm before she dialed the archbishop. It took a long while before she was finally put through.

"Father Giorgos, I have some questions regarding a returning guest."

"Of course."

"What can you tell me about Konstantinos Lykourgos?"

"The shipping magnate." He cleared his throat. "You must understand that what any guest confides in me, or any of us, stays confidential."

"With all due respect, Father, if you want us to find the *Theotokos* you're going to have to make exceptions."

"Mr. Lykourgos is a respected man and has been very generous to the Holy Mountain."

"That's great, and I'm sure he's a wonderful human being, but I find it strange he should visit the Holy Mountain four times in a period of six months. I thought there was a waiting list."

"There is. But exceptions can be made."

"Did you personally make the exception?"

"I did."

"Father, Lykourgos's yacht was spotted anchored outside the monastery just days before the theft."

"I don't see the connection."

"He never sails in Halkidiki."

"Maybe he changed his mind."

"Maybe." Trying to be politically correct and polite was testing her patience. "Didn't you find it strange that Mr. Lykourgos sought your company and the Holy Mountain so often, for the first time in his life?"

"People change."

"But not without a reason."

The archbishop sighed. "If it helps any, and it's about all I can say...Mr. Lykourgos spent a lot of time praying and crying."

"In your company?"

"And alone. We would talk for hours, and then I'd leave him in the same chapel, in the same position, where he would stay for hours on his knees and pray."

"Which chapel?"

"He prayed to the miraculous icon of Panagia Tricherousa at the Holy Monastery of Hilandariou."

"Why there?" she asked.

"Do you know the story of Saint John Damascene?"

"I'm sorry. I don't."

"Saint John was a great supporter of the worship of icons and, with his many writings, was one of the many monks who advocated the use of holy icons. In an effort to silence Saint John, Emperor Leo sent word to Caliph Walid of Syria that Saint John was conspiring to overthrow his rule in Syria."

"Okay."

"The caliph had John arrested and ordered that his right hand be cut off in view of the public. Saint John prayed to Panagia Tricherousa all night and awoke with his hand reattached."

Oh, boy. "Wow. A miracle, indeed."

"Yes."

Switch could picture the father crossing himself at the mere recitation of the story. "So, the icon Lykourgos visited was a healing one, very much like the *Theotokos*."

"Yes." The father still sounded moved by the story. "But the *Theotokos* is not open to view by pilgrims and is practically unknown."

"Did you know that Lykourgos has one of the world's largest private antiquity collections?"

The archbishop was silent for a long while. "I do not busy myself with modern media and such."

"Well, he does. And he's probably one of the very few people who've heard of the *Theotokos*." The monk went quiet again, this time for so long Switch thought he'd hung up. "You there, Father?" He cleared his throat. "He is a good man. Troubled, but a good man."

"I'm sure." Switch rolled her eyes. How could someone so enlightened be so blind? "Father, one more question."

"Hmm?"

"Lykourgos—all those hours of praying and crying—did he tell you what he was so worried or upset about?"

"Yes."

"Can you tell me?"

"No. But I can tell you that he did well to come here. Only a miracle will save him."

"Is he sick, Father?"

"That's all I can say."

Switch couldn't understand the monk's misplaced loyalty. For someone desperate to have the *Theotokos* recovered, he seemed overly defensive of their number-one suspect. "Why are you protecting him?"

"I protect anyone who comes to me for help and forgiveness."

"Even if that means never recovering the *Theotokos*?"

"I am, above all, a man of God. It is my duty to protect His flock."

Switch's eyes rolled so far back she feared they'd never recover. "Thank you for your time, Father. I'll contact you if I have any more questions."

"Good day, Mr. Ramos."

Switch settled back in the lush lounge chair on the deck. If Reno hadn't mentioned any medical records, then that meant there was nothing worth mentioning. But even if Lykourgos was sick, was it remotely plausible to have had the *Theotokos* stolen in hopes of hope? She dialed Reno.

"You again," he said.

"Hey, listen. Did you find any medical records on Lykourgos?"

"Nothing special. Just the usual age-related stuff. High blood pressure, and let me see…" He clicked away on his keyboard. "Allergic to penicillin, high cholesterol, and…that's weird. His last checkup was three years ago, though he'd been consistent with annual visits since 1994."

"Broke a habit of nearly twenty years."

"It would appear so." Reno clicked away. "I can't find anything else."

"Try Europe and overseas."

"Good idea. Give me a few." More clicking.

Switch looked at the octopus at her feet, its tentacles still undulating as it sought an escape. A lot of preparation and treatment were involved in cooking it, and the way her day was turning out, she doubted she'd have the time. Switch picked up the creature and threw it back in the sea. "Another time."

"I found him, or it. Whatever," Reno said.

"Shoot."

"All his files, doctors, and such are at the University of Texas, MD Anderson Cancer Center."

"What was he diagnosed with?"

"Lung cancer, stage three. He received chemo and radiation, but with no positive result. They gave him a year, and this was last December."

"Desperate people do desperate things."

"Would an educated, respectable man believe that an icon and prayer could cure him?" Reno asked.

"Hope dies last." Switch ran her hand through her hair. "I still don't have enough to build a case against Lykourgos. Pierce has given me a week to find evidence the Greek is involved, and without something more substantial, I'll have to let Lykourgos walk."

"Yeah, but…do you really care? I mean, sure he could possibly be behind the theft, but so what?" Reno asked. "Why waste your time on an iffy case and not take a well-deserved time-out?"

"I know you're right, but I like what I do."

"More than you like the gallery, sailing, or, I dunno…just chillin'?"

"I can't enjoy any of that if I can't look forward to it," she replied. "Besides, it gives me satisfaction to know that things are where they belong."

"Paintings in museums, icons in churches—"

"Etcetera, etcetera. Yeah." Switch waved at a passing fishing boat. "I love the hunt and need the challenge, even if I don't always succeed."

"You just described my sex life," Reno grumbled.

Switch laughed. "Might have something to do with your larynx."

Reno laughed loudly, too. "Could be."

"Hey, whatever happened to the video footage I sent you?"

"Should get it back from the lab any minute. There was no way to clear up the image enough to make out faces with my software. The monks' equipment isn't great, and the yacht was too far to zoom in and preserve any kind of quality."

"Let me know as soon as you get it."

"What are you going to do now?" Reno asked.

"Pfff, not much." She moaned. "I've reached a dead end."

"Go swimming or whatever it is you lucky bastards in Greece do."

"Later." Switch hung up and looked around the boat. Everything was in place and scrubbed. Maybe she should go find that octopus she'd thrown back.

She adjusted the mask on her face and had one swim fin on when her phone rang again. She hopped across the deck to where she'd left it, careful not to break her neck in the process.

She checked the ID and flopped on the lounge chair. "Seriously, dude. You need to make more friends."

"You won't *believe* this, dude." Reno's voice was a mixture of excitement and shock. "Unfucking believable."

"Tell me already."

"So, just got the footage back."

Switch felt her heartbeat accelerate in anticipation. This had to be good if Reno was blown away by it. "And?"

"Guess who's standing next to Lykourgos, pointing at the Holy Mountain?"

"Since you're out of breath and about to make a hell of a revelation, it can't be anyone less than Jimmy Hoffa."

"Theodora Quinevere Rothschild."

Switch shot straight up. "TQ."

"The one and only."

"The crazy bitch is in Greece with Lykourgos."

"Uh-huh."

"You sure it's her?"

"Ran it through the FBI facial-recognition software and she's a complete match."

Switch didn't know what to think or feel. Like everyone else in the EOO, she too was all too aware of what had almost happened last year when the crazy bitch tried to kill Jack Harding and the operation it took by the EOO's Governing Trio to recover her. Contrary to many other ops, Switch had no issues with Harding. Live and let live was her motto, and if faking your death to get out of a sick situation was what it took, then so be it. "If you were Lykourgos and looking to steal a priceless artifact, who would you call?"

"I wanna say *Ghostbusters*, but the demon bitch trumps even them," he replied.

"Does Pierce know?"

"Not yet."

"Good. I just found my ticket to this case." Switch wanted to be the first to tell him and reap the benefits. "Thanks, guy. Talk later." She hung up and immediately dialed Pierce.

"I assume whatever you have to say couldn't wait till morning," he said when he answered.

"TQ."

She heard a sharp intake of breath on the other end. Pierce didn't reply for several seconds. "What about Rothschild?" he finally asked, his voice like ice.

"I had the image from the security cam enhanced, and she's right there on deck with Lykourgos, the two of them side by side, staring up at the Holy Mountain."

"What the hell is she doing in Greece with him?"

"Getting paid to steal a virtually unknown and invaluable artifact?"

"She'd know about the *Theotokos*," he replied, his voice rising in excitement, "and she has the manpower and means."

"What she didn't have was the location. Lykourgos gave it to her. He's turned the Holy Mountain into a second home the past six months."

"Very transparent of him."

"Not really. I don't think his initial visits there had to do with the *Theotokos*. As it turns out, he spent all his time crying and praying for a miracle."

"A mira—"

"He's dying. Lung cancer, and he thinks the healing icon can save him."

"Preposterous," Pierce said. "And irrelevant to why you're going to do this job."

"I thought so. I want the icon back in its place and you—"

"I want TQ behind bars in a country where jail is still intended as punishment and not rehab."

"The Greeks have very strict and scary laws when it comes to illicit trading or theft of artifacts," she said. "They take it more seriously than drug trafficking and terrorism."

"I'm aware, and that's why you're going to help me put her there."

"So, I find the icon and bargain with Lykourgos—you know, ask him who he hired to get it and say we'll forget about the whole thing. Either that, or he faces years—or, in his case, months—in jail."

"That's right." Pierce sounded almost giddy.

"He gives you TQ, I get the icon for the monastery, and everyone's happy."

"Exactly. And as far as I know, she doesn't have contacts there to help her out."

"Let's not count on her not being able to cut a deal," Switch said. "We're talking Greek politicians. They've been bought for a lot less than what she can offer."

"You have a point."

"But I'm sure he'll spill, unless he wants to spend the remainder of his short life in prison and publically humiliated. No one wants to step out like that."

"Yes," he replied, with a rare, almost boyish excitement. "Yes, you need to get the icon before he dies, or we'll have nothing on her."

"I need to locate it, first." The challenge amped Switch. She removed the swim fin and got up to pace in order to control her enthusiasm.

"Start at his house," Pierce said.

"I don't think that's necessary. Although Reno couldn't GPS him, he did find his son and daughter in the Aegean, on board the family monster yacht."

"And?"

"If the guy has a few months to live, I think he's going to want to spend that time with his family."

"You think the icon is on the yacht?"

"I think it's wherever Lykourgos is. He needs to see the icon in order to pray to the Virgin. That's the whole point."

"So, we need to get you on his boat."

"If I'm to find the relic, then I need to watch him closely, see where he goes. It's only a matter of time before he runs off to be alone with his…cure." Switch heard Pierce mumble something, and a familiar voice chimed in in the background. "Is that Reno?"

"Yes." A brief pause, then, "According to him, Lykourgos's guard positions are exclusively from his own privately trained ex-military men."

"Damn. I need to be posted near him at least most of the time. What else have we got?"

"Hold on." Pierce sounded frustrated. "You're on speaker."

"Okay, we have steward…" Reno's voice.

"On call all the time," Switch replied.

"Engineer…or deckhand."

"Won't have run of the yacht."

"First mate?" Reno offered.

Switch started to pace. "Too closely watched by the captain."

"Masseuse."

"Eewww, and I'd still have limited access."

"I'm running out of available positions," he said. "How about—"

"Bosun," Switch said. "It'll give me the most latitude to be everywhere, with lots of free time so I won't constantly be monitored."

"No positions available. And he demands male bosuns exclusively," Reno replied.

Pierce cut in. "The later is not an issue. And we can create an opening."

"You're going to…to kill him for the position?" Reno sounded horrified.

"Do you work part-time in a meth trailer?" Pierce. "No one's going to kill the bosun."

"But I can incapacitate him," Switch said.

"Like, break his arms and…and his legs, and blind him?" Reno sounded like he was going to retch. "I don't know how you guys do it. I really don't get it. It's—"

"Good grief, man." Pierce stopped Reno's tirade. "Have you finally managed to push a straw so far up your nose you lodged it in your brain?"

"I'm not going to cut him into pieces and send him to his mother, Reno," Switch said, trying her hardest not to laugh.

"Don't encourage him." Pierce again. "I'm not kidding, you know. I actually walked in once and found him with a straw up each nostril."

Pierce must be on new meds. Switch had never heard him be so open and spontaneous before. Or maybe the mere thought of TQ in a Greek prison had done the trick.

"I was playin'," Reno said. "Hey, I was just playin', Alex."

"She's on a job," Pierce said.

"What, I didn't say Switch? I meant Switch."

"Just go back to your work or whatever you do in there."

"Fine. But only because I want to." Reno sounded like a scolded child.

"I'll take care of the bosun," she said. "It's good timing. The yacht is anchored off the Grand Resort of Porto Carras, so I bet he's getting shore leave. Not a lot of bars and clubs to check. Should be easy to find."

"I'll get the proper CV, pull the right strings, and get you ready to replace him," Pierce said.

"Have Reno send me some of the bosun's stats: picture, etcetera. You get the paperwork ready and I'll move in on the guy as soon as you give me the go-ahead."

"Get ready to move in on him by tonight." Pierce hung up.

CHAPTER SEVEN

Porto Carras, Greece
Next afternoon

To have accomplished as much as he had in less than twenty-four hours, Monty must have assigned a small army to the task of setting up Operation Divine Intervention, Switch mused, which spoke volumes about his passion for bringing TQ to justice. Within a few hours, he'd gotten the necessary approvals from the other two members of the EOO Governing Trio, had obtained a detailed blueprint of the *Pegasus*, and arranged for her to be hired as a replacement bosun after the usual crewmember's unfortunate accident.

He'd even managed to build a very credible resume for her cover, which listed a number of well-known commercial cruise ships among her previous experience. She had no doubt the captains of those vessels gave Alex Ramos a glowing recommendation when Lykourgos had them checked this morning.

Though excited to get the mission under way, she knew this one would contain some unusual challenges. She'd worked on a number of boats before as an op, but never anything as massive as the *Pegasus*, and as bosun she'd have a complex job with immense responsibility. Merely finding her way around the ship would be an issue initially. And Monty had also learned that, in addition to Lykourgos's family, a couple dozen other guests were on board, mostly friends of his wife, daughter, and son. They might make it difficult to effectively search the entire ship.

Whether TQ was still aboard was something she'd have to find out firsthand, as none of the records Reno checked contained any mention of her.

She'd dressed conservatively, in plain black trousers, black button-down shirt, and leather boots with rubber soles, in the event she met the owner before she got her shipboard uniform. While she waited for the *Pegasus*'s inflatable dinghy to pick her up, she scanned the blueprint to locate the crew's quarters and where she'd be staying. She also familiarized herself with the onboard security system, the list of current crewmembers and their backgrounds, and the general duties of a bosun aboard the *Pegasus*, since that position could vary widely from ship to ship.

When the distant buzz of an approaching Zodiac caught her attention, she put the paperwork back into her duffel and stepped onto the pier. Two *Pegasus* crewmembers—both second bosuns, according to the epaulets on their white dress uniforms—had been dispatched to transport her the short distance to the superyacht.

She stepped in and the Zodiac headed off at top speed as soon as she was settled.

"Welcome on board." The attractive thirty-something guy with deliberate stubble who was at the outboard motor smiled and greeted Switch loudly in Greek over the engine's roar. The other man, probably in his late twenties and much shorter, smiled as well and nodded hello.

The *Pegasus* looked enormous from a distance, but close up it was practically a small city. "Good to be here," she shouted back.

In no time, they were disembarking on the rear transom.

"We were told you have plenty of experience, so this should be a breeze," said the tall, stubbled one. "I'm Manos, by the way, and this is Fotis."

Both guys looked friendly and genuinely warm, but Manos looked like he was x-raying Switch.

"Call me Alex," she replied. "I've worked on cruise ships, but I'm a first-timer on a privately owned monster yacht."

"No worries. We'll show you around." Manos smiled, displaying even, white teeth. "It's a good job. Lykourgos is super relaxed and a lot of fun to work for."

"Okay, then. Let's get started with my cabin." Switch hefted her duffel.

They took a crew stairwell two floors down, then followed a long hallway. Manos opened the door to what would be her quarters.

The room had a bunk bed, night table, closet, and what was probably a small bathroom. It wasn't as tiny as she'd expected, but then again, nothing was small about the *Pegasus*.

Privacy was a real concern, however, considering her disguise. "Who am I bunking with?"

"No one," Fotis replied. "We share when we need a bigger staff for longer trips and more guests, but this trip is all about close friends and direct family members."

"Cool." *Thank God.* The last thing she needed was to sleep bandaged up.

"Let's get you changed for the tour and a meet-and-greet with the owner. Your clothes are in the closet," Manos said, carefully scrutinizing Switch again. "You're a bit thinner than the guy you're replacing, but about the same height, so they should fit. If not, we'll hit the crew laundry. Oh, and your radio's on your bunk."

"Does Lykourgos meet with all his new staff members?"

"You bet," Fotis replied. "He doesn't like faces he can't put a name to walking around the yacht."

"Makes sense."

Both men stood at the door, waiting. "Hurry, then," Manos said.

Jesus, were they going to stand there while she changed? "You know what? You guys go ahead. I'll find you on deck."

"Shy?" Manos laughed. "Am I that obvious?"

"What?" Switch asked, confused.

"Just because I'm gay doesn't mean I find every guy attractive."

"Oh." She didn't see that coming. "No, it's not that."

Manos pulled Fotis away from the door. "Let's go. I don't want Alex to think I'm hitting on him."

"Because you would never do that." Fotis rolled his eyes and pointed to his companion. "He's a slut."

"Well, excuse me for burdening you with my exciting sex life," Manos replied. "Not all of us choose to pine away for the impossible. The beautiful, lovely, wonderful Ariadne," he went on, drawing out the words in a comical way. "Way, way, *way* beyond your league, and the faster you realize that, the faster we can all get some sleep." He made a crude masturbation gesture and laughed.

"Move it, flamer." Clearly aggravated, Fotis pushed the taller man out of the room and shut the door behind them.

Switch sighed in relief and had started to unbutton her shirt when the door opened again. It was Manos.

"Just FYI, you're a hell of a good-looking kid." He winked at Switch.

"Thanks?" Switch hoped the bandage wasn't showing.

"Don't be long." He left and closed the door.

She wasn't going to take any more chances. She locked the door before she changed into her dress whites.

"Smile a lot. He likes friendly faces," Manos said as they approached the Lykourgos family on the aft, third-tier deck. They were having brunch beneath an awning and were all being very talkative.

Lykourgos looked just like he did in the magazines, with his thick gray hair and dark eyebrows, only skinnier and paler. She also had a clear view of the wife and son as they approached, but the daughter had her back to them.

"Manos, you bring me good news," Lykourgos said when they got a few feet from the table, and everyone turned to look except for the daughter.

"I like to make you happy," Manos said.

"Mr. Lykourgos, I'm Alex." Switch offered her hand.

Lykourgos, still seated, shook her hand so hard Switch thought he was trying to rip her arm off. Away from the *Pegasus*, one would be hard pressed to peg him as a billionaire in his faded jeans, well-worn shirt and sandals, unkempt hair, and stubble of beard. But that didn't really surprise her. Shipping magnates, even very wealthy ones, were usually a breed unto themselves. Their primary passion was the sea, not money, and they were a generally unpretentious type. For them, yachts weren't vehicles to impress their friends, more like mistresses who fulfilled their innermost desires. "You have a good grip, young man." He finally let go.

Switch grinned, happy to have her hand back. "Thank you, sir."

"So." He clapped. "This is my beautiful family." He gestured around the table, pausing first at his wife. "This is Mrs. Lykourgos."

"Call me Christine." His attractive and elegant wife smiled. She was younger than her spouse, but not by much, and she obviously took exceptional care of her appearance. Her hair was recently coiffed, her makeup perfect, each polished nail exquisitely manicured. The value of the jewelry she was wearing would have fed a small village for years, and she clearly never bought off the rack.

"Nice to meet you, Christine."

"I'm Nikolaos." The young man waved. He was twenty-four and a replica of his father except for hair color.

"Hi," Switch replied.

Lykourgos gestured lovingly toward his daughter. "And this…is Ariadne."

The daughter looked briefly up from her newspaper and gave Switch a quick glance. Then, what she'd seen in that glimpse seemed to register, somehow, and, after a beat, she turned her head, slowly this time, to look at her again. She looked straight into Switch's eyes…then deliberately took a long time to fully assess the rest of her. "How old are you?" she finally asked.

Switch stood at attention with her hands behind her. "Twenty-four." She kept her gaze steady and smiled.

"Ha! You look younger." Ariadne checked her out again, but this time she stopped at Switch's crotch and stared with the curiosity and disinterest of a gay woman. When she saw what she had, or hadn't, expected, she looked up at Switch again.

Switch was used to the scrutiny of strangers when it came to her androgynous looks, but she wasn't used to feeling like she'd been hit by a tornado. Ariadne was, without a doubt, a stunning and sensual woman. Breathtaking. She could see why Fortis had a thing for her. "I get that a lot," she casually replied.

"Where are you from?" Ariadne asked.

"Thessaloniki."

"Aha."

It felt as though Ariadne was looking for questions just to keep Switch there.

"You're one of those lucky guys who don't need to shave," Nikolaos said.

"So they tell me."

"As you can see," Lykourgos said jovially, "my family likes to ask questions. A lot of questions."

"That's fine, sir. I have nothing to hide."

"Manos, show the new kid around and make sure he knows what he's doing," Lykourgos said.

"Yeah, Manos." Ariadne turned to the second bosun and smiled. "Make sure he knows what he's doing." She winked at him.

Great. Now she thinks I'm a gay dude, too.

Manos spent the next two hours walking Switch through the massive ship's seven decks to familiarize her with the layout. Though she'd studied the blueprints and exterior photos Reno was able to snag off the Internet, she hadn't fully appreciated the sheer scope of the *Pegasus* until she saw it for herself.

On the first two decks, Lykourgos had lavishly outfitted the ship with a number of specialty rooms for his guests to enjoy. Two lounges with state-of-the-art sound systems, dance floors, and well-equipped bars had been designed for his children and their friends, while his own guests usually gravitated toward the cigar lounge, sauna/steam rooms, or the massive library, with its oversized leather pub chairs and wide assortment of reading material in several languages. The casino was also a popular hangout, with a roulette wheel, blackjack table, slot machines, and other amenities.

His wife had her own hair salon and a game room with its own bar for her marathon biriba sessions. She also took daily manicures and massages in the spa while on board. Manos warned that she was never to be disturbed there, under any circumstances.

On the graduated upper decks were the two helicopter landing pads and the hangar for Lykourgos's Eurocopter Mercedes-Benz EC145, as well as two pools: a fifty-foot seawater pool with hot and cold Jacuzzis on either side, and a freshwater lap pool. Both had changing cabanas and rows of comfy lounge seating. There were outdoor dining areas there, as well; Switch noticed an abundance of places to dine, or drink, scattered throughout the ship. Each bar they passed seemed to be stocked with every conceivable kind of alcohol and had only the finest crystal glassware.

Once they finished with the recreational areas of the ship, Manos led her past the many guest cabins, all plushly furnished with the finest furniture, linens, flat-screen TVs, and amenities. Lykourgos's son and daughter had enormous staterooms, but the billionaire and his wife's master suite trumped them both.

"When Mr. Lykourgos is in his quarters," Manos said, "a bodyguard is always positioned outside. When he is elsewhere, the room is kept locked and alarmed. Only his family and maid have keycards, and the maid's is locked in the chief steward's safe when she isn't cleaning the room."

Manos knocked twice on the door and announced his name, and a few seconds later, the light on the door changed from red to green. The door opened to reveal a short, heavyset woman in her fifties, dressed in a starched black-and-white uniform.

"Alex, this is Mr. and Mrs. Lykourgos's maid. She's been with them forever." To the woman, he added, "Alex is our new bosun. I'm showing him around."

Switch nodded hello, then looked past her into Lykourgos's suite. Its living-room area had more square footage than the entirety of her boat, and the place was loaded with artwork and artifacts from his collection. She couldn't see into the bedroom or bath.

Too soon, Manos continued on, below deck to the crew quarters, where, in an impromptu meeting in the bosun's office, he introduced her around to the deckhands she'd be supervising. Then they toured the crew's dining area and moved on to the thousand-square-foot galley and food-storage areas. The long, walk-in cooler and pantry seemed to be stocked with enough provisions to feed a small army for six months. Dozens of live lobster swam in their own tank, and Switch could see a handful of sous chefs currently working on other freshly caught Aegean delicacies.

Aft of the galley were the engine rooms and the billionaire's private submarine, capable of diving to three hundred feet. The only area in the underbelly of the ship designed for guests was a cozy lounge with a glass floor, so they could watch the fish and sea creatures swimming by as they enjoyed cocktails. It was accessed by the spectacular spiral staircase that ran through all seven levels of the ship.

"Any questions, come find me," Manos said as they returned to the bosun's office. He fished a clipboard off the desk. "Here is the crew roster and their schedules," he said, pointing to the top page. "And the list of current guests, with a brief description of their likes and dislikes, so you'll know who is apt to need our services. Your first job will be to get the Jet Skis ready. Ariadne and three of her friends want to take them out in a half hour." He started to leave. "Oh, and don't forget to change."

"No problem." As soon as she was alone, Switch flipped to the list of today's guests. Her heartbeat accelerated when she saw Theodora Rothschild among the twenty-six names.

CHAPTER EIGHT

Switch noted that TQ was assigned to the Olympus Suite, one of the premium cabins in the front of the ship. Those doors had all been closed when they'd passed by on the tour.

She found no special instructions for TQ on the guest page, at least not her version of it. Not surprising, since the bitch didn't seem the type to waterski, Jet Ski, or participate in any of the other water-related sports the bosun oversaw. Switch found no notes for planned excursions to shore, either. But one other note on the guest list caught her eye. Beside the name Yu Suk was the notation: Rothschild domestic/Crew quarters 9F.

She needed to access the chief steward's guest records, which would be much more comprehensive. Shouldn't be too difficult, since his office was just two doors down from hers and the locks down here were pathetic.

Switch wished she had time to swing by the Olympus Suite right now, but it just wasn't possible. She'd never get all the way there and back and still have time to get the Jet Skis ready. She shut the door to the hall, dug through the half-empty wastebasket for past guest lists, and discovered that Rothschild had arrived only the day before. The trash didn't go back further than three days, so she had no way to know specifics about TQ's previous visit, when she'd no doubt struck the deal with Lykourgos as they stared up at the Holy Mountain.

This current visit, she concluded, was probably to deliver the stolen icon and receive her payment.

She checked the time and hurriedly changed again, this time

into her casual uniform—a bright-blue polo shirt with the ship's logo emblazoned on the chest, white shorts, and boat shoes. She was thankful young males in Greece had taken to shaving their legs during the hot months, because that meant she no longer had to worry about that when she had to pose as the opposite sex.

She went aft and found the personal-watercraft lockers adjacent to the transom. Another deckhand helped her maneuver four of the Jet Skis to the hydraulic davit, a small crane installed to lower them one by one into the water. She was tying off the last one when a voice hailed her from the deck above.

"Hey."

Switch looked up to find Ariadne bent over the railing, watching her. The sight of Lykourgos's daughter in her barely there bikini, just a few feet away, made her immensely grateful she'd put on her sunglasses. Those dark pieces of plastic were the only things that kept Ariadne from noticing that she couldn't stop staring at that magnificent cleavage. "Beautiful day." She tried to sound pleasantly nonchalant. "You're all set to go."

"Great." Ariadne smiled.

Switch could barely manage the breast situation, but that incredible smile was just too much. She knew she should look away, or say something, or just simply breathe, but she couldn't do anything but gawk at her.

Ariadne frowned. "Do I have something in my teeth?"

"No," Switch mumbled.

"You're staring."

Switch casually put her hands in her pockets. "Oh, that. Sometimes I do that when I'm running a mental checklist." She turned to look at the Jet Skis. "Want to make sure I didn't forget anything."

"Pretty intense."

"Scary, right?" Switch hoped Ariadne was buying it.

"Are you that intense with everything?" Ariadne raised one eyebrow.

Boy, would I love to show you. "No." She shrugged. "Not everything."

"Name something that makes you tick."

Your breasts. I can be passionate about those. "The sea, art, and…" Switch couldn't come up with anything else, at least nothing appropriate. "And that's about it."

"Yeah, I thought so."

"Hmm?"

"Art. So obvious." Ariadne snickered. "Stupid question."

If Ariadne was insinuating something, Switch wasn't getting it. Why would she say art was obvious? Had she been made? Had Ariadne recognized her from her gallery? She didn't think that was possible. She was careful to keep a low profile there, viewing her new pieces always in the back room to avoid being seen by the wealthy visitors she might have to deal with some day as Switch. "Why is art so funny?" She wasn't sure she wanted to hear the answer.

"Well, most gay guys are into art," Ariadne replied.

"Gay gu…I'm…" Switch stuttered.

Ariadne looked away when she heard voices approaching from behind her. "Hey, took you long enough," she called out, and soon another three women stood next to her, all brunettes. They peered down at Switch.

"Guys," Ariadne said, "this is Alex, the new bosun."

"Hi, Alex," they sang in unison.

"Ladies," Switch replied.

"This is Jo, Melina, and Natasa." Ariadne named them from her right to her left.

"How old are you, Alex?" Melina bent over the rail so far she was nearly face-to-face with Switch. The oldest of the women, probably in her late thirties while the others were a decade younger, she was very attractive and had impressive cleavage, too, but Adriane was still the clear winner.

"Twenty-four," Switch replied.

"Single?"

"Yes."

"Since when do you care?" Ariadne asked her friend.

Melina stood upright again and lifted her hands in dramatic surrender. "I'm trying something new."

"Good luck with this one." Ariadne said it under her breath, but everyone heard.

"Be careful," Melina shot back. "You're sounding like a bitter spinster again." She returned her attention to Switch. "Take off your sunglasses."

When she complied, Melina bent over the rail again for a closer look. "I love your eyes. They're an amazing shade of blue."

"Thank you." Switch put them back on, trying hard not to laugh at Ariadne, who was rolling her eyes and looking away in exasperation. "I'm glad you think so." She couldn't help but encourage Melina's flirting. Ariadne's comical frustration was too precious.

"Watch out." Jo pointed her thumb at Melina. "This one's dangerous."

"Dangerously hot," Melina said. The woman didn't miss an opportunity.

"Dangerously desperate," Ariadne chimed in.

"You're just bitter…a little bitter…a spinster, and, oh, yeah… almost forgot…bitter." Melina addressed the others without taking her eyes off Switch.

"You know you can't stop her," Natasa said drolly to Ariadne. "And I don't blame her."

The other three women turned in unison to look at Natasa with shocked expressions.

"My God!" Melina squealed. "She has a libido."

Natasa smiled timidly. "Screw you, slut."

"I'd do him, too," Jo, the petite one of the group, offered.

Switch didn't know where to look. She sure didn't expect her first day on the yacht to be this uncomfortably pleasant.

"How about you?" Melina put her arm around Ariadne. "I know it's not your cuppa gender, but would you, if you…" She waved her hand, trying to come up with the rest of that. "…you weren't so resolutely gay?"

Switch had read about Ariadne's preferences way before she'd ever met her. Lykourgos had given an interview a few years back saying how he supported his daughter's lifestyle and choices. Until now, she'd been handling the playful, girlish insinuations and even open advances just fine, but once Melina involved Ariadne, the situation grew suddenly more awkward. Switch didn't want to hear the answer, because for some reason she didn't want to risk disappointment.

Ariadne checked all of Switch out, as if looking for something, and stopped at her eyes. Her direct gaze was unnerving. "I…I…uh,"

Ariadne stuttered. "I don't sleep with guys."

Melina looked knowingly at Switch. "Well, it's not like she's been *sleeping* with girls either."

"I've slept with—" Ariadne stopped. "It's irrelevant."

"You mean infinitesimal." Jo laughed.

Ariadne took a step back, looking uncomfortable. Why were they ragging on her? Switch wondered. Not all twenty-something women were obsessed with sex. Some had too heavy a burden or responsibilities weighing on them to worry about whether they got laid.

"So, unless you need my assistance…" Switch turned to the Jet Skis.

"We're fine," Ariadne said coldly, sounding almost irritated, as the four women descended the few steps to the transom. But hey, it wasn't Switch's fault her friends had chosen the bosun to have fun with.

She'd started to walk away when Melina stopped her.

"Except for me." Melina waved. "It's my first time, and—"

Ariadne cut in. "No, it's not."

"Like I was saying, it's my first time."

Switch walked back to them. "It's quite easy," she said. "Easier than riding a bike."

Melina laughed like she'd heard something hysterical. "Bike? I can't ride a bike."

"You seem to ride everything else," Natasa said.

Switch didn't like where this was going. "It's very simple, really."

"Show me, will you?" Melina replied provocatively.

"I…" Switch wanted to decline, because drawing attention to herself wouldn't do, but then again, she was already heavily on the map for this bunch and it would be highly unprofessional to say no. "It would be my pleasure."

"Can you give us a few minutes, Alex?" Ariadne asked.

"Of course."

Switch headed away a discreet distance to give the women some privacy, but not before she heard Melina say, "I am so going to score."

"What has gotten into you?" Ariadne asked in a low voice as soon as the bosun was out of earshot.

"I was going to ask you the same. Well, almost the same." Melina peeled off her shirt to reveal a skimpy bikini top. Even though she was wearing sunglasses, Ariadne could see where her friend was looking as she undressed. Alex had his back to them, and Melina was eyeing his tight, firm ass like a lioness scoping out her next meal.

"I'm just having some fun, that's all." Melina folded her shirt. "Where between the breakfast table and the deck did you drop your sense of humor?"

"You made him uncomfortable," Ariadne replied.

"So? It's not the first time."

"Why can't you stick to men of your own standing?"

"Because they're boring and self-involved. We've already gone through this." Melina turned to her, clearly annoyed. "For God's sake, it's not like I'm going to marry him. I simply want to have some fun before the summer's over."

"Weren't the islands enough?" They'd spent most of the previous month skipping between their favorite beaches—on Santorini, Mykonos, Ios, and Paros.

"I don't know if you noticed," Melina replied, "but I spent my nights with you and the others and not with some hot guy." She dropped her shorts. "And I refrained for all of you."

"For us?"

"Remember last summer?"

"You hooked up with some waiter."

"That's right, and I wasn't about to go through the same ordeal again. Listening to you guys go on and on about how selfish and self-centered I am for wanting to spend time with a cute boy toy."

"We hardly saw you last summer. You were constantly off with the waiter when it was supposed to be our annual fun-in-the-sun time. I got three weeks of vacation to make up for the rest of the year in England, and I wanted to have fun. Not worry about who you're with and if they're going to kidnap you." Abductions of kids from rich families had escalated since the economy plunged and remained an ongoing threat. Ariadne wasn't particularly fond of having bodyguards around when they went ashore, but she recognized the need and agreed to the increase in security for her father's sake.

"I'm a big girl, Ariadne, and I refuse to live in fear." Melina caressed Ariadne's cheek with the back of her hand. "You need to start living, too."

Ariadne had to admit her friend had a point. Too many months had passed since she'd been intimate with anyone. She'd been preoccupied with finals and the increased pressure her father had placed on her to learn the intricacies of his shipping empire. "I know. It's just…I don't have time."

"More like you still haven't gotten over that bisexual floozy who broke your heart."

She didn't want to think about the past, though it still stung to remember how thoroughly Eva had used her to get what she wanted. Ariadne had spent a fortune on the woman to keep her happy, mostly on shopping sprees and expensive restaurants. "Be that as it may, I—"

"Well, you know what?" Melina raised Ariadne's chin. "We have a few weeks left and we're going to make them count."

"What do you have in mind?"

"We're going to start with some light and fairly innocent flirting." Melina walked over to the Jet Skis. "Observe and learn." She waved over the bosun, who was standing by the aft pool bar.

"I can't believe you." Ariadne laughed and removed her shorts.

"He's young, handsome in a ridiculously beautiful way, and has a killer bod."

Ariadne observed Alex as he walked toward them. He was definitely a good-looking guy, and had she and the bosun been straight, she would have probably let her hair down and taken advantage of every square inch of him, too. "He's gay, you know."

Melina raised an eyebrow. "He is definitely not gay."

"Look at him. He's too pretty and too charming to be straight." She waved her hand. "And he's into art, for Christ's sake. Even Manos wants to hit that, and I'm sure he's going to have more luck than you."

"Ah, to be young and clueless." Melina adjusted her bikini top so that her ample cleavage was viewable from the moon. "Alex is not gay. I can tell by the way he looks at you."

Ariadne couldn't hide her shock. "Me?"

"Yes, but since you're not into dick, and I am…" Melina licked her lips as Alex joined them.

"Ready?" Alex asked Melina.

Ariadne had to admit that Alex had the most amazing smile. But almost too…something, for a guy.

"Ms. Lykourgos?" Alex interrupted her thoughts. "Is there anything you need?"

"Do you have a sister?" Melina answered for her.

Alex smiled that too-beautiful smile again. "No, I don't."

Melina pressed on. "Cousin?"

"I don't keep in touch," Alex replied, looking at Ariadne and not Melina.

"She's…she's kidding." Ariadne had to turn away from Alex's scrutinizing gaze. "For some reason, her deprived-of-oxygen mind thinks I need a matchmaker."

"I'm sure if I had a sister, she'd be very enamored with you," Alex said seriously. "Though I find it hard to believe you need a liaison to meet someone."

"Don't let the dimples fool you," Melina said. "She's a hard-ass and painfully calculating."

"I don't blame her. The paparazzi and rags will do that to a person's private life," Alex replied.

Satisfied and surprised by the remark, Ariadne couldn't help but smile at the bosun. "And on that perceptive and intelligent note…" She walked over to one of the Jet Skis. "Later, man-eater."

"Where did the other two go off to?" Melina looked around for Jo and Natasa.

"Over at the bar." Alex pointed.

"Shall we…instructor?" Melina practically purred the words.

Ariadne jumped on the machine and revved hard to make sure both Melina and Alex were left soaked.

A few seconds later, Melina and her boy toy were riding alongside her, Melina's arms wrapped tightly around Alex's waist.

"I'm feeling vengeful," Melina shouted over the roar of the engines at Ariadne. Then to Alex, she added, "Make her pay."

Alex smirked. "I don't want to get in trouble," he yelled back, looking over at Ariadne. "She may be a sore loser."

"To the rocks over there." Ariadne pointed. "And back."

Melina practically wrapped her breasts around Alex's neck, much to Ariadne's annoyance. "Beat her, and I'll reward you."

"On the count of three," Alex shouted.

When the bosun reached two, Ariadne gunned the engine and shot ahead of them, swerving the Jet Ski to spray them both as thoroughly as possible.

Switch had a hard time breathing the way Melina was holding on to her. Though an impressively sexy woman wearing nothing but a skimpy bikini was pressed up against her, Switch couldn't take her eyes off the backside of the woman a few feet ahead of them. Thoughts of Ariadne pressed against her instead of Melina distracted her, and she didn't swerve in time to avoid Ariadne's next splash. She was drenched now, and so was her passenger.

"Stop staring at her ass and do something," Melina shouted in her ear.

"Damn right," Switch yelled back.

She opened the throttle and soon they were racing all-out, both drivers trying to splash the other as they sped for the rocks. Switch barely made it there first and had just turned the Jet Ski to race back to the yacht when she saw Lykourgos's helicopter rise from the top deck. Was he going somewhere? If so, then now would be an ideal time to try to get into his quarters. She had to get back on board and ask Manos to relieve her.

Switch reached the transom with Ariadne close behind and cut the engine.

Melina pumped her arms with excitement. "We won! We won!"

Ariadne, like Switch, didn't react to the outcome. She, too, was fixed on the helicopter.

"Is Mr. Lykourgos leaving?" Switch asked.

"No," Ariadne replied. "I'm sure it's that nasty excuse of a human being."

"You mean that horribly cold associate of your dad's?" Melina asked.

"Yeah, the Rothschild bitch."

Holy crap. That close, and Switch had missed her. The helicopter headed off toward Thessaloniki and all too soon was just a speck in the distance.

"You're lucky you didn't have to deal with her," Melina said to Switch.

"Yeah, well, let's just hope she's gone for good." Ariadne frowned.

Switch wanted to ask more, but that would be too obvious and unprofessional.

"And that poor Asian woman who works for her? Christ, I've seen people treat rabid bats better." Melina leaned into Switch from behind, her breasts pressed against her back. "So, where were we?" she asked. "Oh, yeah. My hunk beat you."

"Good ride, Alex," Ariadne said, getting off her Jet Ski.

"Thanks," Switch replied, too distracted by TQ's departure to participate further in the fun and games. "I should probably get back to work." She stepped off her Jet Ski and helped Melina onto the transom. "Manos is waiting to give me the rest of the tour," she lied.

"So, how about your reward?" Melina asked provocatively.

"Keep it PG," Ariadne said.

"Buy me a drink on my day off?" Switch looked around for Manos and spotted him off to the right talking with Fotis, the other second bosun.

"I believe in instant gratification." Melina wrapped her arms around Switch's neck and kissed her softly and soundly on the mouth.

"You taste so sweet," Melina said when she pulled back.

Switch broke away from the embrace and smiled politely. "Thank you for the generous reward."

Ariadne stood off to the side, pretending not to look, but Switch could see her watching them in her peripheral vision. "Imagine what she'll do if you win a medal," Ariadne muttered under her breath.

As soon as she was away from the women, Switch ducked into her quarters to call Pierce.

"TQ was on the yacht when I arrived," she said as soon as he answered. "But a little while ago, before I could make contact, she left here by helicopter, headed in the direction of Thessaloniki. Get Reno on conference."

"Damn it," Pierce replied. She heard him bark instructions to someone, and Reno joined them on the line within seconds.

"'Sup, Switch?"

"Search all of today's flights out of Thessaloniki to see if Rothschild's going anywhere. Private charters included. And trains, though that's less likely," she said. "Then the five- and four-star hotels within the city."

"Doing it as we speak," he replied.

"This is her second visit to the yacht," Switch told them both. "So it figures this was to deliver the icon and get her payment, since she was only on board one day. We have to stop her from leaving the country and I can't get off the boat. Who do we have in the area?"

"I'll have our guy in Neos Marmaras head to the airport, see what he can find out," Pierce said. "And I'll get Allegro on it, since she's in Venice and can be there fastest."

"I'll get into the chief steward's office tonight to retrieve the master records. They should have details on where she stayed between her yacht visits. She may have gone back there."

"Preliminary search is not turning up her name on any of this morning's commercial-flight manifests," Reno reported. "Still checking."

"Gotta run and get back to work. Text me if you come up with anything."

Switch spent the rest of the afternoon attending to her bosun's duties, which consisted primarily of making sure that the entire exterior of the yacht was kept immaculate. On any other ship, that would have meant a lot of hard manual labor scrubbing decks, painting, varnishing, and making repairs. But the *Pegasus* was only a couple of years old, and its numerous deckhands were well trained in their routines and needed little supervision. The job was perfect as her cover, because it allowed her free roam of the ship—she was expected to inspect every square foot of the exterior every day—and since she was the go-to person for guests for their water sports and excursions ashore, she wouldn't be questioned if found in the indoor areas.

As soon as she'd touched base with all of the deckhands she supervised, she made her way to the forward guest quarters to check out the Olympus Suite. If TQ's luggage was still there, it meant she was only going ashore briefly and would be back.

The door to the suite was open when she got there, and a maid she hadn't met yet was inside dusting the living-room area. She seemed very young, barely out of her teens.

Time to turn on the charm. "Hi there. We haven't met yet," she said in Greek. "I'm Alex, the new bosun."

The girl stopped what she was doing and gave her a shy smile. "Sofia. Happy to meet you."

"Still finding my way around." She stepped over the threshold. No luggage anywhere that she could see, but she couldn't very well walk into the bedroom to check there. "Isn't one of Ariadne's friends staying in here? She asked about going ashore later."

"No, a guest of Mr. Lykourgos was here." Sofia looked past Switch toward the hall to make sure they were alone. "Quite a demanding woman, that one. Not sorry she's gone," she added, just above a whisper. "Miss Ariadne's friends are all farther down the hallway."

"Thanks. You sure can get some real demanding bitches as guests on a yacht this size, I expect." Switch winked conspiratorially.

Sofia shook her head. "Of course, but they were saints compared to this one. Nothing was ever right. The pillows weren't soft enough, her clothes weren't ironed right, the food was not up to her standards—and our chef came from the finest restaurant in Athens. I felt sorry for the poor woman working for her. She looked terrified of Mrs. Rothschild the whole time they were here."

"I take it Mr. Lykourgos is a much better employer," Switch said.

"Oh, yes. He's very good to his staff. Not too demanding. You'll see."

"Well, better get back to work. Nice meeting you."

The girl smiled shyly. "Nice to meet you, too, Alex."

Switch wanted to get back into the billionaire's room as soon as possible to make a thorough search, but it wouldn't be easy since he didn't have any plans on the schedule to go ashore any time soon.

At dusk, she ate her dinner in the crew quarters with other members of the staff, chatting with them genially and trying to get a fix on their off-duty routines. Everyone seemed happy to be employed on the *Pegasus* and spoke highly of Lykourgos and Ariadne, who were both described as down-to-earth and unpretentious. A few were less generous in their comments about the wife and son. Christine Lykourgos was a stickler for details when she was aboard: bed linens, ironed just so, were changed daily. Fresh flowers, also replenished every morning, were arranged according to her specifications and placed throughout the master suite and in the game room where she spent most of her day. Her clothes were arranged by type and color, and every item in the private refrigerator in her suite had to be placed with the label facing outward. Son Nikolaos threw almost nightly parties aboard the yacht with his raucous friends, soirees requiring very late nights for his stewards and a massive cleanup job the next morning.

Switch did a late-night tour of the ship to supervise the deckhands, who did much of the exterior mopping chores while the guests were sleeping. About two a.m., she returned to the crew offices to find the hallway deserted and dark. Five minutes later, she was inside the chief steward's office, sorting through the records on the desk and in his computer.

The yacht's extensive guest file for TQ told her that Rothschild had been staying at the Electra Palace in Thessaloniki when she wasn't aboard the *Pegasus*—a detail she immediately texted off to Reno to check out. The file also reinforced Rothschild's reputation as a high-maintenance bitch. Among her demands: stewards and maids were instructed not to speak to her or make direct eye contact. Three large, fluffy, lavender towels of 100 percent Egyptian cotton were required for her bathroom, her pillows must be brand-new, high-quality goose down, and all onboard telephones within earshot of her suite must be disabled during the entirety of her stay. There was a lot more, along with an entire page listing the food and drinks she preferred, as well as those to be avoided. Switch found no indication in any of the paperwork that TQ would be returning to the *Pegasus*.

The other interesting tidbit she learned from her search was that Lykourgos had no timetable for his return to his home and workplace. The schedule for the *Pegasus*'s stay in the waters off Halkidiki was open-ended and she wondered why, since TQ had likely already delivered the icon.

CHAPTER NINE

Venice, Italy
Next day, four a.m.

"To what do I owe this rude awakening?" Mishael Taylor, aka EOO agent Allegro, rubbed her eyes and tried to focus on the digital clock on her nightstand.

"I need you in Greece," Montgomery Pierce replied.

Kristine Marie-Louise van der Jagt rolled over and draped her body over Misha's. "No, you can't go." It was the standard reply her partner of five years gave whenever the EOO called.

They'd had two whole months together without any missions getting in the way. Misha had even taken a long absence from her civilian job as a Formula One race-car mechanic so they could spend some quality time together at their villa. She wasn't anxious to see it end. "Kris says she needs me here." She caressed Kris's hair. "So you know, I guess I'll have to pass."

"Be in Thessaloniki by noon," Pierce said. "Your contact will meet you at the airport with details."

"Can I bring a swimsuit?"

"No."

"Can Kris come with?"

"No."

"Island-hopping a possibility?"

Pierce sighed. "No."

"Sightseeing?" She played with Kris's hair.

"No."

Pierce would ordinarily have hung up by now, but instead he was humoring her. Was he even listening? Or was he preoccupied with Grant? Joanne had softened him up a lot since they'd moved in together. "I got another ticket," she said. He'd always balked at picking up her numerous speeding tickets, so the remark was sure to get a rise out of him.

"Of course you did," he replied.

"For driving nude in clown makeup."

"Of course you were." He clearly wasn't listening. Seconds passed. "You what?" he finally asked when the coin dropped.

"Are you alone?"

"Yes."

"Where's Grant?"

"In her office."

Something was going on with him, for sure. "Are you okay?"

"Why do you ask?"

"'Cause you're still on the phone...with me."

"My blood pressure's a bit low and talking to you fixes that."

Misha laughed. "Hilarious. Did Grant buy you a sense of humor for Christmas?"

Pierce cleared his throat. "Twelve o'clock sharp, in Thessaloniki."

"Yeah, yeah. I'll be there." Misha hung up. "Pierce is being all shades of weird." She shifted to get up.

Kris climbed on top of her and kissed her on the neck. "You don't have to leave for another six hours."

"I know, but I'm wide-awake." She kissed Kris on the mouth.

"Good." Kris straddled her and removed her T-shirt. "Now, take care of your domestic responsibilities before you run off to your professional ones."

❖

Aegean Sea

As a steward brewed her another Greek coffee tableside, Ariadne scanned the latest dismal economic news in that day's *Naftemporiki* and tried to tune out the chatter of her friends. Why hadn't she taken breakfast with her family?

"Good morning." Alex's voice came from a few feet away, to her right.

Her friends looked up when they returned the greeting, but Ariadne mumbled her polite response, too absorbed in her newspaper and too irritated with her friends' new obsession to pay the slightest notice to the bosun. This trip was supposed to be about them having fun and spending time together, not about drooling over one of the crew. Sure, the guy was cute and polite. But hell…no guy was worth this much attention. They'd been talking about little else all morning.

"Is there anything I can do for you this morning, Ms. Lykourgos?" he asked. "Prepare something in the way of water sports?"

"No. Nothing I can think of, anyway."

"We want to take the Zodiac. See if we can move the party to shore." Melina stopped stuffing her face with toast, and Ariadne saw her give the bosun her "I remember what we did yesterday" smile.

"I'm going to pass." Ariadne wasn't in the mood today. "I'm rather tired." Her father had been coughing almost nonstop all night but refused to see the family doctor despite her pleas. He said it was nothing but a cold and sore throat, but it had lasted way too long for that.

"You're kidding," Jo said.

"Sorry, guys, but I'm just going to hang around the pool and read a book."

"You're too young to be hanging around the pool." Natasa poured honey over her croissant.

"And way too young to be this obsessed with reading," Melina added. "How about you, Alex? Would you mind escorting us?"

"I'd love to, but I have a list of things I need to prepare," Alex replied. "Maybe Fotis can—"

"No, that won't do." Melina leaned forward, giving him a better view of her cleavage. "It's you I want."

Ariadne turned her attention from her friends—who were all staring expectantly at the bosun—to Alex, curious what his reaction would be to such a blatant come-on.

"Perhaps next time?" Alex gave Melina one of those charming smiles.

Melina pouted her lips. "I'm holding you to it."

Alex bowed slightly. "Let me know if I can assist you with

anything, Ms. Lykourgos."

"I will."

As soon as he'd gone, she turned to Melina. "Don't you ever feel bad about leading guys on?"

"Why would I?" She laughed as though the question was absurd. "It's beneficial to both parties, after all. I get to have fun, and he gets to have the night of his life."

"Are you really going to sleep with him?" Jo sounded almost shocked.

"Well, of course she is." Ariadne folded her paper and put it down. "When was the last time she passed on a one-night frenzy?"

The other two girls laughed, but not Melina. "I'll have you know that I'm sincerely interested."

All three of them went into stunned silence.

"What?" Melina shrugged. "I like him."

"He's, like, twenty-four," Jo said.

"So what?" Melina replied seriously. "I really like him. I mean, he's fun, gorgeous, well spoken and polite, tastes great, and has…that *look*. In other words, exactly the type of guy I'm in the market for."

"What look?" Ariadne and Jo both asked at once.

"Figures the lesbian asks," Melina replied, "but you, too, Jo?"

Jo was the sweetest, but most naive, of the four of them. She was also the one to most likely spot a unicorn.

"Gentleman by day, and a wild…you know, by night," Natasa said.

"Fuck." Melina sipped her coffee. "The word you're looking for is fuck."

"You said you thought he was interested in me," Ariadne said nonchalantly.

"He'll get over it once he realizes just how uninterested *you* are and how passionately captivated *I* am. He's young. His attention span, unlike his libido, is limited."

"Poor Alex doesn't stand a chance," Jo said.

"Well." Ariadne dropped her napkin on the table and stood. "Good luck to you both." She pushed her chair under the table. "Have fun, guys. I'll catch you tonight."

Though she loved her friends, Ariadne was glad for the day off playing hostess to them. She'd met with her father after breakfast for four hours and was now finally able to relax and sunbathe, away from any further commitments or responsibility. When she reached the upper-deck pool, she found she had the place to herself, just as she'd hoped.

Ariadne took off her wrap, lay back on one of the comfortable chaise lounges, and pulled out her book.

The next thing she knew, she was waking up to the sound of voices. She didn't know how long she'd been out, but when she opened her eyes, Alex was standing a few feet away talking with the two second bosuns. He appeared relaxed but alert at the same time. Come to think of it, Alex always seemed to be on guard, as if looking for something.

She let her gaze drift from Alex's profile to the rest of his body. He was an attractive man, for sure. She could see why her friends were all over him. But there was something almost off about him, and she wasn't sure what. It was as though he was almost too perfect to be real. And he had great legs for a guy.

Alex smiled at her and Ariadne looked away, pretending to hunt for something in her bag.

"Do you need something, Ms. Lykourgos?" he asked from just beside her chair.

Ariadne jumped. "What? No, why?"

Alex had his hands folded behind him. "Because you were looking at me."

How could he know that? Ariadne put her hand to her face and only then realized she wasn't wearing her sunglasses.

Alex picked her shades up off the deck and handed them to her. "You must've dropped them when you nodded off."

Oh, great. Not only had she been caught staring, but she'd also probably been caught with her mouth open and snoring, as well. Her ex used to tease her all the time about that. After twenty-hour workdays, Ariadne would often fall into a semi-coma in the evening and snore loud enough to wake the neighbors. She put her shades on. "Thanks."

"You're welcome." Alex turned to leave.

"So, how do you like it on board *Pegasus*?"

He resumed his "at attention" stance, hands behind his back. "It's a beautiful yacht."

"I think it's too big."

"I agree."

"Do you sail?"

He nodded. "Smaller boats."

Ariadne didn't want Alex to leave. His presence was somehow soothing and unforced. "Would you like to sit?" she asked.

"I'm sure your father didn't hire me to lounge by the pool."

"Don't worry about it, he's a softy. And besides, you're with me." Ariadne smiled.

"Okay, but if I get fired, it's on you." Alex smiled back.

"Deal. A year's compensation."

Alex sat in the chaise next to hers.

"I'm sorry about yesterday's debacle, by the way." She tucked her book back into her bag.

"Debacle?"

"My friends can be obnoxious, though they mean well."

"I think they're fun." Alex snickered. "I, for one, had a great time."

"Melina can be pushy."

"She's just enjoying the summer."

"She likes you."

"I gathered." He seemed, from his casual demeanor, to dismiss the attention as insignificant.

"I mean, a *lot*."

"Oh." Alex frowned. "That's not good."

"Yeah, I didn't think so." Ariadne smiled. "Just tell her the truth."

"The truth being?"

"That you're not into women."

"That would be lying," Alex replied.

Ariadne sat up. "You mean you're attracted to women?"

"Absolutely." Alex didn't sound at all offended. "You insinuated otherwise yesterday when we got interrupted."

"I just assumed you were…Never mind. I was wrong."

"Disappointed?"

"I'm not sure," she replied honestly.

"Hmm. I'm sorry. If you need a gay bosun to talk to, I can get you Manos." Alex was clearly kidding.

"Don't be silly. I have plenty of gay male friends." She smiled. "But in my defense, Manos thought you were pitching for his team, too."

"Nope. I'm all about women."

"So, what's wrong with Melina?" Ariadne had no idea why she was pushing the topic. She wanted to hear something from him, but she wasn't sure what.

"Nothing, nothing at all. She's attractive, witty, and very sexy."

Ariadne shrugged. "I guess. So what's the problem?"

"There's…" He paused, as though deciding how to answer.

"Oh, how insensitive," she said. "It didn't even cross my mind you might be involved."

"Because I'm young?"

"Yeah. No…I mean…I don't really know why," Ariadne muttered, frustrated over why she seemed incapable of expressing herself at the moment with any reasonable eloquence.

"But you're right. I'm not currently involved," Alex said.

Ariadne found that information uplifting for some reason. "And Melina, then?"

"You don't give up, do you?" Alex chuckled. "Are you trying to set me up with your friend?"

"Maybe," Ariadne lied. "Interested?"

"It would be wrong."

That wasn't a no. "Because you work here?"

"Among other reasons." Alex gazed out at the sea. "I'm interested in art, though."

A not very subtle change of topic.

"You sound like my father," Ariadne said.

"Is that bad?"

"It's just him, and I love everything about him."

"He has a world-renowned private collection, and boy, what I wouldn't give to see it," Alex said wistfully. He seemed as passionate about art as she was about the family business.

Ariadne could deal with any fault in a friend or partner except one. She could not handle anyone who lacked passion about something, anything. "Hey, I have an idea."

"Oh?"

"I can show you some of his private collection," she offered. "If you don't mind my company, that is."

"Only a fool would mind your company." Alex's penetrating blue eyes remained fixed on hers, with a familiar softness that didn't make sense. This wasn't about a guy trying to get laid. This was about being unable to say what you want. Alex was different than any man Ariadne had ever met.

"So, anyway..." She snatched up her bag and pretended to fish for her book. "Just say when."

"I have a break in forty-five minutes," Alex replied at once.

"It's a da...see you then."

Alex stood. "I look forward to your company," he said seriously, and started to go.

Was he hitting on her? Was Melina right? "Hey, Alex," Ariadne called out when he was still a few feet away.

He turned. "Yes?"

"I'm...you know I'm gay, right?" She needed to hear herself say that.

"So am I." He laughed. "And I'm especially cheerful about our date."

"No, I mean—"

"I know what you mean." Alex smiled.

CHAPTER TEN

Forty-five minutes later, Switch found Ariadne dressed and waiting for her where she'd left her by the pool. She'd apparently gone back to her room to ditch her bag and change into shorts and a polo. She managed to look amazing in everything, and that was worrisome. Ariadne was the type of woman Switch had always wanted but never managed to meet. Not because she didn't go out enough, or because the women she occasionally saw were inferior; Ariadne was the full package. She was beautiful, dynamic, determined, and so far seemed to be the type who would not only endure Switch's need for adventure but also seek it out herself. None of the women Switch had dated were the whole package, and the fact that Ariadne *was* depressed her, to say the least. The woman was unattainable, and Switch was in the wrong body at the wrong time. If only they had met under different circumstances, she could have at least pursued a long sexy evening, maybe even a whole weekend with her. That was usually enough to get any flirtation out of her system, though she wasn't sure even that would work with Ariadne.

Ariadne looked at her watch. "On time."

"Always."

"Okay, then. Let's go." Ariadne led the way to the forward suites. "I say we start with my room."

"You keep art there?"

"Sure. Dad's collection is just too much to fit in one place, and he loves to be surrounded regardless of where he is."

"I like him." Switch truly admired anyone who had as big an appetite for art as she.

Ariadne inserted her red keycard into the door and led the way inside.

"Impressive." Switch hardly knew where to look first. She was surrounded by paintings and sculptures representing many of the best-regarded artists of the twentieth century: Picasso and Matisse, Warhol and Pollock, Chagall and Klimt, Dali and Miró. Many of the pieces depicted women, and Switch recognized most of them. Some had gone for record prices at Sotheby's or Christie's and made headlines worldwide. Others were lesser-known works that only serious collectors or art historians would be familiar with, since they'd never been well publicized. Lykourgos had no doubt acquired these from another private collector or through some other means.

She approached an oil on canvas painted by Modigliani. "This is *Nude Sitting on a Divan*, if I'm not mistaken."

Ariadne came to stand beside her. "You do know your art. Dad acquired it a few years ago at Sotheby's, along with..." She glanced around and pointed to a bronze sculpture of two naked figures embracing. "That Matisse."

"And I recognize this Picasso," Switch said as she stepped to the next painting, which was more than five feet tall. "But I can't recall its name." In fact, she knew a lot about *Nude, Green Leaves and Bust*, one of the artist's major works, except who'd acquired it. The buyer, who bid by telephone, had wanted to remain anonymous. "What can you tell me about it?"

"This one I know well," Ariadne said. "Picasso painted this in 1932 and called it *Nude, Green Leaves and Bust*. It's one of a series he did of his mistress, and it was in a private collection for several decades until it was sold at Christie's three or four years ago. For a while, it held the record as highest price paid at auction for a piece of art."

"You make a wonderful tour guide." Switch smiled and glanced at the next painting. "What do you know about the Warhol?"

"This one has a great story behind it," Ariadne replied, excitement in her voice. "It's *Turquoise Marilyn*, and it's one of five Marilyn Monroe canvases he did in 1964, each with a different colored background. What separates this from the others is that it's the only one without a bullet hole in the forehead."

Switch knew the story but feigned ignorance. She had to refrain from volunteering more than an art-loving bosun would know. "Bullet hole?"

"A woman named Dorothy Podber saw the paintings stacked against each other—except for this one—at Warhol's studio in Manhattan and asked if she could shoot them. Warhol thought she meant, you know, with a camera, so he agreed. Instead, she put on white gloves, pulled out a revolver, and...*pow*, right between the eyes." Ariadne laughed. "The other four are known as the *Shot Marilyns*."

Switch laughed, too. "More, please."

Ariadne took her around the room, regaling her with what she knew about each piece.

Though she wasn't any closer to finding the icon, she was enjoying every minute of the tour. Letting Ariadne take the lead gave Switch a good excuse to gaze at her, to stare at her mouth, her mannerisms, the way she touched her hair when she got excited. "I see your father's enthusiasm has rubbed off."

"Stories about artifacts and paintings were my bedtime stories," Ariadne replied. "I grew up hearing about what he'd just purchased, of course, but mostly he talked about the elusive treasures he hoped to find. He'd make up such remarkable stories about those, since very little is known about them."

"I'd have killed for stories like that growing up."

"What were yours like?"

I had none, because they don't tell you stories in orphanages and certainly not at the EOO. "Oh, you know, the boring *Snow White* and *Red Riding Hood* variety."

Ariadne smiled. "Hey, those aren't bad. As a matter of fact, I've read and watched the Disney versions of them all."

"So, you're into damsels in distress, knights in shining armor, princes and princesses." Switch was surprised.

"There's nothing wrong with that."

"You just don't seem the type who needs saving."

"I need it, all right. I just don't care to admit it."

Switch crossed her arms over her chest. "What do you need to be protected from?"

Ariadne didn't answer for several seconds. "It's more a matter of wanting. I want someone who'll fight for me and go out of their way to defend me, even when I'm wrong."

"I'd think there would be a line of volunteers backed up all the way to Athens."

"And there is. Only they're there because of who my dad is, not because of who I am."

"You're a beautiful, bright woman."

"Who hasn't proved herself, yet." Ariadne shrugged. "But my time will come."

"So you think you have to prove yourself before you can deserve what you ne…want."

"Of course," Ariadne replied, matter-of-factly.

"Interesting and…futile," Switch said.

"Is it?"

"Very few get what they deserve, and even fewer deserve what they get."

Ariadne frowned. "Are you saying I'll never find the right person?"

"I'm saying the right kind of love doesn't have to be earned or deserved. It just happens. Call it chemistry or destiny."

"Right kind of love. Is there a wrong kind?"

"The wrong person can never give you the kind of love you want. Even if they love you to the moon and back, it'll never suffice because you don't want to see it."

Ariadne nodded. "You're a romantic."

"I am."

"It figures. Anyone who loves art this much must be."

"That makes you a romantic, too."

Ariadne appeared skeptical. "I don't know."

"Exactly. You don't know it yet."

Ariadne looked pensive as she gazed around the room and then back to Switch. "For once, Melina might be right."

Switch, confused, raised an eyebrow.

"You could be exactly what she's been waiting for," Ariadne said.

"The question is," Switch met her eyes, "is she what I've been waiting for?"

Ariadne looked away. "Ready for the next room?"

"Lead on."

As they headed out of the suite, Ariadne paused momentarily to open a drawer of her desk. Switch saw her slip a blue keycard into her pocket.

"My brother's in his room," Ariadne said as they headed to the next door down the hallway. "I gave him a heads-up we were coming." She knocked twice and the door opened almost immediately.

Nikolaos waved them both inside and went to fetch his sunglasses off his desk. "I was just heading out. Good timing." He nodded hello to Alex as he left.

Nikolaos's room was just as impressive as his sister's, with a wide collection of art and artifacts, mostly Byzantine icons, crosses, mosaics, and relics.

"My brother isn't a fan, but he endures it for my father's sake."

"Yes, well. Not everyone gets it."

"He thinks art and collectors are pretentious."

"Some are," Switch replied. "But others love it in earnest."

"What turned you onto art?"

"The world around me. I can see art everywhere. It's just that, sometimes…" Switch laughed.

"What?" Ariadne pressed her.

"Sometimes I want to fix it," she explained. "Rearrange things, like leaves or stones, even trees, to make the end result perfect."

Ariadne smiled. "People as well?"

Switch looked at Ariadne. "Yup."

"A perfectionist, too."

"Unfortunately."

"Is anything ever perfect for you?" Ariadne stopped smiling and locked eyes with Switch.

"Yes." They were stuck looking intently at each other and she couldn't break away. "You. You're perfect," Switch finally whispered. *Fuck, did I just say that?* "I mean, perfectly okay."

Ariadne eyed Switch suspiciously. "Thanks, I guess."

"So, where to next?"

Ariadne led her to the master suite. "My parents'." She knocked on the door, and when no one answered, she inserted the blue keycard she'd taken from her desk.

"I hope we don't get in trouble."

"You worry too much," Ariadne said.

The master suite was amazing, but she'd already scoped out the living room area while talking to the maid. What she couldn't wait to see was the bedroom.

After perfunctory *aahs* and *wows* over the pieces she'd already seen, Switch looked over to the closed door. "What's in there?"

"The bedroom. That's next on our tour." Ariadne opened the door, and a world Switch thought existed only in secret museums was unveiled.

The massive room, nearly as large as the outer living area, was filled with rare and spectacular paintings and artifacts. Most of them she'd only heard rumors about. "This is…it's…" Switch was at a loss for words, and she had to concentrate hard to remember what she was there for.

"You should see what's still back at the house."

"Does he usually travel with so much?"

"Not like this, but since he decided to spend the summer on the yacht, he moved a lot of the pieces here." Ariadne stood a few feet in front of her.

"Lots of icons."

"He's quite religious."

"Clearly."

"He bought another one the other day, one virtually unknown to everyone."

Jackpot. "Oh?"

"Yeah the, the…um." Ariadne snapped her fingers. "I can't come up with it right now."

I can. "Which one is it?" Switch asked casually.

"I don't see it here…or anywhere, for that matter." Her puzzled expression told Switch this was an unusual occurrence.

"Huh. Maybe he resold it, or…had it taken back to his house."

"Yeah, maybe." Ariadne looked around again, as if refusing to believe it wasn't there. "But I doubt it. He'd want to have it here, since he went completely gaga over it and just acquired it."

"Maybe he has a secret room?" Switch joked and hoped she wasn't pushing her luck.

"Who knows?" Ariadne replied, as though the idea wasn't out of the realm of possibility for her father. "I wonder why he doesn't have it on display. He tells me everything." She scanned the room again to make sure the *Theotokos* wasn't there.

"Everyone has secrets," Switch said, more to herself than to Ariadne as she looked around as well.

"Well, I've shown you all there is," Ariadne mumbled, her back to Switch.

If it wasn't here, and it wasn't in the previous bedrooms, and Lykourgos needed to see the icon to have it cure him, then where the hell could—? Switch felt before she saw Ariadne in her arms.

Ariadne had apparently backed up into her, and Switch had instinctively put her arms around her.

"I'm sorry," Ariadne said, but didn't move.

"No problem." Switch knew she should release her, but her hands seemed unwilling to let go. Their bodies fit perfectly together.

Ariadne tilted her head back to look at Switch. "I wasn't looking."

"Neither was I."

Ariadne smelled so good that Switch was tempted to nuzzle her hair.

"So, uh…" Ariadne pulled away and Switch felt a cold void. "This concludes the tour." She moved toward the door.

"You have no idea how much this has meant to me." Switch followed her out of the room.

They walked silently back to the upper deck. Switch should've been concentrating on where else the *Theotokos* might be, but instead she couldn't stop thinking about the feel of Ariadne against her.

"Well," Ariadne said when they reached the deck. "I'm glad you enjoyed it."

"Thank you." Switch avoided eye contact, too afraid Ariadne would see her thoughts. "You were the perfect guide." She straightened her collar.

"Thanks." Ariadne scratched her nose, a sign she felt uncomfortable.

"I have to get back to work," Switch said abruptly, and walked past Ariadne. She kept going until she was alone in her quarters.

CHAPTER ELEVEN

Aegean Sea

"How are you ladies this splendid morning?" Kostas greeted his wife and her guests, who had moved today's biriba game to the sixth-tier outdoor lounge, under a canopy. Two stewards stood at the ready to service their needs, and more would join them when it was time to set up lunch. Though he took his responsibility as host seriously, he was there primarily to make sure Christine would be well occupied for the next hour or so and unlikely to return to their suite.

The women all gave him polite replies and greetings and quickly resumed their gossip and card game.

So far, he'd successfully managed to keep his illness a secret from his family, but both his wife and daughter were growing more concerned by the day about his frequent coughing spasms.

Whenever his family was preoccupied and he could slip away from business matters, Kostas went to his room and prayed to the icon, asking the Holy Mother to bless him with her healing powers. Though he could detect no change thus far in his condition, that only meant he'd not yet prayed hard enough or long enough. His faith in the *Theotokos* was unshaken, because he could feel its miraculous powers every time he touched it.

He was happy to see when he let himself in that the maid had come and gone, so he would not be interrupted. Nikolaos had already gone ashore for the day, and Ariadne was planning an outing away from the yacht as well.

Kostas went into the bedroom and opened the wall panel that concealed his panic room, a steel-walled enclosure intended as a secure location for his family in the event pirates or other desperate individuals ever overtook the yacht. The man who'd installed it was the only outsider who knew about this secret hiding place. It had a thick, reinforced steel door and was accessed by a code known only to his family. The room was well stocked with food, water, guns, ammunition, and communication devices but was otherwise unused, so he kept the *Theotokos* there when he wasn't praying to it.

He kept his other valuables in his wall safe, which was hidden behind another ancient fresco. The safe held gold bricks, valuable gems and jewelry, important papers, and a handful of precious items from his artifact collection. These included unpublished biblical papyri dating back to the time of the Library of Alexandria, a number of Dead Sea Scrolls, and five of the eight Imperial Fabergé eggs considered lost for nearly a century.

Kostas reverently removed the case containing the panic room's newest treasure…the *Theotokos*…and placed it gently on top of the bed. He was almost shaking with awe and anticipation, as he did every time he neared the magnificent representation of the Holy Mother.

He knelt beside the bed, unlatched the case, and slowly pulled back the linen covering the icon. For a long moment, he didn't breathe. He merely gazed at her, as though seeing her beatific face for the very first time, because each time, he felt her blessed presence even stronger than the time before.

She would heal him.

Kostas placed his fingertips on the bottom of the halo surrounding her face, bent his head, and began to pray. He began with the Orthodox prayer to the Virgin Theotokos, then added his own. "Oh, Holy Mother, I implore you to look with favor on your faithful servant and bless me with your healing." Tears began to stream down his face as the power of the icon washed over him. "My family needs me, Blessed Virgin," he cried out, his voice breaking. "I ask of you…I beg of you, be merciful."

❖

Thessaloniki, Greece

Allegro wiped the sweat from her forehead. Though it was seventeen hundred hours, temps were still in the high nineties, which was a radical change from the mild weather she'd left behind in Venice. She'd been sitting on the same bench outside the Electra Palace Hotel for hours to get a feel of the area and keep an eye out for TQ. Her orders were to report The Broker's every move, but five hours later, the deranged virus of a woman still hadn't made an appearance and her patience was wearing thin. "I need a cold *frappé*," she said under her breath to no one in particular. "And a long, cold shower."

A young kid, probably not more than ten or twelve and dressed in dirty, worn clothes, walked up to her and said something in Greek.

"I have no idea what you're going on about," Allegro replied.

"Money," the boy said in English, and held out his hand.

The city was swamped with underage gypsy beggars and Allegro had no small change, just a two-euro coin and some five- and twenty-euro bills. "Listen, get me a *frappé* from over there…" She pointed to an outdoor café as she reached for the coin, "and I'll give you five euros."

The cold coffee only cost one-fifty, so she was sure the kid would come back with her *frappé*. But the little guy shrugged like he didn't understand and kept his hand an inch from her face.

"You know, I really want to like kids, but most of you make it real hard." She pulled out the coin. "Here." She gave him the two euros. "Now get as far away from me as possible and tell whoever spawned you to send you to school."

He stuck his tongue out and ran off as fast as his bare feet could take him. The boy kept looking back at her as he ran, and Allegro saw him bump into the backside of a woman exiting the Electra Palace. He dropped the coin and had started to pick it up when the woman turned and looked down.

"Well, hello, freak show." Allegro recognized TQ. She had two men at her side, one tall and thin, the other squat and bald.

She immediately pulled out her cell and started taking pictures to send to Reno. She was far enough away they wouldn't notice her, but her zoom was good enough to get very usable images.

The bitch stepped on the kid's coin and wouldn't move. The boy tried to move her foot, but she kicked him in the face and yelled something. Bystanders glanced their way, but no one stopped to say or do anything. Gypsies were known to be menacing thieves throughout the Mediterranean, and they often worked in groups.

As the boy wiped his bloody nose and got up, her two goons stepped in front of TQ. The boy ran for his life and TQ laughed. She bent down, picked up the two-euro piece, and put it her purse.

"I guess some never get over poverty." Allegro followed the trio as they headed down a busy sidewalk, and ten minutes later, they stopped at an upscale lounge bar facing the water and took seats outside under a huge umbrella.

Allegro took a table close enough to hear them, grateful that the olive skin and caramel eyes of her Persian heritage helped her blend in like a native. When the waiter came for her order, she said simply, "*Frappé.*"

It wasn't long before TQ and her goons ordered as well and got down to business.

"I can't believe the fool," TQ said. "He has such a treasure and won't show it the respect it deserves."

"Why do you care?" the bald one asked. "It's not like he'll have it for much longer."

TQ sighed. "Yes, but we don't know how much longer he'll need it for his voodoo ritual, which makes it difficult for us to determine our next move."

"I say we move as soon as possible."

"Yeah, the guy could croak any day, and then what?" the tall goon added. "We'll never know what happened to it or where to look for it."

No one spoke while the waitress set their drinks down.

"I know all this, imbeciles," TQ continued after she'd gone. "But I haven't heard back from my contact yet. If he doesn't locate the icon, we can't make any kind of move."

"You sure we can trust him?" the bald guy asked.

"When am I ever not sure?" TQ rolled her eyes. "Few have fooled me, and they were way above his status."

"And they've…departed." The skinny one laughed.

"All except one."

"She means Jack."

"I know who she means," the bald guy replied.

"It's only a matter of time." TQ frowned.

"But you prom—"

"I *said*, it's only a matter of time." TQ glared at both men angrily, and Allegro watched them shrink back from her. "But…" She smiled then, a cruel smile devoid of warmth. "First things first."

"Want me to contact him?" the skinny guy asked.

"Yes, do that. Tell him if he takes any longer, you're going to remove his testicles and mail them to his mother."

❖

Near Colorado Springs, Colorado

"Jack, your phone's ringing," Cassady called from the kitchen.

"I hear it." Jack pretended to be busy fixing a problem with her PC. "Can't right now."

Cassady came in and walked over to the table where she was sitting to look at the caller ID. "It's Landis."

"Oh." Jack looked up. She'd rekindled her long friendship with Landis Coolidge, aka Agent Chase, when they'd worked together to free Cassady from the clutches of Andor Rózsa, the madman who'd unleashed his deadly Charon virus on the world. Recently, she'd left several messages asking Landis to come visit them, but her friend was apparently away on a mission. "About time."

Cassady pressed the answer button and handed the phone to Jack.

"Where the hell have you been?" Jack asked.

"At the office," Montgomery Pierce replied.

Jack shot Cassady the look of death. She placed her hand over the mouthpiece. "You're gonna pay," she whispered.

"Man up," Cassady replied, and left the room.

Jack cleared her throat. "I thought you were someone else."

"I see."

Jack played with the mouse. "So, what's up?"

"Not much. Nothing much changes here," Pierce replied. "How about you?"

Jack prayed for a zombie apocalypse or some kind of disaster to occur so she could hang up. "Oh, you know, laundry…dishes…a bit of vacuuming, and all that other exciting shit that domestic life includes."

Pierce laughed. "You'll never be the domestic type."

"I know, right? I mean, how do so many women do it, day in, day out?"

"They're not you."

"What's that supposed to mean?"

"It means you're too talented to be sitting at home folding underwear."

"I don't think my resume can get me an office job." Jack was already getting irritated.

"But you enjoy working with the kids, right?" he asked, referring to her long-time passion of counseling troubled teens.

"It's okay, but it's only part time, and then…well, it's back to dishes."

"You're probably not ready to hear this, and definitely not from me, but…" Pierce paused. "I think I have a solution."

"I'm not going to work for you."

"I'm aware. I understand, and I don't want you to."

How refreshing. "So?"

"Can we meet in person?"

She didn't see that coming. "I…I, uh…when?"

"This week. Whatever day works for you."

"Friday?"

"Great." Pierce sounded sincerely pleased. "Promise you'll try to keep an open mind."

"I won't promise anything."

"I'll take it. See you Friday." He hung up.

"Damn it," Jack said.

"What happened?" Cassady walked in.

"Pierce wants to meet Friday."

"And?"

"I said I'd do it."

"Is that why you're agitated?" Cass asked.

"No." Jack sulked.

"Then what?"

"He hung up before I did. I hate that."

Cass came over and sat on her lap. "Poor baby." She kissed Jack. "Did Daddy hurt your feelings?"

Jack got up with Cass in her arms. "I told you what would happen the next time you teased me." She carried her to the bathroom.

"No!" Cass struggled, but only halfheartedly.

Jack turned on the cold water to the shower. "Yes." She set her down, right under the cold stream.

"You suck." Cassady laughed. "Oh, God, what's that?" she said seriously, looking down.

"What?" Jack peered into the shower to see what she was looking at, and as soon she did, Cassady pulled her in.

"You suck more." Jack adjusted the temperature and grabbed Cass by the waist. "Since we're already wet, why not get wetter?" She bit Cass's ear.

CHAPTER TWELVE

Aegean Sea
Next morning

"You have to ask him to come," Melina pleaded across the breakfast table. "Please, don't say no."

"But it was going to be a girls' day out," Ariadne replied. She was looking forward to their shore excursion to a private, secluded beach, but not if Melina got her way.

"Every day is a girls' day out. Come on, I've been good this trip. No men, hardly had a drink, and I haven't smoked at all."

Ariadne lifted an eyebrow.

Melina sipped her coffee. "Weed doesn't count."

"Uh-huh." Ariadne, together with Jo and Natasa, had made Melina promise to stop smoking, and so far she was making a worthy effort. "I've arranged for Manos to set us up and hang out," she told the others.

"Oh, yay!" Jo said. "He's a hoot."

"But why?" Melina frowned.

"I thought you liked Manos," Ariadne replied. "You've spent the past two summers clubbing and barhopping with him."

"Yeah, but that was different," Melina said. "And I'll have enough girlfriends with me today."

"Manos will be disappointed."

"So invite both," Natasa stopped eating just long enough to mumble.

"Yes, Manos can take my place while I get to…know Alex better and…" Melina looked at Natasa. "Your eggs are not going to hatch, you know. Take a breather."

"Mind your own hormones and let me eat. I'm PMSing," Natasa snapped.

"And this is why Alex has to come along." Melina turned back to Ariadne. "Estrogen overload is not good for me."

Ariadne had deliberately asked Manos to come set them up for the barbecue and day at the beach. For some reason she couldn't explain, she wanted to put some distance between herself and Alex and had avoided inviting him. He was a nice enough guy, but something about him bothered her. And the biggest problem was, she wasn't sure if that was his fault or her own.

He was gentle, polite, interesting, and interested, so why did Ariadne feel awkward around him? Men were always fun company and they never made Ariadne feel uncomfortable, even when they flirted with her. But Alex did, and that was annoyingly unfamiliar and unnatural, because that sensation was reserved for women.

"I really don't think he can make it, anyway," Ariadne lied.

"Hey!" Melina yelled and waved. "Alex! Over here!"

Alex, who'd been nearby talking to one of the deckhands, hurried toward them at a jog since Melina was shouting and floundering in the chaise like a dying fish. "Is everything okay?" He looked concerned.

"Yeah…well, actually no." Melina smiled. "I hear you're too occupied to assist us with today's beach barbecue."

Alex searched Ariadne's eyes before he answered. "Yes, that's correct." He smiled politely at Melina.

Melina shoved Ariadne. "Well, don't just sit there. *Do* something."

Ariadne sighed. "I'll talk to my father about changing your schedule for today," she told Alex without looking at him.

"I'm sure Mr. Lykourgos needs me around." Alex clearly understood she didn't want him to come along to the beach.

"*I'll* talk to him." Melina started to get up.

"No." Ariadne stopped her. "I'll take care of it. I'm going to meet with him in an hour anyway."

"So, Alex…" Melina turned toward him with a provocative smile. "Get your…whatever you swim in ready."

❖

Halkidiki, Greece

Switch and Manos had to make two trips in the Zodiac to carry everything required for the women's upscale barbecue on the beach—portable tables, folding lounge chairs, barbecue grill and supplies, two coolers with ice and drinks, and more coolers with the wide array of foods the chef had sent along. In addition to the souvlakia, pancetta, octopus, and fresh fish destined for the grill, he'd prepared tzatziki, spanakopita, dolmades, taramosalata, horiatiki, freshly baked flatbread, and the beetroot, feta, and lentil salad that was Ariadne's favorite.

As she finished setting everything up, she sent Manos back in the Zodiac for the women. The beach they'd chosen was as good as private, since they were the only ones in sight. Tourists and locals tended to congregate on the easily accessible stretches of sand, especially those with a beach bar nearby. The temps were pleasant here with the steady breeze, much cooler than in the city, and the sea was a clear, azure blue. Conditions could not have been more perfect for a day ashore.

The Zodiac returned just as Switch finished setting up the lounge chairs under the shade of some pine trees. When she saw the women stepping onto the beach, she was glad she was wearing her shades.

Melina headed straight for her, wearing a broad, anticipatory smile and little else. She'd seen a lot of barely there bikinis, but this one was a mere thong that left Melina's bare ass exposed, and the top didn't have enough material to cover a mouse. If she coughed, her nipples would be exposed.

Jo and Natasa, walking behind her, wore bikinis that were only marginally less distracting. It seemed as though they were all in a contest to expose as much flesh as possible.

But it was Ariadne who took her breath away. She stepped off the Zodiac with her black bikini provocatively outlined under a sheer, see-through top, her blond hair shining in the sun and blown away from her face by the breeze. At that moment she could have been a model for some Greek tourism ad, and the world would have rushed to come find her.

Switch could have stared at her like that all day, though the sheer top made her feel like a voyeur peeking into Ariadne's bedroom, but Melina was determined to gain her attention.

"Too bad you're wearing shades," Melina said. "I can't see if my new outfit has blown you away, or blown you away."

"You forgot the third option," she replied with a smile, enjoying the look of confusion on Melina's face as she walked away to help Manos secure the Zodiac.

The women spent an hour or so having drinks and chatting, then drifted off to do their own thing: Jo pronounced herself DJ with the portable CD player, Natasa got engrossed in her book, and Melina spread her towel by the water for some sunbathing.

Ariadne went for a walk along the beach.

Something was evidently troubling her. She was distant and preoccupied today, no matter how hard her friends tried to cheer her up. Maybe her father's illness, together with her imminent future as head of the company, had started to weigh on her. Switch couldn't blame her; taking over the Lykourgos empire was a big responsibility for a young woman, a woman who still needed the space to grow, discover, and live, before she chained herself to a desk and familial responsibilities.

"She's gorgeous, isn't she?"

Switch hadn't heard Manos approach. "Ms. Lykourgos is very nice." She tried to keep it professional.

"Her name is Ariadne," Manos replied. "So use it. She prefers it."

"She hasn't given me permission to do so or complained about me using the polite form."

"How peculiar," he replied with a puzzled expression.

They watched Ariadne climb up onto a high rock and sit, staring out over the water toward the yacht.

Manos turned to Switch. "Fotis wants to kill you, by the way. According to him, if you hadn't been asked along, he would have."

"Desperate for a day at the beach, huh?" she asked.

"Desperate to be around Ariadne." Manos laughed. "He's had a thing for her since he started working for the family seven years ago. He was devastated when Ariadne couldn't make it last summer because her dad sent her to the Maldives instead."

"Poor guy."

"I'd watch my back if I were you," he said seriously.

"Oh?"

"Fotis has gotten it in his head that Ariadne is into you."

"She's gay."

"Yeah, so? Gay women are different than us. They like to mix it up now and then."

"That's not true."

"Most lesbians I know have been with a guy or two, or more."

Then they're bisexual, not lesbian, she wanted to say. But she wasn't in a position right now to debate the issue. "I know plenty who haven't."

Manos smoothed back his hair. "Anyway, who cares what they put where? We guys are pretty set on our needs."

Just then, Melina called Alex over.

"The busty one beckons." Manos laughed again. "She's fun, and a wild one. You should hit the clubs with her. You're guaranteed to score."

"I'm not interested in her."

"Of course you're not." He slapped Switch on the stomach. "Or at least I should hope not, because I'm not getting a bisexual vibe off you. Besides, it would be a real shame to see you giving it to the wrong side for an extra tip."

Manos thinking she was a gay dude wasn't really a bad idea. Maybe she could use that to her advantage concerning Melina. "Yeah, that would be a shame." She went to see what the busty one wanted.

❖

Ariadne lost all track of time until her stomach grumbled, reminding her it was time for lunch. She headed back to her friends and spotted Melina draped around Alex's neck. He was sitting next to her towel on the sand, looking uncomfortable.

"Jeez, take a hint, Melina," she mumbled under her breath.

"Who's hungry?" Natasa asked loudly when she spotted Ariadne.

"You're clearly ready to devour everything we brought with."

Melina was joking, and Natasa snapped back. "Keep it up and you'll be on the menu, too."

"You either got miraculously pregnant since yesterday, or you gained five pounds," Melina said.

"She called you fat." Jo chuckled.

"She's jealous because I'm young and she's decrepit," Natasa replied.

"Play nice," Ariadne said when she reached them.

"I am kinda hungry." Melina moved closer to Alex. "But not for food."

"Okaaay." Ariadne turned back toward the beach. "I obviously returned too soon."

Alex immediately got up. "Are you ready for lunch, Ms. Lykourgos?"

Manos joined him. "We can get a fire started." He looked at Alex. "I, for one, am gifted when it comes to building up heat."

"That's great," she replied, without enthusiasm. *Just great.* Now the gay guy is hitting on Alex, too. Ariadne wanted to hurt someone but didn't know who. Why was everybody enjoying themselves except for her? Even Natasa, the hormonal mess, was being happily entertained between her book and Melina's over-the-top effort to seduce the bosun.

"Well, I'm going for a swim first." Melina had put on a shirt while she was gone, and she now made a big show of taking it off again. "I bought them so I can flaunt them," she said to no one and everyone.

"They're gorgeous," Manos replied. "Aren't they, Alex?"

"I...yes, they're definitely impressive."

"Care to join me?" Melina asked him.

"I...uh...I don't swim."

"Oh, and why is that?"

Alex looked away. "I didn't bring anything with me."

"Swim in your briefs." Melina's voice dripped with seductive intent. "I won't mind."

"I'd love to but...but..." He was clearly uncomfortable, and growing more so by the second.

Natasa cut in. "Just go for a swim already. He doesn't want to."

"She gets cranky when she's hungry. You know, all that feeding for two." Melina waved Natasa off. "So...you know where to find me if you change your mind," she said to Alex.

Ariadne was glad someone had stopped Melina's desperate attempt to be all *come hither.* It was seriously beginning to get on her nerves. She lay on her towel and shut her eyes as Alex and Manos started lunch preparations.

The morning meeting with her father had been exhausting; it was as though he was trying to quickly cram as much information about the company down her throat as possible. His whole demeanor had been different since her return from Oxford, she realized. Once a hurried and impatient man, always preoccupied with business matters, he'd turned into a mellow and almost too-sentimental version of himself, spending much more time devoted to his family. He'd tear up now at the smallest thing and not be concerned about who witnessed it.

But his recurring cough really worried her. Although his GP had apparently said he was fine, it seemed to be getting worse. Could her father be lying about the results? Maybe she should just call the family doctor and plead for the truth.

"Mind if I sit?" Ariadne opened her eyes to find Alex hovering over her.

"Wouldn't you rather swim?"

"I don't know how." He shrugged, as though embarrassed by the admission, and settled onto the sand beside her.

"You sail, but you can't swim?" Ariadne sat up. "I find that hard to believe."

Alex didn't say anything for a long while. "Have I done something to offend you?" he finally asked.

"No, why?"

"It's clear you don't want me here."

"That's not true, it's…it's about Melina," she lied. "I don't like to see her making a fool of herself. I just wanted a girls' day at the beach, and her hormones are getting in the way of that…again."

"You shouldn't worry about her so much," he said. "She's a grown woman and she likes to flirt. She's harmless."

Ariadne played with the sand. "I don't know. I guess."

"I think something else is bothering you."

Why was he pushing? "Listen, you're a sweet guy, Alex, but I'm not in the market for a new friend. I can't even handle the ones I have."

"I'm sorry. I didn't mean to pry," he said gently. "It's just that you look concerned. Worried, actually."

Even her friends hadn't noticed. Damn him. "Maybe because I am," she blurted out.

"You're too young to worry so much. But then again, you're also your father's daughter."

"What's that supposed to mean?" Why was she being so defensive?

"Everyone knows you're being groomed to take his place. That's not a light responsibility."

"No, it's not, and it's also not age related. His shoes would be too big to fill even if I were twenty years older."

"You're right," he replied. "It's not going to be easy."

Alex was the first person to openly tell her that. Until now, everyone stuck to the usual clichés: *you'll manage, you can do it, you were born for this, piece of cake, etc.* But no one had acknowledged what really lay ahead for her.

"You're going to have to sacrifice a big part of your life to maintain, let alone expand, your father's legacy," he said.

"I know," Ariadne muttered. "I know."

"Is it what you want?"

"I can't remember ever wanting anything else. I love this company."

Alex nodded. "Then it'll be a bit easier to make sacrifices."

"I'm not ready to think about all that. Not yet."

"The sacrifices?" he asked.

She shook her head. "Losing my father. I can take any amount of work, sacrifice anything to make him proud, but I'm not ready to lose him." Tears sprang to her eyes at the mere thought of her life without her father around. It was incomprehensible.

"I'm sorry about his—"

"I don't know what I'd do if anything ever happened to him. And now he has this cough, which he tells me, according to his GP, is nothing, but…" Ariadne kicked the sand at her feet. "I'm being paranoid, right?"

Alex didn't say anything right away. He just stared out at the sea. "I don't know," he finally replied. "But either way, he won't be around forever. Someday you'll have to face your world on your own." He remained gazing out at the water and sounded like he was talking to himself, rather than her.

"Have you lost a loved one?" Ariadne asked.

"Yeah. Before I got the chance to love them," he replied cryptically, and got to his feet. "I'm going to see if Manos needs help."

"Yeah, okay."

"And I'm sorry if my presence here today bothers you. I can have Manos take me back after lunch."

She put her hand to her eyes to shield against the glare as she looked up at him. "No. Please, stick around. It's fine."

Alex bowed. "As you wish." He smiled.

"Manos is hitting on you, you know."

"I'm aware."

"Does everyone hit on you?" Ariadne feigned frustration.

"Not everyone," he replied with a serious expression. "Not you."

"You're a guy."

"And if I wasn't?" Alex asked.

"I guess I…I'd…" *Drag you to my bedroom.* "It's all hypothetical. Consider it impossible."

"I agree with *hypothetical*." Alex walked away.

Why the hell couldn't she meet a woman like Alex?

CHAPTER THIRTEEN

Switch watched the rest of the group eat and chat for a while and then wandered off for a walk. A day on the beach was nice, especially in Ariadne's company, but that also meant wasting time better spent searching for the icon. Lykourgos had remained on the yacht with his wife, but they certainly would've left the master suite for much of the day, and that was exactly where Switch needed to look again. If the *Theotokos* wasn't in plain sight, then it must be in a safe, and she was sure any safe had to be hidden somewhere in that room.

She'd been surprised, almost shocked, to learn that Ariadne had no idea her father was sick. Did that mean that no one in the family knew? Could that be one of the reasons he'd sought out American doctors and hospitals? Was it even *possible* for his wife not to have figured it out? His wife *had* to suspect something. Only someone completely self-involved could overlook the clues that something was wrong with him: the guy coughed half of the time, and when he didn't, he looked pale and weak. Then again, she concluded, people often saw what they wanted to and could convince themselves of anything.

And then there was the mystery of why Ariadne didn't want her around. Although she seemed to enjoy their talks, she often seemed uncomfortable in Switch's presence, and even more so when her friends were around. Why?

A new possibility occurred to her. Maybe Melina was indeed the problem, but for different reasons than the obvious. Maybe Ariadne found the attention Switch was getting from Melina frustrating because *she* had feelings for the older woman. Jeez, why hadn't she thought of that before? It would explain the jealous outbursts and the way they were always teasing each other. Ariadne had feelings for her straight friend and couldn't bear to see Melina throwing herself at men.

Switch's cell went off. The caller ID told her it was Pierce. "Go ahead. I can talk."

"I have Allegro stationed outside Rothschild's hotel. She followed her yesterday and got some very useful information."

"Okay."

"TQ plans to steal the icon from the Greek. Apparently she has someone on the inside to help her."

"And we don't know who."

"No," he said. "Only that it's a guy."

"I have to find the icon before he does, or we're screwed."

"You are not going to let that bitch get away," Pierce shouted. "I don't care what you have to do, but I do not want that woman leaving Greece."

She'd never heard him so wound up, as if all of this was deeply personal, somehow. "I'll make it happen, Pierce. Relax."

"Do *not* tell me what to do."

"What's going on? There's more, isn't there?"

He was silent for a long time.

"Pierce?" Switch asked. "You there?"

"She said she's going after Jack."

"The woman really has letting-go issues."

"I cannot allow that."

"We won't let that happen. I'll do everything in my power to put her behind Greek bars."

"And if that doesn't work, then you..." Pierce sounded so angry he could barely talk. "You do what you have to, to make sure she never leaves Greece."

"I understand."

"Do you?" he shouted.

"Yes."

Pierce was giving Switch permission to off Rothschild if she couldn't have her arrested. "Wouldn't it save us all time if I began with the second scenario?"

"Nothing would give me more pleasure than to dance on her grave," he replied.

"But?"

"If she can rot in a Greek prison, publically humiliated before we terminate her, even better."

"Then that's what we'll do." Switch tried to sound upbeat.

"Let me know when you have news."

"Will do."

"Allegro is on call in Thessaloniki. If you need backup, Reno will patch you through."

"Got it."

❖

"Where's Alex?" Melina asked.

"Over there," Ariadne said. She'd been watching him talk on the phone, and from the look of it, it wasn't a pleasant call.

"Hey! The party is over here," Melina shouted, and waved.

Alex turned to look at them and waved back.

"So, are you going to make a move, or what?" Natasa asked Melina.

"I was kind of hoping he would," Melina replied.

"I don't see that happening any time soon." Jo got up to stretch. "You don't crap where you eat, so I can't blame him."

"Yes, well, my summer vacation is quickly coming to an end, and I'm not going to sit around and wait for him to get over his moral hang-ups."

"You go, girl," Natasa said. "Show him what a desperate housewife is capable of."

"Damn right. I…" Melina did a double take. "What did she just call me?"

"Hey, Alex!" Jo said loudly, to signal to the rest he was close enough to hear them talking about him.

"Hey, Jo. Where's Manos?"

"Sleeping somewhere under a tree."

"Slacker," Alex said.

Jo had been playing some upbeat dance-club music on the CD, and just then a new track started, one with highly provocative lyrics.

Melina jumped to her feet and immediately began to dance, her eyes hungrily fixed on Alex. "Dance with me," she said as she grabbed him by the hand and pulled him away from the others to an open stretch of beach. Her tone was more demand than request, and though initially hesitant, he soon joined in, laughing at her unbridled flirtation and twirling her around in the sand.

Ariadne tried to tell herself Alex was just doing his job, complying with his guest's requests with charm and enthusiasm. She'd be angry with any *Pegasus* crewmember who didn't do the same, wouldn't she? But as the dance continued, her irritation grew. Melina had her arms draped around Alex's neck now; she whispered something in his ear that made him smile and lean closer, near enough for Melina's ample breasts to be pressed tightly against his chest.

The song seemed endless, and when it finally finished, Alex took a step back and said something to Melina she couldn't hear. The pair rejoined the others, and Melina plopped back down on her towel. "Would you please put some lotion on my back, Alex?" she asked as she lay facedown.

"Sure." Alex knelt next to her and picked up her tube of suntan lotion.

"You can undo my top." Melina's voice oozed with sexual intent. "I want you to get me *everywhere*."

Alex unclasped it with a quick flip of two fingers.

"I see you've had plenty of practice."

"I can't complain," Alex replied.

No sooner had he started to apply the cream than Melina began moaning like a caged beast. "Oooo. Mmm. Grrrr."

"Seriously?" Ariadne could see Alex was trying hard to keep a straight face.

"Is that supposed to be sexy?" Natasa asked.

"Stop talking. I'm concentrating," Melina replied.

"On what, animal sounds?"

"On…those…marvelous…hands." She moaned between each word.

On closer inspection, Ariadne could see that Alex did have beautiful hands for a man, and his touch seemed gentle yet powerful. She wondered what they would feel like on *her* back.

Alex finished and put the cap back on the tube. "Anything else I can do for you, ladies?"

"Me! Me!" Natasa and Jo said in unison.

"Me first," Jo insisted.

While Alex applied cream to the other two women's backs, Ariadne lay belly down on her towel and stared at the sea. What she wouldn't give for a massage on her tense shoulders.

"How about you, Ms. Lykourgos?" Alex said from beside her a few minutes later.

"Sure, why the hell not?" she mumbled without looking at him. "But don't unclasp my...*oh*." Ariadne lost track of what she was saying when Alex touched her back.

"I won't," Alex whispered close to her ear.

The combination of his hands pressing on her shoulders and breath close to her ear made her shiver.

"Just relax," he whispered again, but this time his voice was even gentler and somehow different.

He took twice as long with her lotion massage as he had with the others, but Ariadne didn't intend to complain. She couldn't remember the last time she felt so loose and peaceful.

"Why does she get the deluxe package?" Natasa asked.

"Because she's the boss." Alex sounded hoarse.

"Enjoying much, Ariadne?" Melina asked.

"Ye..." Shit. Her voice cracked. Ariadne cleared her throat and turned her head around to look up at Alex, kneeling over her. She shaded her eyes to see him better. "Thank you," she said formally.

He didn't move for several seconds but remained there looking at her, his eyes half closed. Who was he trying to impress? And why wasn't he getting the message? Ariadne had made it clear she wasn't interested in men.

How could this guy be so sensitive and perceptive when they were alone, and such a player when they were around others? He'd had his hands all over each of them and seemed to revel in the fact that her friends were drooling over him. And now he was looking at her, as if to say, *I can have* you *as well as your friends*.

Irritated, Ariadne grabbed a magazine Jo had brought along. She wanted to say, *Stop looking at me like that and go away*. "So..." she said. "Maybe you should start picking up."

"Of course." Alex got to his feet and walked away.

❖

Switch continued to think about how Ariadne's body had felt until well after they returned to the yacht. Fortunately or unfortunately—she wasn't sure which—Ariadne kept an even bigger distance between them after they left the beach. On the one occasion when they'd inadvertently bumped into each other on the Zodiac, Ariadne had jumped like Switch had the plague and had moved as far away from her as she could in the small dinghy. And she alone among the women hadn't bothered to thank Switch for the outing once they were back on the yacht.

And when Melina had asked Ariadne where and when that evening they would all meet up again, Ariadne answered that she had a meeting with her dad and would be busy till late. After which she'd snatched up her beach bag and run off without saying a further word to anyone.

It was just as well. She needed to concentrate on the icon and Pierce's personal vendetta and not spend any more time analyzing Ariadne's reactions to her. If Melina was interested in Switch instead of Ariadne, there was nothing she could do about that. Nor was she hired to play matchmaker.

Her work onshore and the trip back on the inflatable required a quick stop in her cabin for a change into clean, dry clothes. She'd just started her rounds on deck when Lykourgos called her over from a lounge chair by the pool bar. Ariadne was with him and didn't seem too happy.

"What can I do for you, Mr. Lykourgos?" Switch asked.

Ariadne practically made a show of looking the other way.

"The girls tell me they were very satisfied with your services on the beach," he replied. As before, Kostas Lykourgos looked nothing like the billionaire he was. Today he was dressed in a pair of faded khaki shorts and a dark linen shirt that needed ironing and only emphasized the dark circles under his eyes. The guy really didn't look well, though he seemed in excellent spirits.

"I'm glad." Switch smiled politely. "It was a pleasure to spend the day with them."

Lykourgos laughed. "Are you sure? They can be a handful, especially that Melina."

"They were wonderful company, sir."

The billionaire gave him knowing smile. "Ariadne tells me she has a thing for you?"

Switch's heartbeat accelerated. *Please don't let that be true.* She *so* needed Ariadne to not be interested in her as a guy. "Oh?"

She glanced at Ariadne, who said testily, "Not me. Melina."

Thank God. "Oh, yes. She's made that quite clear."

"They all seem to think you're a nice guy," Lykourgos said.

"Yeah, a real charmer." Ariadne's voice dripped with sarcasm.

Lykourgos put his arm around his daughter. "She's a difficult one," he said proudly. "Just like me, she's difficult to please."

"I call it being selective," Switch replied. "A very positive quality, in my opinion."

Lykourgos laughed loudly. "I like him." He looked over at his daughter.

"Like I said," Ariadne repeated drolly. "A real charmer."

"So." Lykourgos clapped. "Although the others like you, my girl seems to have a problem. Have you done anything to offend her?"

You're kidding me. I'm going to lose my job because of a spoiled brat who thinks it's my fault her straight friend prefers dudes? "I don't think so, sir, but…" Switch looked at Ariadne. "My sincerest apologies if I have."

"He hasn't offended me, Dad." Ariadne visibly squirmed in her chair.

"Good." He clapped again as if to say, *I'm glad we got that settled.*

Ariadne took this as her cue to leave. "I'm meeting the others in Melina's room. If you—" She'd started to get up, but Lykourgos immediately put his hand on her arm.

"Not quite yet, my dear." He turned to Alex. "I want you to escort the girls tomorrow night on Santorini."

This escorting gig was turning into a nightmare. Not only was it taking Switch away from the yacht she should be searching, but it was also giving her more time with a woman who suddenly couldn't stand her. "With all due respect, sir. If your daughter doesn't like me, maybe it would be preferable to send Manos or Fotis."

"My girl has a great radar when it comes to business and associates, but not when it comes to her personal matters. She will do anything to keep her friends or partners happy, and that worries me. So, if she doesn't like you, then that means you're the right person to keep an eye on her. Manos and Fotis are nice boys, but…they get too involved in having fun."

"Dad—"

Lykourgos went on as though he hadn't heard her. "You are to stay with her and her friends at all times."

"Sir—" Switch started to protest as well, but Lykourgos apparently wasn't going to be swayed.

"Do you drink?"

"No, sir. Never on the clock."

"Excellent. She will have her bodyguard along, as well."

"Oh, great. It'll be a super-relaxed evening." Ariadne pulled away from her father. "Anyone else you want to send along? Maybe the navy?"

"Not necessary, at least I don't think so," he answered seriously. "So." He clapped again. "It's settled." Lykourgos got up and left without another word. Clearly, he was used to getting his way.

"I'm sorry if I've done anything to upset you," Switch said when they were alone.

"How can you be so sensitive and…and normal when we're alone, and a complete jerk when we're not?" Ariadne asked.

"Excuse me?" Switch replied, genuinely surprised.

"You act like you want to prove to the others that you can have a gay girl. I've got news for you: you can't, never will, never gonna happen."

"I never—"

"You go out of your way to put on a show every time they're around. It's not bad enough you have them drooling over you, but you want to show them you can sway me as well."

Switch was having a little trouble following. "I have never tried to sway you, nor do I feel the need to do so. I am merely being polite and accommodating. I thought you enjoyed my company, but I was obviously wrong."

"Your company, yes. Not your groping hands."

Had she really gotten that carried away? Maybe so. She'd had some moments there when she had been lost in the feel of Ariadne's warm skin beneath her hands. "You could have stopped me. I only continued because I thought you were enjoying it. It wasn't sexual, and…" Switch tried to compose herself. "I did not grope you."

Ariadne continued like Switch hadn't spoken. "You were all over Melina, though."

"Don't you mean she was all over me?"

"I didn't see you stop her."

Boy, did Ariadne have it bad for the other woman. "As a matter of fact, I did," Switch said calmly. "Look, you have nothing to worry about. I do not intend to do anything with Melina, Ms. Lykourgos."

"Frankly, I don't give a damn. Maybe you should, so both of you can get whatever pent-up tension you have out of your systems."

"With all respect," Switch replied, "I don't think I'm the one with the pent-up tension."

"What's that supposed to mean?"

"That you might want to try being honest with yourself and face reality."

"Really? You sound like you're aware of something I'm not," Ariadne said. "I sincerely doubt you know me well enough to determine whether I'm capable of facing reality."

"I hardly know you, but it doesn't take a genius to see you're terrified of what you want." Switch was past trying to be courteous. "Money can't buy you everything, and certainly not guts."

"How dare you make such assumptions. You've been here, what, a week?" Ariadne got up and started to pace. "And I don't have guts to do what, by the way?"

"To put aside your fears and take what you want, or at least find out if it's attainable."

"Oh…my…God." Ariadne strung out each word. "You really think I'm fighting some heterosexual desire to pounce on you. You are the most typically chauvinistic, homophobic pig I've ever met. Your limited understanding of…of *everything* has you thinking you're so hot that one night with you and I'll be all…" Ariadne fanned herself with her keycard. "Oh, gosh. How could I have gone without for all these years?"

Ariadne was getting it all wrong, and frankly, Switch didn't know what was going on. When did the discussion go from Ariadne 'fessing up to her desire for Melina to Switch being a chauvinistic pig that wanted to change her? "I don't think—"

"Don't you realize it's men, especially men like you, that make even straight women want to jump the fence?"

Switch shrugged. "And you're hoping Melina jumps that fence before she jumps me?"

"Women like Melina will sleep with anyone, so don't flatter yourself. It's not about you. It's about what's in your pants."

Silicone? "I told you already," Switch said. "I'm not interested in her."

"Of course not. You're obsessed with the one who doesn't want you."

"That's—"

"Look, it's never gonna happen. I don't do guys, and not you or any other guy will change that."

"I never said—"

Before she knew what hit her, Ariadne had grabbed Switch by the shoulders and pinned her against the wall.

"And here's your proof," Ariadne said, and kissed Switch on the mouth. First hard, and when Switch didn't react, Ariadne slowed down.

Switch's brain told her to push Ariadne away, but her body wouldn't listen. Instead, she remained against the wall, hands to her sides, too afraid to lose control if she touched Ariadne.

She tried to focus on why she was there. And she did, long enough to switch Ariadne's keycard from the front right pocket of her shorts—the outline against her tight shorts was unmistakable—and into the left front pocket of her own.

Then Ariadne sucked and licked her lower lip, and slipped her tongue between Switch's lips to part them.

That pushed Switch over her limit. She wanted to kiss Ariadne back so much her head hurt. She groaned and grabbed Ariadne's face to stop her. "Please." She was breathless. "Please, don't." She stepped to the side.

Ariadne smiled but looked confused. "Nothing. I felt nothing."

"That's…" Switch moved farther away. She needed to distance herself, but she didn't know if it was because of disappointment or fear. "That's great." She turned to leave. "Have a nice evening, Ms. Lykourgos."

CHAPTER FOURTEEN

Ariadne took a roundabout way to Melina's room, pausing for a long time on deck to stare out at the sea, as though it held the answer to why she'd just kissed a guy.

What had possessed her to kiss Alex, and what the hell was she thinking? The last time she'd kissed a boy was in high school, and she'd had no desire to do so again. Nothing about the opposite sex turned her on, and she was sure Alex would get the message, too, if Ariadne kissed him. But what had been an irrational, almost aggressive outburst of frustration ended up leaving her exasperated and confused. Exasperated because Alex had pushed her away, and confused because there was something unusual about him. The way he smelled, the softness of his lips and skin, the sound of his soft moan, and his voice at that moment.

Ariadne trembled at the memory of his breathless voice. Why hadn't he returned the kiss, if he was set on making a point? Was the kiss that bad, or was being the aggressor a role he thought was reserved only for men? And what would she have done if he'd returned the kiss?

Ariadne touched her mouth and remembered Alex's full lips under her own. He hadn't even kissed her back and Ariadne felt… "What the hell?" she said out loud. "What's wrong with me?"

Unable to be alone any longer with her thoughts and anger over what she'd done and felt, she headed to Melina's room. Her friends lay sprawled out on the floor on pillows, with a bottle of wine and various cheeses on a tray.

"The girls said I was allowed to drink." Melina held up her wine.

Ariadne sat on the comfy armchair. "Oh, nice," she replied distractedly.

"You okay?"

"Fine." She plucked at the fabric of the chair.

"No sermon about how many I've already had and how it's killing my brain cells and compromising my senses."

Ariadne shrugged. "You're a big girl."

"Okaaay," Melina said with mock seriousness, "everyone back away and don't stare in her eyes. It makes them nervous."

The others laughed.

"Don't mind me, okay?" Ariadne said. "I just need company but don't feel like talking right now."

The girls gave up trying to cheer her and talked instead about the usual things: their jobs, office gossip, celebrity gossip, their plans for the coming winter, and, of course, guys. Melina didn't need much encouragement to start in about Alex.

"He's not your average guy." Melina took another sip of wine. "He's…something, but I don't know what."

"He's almost too sensual in a way," Jo said. "Too…I don't know… his eyes are…I mean, the way he looks through them. It's like there's more to it than with most."

"He's a metrosexual, darling," Melina replied.

"He shaves his legs." Natasa frowned disapprovingly.

"And thank Gillette for that," Melina said. "I can't stand hairy men."

"I like them hairy." Natasa grabbed another cracker and a big slab of cheese. "Not too hairy, but I like some hair."

"I agree with Melina. I'm not into hairy butts and shoulders." Jo made a disgusted face.

"That's because you guys want a woman with a dick," Natasa said. "I like mine all man."

"Yeah. Nothing like fucking a gorilla," Melina replied.

Ariadne had to laugh.

"How about you?" Melina took another sip of wine and pointed at her with her glass. "You like them hairy?"

"I like women, remember?"

"Shaved, trimmed, or forest? I mean, when you go diving for the pearl?"

Ariadne laughed. "Shaved or trimmed are both fine. My internal compass gets confused in a forest."

"Butch or butchless?" Natasa asked.

"It's called femme," Melina said.

"Butch, but no macho crap," Ariadne replied.

"And what else?"

She thought about it for a moment. "Sensitive, gallant, protective. Not a player, but definitely a challenge. Someone who keeps me on my toes."

"You know…" Jo sat up. "If Alex was a girl, he'd *so* be your type."

"But he's not, and he's exactly *my* type," Melina was quick to add.

"Yes, we all know you like them young." Natasa finished off the last of the feta.

"They're easier to mold." Melina winked. "And so much easier to train."

"Get a dog," Natasa said.

"We can't all be bear lovers," Melina replied.

"I wonder how he kisses." Jo lay on her back with her feet on the couch. "Do guys kiss differently than women?" She looked at Ariadne.

"Is that a proposition?" Melina asked. "If you want Ariadne to kiss you, then say so."

"Yuck." Jo threw a couch pillow at her. "She's like my sister."

"Yuck, indeed," Ariadne said. "But, yeah, girls are different. Not that I have a lot of experience with guys, but women are sincerely passionate. It's not like they need to prove something. With girls, kissing is just as exciting as sex. With men, it's a three-second prelude to your breasts or panties."

"My ex was like that." Natasa sighed. "The hit-and-run type. We'd be kissing one minute, then scrambling around on the floor to find his briefs the next."

"How many guys have you kissed?" Jo asked Ariadne.

"I…" How she wished it had still been just one. "Two."

"Was it that bad?" Melina asked.

"The first time was in high school. It left me indifferent, like kissing a fish."

"And the second?"

"It was, uh…like kissing a girl."

"So you liked it," Jo said.

"Well, duh." Natasa rolled her eyes. "She said it was like kissing a girl."

"When was this, and who?" Melina asked.

"I really don't want to talk about it. It was a horrible mistake and one I want to forget," Ariadne replied.

"Koo Club's the place for forgetting," Natasa said, referring to the trendy Santorini nightclub they planned to hit the next evening. "Your dad told me Alex was going to be our chaperone."

"Chaperone, my ass. He's going to be my primary objective." Melina smiled. "And I don't want anyone coming to look for us," she added, looking pointedly at Ariadne.

"Go crazy. Have at it, bonk till you drop, etcetera, etcetera. You have my blessing." Ariadne joined her friends on the floor. "Pour me some of that, will you?" she asked Jo, who was nearest the bottle of wine. "And can we talk about something else, please?" She needed a distraction from the memory of Alex's kiss and Melina's plans for him.

❖

Switch felt her pocket to make sure the keycard was still there. She could remember taking it from Ariadne, but only vaguely. She wasn't sure *what* had just happened and was even more confused about the *why*, but what *was* clear were the repercussions. Her whole body still buzzed and her lips tingled from the lingering sensation of Ariadne's mouth. Switch had wanted to disregard the mission, forget the icon and TQ, and surrender to those lips. She'd wanted to scream that she was a woman, tell Ariadne the truth, but the truth would have been dangerous for her and obscene for Ariadne.

What bothered Switch the most were Ariadne's reasons and intentions. Ariadne had probably had to endure plenty of guys coming on to her, so why was she so concerned about proving to Switch how impossibly gay she was?

She couldn't think about that now. She had to focus on taking immediate advantage of having this keycard. Ariadne was going to meet her friends in Melina's room, and Lykourgos and his wife were topside having dinner, so it was the perfect time to get into the master suite, but she had to work quickly.

She headed toward the wing where the Lykourgos family stayed. No one was about. After knocking, not too loudly, on Ariadne's door, and getting no response, Switch used the borrowed keycard to slip inside.

The blue keycard to the master suite was back in Adriane's desk drawer, as she hoped it would be. She retrieved it and used it to get into Lykourgos's room, after knocking again first to make sure no one was inside.

The master suite was tomb quiet, so she started a quick but methodical search of the main living room, checking behind every painting, tapping on walls for inconsistencies, examining the desk for any latches or buttons that might release a hidden passageway or chamber. She couldn't waste time. Though Europeans in general and Greeks in particular could linger over a meal for hours, Lykourgos or his wife could easily decide at any time they needed to retrieve something from their quarters.

Once she'd exhausted likely possibilities in the living room, she headed toward the back of the suite, bypassing the bathroom for the bedroom just beyond it.

She found the enormous wall safe, hidden behind a massive ancient fresco, five minutes later. Though she'd been trained to open a lot of different kinds of locks and devices, she had no chance of getting into this vault because she'd never seen anything quite like it before.

The *Theotokos* had to be in there.

But she'd need Allegro's expertise to get it out.

Switch checked her watch. She'd been in here almost a half hour. Time to leave. She'd taken a few steps out of the bedroom when she heard the distinct click of the lock to the doorway entrance.

She glimpsed that the light had changed from red to green as she ducked into the bathroom, the nearest hiding place.

Not a good choice, she realized immediately.

If Lykourgos or his wife had come back to use their own john, certainly a reasonable possibility, she was screwed. The shower was made of semi-transparent glass, so the only place for her to hide was behind the door.

She held her breath and waited, peering through the tiny crack between the door and frame.

A few seconds passed. All was quiet, though she was certain someone had come in.

Then a noise, but scarcely there—the brush of shoes over Lykourgos's oriental carpet.

A male figure passed by her extremely narrow field of view, headed toward the bedroom.

But it wasn't Lykourgos.

It was Fotis, her second bosun.

And also, apparently, TQ's man on the inside.

She didn't think he'd even be able to *find* the safe—the latch for the panel that hid it was pretty well concealed. And even if he did, he'd probably never be able to open it.

But she certainly had to eliminate him as a threat to her getting the *Theotokos*.

Very slowly, she slipped out of her hiding place and peeked into the bedroom. Fotis was searching the walls, all right. Not the right one, at the moment, but perfect for her because he had his back to her.

She slipped out of the master suite, closing the door silently behind her, and went next door to Ariadne's quarters. A soft knock. No answer, so she used Ariadne's red card to get in again and put Lykourgos's blue card back in the desk drawer where she'd gotten it.

Switch left Ariadne's red keycard on top of the desk, hoping that she'd think she'd just forgotten to take it with her, and went back into the hall, not too close to the master suite, but where she could keep an eye on the door.

She called the first mate on her radio and asked him to patch her through to Lykourgos.

"Yes?" His voice came through less than a minute later.

"I'm sorry to disturb you, Mr. Lykourgos," she said, "but I was headed to see your daughter and her friends to make arrangements for tomorrow when I saw my Second Bosun Fotis going into your suite. I just wanted to make sure you authorized him to be there. It seemed unusual."

"I did not. I'll be right there," Lykourgos said. "If he tries to leave, detain him."

CHAPTER FIFTEEN

The women were heatedly debating which celebrity was most fuckable when a knock on the door interrupted them.

Melina got up to answer it. "Here for the party?"

Manos walked in and shut the door behind him. "So, what happened?" he whispered, looking at Ariadne with a worried expression.

"What are you talking about?" Ariadne asked.

"Fotis. What did he do?"

Ariadne got up and so did the others. "I have no idea what you're talking about," she replied. "Fotis hasn't done a thing."

"We haven't seen him since this morning," Jo added.

Manos pulled his hair back in obvious distress.

"Speak up, already. What's going on?" Ariadne took a step toward him. "Is he all right?"

"Your dad's muscle just escorted him off the boat."

"Why?" Ariadne asked. "What happened?"

"I couldn't hear most of it. Your dad told me to mind my own business, but what I got from hiding around the corner is that Fotis will be arrested if he ever sets foot on the ship again. I heard your dad say to Alex that he was thankful Alex had reported him, that he'd done the right thing."

"Oh, my God. Reported him for what?" Natasa asked. "He'd never hurt anyone. Fotis is such a sweet guy, and he's been around forever."

Manos looked like he was about to cry. "Yeah, I know." He bit his nail. "I want to ask Alex, but I don't know him that well, and I don't want to get in trouble for interfering. Your father was pretty upset. I can't remember ever seeing him that angry."

"Why would Alex get Fotis fired? What the hell is going on?" How much stranger could this day get, and how much more trouble could this Alex possibly cause? It was as though everything had gone to pieces since he'd set foot on the boat, Ariadne's sanity included. She'd had enough of the new bosun screwing up their summer and her peace of mind. "Where is he?" Ariadne pushed forward. "I want to talk to him."

"I think he went to his quarters." Manos got out of her way. "But I'm not sure."

Ariadne slammed the door on her way out. She stomped to the crew quarters on the other side of the yacht, fuming the whole time. *How dare he come here and screw up all our lives?*

She reached Alex's room and didn't bother to knock. "I want to—"

Ariadne's breath caught in her throat. She couldn't believe what she was seeing.

Alex stood next to the bed, wearing only a towel from the waist down. Nothing else. "What the—?" Alex quickly grabbed a T-shirt from the pile on the bed and put it on. "Shut the door, please."

Ariadne, in a trance-like state, shut the door, never taking her eyes off Alex.

"You…you…you're…"

"I'm a woman."

Ariadne nodded, still unable to speak. She looked from Alex to the spandex torso bandage on the bed.

"Say something," Alex said.

"I don't know how to react."

"Would you like to sit?" Alex pointed at the only chair in the room. "I'll explain."

"I can't sit just yet," she mumbled. Ariadne couldn't stop looking at Alex's chest, covered or not. The image of those breasts—not too large, but beautifully shaped—was burned into her memory.

Alex looked down at herself. "I know I have no right to ask, but please don't tell anyone."

"Why? Why are you a woman? I mean, why did you lie?"

"Because your father hires exclusively male bosuns."

"You wanted the job that badly?" Ariadne pointed at the compression tank top on the bed.

"Yes."

"There are so many other positions you could have applied for."

"I wanted this one," Alex replied.

"I don't know what to say."

"Say you won't tell your father, or anyone else."

"But I have to tell him."

"It'll get me fired, and…" Alex sat on the bed. "He's already upset with Fotis. This will push him over the edge. I'll never work on another yacht again."

The initial shock had started to wear off, and Ariadne began to feel a sense of betrayal, instead. "You can't go around lying and misleading people."

"I never meant to harm anyone."

"What happened with Fotis?"

Alex looked up at her. "He stole your brother's keycard to break into your parents' suite. I was on my way to find you to make arrangements for tomorrow night, since…since we hadn't gotten the chance, earlier…when I saw him going into the room."

Ariadne looked away. Alex referring to their earlier argument and kiss disconcerted her even more than she already was, and she didn't want to think about all that right now. "What was he doing there?"

"I don't know, but I immediately called your father and he came right down. We went into the suite together and found Fotis in the bedroom. He wouldn't say much at all, other than he'd taken your brother's card."

"He never said why he was there?"

"No, but we found him moving paintings around, and drawers had been opened."

Ariadne couldn't believe it.

"Your father had him escorted off the yacht."

She needed to sit for a moment. This was all too much to take in. Ariadne took the chair, a few feet away from Alex. Fotis had been with them…six or seven years, at least. Was good at his job, always polite and attentive to her, and he'd even partied ashore many times with her brother. The Greek economic crisis had driven many to take desperate measures, but she'd never imagined Fotis could be one of them. "This has been a hell of a summer" was all she could think to say.

"Are you going to tell them?" Alex got up like she was ready to face bad news.

"I…" Ariadne nodded. She didn't know how she was going to keep this a secret from her father and friends.

Then she looked at Alex's worried expression and considered the ramifications of that decision. If she agreed to remain silent, then she'd have to keep her word. Was she willing to lie for a stranger? And could she trust Alex enough to become an accomplice in this game of changing sexes? "No," she said finally, and got to her feet as well.

"No?"

"I won't tell anyone."

Alex sighed in relief. "Thank you. It means a lot to me."

"I sure hope so, because I don't like lying and fooling people I care about." Ariadne moved to the door. She needed to be alone and hopefully not flip out when the realization of what she'd seen and agreed to really sank in.

"I'm sorry if I…freaked you out." Alex approached her. "But you should've knocked."

"You did, but…" Ariadne frowned as realization dawned. No wonder she'd been so confused about her attraction to the bosun. "In retrospect, it makes absolute sense."

"Oh?" Alex looked surprised, almost troubled.

"You make for a convincing guy, on a superficial level."

"Too polite, too sensitive?"

"I'm not sure." She searched Alex's face. "It's the way you…" Ariadne suddenly felt exposed.

"I what?" Alex came closer. "The way I what?" she repeated when Ariadne didn't answer, her gazed fixed on Ariadne's mouth.

"I should go." Ariadne opened the door. "Keep it locked from now on," she added before she shut the door behind her.

❖

Thessaloniki, Greece

TQ paced her suite with the phone in her hand. "Well, that's just brilliant." She fumed at the setback. "That's what you get when you work with moronic amateurs," she said to Thanos, the skinny one of her pair of goons and the man responsible for contacting and hiring the second bosun.

"He's worked for Lykourgos for seven years. He was our safest bet," the man replied.

The icon was slipping through her fingers with every second that passed. "We need to come up with something fast, because I'm not going to leave without it, and you're not going to live if I don't get it."

"I have something in mind," he offered hesitantly.

"My patience is wearing thin, so get on with it. What is it?"

"An exchange."

"For?"

"His daughter."

"That ungodly creature." TQ liked the idea of anything bad happening to that icy bitch.

"He'll do anything for her. And it's not like he can run to the police. What's he going to tell them?"

"He'll never confess to being behind the theft of the icon," TQ mumbled to herself.

"It would destroy him. So, we take the girl and contact him right afterward. Tell him he can have her back if he agrees to cooperate."

"Don't spell everything out. This is not prime-time TV."

"Sorry."

"If you in any way involve or even so much as imply my name…"
She let the threat go unfinished, so he could imagine the worst.

"Yes, I know."

"I want that icon on my desk in forty-eight hours."

"It'll be there."

"Not if you're still on the phone. Move it!" she shouted.

TQ had to trust that these idiots knew what they were doing, because she didn't have a choice. Neither did she have the array of helpers and contacts she did back in the States. Here in Greece, she had only two men to rely on, and that made her nervous.

A tiny part of her wanted to forget the whole thing and leave, but quitting wasn't what had gotten her this far up the ladder. She'd become too powerful and feared to back down from a challenge this trivial. And what an addition this relic would be to her collection. She already had one of the world's largest, but this one would put her in first place. The prospect made her almost giddy. "Girl!" she shouted.

Her Asian Cyclops came running to her side, like a well-trained dog. "Madam?"

"Where have you been cowering?"

"I have been polishing your jewelry, as you instructed. I am almost finished."

TQ laughed. "Are you, now?"

"Yes, Madam."

TQ bent to the smaller woman's height. "Would you like the rest of the day off to roam this wonderful city? It's hot enough to remind you of your lice-infested country."

The servant's smile at the question was so broad she looked like the Joker. "Yes, Madam. I would like that very much."

"Hmm, I thought so." TQ smiled, enjoying the torture, and sat at the desk.

"Can I go now, Madam?" the girl asked expectantly.

TQ laughed so hard she had tears in her eyes. "You stupid cow." She laughed harder.

"Madam?"

"Why in my name would I let you do that?"

"I don't—"

"Start polishing from the beginning."

The woman hung her head in defeat and walked away.

"Life is good." TQ sat back in the chair and stared out the window at the Aegean, feeling content and exhilarated at the prospect of owning the *Theotokos*.

CHAPTER SIXTEEN

Colorado Springs, Colorado

Jack arrived at Southside Johnny's fifteen minutes early to check the bar and possible exits, something she always did when visiting a place for the first time, let alone to see someone she didn't trust. She sat at the bar and played with the car keys as she waited. She had no reason to feel this nervous. It wasn't like Pierce and his posse were coming to kill her, at least not this time. But the idea of being alone with this man, who professed to being her father, both terrified and aggravated her.

She'd made a very successful career of hating Pierce but because of stupid genetics was now made to feel obligated to see him. If she didn't love Cass so much, she'd have never agreed to this appointment.

Although that explained the aggravation, it did nothing to help her understand where the fear was coming from. It wasn't like she had to accept him or believe anything he had to say, so why did she feel like she was about to fail some test?

"Glad you could make it," Pierce said from beside her.

Jack didn't turn to look at him. "I said I'd be here."

Pierce sat on a bar stool next to her. "Is this okay?" he asked tentatively.

"None of this is okay, but we're here now." Jack took a sip of Black Label.

"What can I get you, sir?" the bartender asked.

"Orange juice." Pierce turned to Jack. "I stopped drinking."

"Oh, good. I don't have to worry about that," she replied, her voice dripping sarcasm.

"So should you."

"I stopped two years ago," she said. "It doesn't mean I can't have one now and then."

"As long as you've got it under control."

"Really?" Jack turned to glare at him. "Are we going to discuss my drinking habits? Don't you think it's a little too late to play the concerned card?"

"It was just advice." Pierce looked away.

"Not looking for it."

"So how's life at home?" he casually asked.

Jack relaxed and sat back. If she was going to get through this ordeal, she might as well try to keep it friendly. "Like I said. It's fine when Cass is there, but this part-time gig doesn't cut it."

"Would it be enough if it were full-time?"

"No," Jack replied honestly. "Maybe I need more time to deal with the fact that I'm no longer Phantom, or Silent Death, or whatever the hell else they've baptized me." The former was her op name, the latter the name she'd been known by when she'd left the EOO and taken jobs for the underworld.

"I won't argue with Silent Death." Pierce took a sip.

"But you're okay with Phantom."

"Phantom had a cause," he replied.

"So did the other."

"Silent Death killed for money, regardless of who or what."

"So did Phantom."

"That's not true," he said. "Phantom fought for those who couldn't, gave voice to those who weren't allowed to have one."

"But killed, nevertheless."

Pierce took another sip. "I won't deny that." He put his glass down and took his time centering it on the cocktail napkin. "Killing is terrible even when someone deserves it. You never get over it. I know I haven't." He took another sip. "I still have nightmares of the first time I pulled a trigger. I was twenty-one and thought I could singlehandedly save the world. All those years of training and studying and finally, there I was, in the field and ready to do anything to please the organization that had raised me."

"Indoctrinated you," Jack said.

"Yes, that too." Pierce frowned. "It was 1971 in Italy, covert CIA-

NATO Operation Gladio. It was a Cold War action intended to prevent Soviet infiltration and expansion."

"A stay-behind."

"Indeed. Secret armies were set up all across Europe, but some of them went rogue. Conducted assassinations, bombings, even coups, and made them look like the communists were responsible to stir up anti-leftist sentiment. The rest of us kept to our directive, though we had significant latitude to do whatever it took to prevent attacks by pro-communist groups."

Pierce took another sip of his juice. "Anyway, two of us were on the lookout for a Red Brigades attack in downtown Palermo that we'd gotten intel about. They planned to destabilize the government through bombings, kidnappings, you name it. We were hiding in the shadows a few feet away from this upscale club when a car stopped and dropped off a child, no more than twelve years old, in front of the door. Of course, we found it strange and called it in. They got back to us that Emilio Colombo—at the time, the prime minister—was inside the nightclub with his wife and friends."

Pierce went quiet for several seconds. "The child never moved, even when the doorman tried to shoo him away. We stood there, until finally, at two a.m., Colombo came out. The boy waited for the doorman to send for the prime minister's car and then opened his sweater. Phil and I saw it right away; the boy had a bomb strapped to him. Phil got in front of me and lifted his M16 to take the shot. I waited. The boy was getting closer. *Take it*, I said, but Phil just stood there, his hands shaking."

Pierce signaled the barman. "Give me one of those." He pointed to Jack's Johnnie Walker and downed the drink as soon as it was poured.

Jack had never seen Pierce this undone. "You don't have to—"

"I have to. I have to tell someone."

Jack nodded. She understood the feeling of redemption all too well, even if all it provided was a false sense of self-forgiveness.

"Phil wouldn't take the shot," Pierce said. "Said he wasn't sure. But the boy was less than five feet away from Colombo, so I took it for him. It was the first time I'd shot and killed anyone. Shot to the head." Pierce made a gun with his hand. "Bam. Just like that, a child was dead." He looked away and stopped talking.

"It's rough," Jack finally replied. "Killing a kid is the worst. But you didn't have a choice. You did what you had to. He was a suicide bomber, and who knows how many he'd already killed, or would have, if you hadn't stopped him." Jack was running out of consolations. "It happens. Sometimes you don't have a choice."

"As it turned out, what we saw shining in the dark and thought was a bomb was in fact dark plastic wrap. The boy was concealing flowers he apparently intended to give to the PM." Pierce wiped his eyes.

"Fuck." Jack was on the edge of her stool and didn't know how she'd gotten there. "That's…" She leaned back, at a loss for words. "I'm sorry."

"That was my first mission. I was twenty-one the first time I killed."

"Why tell me?" Jack asked. "Why now?"

"I've made mistakes," he replied. "Mistakes I've never learned to live with, killing the boy being one of them. But there are three things I don't regret."

"I—"

"One being the organization. I regret what happened that night in Italy and always will, but I do not regret having spent my whole life trying to make up for that, because in my pursuit for redemption I have saved so many innocent lives."

"You would have never killed him if it wasn't for the organization," Jack pointed out.

"The EOO didn't make me pull the trigger. My ego and eagerness to prove myself did."

"But they put you in the position to have to make that mistake."

"They gave me the expertise to know and do better. The mistake was mine."

"Either way, you wouldn't have had to deal with that otherwise."

"Maybe not. Then again…you know, better than I do, what happens to orphans who don't get adopted. And back then it was worse. Very few people adopted, and even fewer were willing to foster-parent. I would've ended up on the street at eighteen with nothing but a bitter attitude and a chip on my shoulder. What kind of future do you think I'd have had then?"

"You'll never know."

"How do you think *you* would've turned out?"

Jack shrugged. "I wasn't an easy kid," she replied honestly.

"No, you weren't. Like me and…Celeste, you were born for trouble."

"She did what she had to." Jack didn't want to hear anything negative about her mother. Despite their geographical distance, she'd become quite close to Celeste during the nearly two years that had elapsed since she'd found her in Sainte-Maxime, France.

"My point." Pierce wiped his forehead although the bar was quite cool. "I took you from her to give you a future where you didn't have to face prostitutes and pimps, drugs and thugs. I couldn't risk you becoming like them. You were better than that, and you were my daughter."

"So, facing terrorists and drug lords is preferable?"

"Of course not. But at least I taught you to fight them, not join them."

"I…" Jack wanted to argue but couldn't come up with anything other than, "I just wanted to have a normal life." She sighed. "That's all."

"No one has a normal life. Everyone faces shit, regardless of who their parent is or how they grew up. You had an organization backing you, friends—some who turned into sisters—a great education and all kinds of activities, the best health care, and…everything."

"But a family."

"We *are* a family. All of us here are tied together. Bound to each other by secrets and solidarity. We give our lives for each other and never ask why. That sounds like a hell of a family to me."

"You never told me you were my father."

"That was my mistake. I kept waiting for the right time, but…"

"It never came."

He shook his head. "It did. Plenty of times. I simply found excuses to not see it."

"Why?"

"I was afraid. I feared we'd get too close, that I'd have someone to lose. I dreamed of and feared your arms around me, calling me Daddy." Pierce took off his jacket. "I figured as long as I kept you at a distance, I'd be able to cope with leaving you behind if something happened to me."

Strangely enough, Jack could understand that, because it was her biggest fear with Cass.

"But I was wrong, and that's one more blunder on my pile of mistakes."

"Not that simple, is it?" she asked.

"When is it ever?"

Jack downed the rest of her scotch. "What are the other two?"

Pierce looked at her. "The other two things I don't regret?"

Jack nodded.

"Breaking the rules to be with the woman I fell in love with more than forty-five years ago."

"Did she know?" Jack asked. "Back then, I mean?"

"She had no idea until five years ago."

"What a waste of time." Joanne Grant obviously had much to do with Pierce's softening in recent years. When he'd taken Jack back to their home to recover from the torture TQ had put her through, she'd seen firsthand how devoted they were to each other.

"Yes," Pierce said. "But they've been the best five years of my life, and that's got to count for something. At least I get to feel loved before I die."

"Yeah." Jack thought about Cassady. "Being loved is… everything." She checked her watch. "I have to meet Cass in five minutes." She was actually disappointed to leave.

"I understand."

"Maybe…maybe we can do this again."

Pierce's face lit up. "I'd very much like that, Jaclyn."

Jack smiled back. "So." She got up. "I guess…"

"The third thing I don't regret is you," he said quietly. "Watching you grow up, play, fall asleep, being with you even if you didn't know it are the happiest memories of my life."

Jack tried to hold back the tears that sprang to her eyes. "I…I have to go." She plucked at the barstool's upholstery.

Pierce cleared his throat. "Of course."

"Okay." Jack held out her hand.

Pierce took it and held it in both of his. "One last thing."

Jack raised her eyebrows.

"TQ."

Jack froze. "What about her?"

"I have one of our own, Switch, on assignment in Greece to recover a stolen icon. Turns out TQ's behind it."

"So?"

"Allegro is Switch's backup. She overheard TQ say she wasn't through with you. That it was only a matter of time before she got 'the one that got away.' She mentioned you by name."

"Where in Greece?" Jack asked.

"That's not important," he replied. "I'm only telling you because you need to watch your back."

"Where?" she repeated, more forcefully.

"I do not want you to do anything stupid. That woman is crazy."

"Where, Pierce?"

He took a deep breath and let it out. "Last seen in Thessaloniki."

Jack pulled her hand away.

"Jaclyn, please. Don't go looking for trouble."

"No worries." Jack smiled. "We should do this again."

"How about next week?"

"I'll call you."

CHAPTER SEVENTEEN

Fira, Santorini Island, Greece
Next day

Ariadne managed to successfully avoid any contact or confrontation with Alex on the boat ride from the yacht to Fira. Alex had kept as far away from her as possible on the Zodiac, and Ariadne had avoided any direct eye contact. It was as though both felt too uncomfortable with the previous night's revelation to want to acknowledge it. Ariadne had kept her word and hadn't told anyone, not even Melina, who'd talked her head off about what she intended to do tonight to get Alex in bed.

Once ashore, they all checked into the Aressana, an ultra-modern five-star spa hotel with luxury suites, to leave their overnight luggage and change for the club. Ariadne and the other women had adjacent rooms, and her father had booked Alex one as well, down the hall from Ariadne's.

Ariadne had chosen one of her black cocktail dresses, suitable for a warm summer evening and one of the more elegantly provocative ones in her collection. The form-fitting minidress had a strapless bodice that cut a low V in front to expose cleavage, and a see-through mesh panel in back that dipped almost to her ass. She'd just finished putting on her earrings when Melina knocked on her door.

"Time's a wasting," she said from the hall.

Ariadne opened the door. "You look great."

Melina had opted for a deep shade of red, guaranteed to draw attention, for her look for the evening. The halter-style dress had a narrow V that plunged nearly to her navel, the two sides held together only by a thin gold chain. The innermost portion of each breast was visible, the nipples barely covered. "Don't I always?"

"True," Ariadne said.

"And you look completely edible." Melina caressed her shoulder. "Love the earrings."

Jo and Natasa appeared at her door as well.

"Figures." Natasa frowned.

"What now?' Melina asked.

"You all look great and I feel like a wet mop." Natasa was as fashionably elegant as her friends in her loose, caftan-style black dress, but her choice covered far more of her figure than the others'. It fell to just above her knees and concealed her bodice entirely.

"But you look wonderful," Ariadne said, to fix her obvious unstable mood.

"I'm fat, ugly, and we're all gonna die, so what does it all matter?" Natasa sulked.

"Period?" Melina asked.

"Yeah, so careful what you say." Jo stepped back to put some space between her and Natasa. "She could go off any second."

"Too bad." Melina straightened her dress. "The club is going to be full of hot, warm bodies."

Natasa sighed ruefully. "And I, as usual, will be on the sideline."

"There's always the porn channel," Melina said.

"Screw y—"

"Ready, ladies?" Alex came to stand behind the others, facing Ariadne.

Ariadne's friends turned to look.

Alex wore faded, low-slung jeans and a tight black V-neck T-shirt that showed off her slender, yet athletic build and well-defined arms. Ariadne had seen her practically naked the night before but had been too shocked to register her body well. Alex's hair was still moist and deliberately tousled, instead of the tight male style she kept during work. She looked dangerous, naughty, and *for Christ's sake*, gorgeous.

They all stared at Alex for what seemed like forever, until Melina finally said, "You look delicious." She dropped her gaze to Alex's crotch. "Simply irresistible."

Melina's insinuations had started to get on Ariadne's nerves, and not in a benign way. "Careful what you wish for, Melina," Ariadne said, and Alex looked at her. "You might not know what to do with it, if you get it." She deliberately looked at Alex's crotch, too.

"You do know who you're talking to, right?" Melina replied, and laughed.

Alex checked her watch. "Whenever you're ready," she said, and headed toward the gate to the street, where the car she'd hired was waiting.

How could Alex stand to lie to all these people? And how dare she lead so many people on? Melina was obsessively in lust, Jo wanted to blow her mind and then Alex, Natasa was convinced she could persuade Alex to quit shaving, and never mind her father, who sincerely seemed to like the new employee, especially after yesterday. Right now, Ariadne was finding it impossible to remember why she'd agreed to help this fraud.

❖

The Koo Club maintained its distinction as the trendiest bar on Santorini through its exotic cocktails, great service, well-muscled, hunky bartenders, exceptional DJs, and a layout designed to appeal to any type of patron. The indoor space offered a two-story ceiling with ornate arches, crystal chandeliers, and disco balls strung over a bar that ran the length of the room, so those getting drinks could watch the action on the massive dance floor, built to accommodate three hundred partygoers.

Those who preferred to sit outside and marvel at the spectacular sea views were accommodated on two enormous terraces. Patrons at the lively high-walled courtyard lounge, with its own bar and dance floor, could relax on comfy couches shaded by palm trees, while the wide terrace one floor above provided table and banquette seating for clientele who liked a quieter, more upscale experience.

Switch had arranged their reservation on the upper terrace the day before, after she received a call from Jo with specifics. During their earlier island-hopping vacation, the four women had spent a good deal of time checking out the current status of the nightclubs on the island and decided The Koo Club was their favorite. Celebrity sightings were commonplace and the clientele was usually well dressed, the men in trendy T-shirts and jeans, the women in sexy dresses.

The women requested lounge couch seating with a low table overlooking the sea, close enough to the dance floor for body checks, as Jo put it, but far enough to hear themselves over the music. The bodyguard that Lykourgos sent ashore with his daughter kept a discreet distance from the women but never took his eyes off Ariadne. Manos had also ridden over with them on the Zodiac, because he had the night off for shore leave.

So far, Ariadne's friends hadn't let on that they knew anything, and for some reason Switch couldn't understand, she trusted Ariadne to keep her secret.

She'd never had a problem convincing anyone she was a guy on the occasional mission that called for it, so she'd expected Ariadne to react a lot stronger, be more shocked or upset than she had. Her remark at the end about how she "half expected it" was what troubled Switch the most. Was she losing her touch? Was Ariadne a lot more perceptive than most, or was Switch simply different around her?

She stood at the balcony's bar where she could see the girls, who were chatting away at the table. Ariadne was stunning tonight, which made it almost impossible to avoid looking at her.

She'd taken her glass of soda and settled in a quiet corner to observe, when Manos stepped up to her.

"Boy, was I wrong," he said.

"About what?" Switch asked, never taking her eyes off Ariadne.

"You being gay."

Switch smiled. "I never said I was."

"I know."

"What gave it away?" Switch asked.

"The way you look at the boss's daughter."

Switch straightened and glanced casually around. "Just doing my job. Making sure she has what she needs."

"I don't think she needs what you want to give her." Manos winked.

"It's not like that," Switch lied. She could think of little else since she'd showed up at Ariadne's door to pick them up. "Besides, she's not interested."

"You'd think so." Manos checked himself in the big mirror behind the bar. "But she seems to be ogling you just as much, practically from the beginning."

"Well, I doubt it's because she wants to—"

"And let the games begin." Manos gestured toward the girls.

Three guys stood over the women's table with drinks in their hands. The tallest one said something that made them all laugh, and soon the men were cozied up next to the four women, the tall one struggling to squeeze himself next to Ariadne.

"It's always that way," Manos said. "Guys flock around them."

"Don't blame them." Switch turned her back to them.

"Tall Guy just put his arm around your girl."

"Don't call her that." Switch fumed. She felt like picking Manos up and throwing him across the room.

"So anyhoo, since you're going to sulk all night and I'm not going to have the entertainment I expected with you…" He fixed his hair. "I'm off to funner and gayer times." And with that, he walked up to an equally searching twink.

Switch went down the stairs and walked around, pushing through countless bodies while the club music's heavy bass beat pounded through her body. She avoided looking up at the table where the girls sat and instead struck up a conversation with a cute brunette who came to stand beside her at the edge of the dance floor.

"First time here," Switch was saying, when suddenly someone was shoving her from behind onto the dance floor.

"Dance with me," Melina said loudly over the music, then turned her back to Switch and started to gyrate against her.

Switch danced to avoid looking stupid and uncomfortable, and soon enough Natasa and Jo were on the floor with two of the guys she'd seen earlier. She instinctively turned to look up at the balcony for Ariadne, who was still at the table and seemingly absorbed in whatever Tall Guy was saying.

"The guy is wasting his time," she blurted out.

As if Melina knew immediately what Switch was referring to, she said, "He's trying to fix her up with his sister."

Just then Ariadne stood to greet an attractive blond woman with short hair, about her age. They remained standing while they talked, and a few moments later, Tall Guy left.

Switch turned her back so she didn't have to look at them and checked her watch. Her appointment should be there soon, and frankly, she couldn't wait to have a reason to leave this scene for a while and talk about something, *anything*, that didn't include Ariadne.

"Let's go get a drink." Melina pulled her away from the dance floor and back up the few stairs to the balcony.

"I don't—"

"It's a euphemism." Melina dragged her to a quieter spot not far from their table. "So, here we are, finally alone," she said in Switch's ear, then licked her neck.

Ariadne stood a few feet away in discussion, and although Switch didn't want to see what she was up to, she couldn't help herself.

Ariadne was looking over her company's shoulder as well. Right at her. Eyes locked on each other, Switch was incapable of breaking the fragile contact.

Melina grabbed her face. "I love the way you dance. The way you move is so sexy." She rubbed herself against Switch. "I love a man who knows how to move."

When Melina placed her hip against Switch's crotch, Switch tried to pull away. "I—" she started to say, when someone wrapped their arms around her from behind.

"Naughty boy," said a familiar voice in English. "I can't leave you alone, can I?"

Switch turned to find Allegro and sighed in relief. "It serves you right for being late," she replied in English under her breath. Allegro was dressed in tight black jeans and a yellow polo.

"Who is this?" Melina kept to English as well. "And where did you pick up an American accent?" she asked Switch.

Allegro put her arm around Switch's waist. "We went to college together in Boston."

"And who are you?" Melina eyed her suspiciously.

"Angie." Allegro frowned. "And who are you?"

"Melina, and you're interrupting."

"Seriously?" Allegro feigned irritation and turned to Switch. "Something I need to know, darling?"

"Darling?" Melina repeated incredulously.

Allegro wrapped herself around Switch. "I usually call him Monkey, but I reserve that for sexier moments. You know, when I have him hang from the chandelier."

Switch was glad Allegro had gotten her away from Melina's clutches, but what the hell was she doing? It was a well-known fact to everyone in the EOO that Allegro was a pain in the butt. Switch had worked with the unpredictable nut before, since they were both stationed in Europe, and every single time they got into trouble that could've been avoided.

"Oh?" Melina stepped back and gazed at Switch. "You never said…"

"You never asked." Switch smiled, trying to keep it light.

Melina frowned. "I'll leave you two alone, then." She disappeared inside the club.

Ariadne had apparently noticed something was wrong with her friend, because she leaned into her blond companion to say something and went after Melina.

"I did you a favor, right?" Allegro asked. "It was obvious you didn't want what she was selling."

"Of course not, but…do you always have to push it? I mean, Monkey? Chandelier?"

"Nothing wrong with a healthy sex life, and don't tell me you've never hung from one."

"What…? No, I haven't."

"Why is everyone so boring?" Allegro sighed.

"Poor Kris," Switch said. "I don't even want to know what you make that woman do."

"Well, there was that time on the trapeze—"

"Don't want to know."

"And I thought Greeks were uninhibited."

"No comment."

"So how've you been?" Allegro glanced down. "Still stuffing your pants, I see."

"Don't start."

Allegro always kidded her about that. "You know me. Can't resist a cock tease."

"Let's go inside. I should be keeping an eye on them."

"I saw Lykourgos's daughter go in a minute ago."

"Never miss a thing, do you?"

"Not when it's blond and beautiful."

"I'm sure Kris appreciates that," Switch said as they moved inside.

"Bite your tongue."

Switch laughed. "Whipped, much?"

"You have no idea. She won't even let me look at magazine-cover girls too long."

The club was pumping with music and bodies, and they had to push their way through. "It's an estrogen and testosterone bowl of hormones in here," Allegro said. It was past midnight and the clubgoers were revved and ready for action. The warm summer breeze, the lowly lit bar and its sensual décor meant that bodies were all up against each other, and couples were making out in every corner.

"Hey, there's the woman who was groping you earlier," Allegro said when she spotted Melina, "and she's talking with Lykourgos."

"They're friends. Good friends."

"That's complicated."

"You bet."

"Sucks to be you," Allegro said. "You couldn't do her even if you wanted to, not without revealing your silicone valley."

"It's not her I'm interested in."

"So there is…" Allegro stopped. "Oh, shit. You're into the Greek's daughter."

"She's amazing."

"Jeez, stop staring like a love-struck idiot."

Switch looked away from the two friends talking so fast her neck hurt. "I don't know what you're talking about."

"Well, you've got taste."

"And she knows I'm a woman. She walked in on me last night. I told her I really wanted the job."

"Holy crap," Allegro said. "How did that go down?"

"She wasn't surprised, she said."

"What if she—"

"She won't. She promised not to, and I trust her, even though she wasn't happy with having to lie to everyone and probably hates me for asking her to."

"I met Kris on a job."

"You've mentioned."

"But your deal is a lot more complicated. Her friends think you're a guy, so does her father, she's a public figure, and she thinks you're a filth bucket of a liar." Allegro exhaled theatrically. "Not to mention she has more money than God."

"What's that got to do with it?"

"Look at her. She's a different breed, and you're…"

"I'm what?"

"Don't get me wrong. You're cool and all that, and kinda cute for either sex, but…where do you even start to impress a woman like that after the sex gets normal? Women like her are used to getting what they want. It's all about money and luxury, and they probably have caviar before breakfast. How do you keep a woman like that happy unless you let her pay for…practically everything? That's gonna get old really fast, knowing you, and eventually get on her nerves."

"Thanks for sketching out such a pretty picture." Switch really felt depressed now.

"Just sayin'."

"Say it inside your head."

"And she's gay, you know," Allegro added.

"Really? 'Cause it's only all over the rags and public knowledge. Gee, no flies on you."

"Cool it, stud, before I break up with you in public. And I'm not afraid to make a scene."

Switch cleared her throat. "Let's talk shop." She briefed Allegro on her search of Lykourgos's suite, detailing all she remembered about his safe. They then made plans to get Allegro on board to crack the vault the very next night; Switch had seen on the schedule that Lykourgos and all his guests would be ashore for a big dinner he'd booked at a pricey restaurant.

"I'll get a steward's uniform for you, and—"

"Hey, don't look now," Allegro said, "but Ariadne, or however you pronounce that, is coming this way."

Switch's heart rate accelerated as she turned to see. "And she doesn't look happy."

"Melina's really upset, you know," Ariadne said as soon as she reached them.

Allegro grinned. "Hi, I'm Angie."

Ariadne checked Allegro out from top to bottom. "Good for you,"

Ariadne replied in her British-inflected English and turned to Switch. "Does she know?" Ariadne pointed to Allegro.

"Yes."

"Know what?" Allegro was clearly puzzled.

"That I'm a woman," Switch replied without looking at Allegro.

"Oh, that little thing." Allegro waved it away. "I'm versatile that way."

"You could've had the decency to at least tell Melina you were involved." Ariadne was fuming. "Now I have to spend the evening picking up her pieces."

"I tried to make it clear I wasn't interested."

"She can be a flirt at times." Allegro tried to help. "But never on the job."

"I wouldn't be so sure," Ariadne shot back. "I think he loves to fool people into wanting him, to see how far he can take it."

"She," Allegro said. "Trust me, she's all woman."

Ariadne looked like she might blow a fuse. "How refreshing that you have to stand up for her," she said to Allegro, "while she just stands there tongue-tied." She turned to Switch. "She doesn't even have the figurative balls to do that herself."

She'd had enough. Ariadne had just taken it too far. "I never led anyone on," Switch replied, louder than normal. "And definitely not your friend. Besides, you should be happy she's angry with me. Maybe you can finally make your move."

"On who?" Ariadne glared at her, obviously pissed. "You?" She sounded almost disgusted.

"Of course not," Switch snapped. "Your bestie Melina, whom you've been drooling over."

"This is all too Greek for me." Allegro took a few steps back.

"Are you insane?" Ariadne almost choked. "She's like a sister."

"Her flirting with me wouldn't have bothered you if that were true."

"What bothered me…" Ariadne stopped and looked at Allegro. "Forget it. I'm over it." She looked back toward the dance floor. "Now, if you'll excuse me, I have someone a lot less dense waiting for me." She walked to the dance floor and grabbed the blonde with the short hair by the hand.

"Mind if I point out the obvious?" Allegro said from behind her.

"Yes."

"I'm glad you asked." Allegro came to stand next to Switch. "I didn't understand a word, but one thing is clear."

"I don't want to know."

"She likes you. A lot."

Switch almost laughed out loud. "Were you in another club just now?"

"I'm serious. She's hot for you."

"So hot she's kissing another woman?"

Ariadne was leaning against the bar. Her blond companion wrapped her arms around her and kissed her throat, then took her by the hand and led her toward the exit.

"She's angry and jealous," Allegro said.

Switch wanted to rip the blonde's face off. "I don't care what she is. Let's get out of here. We need to finish planning for tomorrow night."

"I need to hit the can first," Allegro said.

"It's on our way out."

Allegro entered the ladies' room just as Ariadne came out.

"I can't catch a break," Ariadne mumbled when she saw the two of them.

"Don't let me stop you," Switch replied sarcastically. "Don't want to keep your date waiting, especially since she seems the impatient type." *What the hell?* she thought as her words registered. She seemed to suddenly have no control over what was coming out of her mouth.

"At least she's my type," Ariadne replied with equal vitriol.

"Meaning?" Switch crossed her arms over her chest.

"A woman who doesn't want to be a guy."

"I never said that binding my breasts and sticking silicone junk down my pants was a thrill. It's just something I have to do."

"Have to? You don't have to. You choose to."

Switch wanted to pull her hair in frustration. "You just don't understand."

"How you prefer to live a lie? No, I get it. The majority of people around me do that for a living. They hide behind pretty fake things, like their fixed faces. They surround themselves with beautiful, meaningless stuff and lead perfectly bogus and superficial lives. Trust me, I get it. I just thought you were different, but as it turns out everything about you is as sincere as all the Botoxed lips in here."

"You…you don't under—" How she wished she could explain, but that would compromise her mission. "I'm not fake and I'm not a poser. I wish I could've been honest with you, but—"

"You've lied about everything, even stuff you didn't have to lie about. You could've told me you were involved, and you could've mentioned that you've…" Ariadne flapped her hands in exasperation. "Are you even Greek? Because you sure didn't sound like it back there."

"I'm was born in Greece, but…" Switch wanted to tell her everything but instead looked away.

"There's always a but. You can't even answer a simple question."

A big group of people began to push past them and Switch tried to get out of their way, but the hallway was too narrow. Before she knew it, she was pressing Ariadne against the wall. "I'm sorry." She pushed her hands against the wall so she wouldn't crush Ariadne. "I can't move." Switch was abruptly pushed even closer against Ariadne, until their faces were only an inch or two apart.

Ariadne moaned.

"I'm sorry, did I hurt you?" Switch asked.

"No." Ariadne whispered. "I…uh…"

Switch felt Ariadne's breath on her neck. She shivered involuntarily and closed her eyes to clear her head, to distance herself from the enticing vision of those lips, too near her own. She was breathing so fast she was getting light-headed. "I'm…I…you're…" Switch stopped mumbling when she felt Ariadne's lips caress hers.

Soft, so soft, and so wet. This time, Switch couldn't hold back. She pulled Ariadne into her and took her mouth with the same slow rhythm.

"What's your real name?" Ariadne mumbled against Switch's lips.

"Alex…my full name is Alexandra." Switch slurred her words and took Ariadne's mouth again. She felt Ariadne begin to buckle and grabbed her ass to pull her harder against her.

Both moaned at the feel of the other. Ariadne bit Switch's lower lip, then licked it. "I could kiss you for days."

"You're driving me crazy," Switch managed to say and opened Ariadne's mouth with her tongue to taste her. They were shaking so much it was ridiculous. Switch had to break the kiss or come in her pants. "I…"

"Do you want me, Alex?" Ariadne asked provocatively.

"So much."

"Good." Ariadne pushed Switch away. "Now you know what it feels like," she said, breathing hard, "to screw with people's feelings."

Switch had never landed harder in her life. She stared in disbelief as Ariadne straightened her dress.

"You have got to be fucking kidding me," Melina said from behind them.

CHAPTER EIGHTEEN

Near Colorado Springs, Colorado

Cass checked the caller ID and sighed. "Here we go again," she grumbled to herself before she answered. It wasn't that she minded talking with Pierce. She quite enjoyed it, actually, but his constant asking about Jack in roundabout ways had started to get old. "I thought you guys talked it out," she said right away.

"Good evening, Cassady," Pierce replied.

"Jack told me she enjoyed your get-together yesterday."

"Really?" Pierce sounded jovial. "I'm very happy to hear that. She's difficult to figure out."

"Not if you know her. She would've left five minutes after your arrival, otherwise. You know Jack doesn't do anything for the sake of appearances."

He chuckled. "She's certainly no diplomatic guru."

"Can I ask her to call you back when she gets in?"

"Where is she?" The tone of his voice changed instantly from cheery to concerned.

"She mentioned something about getting her car looked at. Something about the headlights and a stop after at the grocery store."

"How long has she been gone?"

"What's going on?"

"How long?" he repeated.

"A couple of hours." The sudden change in his demeanor was making her anxious, too. "What's going on, Monty?"

"I…I warned her about TQ when we met."

"What about TQ?" Cass's heart boomed at the mention of The Broker. It had taken months for Jack to fully recover from the beatings TQ's goons had inflicted on her.

Pierce told her what Allegro had overheard. "I'm afraid she might do something stupid."

"Then why did you tell her?" Cass was upset with him and didn't care if he knew it.

"Because I need her to be careful. That deranged witch is capable of anything, and both of you need to be aware that she's not letting go."

"This is never going to stop, is it?" she asked. "It's like some evil force can't stand that we're together. Ever since I met her, it's been nothing but abductions, serial killers, mad scientists, and—"

"Always something, I know."

"Trouble follows her everywhere, and if it doesn't, she goes looking for it."

"She was trying to protect you when she gave herself up to Rothschild."

"I know…I know."

"I would've done the same," he said.

"Knowing she got her genetic defects from you is not consolatory. If she gets in trouble again, I don't know what I'm going…" Cass stopped when she heard the door shut.

"Honey, I'm home," Jack sang out.

"She just walked in," Cass told Pierce, and sighed in relief. "Where have you been?" she said sharply to Jack when she entered the living room.

"Did I forget to mention?" Jack shrugged. "It was my weekly visit to my other girlfriend. The one who looks happy when I come home."

"Funny, real funny," Cass replied, smiling. "Anyway, Monty is worried about you and it rubbed off."

"Worried?" Jack asked, her face the picture of clueless innocence. "Why?"

"So, anyway…" Cass returned to Pierce, who'd been silent. "She's back."

"I heard. Does she seem all right?"

She studied Jack, who was humming some tune as she carried groceries from the car to the kitchen. "She seems fine." Cass relaxed. "Her usual 'I'm headed to the kitchen to burn or break something.'"

"She needs a real job," he said. "She's too overqualified to be a domestic princess."

"I know, but every time I broach the topic she waves it off or storms out of the room. And frankly, I can't picture her doing a nine-to-five."

"Of course not. She needs to do what she loves. Something other than guiding runaways."

"She'll figure it out." Cass had to believe Jack would come up with something fulfilling, because she feared the eventual consequences on both Jack and their relationship if she didn't. Jack's less than satisfying day-to-day existence was starting to show. She was moody and bored, and it often felt like she was trying to pick a fight just for the hell of it. Jack needed to get out, find something to make her feel important. She wasn't interested in making friends, and Landis—the only one she did have—was unavailable most of the time, either away on a job or busy taking care of her partner, Heather, and Heather's sick brother. "I hope sooner than later."

"I have a proposition," Monty said. "But I don't think our relationship is ready for that discussion."

"Not if it concerns the EOO." The organization was usually the catalyst for any disagreement between her and Jack. Jack had tried every way possible to convince her to give up her job; she'd never understand why Cass still felt committed to the organization, even after having endured two life-threatening abductions in a row. And Cass, for her part, couldn't stop trying to bridge the gap between her partner and father, despite their fractured history.

"Well…keep an eye on her," Pierce said.

"I always do. Do you want to speak to her?"

"No. I've worried you both enough. Just say hi. I'll catch her later."

Cass hung up and walked to the kitchen. "Monty was concerned after updating you about TQ."

Jack turned to face her. "Is that why you're upset?"

"Why didn't you tell me?"

Jack put the milk in the fridge and walked up to her. "Because I'm done living in fear. We need a break from all this paranoia, and talking about her would just screw things up. I don't know about you, but I've been enjoying our normal life."

"Me, too." Cass softened. "But I need to know if someone's a threat to you."

Jack cradled Cass's face in her hands. "Cass, our address and names are unlisted, and we're both very capable of dealing with threats. I'm not going to sit around biting my nails in fear and hiding away because of TQ, or any TQ for that matter. We deserve a normal life."

Cass knew exactly what Jack meant. It had taken them too long and they'd had to fight too hard to get where they were, and she didn't want to go back to living in dread, either. "I know," she finally said. "But we need to be careful, that's all."

"That's all, indeed." Jack kissed her.

"I gotta say, you're taking this very well."

Jack shrugged. "I'm just tired of running from and after fucking idiots. I'm not thirty anymore."

"So you're not going to do anything stupid?"

"I can't promise that," Jack replied seriously. "I mean, look what happened to the frying pan." Two days earlier, she'd thoroughly blackened Cass's favorite frying pan and set off all their smoke alarms when she decided to cook them a stir-fry dish.

Cass smacked her on the butt. "You know what I mean."

"I love it when you spank me."

"Jack." Cass waited.

"I promise." Jack kissed her on the nose. "Nothing stupid."

❖

"And?" Joanne asked expectantly as Monty hung up the phone.

"Sounds like she's keeping a cool head for once, at least for the time being," he replied as he rejoined her on the couch. "And now Cassady will be keeping a close eye on her. I'm sure she'll let us know immediately if Jaclyn decides to do anything."

"We should take Cass off active reserve for a while," Joanne said, referring to the list of available agents they could call upon when new assignments arose. It was updated daily and usually only exempted ops already in the field, those just back from a long or grueling mission, and those recovering from injuries.

"Agreed." He put his arm around her and pulled her close. "I'll tell David," he said, "but not right now." He kissed her cheek. "I'm much too comfortable to worry any more about business unless the phone rings."

Since his recent heart issues and high blood pressure had surfaced, Joanne had insisted he scale back some on his responsibilities. Work more normal hours whenever possible and spend more time relaxing. At first, he balked at the idea. His job had consumed his life for *all* of his life.

But he couldn't deny her anything, and now he wondered why he'd ever hesitated. Their cozy home was a sanctuary, and their relationship had fulfilled him in ways he never imagined possible. He was only sorry he'd waited so long to tell her how much he loved her. He regretted all those wasted years that he could never get back.

For many months, he'd toyed with the idea of proposing. The whole organization knew about their involvement, anyway, and laughed at the long-standing rule against fraternization among ops. *What stopped me?* he wondered as Joanne put her head on his shoulder and sighed contentedly.

Jaclyn, he realized. He wanted her to be there if he married Joanne, and she wasn't anywhere near ready to fully acknowledge and accept him as her father, though their recent meeting had given him hope that she might, in time.

"What shall we do this evening, my love?" he asked. "Whatever you like."

"I like *this*," she quietly replied, and snuggled closer.

CHAPTER NINETEEN

Santorini Island, Greece

Ariadne knocked repeatedly on Melina's door but got no response from within. Her friend had stormed out of the club after she'd seen Ariadne and Alex kiss, and although she'd run after her to talk, Melina obviously had no interest in listening. Ariadne had glimpsed her getting in a cab, so she took the next one, a couple of minutes later.

She'd assumed Melina had gone back to the hotel, but maybe she was wrong. She tried the door handle, and when that didn't work, she headed to the reception desk. The guy on duty told her Ms. Pappas had picked up her keycard fifteen minutes earlier, so Ariadne went back to Melina's room and tried again.

"Open up. I know you're in there." She kept her voice low so she wouldn't create a public scene. "I know you picked up your key a few minutes ago."

Silence.

Ariadne knocked again. "Let me explain. Just give me a few minutes to tell you what happened."

Just then, Natasa and Jo showed up in the hallway.

"What's the deal?" Natasa looked grumpy. "Your bodyguard told us you guys ran off, and let me tell you, right now, he's not too happy."

"Where's Melina?" Jo asked.

"In her room. She won't open the door."

"Shit, what happened? Is she okay?" Jo asked.

"She's upset."

"Why?" Natasa eyed her suspiciously. "What did you do?"

"What makes you think it's her fault?" Jo asked her.

"Because she'd never shut Ariadne out. Melina always talks to her." Natasa pointed at Ariadne.

"Well, I think you're jumping to—"

"Natasa's right," Ariadne said. "It's my fault."

"What happened?" Jo approached her, concern etched on her face. "You guys never fight."

"I hurt her feelings, but...I didn't mean to."

Natasa put her hands on her hips. "What did you do?"

Melina threw open the door. "She kissed the one guy she knows I find interesting enough to want to get to know."

Jo and Natasa both looked at Ariadne with shocked expressions.

"You kissed a guy?" Jo asked loudly.

"Well, fuck me," Natasa whispered.

"They were all over each other," Melina shouted. "Practically fucking in public."

"No!" Both women gasped.

"Can I talk to you in private?" Ariadne had never seen Melina more hurt and angry.

"What for? A blow-by-blow account of how and why?"

"Yes."

"I'm not interested."

"You should be," Ariadne said, "because it's not what you think."

"Please tell me she's not going to say she tripped and her tongue landed in Alex's mouth," Natasa said to Jo.

"Shut up and let her speak," Jo replied.

"Look, I'm very sorry you had to see that," Ariadne told Melina. "But I can explain. It's definitely worth five minutes of your time."

"Let her inside," Jo said. "She owes you an explanation."

"I think they should talk it out right here." Natasa moved closer. "All of us need to know how a sworn lesbian stole your boyfriend."

"I didn't steal anything," Ariadne said, exasperated. "And certainly not a boyfriend."

"It was a matter of time." Melina scowled. "That is, until you decided to experiment with dick."

"You're so wrong."

"Tell me how I'm wrong, Ariadne." Melina was close to tears. "Because I know what I saw."

"What you saw was…" Ariadne couldn't finish. She wanted to tell her everything, blurt it all out, but some invisible force held her back.

"Screw the idiot," Natasa said. "You deserve better than—"

"It's not him I'm upset with, or disappointed in." Melina looked at Ariadne. "It just makes me sick to my stomach that my best friend betrayed me."

Jo cleared her throat. "Well, in all fairness, he didn't exactly throw himself at you, and he pretty much kept his distance. If you ask me, it was rather clear he was into Ariadne from day one."

"Seriously?" Natasa turned on Jo. "Are you set on making her feel worse, or are you just challenged in some way?"

"Neither," Jo replied quietly. "I'm just being fair."

Ariadne wanted to scream, to tell them to shut up, because they had no idea what was going on. "Melina, Jo's right. He's really not worth it. What I did…it was wrong, and…I don't know why I let it happen. It was stupid, selfish, and insensitive."

"Yes, it was." Melina said, still quite angry.

"I needed to prove something to Alex. He made it clear the other day that he was interested, and I guess I needed to defend my sexuality by proving him wrong."

"And?" Melina asked. "Did you?"

"Does it matter?"

Melina looked defeated. "No, I guess it doesn't."

"You're not going to let a guy come between you," Jo said.

"And a hairless one at that," Natasa added. "I tell ya, there's something fishy about a guy who feels the need to shave."

All of them laughed, lightening the mood.

Ariadne turned to Melina. "I'm really sorry. I never meant to hurt your feelings."

Melina shrugged. "I know. It's just that you're so young and beautiful and I'm…I see myself getting older every day. The prospect of getting serious with an attractive, younger guy blinded me. I figured he'd look cute on my shoulder."

Jo rolled her eyes.

"Like a hairless wrap," Natasa said.

"Let it go, already."

"Can't. Any guy who shaves more than I do must be a douche."

"You never answered." Melina tapped her finger on the door. "How was it?"

Ariadne blushed at the memory. "You mean…"

"Yes, yes, she means the kiss," Natasa said. "She's not asking about the cab drive here."

"She liked it." Jo smiled smugly. "I can tell."

"I knew it," Melina said. "I was sure he'd be a hell of a kisser."

Ariadne tried to keep her expression neutral. Her friends knew her so well she'd get caught lying if she so much as twitched. She focused on the spot between Melina's brows. "I never said that."

"The fact that you didn't say how much it sucked is enough," Jo insisted.

"Does that make you strai…does that make her straight?" Natasa asked Melina and Jo.

"No," Ariadne blurted. "The kiss sucked, and…and I'll never be attracted to guys."

"Hmm." Natasa crossed her arms. "Denial is one of the three steps to—"

"Guys, I'm beat, and I need to get some rest, so if you'll excuse me." Ariadne had to get away from there to deal with what had happened, and what hadn't happened, and she was desperate for a cold shower. "Are we okay?" she asked Melina.

"Not yet." Melina smiled. "But we will be by tomorrow."

Ariadne exhaled in relief. "Sh…he's not what you think." She kissed Melina on the cheek. "And definitely not the man you were hoping for."

Though she headed off toward her own room, Ariadne was too unsettled to sleep, so she detoured to the hotel's fairly busy pool bar. Once she got her gin and tonic, she chose a bench off to one side, in the small garden. She wasn't in the mood for small talk and was actually more upset with tonight's developments than she cared to admit to herself, let alone her friends.

She'd screwed up on so many levels. First with Alex, and then with Melina. She didn't know what had possessed her to say all that to Alex, and she didn't know where she'd found the strength to break that kiss.

She was mortified to realize that her frustration had more to do with how Alex had toyed with *her* than with how she'd behaved with Melina. Had she misread Alex's interest in her? She did have a girlfriend, after all, and if she'd misjudged Alex's intentions, then why didn't Alex pull away when Ariadne kissed her on the yacht…Wait a minute. She *had*. Alex had been the one to stop things. But then, why not tonight? Especially with Alex's girlfriend there?

Ariadne rubbed her temples. Everything about this woman confused and terrified her. She'd never met anyone she wanted to smack and sleep with at the same time, and she'd also never met a liar she wanted to protect and defend.

Everything she thought she knew about Alex had been bogus. And why would an obviously well-educated woman want to work as a male bosun, anyway? Something was off, and Ariadne wanted to be angry and suspicious, but all she could feel was desire for the beautiful liar.

"Typical," Ariadne said out loud. The one time someone's mind and manners turned her on as much as their beauty had to be an involved fake. And on top of that, after tonight, her friends would likely consider her a trysexual man stealer. Would she have the courage to let them believe that, or would she eventually tell them the truth and clear her name?

"The bartender told me I'd find you here."

Ariadne jumped when she heard Alex's voice. She turned to look at her.

"I'm sorry I startled you," Alex said.

"There's a reason I'm hiding here."

Alex sat beside her on the bench as though she didn't care about Ariadne's need to be alone. She sighed and leaned back. "I know, but we need to talk."

"Your secret is still safe," Ariadne said. "Other than that, I don't see what else we need to discuss."

"How's Melina?"

"She'll be fine."

"How about you?"

"What about me?"

"I know how you must hate lying to your friends."

"Doubtful. Because you wouldn't have put me in the position to do so if you had even the smallest insight into that."

"I have my reasons." Alex avoided eye contact.

"I know something's going on, because there's no way someone like you needs to so desperately work as a bosun."

"Like me?"

"You're too educated…too refined, to be doing this. You have a certain air. The way you move…everything about you, really, doesn't fit the 'woman struggling to survive' profile."

Alex's startled expression confirmed her assessment.

"Don't look so surprised," Ariadne said. "It's my job to read people and situations. It's why I'm good at what I do."

"As your father warned me," Alex replied.

Ariadne sipped her drink. "So, what are your reasons?"

"I needed the job, but…not for the money."

"What then?"

"The…" Alex rubbed her face. "I don't want to lie to you. Not again. So please, let's not talk about that."

"Does this have to do with my father?"

"It has to do with me. Just know that I never meant to hurt your feelings or play with your friends, and I'm sincerely sorry for everything."

"Does your girlfriend know?" she asked.

"That I kissed you?" Alex smiled that wonderful smile, and Ariadne found herself once again completely captivated by her mouth.

She nodded, unable to speak or move her gaze from Alex's lips. How did she go from being furious with this woman to wanting to kiss her in mere seconds?

"She saw us." Alex shifted to look at her.

"So, why are you smiling?"

"Am I?" Alex asked.

"Yes."

"Angie and I have an arrangement."

"Ah, one of those." Ariadne felt inexplicably disappointed. "I never understood those relationships."

"We have an arrangement that we pose as each other's girlfriend when we want to get out of an uncomfortable situation."

"You mean…?" Ariadne felt a flutter in the pit of her stomach.

"She got me out of a tough spot with Melina."

"Oh."

"Yup."

"That explains a lot."

"Does it?"

"Angie doesn't strike me as your type. She's too…"

"Butch?" Alex asked, still smiling. "Maybe I like butch."

"Yeah, maybe." Ariadne picked at her dress. "Do you?"

"I like smart women who aren't afraid to go after what they want or afraid to get dirty. Women who feel just as comfortable in sweats and sneakers as they do in a cocktail dress and high heels. I like women who share my passion for diving and sailing."

That's me, that's me. "I see."

Alex looked from Ariadne's eyes to her lips.

"So, Angie saved you from Melina, but not from me." Now why did she have to say that?

"That's right."

Don't push it. "Why not?" *Too late.*

"She's a very perceptive woman." Alex grinned.

Ariadne's cheeks burned. The combination of Alex's melancholic smile and subtle charm was irresistible. "I'm sorry I said those things to you earlier and pushed you away like that. I had no right to play with you, but I got really angry when I found out you had a girlfriend and still wanted to…kiss me."

"I wanted more than that," Alex replied.

The words reignited the fire from earlier, and it was spreading dangerously fast from Ariadne's abdomen to the juncture of her thighs. She wanted to say something casual to douse the heat, but nothing came out. There was nothing flippant about how Alex made her feel.

"Was that kiss all about punishing me?" Alex asked.

Ariadne wanted to lie but couldn't. "No."

"I am very attracted to you, Ariadne, and I think you know that, especially after tonight."

Can we stop talking and go to my room for hot sex and then plan our future?

"Please don't say anything, because whatever your response…" Alex tucked a stray strand of hair behind Ariadne's ear and she shivered. "It will upset me." She got to her feet. "Maybe in another place and time we could've gotten to know each other…dated, but we have too much going on in our lives. Too many barriers."

"I don't know anything about you, but don't presume to know what my life is like."

"Frankly, I don't think you understand the price you're going to pay for being the Lykourgos heiress."

"What's that supposed to mean?"

"In order to take your father's place and live up to his role, and your brother's and mother's expectations, you're going to have to change your priorities. Your mother and brother will become your responsibility, and so will your father's empire."

"So?"

"You grew up in a loving and healthy family environment, which creates a sense of obligation. One that I respect," Alex said, "but can't relate to, because I never had that."

"I still don't understand."

"Whoever you choose to be with will have to accept that they will always be in the shadows of your responsibilities and commitment toward your family."

"They will be part of them, not a…a sidekick," Ariadne said.

"You're fooling yourself if you think that," Alex replied. "You have such a rooted sense of responsibility and loyalty toward your family that no one will ever measure up to, and frankly, not everyone wants to be a responsibility. Some want to be more than an obligation, more than part of a collective commitment."

"I don't understand why that's a problem."

"Because anyone who loves you and not your money will tire of taking a backseat."

"I wouldn't want them to." Ariadne got up as well. "I'd tire myself with someone who wouldn't stand up and take the wheel."

"Has your father ever given up the wheel? To you, or anyone, for that matter?"

"He trusts my judgment. He listens to me about work and he appreciates his advisors' input."

"And who has the final say?" Alex asked.

"He does, of course."

"And does he listen to you, or whomever, when it concerns family matters?"

Her father was flexible when it came to most things, but not when it came to how family matters should be dealt with. According to him, his ways were always the wisest, because he was chief executive and owner of the family as well. "No," she admitted.

"How do you feel about that?"

"It's frustrating at times, but..." She shrugged. "It is what it is. It's how it's always been."

"And how it will always be. Only you're next in line to hog that wheel. You may think you want someone to take the wheel now, but deep in your heart you know you won't be able to."

Maybe Alex was right. Her father had already started to call her a control freak, and even domineering. "Be that as it may—"

"I don't do well in the backseat, Ariadne," Alex said quietly. "And I sincerely hope you don't fall for someone who does, because anyone willing to get comfortable in the back probably deserves to be there, but not with you."

Ariadne didn't know what to say, and Alex looked around as well. An uncomfortable silence descended upon them.

Alex finally looked at her watch. "It's late, and..." She suddenly covered her watch with her hand and sighed. "I really hate clichés. I'm going to leave now because I'd like to be alone, and I think you want that, too."

She left and Ariadne sat back down on the bench. Was she really becoming her father? And if so, was that what she wanted? And if not, could she be something other than the gentle tyrant she was being groomed to be? What if Alex was right? Had all her ex-partners settled into a subservient position just because of who she was and what she could offer?

What bothered her more than anything was that the one person who had managed to melt Ariadne with her kisses, had taken the time to look close enough to have an opinion, and then had the guts to stand up to her and tell her what she thought was too busy with her own life to want to give Ariadne a chance.

CHAPTER TWENTY

Thessaloniki, Greece
Next day

TQ frowned when her servant drew back the curtains in her room and exposed the vista she'd be subjected to until she recovered the *Theotokos*. She'd traded her magnificent terrace view of the harbor at the Electra Palace for a brick wall, in a hotel that under ordinary circumstances she'd refuse to even set foot in.

But it was necessary, she kept telling herself. Lykourgos was a very powerful man in Greece, with connections everywhere, including the highest levels of the government and law enforcement, no doubt. Once his daughter went missing, he'd likely use those resources to find her, so she'd had to move to an inferior hotel that wouldn't demand ID at check-in.

She scanned the room. It wasn't even a suite, though it was the best the hotel had to offer. Cheap tourist art, inferior linens, an antiquated television. Not even a goddamn minibar or coffeemaker, for Christ's sake, and forget about room service.

"Go out and get me some sheets I can actually sleep on," she told her Asian Cyclops. "And a summer comforter," she added, not wanting to guess how long it had been since the hotel had washed the monstrosity of a bedspread currently on display, or what it had absorbed and been stained by in the interim. "Up to my usual standards."

The girl looked terrified. "Madam, I do not know the city, or the language, or—"

TQ turned to glare at her, and the servant immediately bowed her head and stopped talking. "Learn fast, or your next trashy romance will be in Braille. You have an hour."

The girl bowed deeply and ran to get TQ's purse. She brought it over and TQ gave her several fifty-euro bills.

"Get a decent espresso machine, too, and the kind of coffee I like," she yelled after the girl as she hurried toward the door.

TQ went to the window and stared out. The white-brick building opposite was shuttered, the electronics store it had once contained long closed because of the struggling economy. Three floors below, the street was crowded with cars, scooters, and pedestrians, and the noise level was an added irritant.

How she wished she were back in the States, surrounded by her treasures in her plush Houston penthouse. And where her significant contacts and resources kept her from ever having to resort to hiding in such a dump.

The *Theotokos* was worth it. But Lykourgos had better act quickly to meet her demands. Even her patience had its limits, and this place would push her into the red zone in a hurry. She was already feeling the need to take out her frustrations on someone, and it took so damn long to adequately train a new servant.

❖

Off Santorini Island, Greece

As Switch made her rounds on the *Pegasus*, she tried to at least catch a glimpse of Ariadne, but the woman was nowhere to be seen on the yacht. She'd spotted Melina and the other two by the pool but had avoided contact. And besides, the glare of death coming off Melina hadn't been exactly inviting. It had been made clear to her early that morning that keeping her distance was prudent after the previous night's events. Switch was supposed to have taken the girls back to the yacht, but they'd summoned Manos instead, at Melina's insistence. She'd taken the other Zodiac back alone.

In the early afternoon, she broke down and asked Manos if he'd seen Ariadne, and the second bosun's reply had been cold, albeit helpful. The women had apparently updated him on what had happened and he clearly sided with them, probably out of loyalty.

According to Manos, Ariadne was planning to spend the day in her room, with the exception of the meeting she'd had earlier in the morning with her dad.

Switch's bittersweet time around Ariadne was ending. After tonight, she'd have no reason to see her again, and although that meant distancing herself from the impossible object of her affection, she'd soon have the space to get over the woman who was fast becoming an obsession.

The rest of the day had been uneventful, so Switch was happy it was almost time for the family and guests to go ashore so she could get down to business and back to her life.

Though the initial schedule she'd been given called for her and Manos to ferry the Lykourgoses and their guests in the Zodiacs for a lavish dinner ashore, she ended up getting a few hours off instead, a fortuitous turn of events that would make getting Allegro onto the *Pegasus* a bit easier.

Taking guests ashore by dinghy was standard for most luxury yachts, but different arrangements were made once Lykourgos found out that the Ambassador Aegean in Akrotiri had its own private helipad. He'd arranged to host his banquet at the new luxury resort and had booked rooms for all his guests there, so the decision to ferry them by helicopter instead was a no-brainer.

Switch went up to the helipad to watch the departures, keeping mostly hidden in the recesses of one of the poolside cabanas nearby so she wouldn't precipitate any protracted scene involving Ariadne or Melina. Tonight's operation had to proceed without a hitch, and the more people off the boat, the better. Because the family and all guests would be away overnight, many of the stewards had a rare night of liberty and were going ashore as well.

Fortunately, one of them was the chief steward, which lessened the chances she and Allegro would be caught breaking into his safe to get the blue keycard for the master suite. She certainly couldn't try to get Ariadne's a second time, or Nikolaos's, and Lykourgos and his wife would surely keep theirs with them, even off the yacht. So the maid's card was the only one possible.

She spotted Ariadne emerging from the side stairwell and froze to stare in wonder at how stunning she was tonight. Clad in an elegant turquoise gown, her hair up, gems around her throat, she looked like a modern-day princess. The rest of her friends had dressed formally for the occasion as well, but none could compare.

Lykourgos came next, his wife on his arm. Christine was impeccably groomed, as always, and he was hardly recognizable in his expensive navy suit, pale-blue shirt, and silk tie. He'd even shaved, and his hair, for once, didn't look as though he'd just rolled out of bed. Smiling and apparently eager to get the party started, he hustled them all with a wave of his arms toward the chopper as its rotors started.

Switch watched them all board, and soon the helicopter was headed toward the island. Two more trips were required to ferry Nikolaos and the rest of the guests to the resort. By the time they were gone, the chief steward and other crewmembers with the night off were in a dinghy also headed ashore. As soon as they were out of sight of the yacht, Switch went below and commandeered one of the Zodiacs for herself, taking along the steward's uniform she'd lifted earlier from the crew linen closet for Allegro, in case anyone questioned them.

She'd arranged to rendezvous with Allegro at a secluded beach some distance from the resort where Lykourgos was hosting his event and found her waiting impatiently with a small backpack containing her safecracking tools. Allegro changed into the steward's uniform en route, but by the time they got back to the yacht, it was full dark out, and the transom area was deserted.

They tied off the Zodiac, and Switch led the way to the below-deck offices via a freight elevator used to transport food to the galley. Manos's tour and her rounds aboard the *Pegasus* had given her ample time to scope out the lesser-used avenues of transit on the ship, where they were less likely to encounter anyone who might challenge an unfamiliar face.

The crew offices were all dark and the hallway deserted. Switch picked the lock on the chief steward's door in a few seconds, and it took Allegro only another couple of minutes to get inside his safe for the keycard to the master suite.

"I hope the big-boy version is more of a challenge," Allegro said as she handed the blue plastic to Switch with a grin. "I could have phoned this one in."

They headed to the family's quarters via the crew stairwell that the maids and stewards used. After slipping into Lykourgos's suite undetected, Switch led the way into the bedroom.

Allegro let out a low whistle when Switch opened the panel that hid the massive wall safe. "Now you're talking." She set to work and had it open in less than ten minutes. "Voilà. Save the applause, please."

The wall safe contained enough gold and jewels to finance a small country, along with a wealth of other treasures. But the *Theotokos* wasn't one of them.

"It's got to be here," Switch insisted as they stared at the safe. "Where else could it be?"

Allegro took a couple of steps back and started looking the room over, meticulously scanning the walls. "My guess? A yacht this size? Some kind of hidden room, maybe. You know, in case of pirates."

"I didn't keep searching after I found the safe," Switch said. "I was just so sure it would be in there."

"You start over there." Allegro pointed to the opposite wall. "I'll take this side."

They focused on the myriad of large art panels that ringed the room, since one had hidden the safe, and after much searching, Switch found the subtle trigger to the one that hid Lykourgos's safe room. When they swung back the panel, they found a solid-steel door, with an electronic panel beside it that looked much more complex than the one Allegro had just cracked.

"Three for three, coming right up," Allegro said. "Stand back, and watch a genius at work."

Despite the boast, Switch began to get nervous when twenty-five minutes had passed with Allegro still sweating over the high-tech electronic lock. "Problems?" she asked.

"Why? Got somewhere else to be?" Allegro shot back with annoyance.

"Someone's touchy about their less than successful attempt at showing off."

"Look who's talking, Ms. 'I can't help but screw Lykourgos's daughter in public for the world to see.'"

"I didn't screw her," Switch said.

"Came close enough."

"Hey, I—"

"Really slick," Allegro said. "With one of the country's public figures? I wouldn't be surprised if it ends up in the papers. You just know someone taped it. I'm sure Lykourgos is going to be thrilled when he finds out the bosun is banging his daughter. Not to mention Pierce."

"He won't find out."

"I sure as hell hope not. You know how he is about discretion and publicity." Although all ops' identities were protected, Pierce was strict about his people avoiding the media because you never knew who your next client or what your next job would be, and being made on the job was a big no-no.

"If someone had taped us," Switch said, "it would be out there by now."

"Maybe you got lucky this time, but I'd stay away from her if I were you."

"We're out after tonight, so enough with the oration."

"Shhh." Allegro hushed her as the decoder ran another number. "You guys looked hot together," Allegro said when the code failed again. "She's got it bad for you, too."

Switch's heart fluttered. "You got that from a kiss in a dark hallway?"

"Hell, yeah. You mean you didn't feel it?"

"I…I did, I guess." Switch looked out the large window at the blue sea.

"Hey, hey. Stay focused." Allegro ran another algorithm. "I need your head here, not between Ariadne's legs."

What a sweet image. "I wasn't—"

"The hell you weren't. I know that lo—"

Both of them froze when they heard the loud *click*.

"Bingo." Allegro stood and bowed. "I present to you, the virtuoso that is me." The lights to the safe room were connected to the code, because the room lit up as soon as the door slid back. Switch entered while Allegro stayed behind as lookout.

The safe room contained boxes of food and a large supply of water, as well as other emergency essentials, but she spotted the *Theotokos* at once. It was hard to miss, with the shrine built around it. The gold icon was centered on a pedestal, surrounded by candles, other smaller icons, and a picture of Lykourgos and his family. A kneeling bench had been placed in front.

"The dude really believes in all this," Allegro said from the door.

"Hey, whatever gets you through," Switch replied. "At least his drug of choice is harmless."

"There's nothing harmless about religion."

"You mean there's nothing harmless about the bull crap around it. Religion without the circus of church and politics is nothing more than faith and a source of strength for those who choose to believe in it."

Allegro shrugged. "Whatever. It's not my choice, anyway."

Switch carefully lifted the icon from its stand, surprised at its weight. "I'm sure this came in something." She looked around and found a hardcover case on a shelf. She placed it in there and secured the case. "Part one is done," she said. "Part two, confront Lykourgos."

Allegro closed the door to the safe room and they left everything as they found it, then made their way back to the transom where they'd tied off the Zodiac.

Allegro got in and Switch handed over the icon. "Be careful with it. It's priceless."

"Hey, if I can find and return a huge-ass diamond, then I can handle a piece of gold." Allegro was never shy about touting past accomplishments, and her recovery of the famed Setarehe Abi Rang, or Blue Star Diamond, was one of the EOO's finest achievements.

Switch jumped into the Zodiac, too, and started the engine. "Let's get it away from here before someone sees us."

As they beached the inflatable on shore, Switch's cell vibrated. The caller ID told her it was Pierce.

"We have the icon," she told him as soon as she answered.

"Good job," he replied. "But we've got a hitch. TQ's in the wind. Dilbert lost her when she switched hotels in the middle of the night, and we haven't managed to track her down yet. I'll let you know when we do."

CHAPTER TWENTY-ONE

Off Santorini Island, Greece

Kostas waited until his guests had all left the festivities, the older generation retiring to the rooms he'd booked for them at the Ambassador, and his children and their friends to their nightclubbing after parties. Then he escorted his wife to the suite he'd reserved for them both.

As he slipped his keycard into the lock, Christine said gently, "You needn't bother with seeing me inside and comfortable, darling. I know you want to get back to the *Pegasus*. Go on. I'll be fine."

"I love how you know me so well." He kissed her.

"As long as she's your only mistress." She laid her hand on his chest and smiled up at him with such love and trust that his heart warmed. "I can live with that."

"You are my greatest treasure, now and always." Kostas kissed her again and opened the door for her. "Sotiris will be outside, if you need anything." He'd arranged a room for the family's bodyguards on the same floor they were staying and had notified Christine's to stand watch until he saw her lights go out. He beckoned the man over before heading to the hotel's helipad.

As he and his own bodyguard flew back to the ship, he stared up at the clear night, full of stars. He always preferred sleeping aboard the *Pegasus* to anywhere else, even his ornate, comfy bed in suburban Athens. He was born to be at sea and felt most at home there, but tonight he was especially eager to get back aboard his yacht.

He'd awakened this morning with a vigor and robustness he

hadn't experienced in many months; the *Theotokos* was healing him. When he'd dressed for dinner, he'd seen color in his cheeks again, and even after many hours entertaining his guests, he wasn't tired at all. Oh, his cough was still there, but that was better, too. He'd had just two minor episodes all evening.

He needed only to continue venerating the icon even more fervently than before, and soon all of his cancer would be eradicated. Then he could return the *Theotokos* to the monastery.

As soon as the chopper landed on the upper deck, Kostas headed to the master suite. "I won't need you any more tonight," he told his bodyguard when they reached the door. "It's been a long day. Get some rest."

"Thank you, sir. Good night, Mr. Lykourgos," the man said, and headed away toward the crew quarters.

Kostas hurried to his bedroom, his heartbeat accelerating with anticipation. He opened the panel and punched in the code, and the door slid back.

It wasn't there.

The pedestal was just as it was, and the rest of the room was the same as he'd left it.

But the *Theotokos* was gone.

In disbelief, he ran to the pedestal and searched frantically behind and around it.

Then he noticed the case for the icon was missing, too.

Either Fotis had gotten back on board or someone else had been here.

He hurried to the shipboard phone and rang his head of security. "Seal off the ship immediately," he shouted. "Don't let anyone leave. There's been a theft from my suite." His hand shook from anger and frustration, and he gripped the phone tighter. "Assemble all personnel immediately on the aft main deck."

"Sir, I believe some of the stewards are ashore on leave," the voice on the other end said.

"Get them back here, now! I want answers!"

Kostas searched the safe room again after he hung up, though he knew it was futile. He just still couldn't believe the icon had been stolen.

Almost as an afterthought, he opened his wall safe to see if the thief had gotten in there, too, but the contents seemed to be just as he had left them.

How? And who? He hurried up to the aft deck, praying some member of his crew had a clue that could tell him what had happened.

After all the staff on board had gathered, he told them about the theft and asked them all loudly whether anyone had seen someone near the family's quarters that night, or a stranger on board. No one stepped forward. He then asked, even louder, whether anyone had seen anything at all suspicious or unusual. More silence.

So, he spoke to each of the assembled deckhands, stewards, engineers, and other staff in turn, one by one. He studied their faces and mannerisms as he did, trying to find some sign of deceit, though he'd been blind to Fotis's betrayal until he caught him in the act.

Every face he talked to was familiar. Long-time employees, most of them. Trusted. No one seemed uneasy under his questions. If a new traitor was on board, he couldn't tell who it was.

"Someone has to know something!" he shouted after he'd questioned everyone present. But no one, apparently, had information to help him.

He hoped that when all the staffers on shore leave had returned, one of them might be more helpful. But two hours later, when all crewmembers but one had been accounted for and questioned, he was no closer to finding out who was behind it.

"Where is Alex?" he asked his security chief when informed about the missing bosun. "Why hasn't he returned to the ship?"

"He didn't answer the cell number he gave us," the man replied. "We left a message to return to the ship ASAP, but he hasn't responded, and he didn't tell anyone where he was going."

"Let me have that number. I want to call him myself."

❖

Akrotiri, Santorini Island, Greece
Next morning

Ariadne rose early, edgy and in need of distraction. She'd humored her friends the night before and barhopped with them in Fira again after her father's banquet, though she'd really been in no mood for loud music and busy clubs. Not that they'd noticed. She'd ended up spending most of her time in quiet corners chatting with her bodyguard, while her friends danced and flirted. Melina seemed to be enjoying the much-needed ego boost and was feeling a lot better with all the attention she was getting.

Ariadne's only amusement had been when she'd run into the blonde again from the previous night of clubbing, a woman whose name she'd completely forgotten. She'd been so preoccupied with Alex at the time that she couldn't focus on what Niki was saying, though she'd been about to leave for a quieter bar Niki had suggested when she ran into Alex outside the ladies' room.

Niki was pleasant and attentive both nights, and obviously interested in her, so Ariadne took her up on her offer for breakfast the next morning. She was in no hurry to return to the yacht and could use the flirty diversion.

This morning she'd gotten up at six thirty and, too restless to wait for her friends to awaken, wandered down to the hotel's restaurant for coffee and found Melina having breakfast.

"Couldn't sleep?" Ariadne asked when she approached.

"I'm depressed." Melina rested her head against her hand. "I'm not ready for the summer to be over."

"In other words, you're not ready for reality."

"Why do guys flock to gay women? It's not fair."

"Now I understand where the depression is really coming from," Ariadne said. "It's because we're not interested. Straight women try too hard, and guys need a challenge."

Melina mulled over that for a few seconds. "Hey, let's get out of here." She perked up. "Just me and you, and you can tell me all about how your breed lures our men."

"I have a breakfast appointment at nine."

"Oh, yeah. That Niki woman."

"Yup."

"Are you into her?" Melina asked. "Or is this a quest for redemption?"

"Redemption?"

"You know, for kissing a guy."

"Neither," Ariadne replied. "I thought it would be nice to chat over breakfast. She's fun."

"If it were a nice chat and fun you were interested in, you'd be having breakfast with me. You're not fooling me, Lykourgos. You want redemption."

What if she did? There was nothing wrong with spending a few hours with someone interested in her, and she could surely use a break from Alex. "Yeah...maybe I do."

"Okay, so I'll leave when she shows up."

Ariadne liked the idea of some time alone with Melina. "I'll call Lambros, tell him to get ready." She always notified her bodyguard. Not because she wanted to, or thought it necessary, but because it was father's orders.

"Just me and you, please?" Melina stuck out her lips in a pout. "Just this once?"

"But Dad—"

"Call Lambros when you get to your appointment. But let's just have an hour alone."

"You're right. Come on, let's go."

Melina got up. "Maybe I need to try for faux lesbian," she said. "I think that should be my strategic approach."

They walked around the small village with its picturesque tavernas and quaint shops. Ariadne had her first cup of coffee at one stop, and around eight thirty, they headed to the Seagull café at the harbor for her breakfast date with Niki.

They were early, so Ariadne plucked a complimentary newspaper from the stand and chose a table close to the water, around the corner from the entrance so they wouldn't have to deal with the noise of tourists and traffic passing by.

"Could we get any farther away from the waiter and everyone else?" Melina asked.

Ariadne looked around. "Who's everyone else? You mean the only other couple here?"

They settled in, and Ariadne lost herself in the financial page while Melina talked to herself about the earrings she'd bought that morning and which dress she planned to wear them with.

Both women looked up when they heard a speedboat approach. Niki and her brother waved at them.

"She brought her brother." Melina pouted.

"He's probably dropping her off."

The boat pulled up to the seawall, close to the table where they were seated.

"Hi there," Niki's brother Phaidon said. The tall young man had hit on Ariadne at The Koo Club, but had been gracious when he'd found out she was gay and instead introduced her to his sister. "Is Melina your new guard?" he asked, looking around as if searching for someone.

"Hi, Phaidon." Melina smiled. "And yes, she's my responsibility today."

"I hope you don't mind. Big brother wanted to join us for a bite," Niki said.

"Not at all. The more the merrier," Ariadne replied.

"See, good thing I came along." He grinned at her. "Or you'd be filled with regrets for rejecting me."

Niki spread her arms and twirled. "So, how do you like her?" she asked, indicating the shiny Sunseeker Comanche they'd ridden up in.

"She's a beauty," Ariadne said.

"Looks fast," Melina added.

"Want to go for a spin before we settle for breakfast?" Niki asked.

"Yes!" Melina exclaimed. "I love speed."

Ariadne didn't respond. The siblings looked benign and sweet, but she wasn't crazy about the idea of getting into any kind of contraption with someone she didn't know, let alone a boat with that much horsepower.

"Just a short ride. I promise not to go fast," Phaidon said as though he'd read her mind.

Niki urged her. "Trust me. He's a safe driver."

"Come on." Melina rose and pulled her hand. "Let's go, already."

Ariadne got up. "Okay, okay. But only once around the harbor."

"You won't need more than that to appreciate my baby," Phaidon said proudly.

He helped both her and Melina onto the speedboat, and Phaidon started off slowly until they were away from the shore, where he picked up a pleasant speed.

"Over to those rocks and back," he yelled over the engine's roar, pointing toward an outcropping several hundred meters distant.

"Go for it." Melina stood beside him with her arms spread like she was rehearsing for a role in *Titanic the Sequel*.

Ariadne remained seated at the rear of the boat, with Niki next to her. Discussion was impossible over the roaring engine, so she lifted her face to the warm sun and luxuriated in the smell of the sea and the feel of the spray. They had just reached the rocks and were going around them when Ariadne felt a pinch behind her neck. "What the...?" She smacked her neck. "Something bit—"

CHAPTER TWENTY-TWO

Switch had seen the first mate's and Lykourgos's cell numbers pop up on her caller ID the night before, but she hadn't answered the calls. Instead, she listened to the voice mails, asking all personnel to return to the yacht. The tone of Lykourgos's voice made it clear he'd already discovered the icon was missing, so it was a good thing they had moved when they did. The first phone call had come less than an hour after she and Allegro had left the boat. There was clearly no reason for her to immediately return to the yacht, because when she did it would be on different terms, and she needed to be prepared.

After checking into a small hotel overnight, Switch headed back to the yacht to confront Lykourgos, while Allegro arranged for a private helicopter charter later that morning to return the icon to the monastery.

Switch had just stepped off the Zodiac and onto the yacht when Manos came running toward her.

"Where have you—" Manos stopped himself when he drew nearer and got a better look at her. "I'm sorry, I thought you were…" He peered intently at her. "Alex, is that you?"

She'd dressed in dark jeans and a black blouse, unbuttoned enough to show cleavage. And her hair was tousled in a feminine style, the way she usually wore it, instead of combed to the side and slicked back from her face.

"Hey, Manos." She smiled. "Yeah, it's Alex."

"Oh, my God." He gasped. "You're a woman."

"Surprise," Switch said.

"Well, fuck me."

She chuckled. "You're not my type."

"Neither are you...anymore." He half smiled, clearly puzzled.

"Where's Lykourgos?"

"In his office, screaming at everyone. Where were you, by the way? He summoned us all back last night."

"About a missing icon?" she asked.

"So you heard."

"You could say that."

"He asked about you and was infuriated you didn't show up. If you ask me, you and Fotis are his number-one suspects."

"I'm not a thief, Manos." Switch smiled.

"Yeah, well. Tell him that."

Switch turned to leave. "Later."

"Does he know you're a woman?"

"Nope."

"By the way, *why* are you a woman?" Manos asked.

"Born that way."

"I mean, why pose as a man?"

"I have my reasons." Switch went forward to find Lykourgos. She ran into a few of the guests and personnel, and all of them stared at her, either in disbelief because they recognized her or because an unescorted stranger was on board.

Switch knocked on Lykourgos's office door.

"Who?" His tone was angry and irritated.

"It's Alex."

"About damn time," he said loudly while he buzzed her in. "Where have you—" He stopped when Switch entered the room. "Alex?"

"Yes, sir." Switch shut the door while Lykourgos sat with his mouth hanging open. "I know it's a bit of a shock."

"You're a woman." He sat back in his chair as if to put distance between himself and reality. "What in the hell is going on?"

"I took the *Theotokos*."

Lykourgos blanched. "How do you know about the *Theotokos*?"

"Mr. Lykourgos, I'm a private contractor." Switch stepped closer to his desk. "I work for a company that Mount Athos hired to recover and return the priceless icon you hired someone to steal."

"No!" Lykourgos shouted. "No, no, no!" He got up and placed his hands on the desk. "I will give you any amount of money to return it to me."

"I'm not interested in money," Switch replied calmly.

"I need it." He fumed between tight lips. "I need it just a while longer. I never meant to keep it. I would never deprive others of its powers, but I have to keep it with me until I'm better."

"I know you want to believe it will cure your lung cancer, but I cannot return the icon to you under any circumstances."

"How do you know about my illness?" He looked surprised.

"I'm afraid you don't understand how far-reaching this organization is, Mr. Lykourgos. There is nothing and no one our means can't find. If you put the CIA together with Interpol you'll still come up with only a fraction of what we can do."

Lykourgos dropped into his chair. "Does this mean I'm going to be arrested?"

"That's up to you."

Lykourgos eyed her suspiciously. "You said you don't want money. So, what then?"

"I want your cooperation to arrest Mrs. Rothschild, the woman who helped you steal the icon."

"How do you...?" He stopped. "Never mind." He was apparently convinced about the EOO's power.

"We have been trying to catch Rothschild in the act for years. She is behind everything wrong with this world, from slavery to trading in weapons and human organs. Every time we get close to taking her down, she reaches in her pockets and buys a cop, an agent, a politician, or a witness. We need to stop her and you can help us do it. In exchange, you get to keep your freedom and our discretion."

"But can the monks have me arrested for an icon that presumably doesn't exist?" he asked.

"They're willing to expose its existence if the thief doesn't cooperate, or if we don't have it back in its place by tomorrow," Switch lied. "Basically, they're willing to go to any lengths to get the *Theotokos* back, and if the police get involved, just like us they will conduct the same pattern of research that will lead them to you." She was bluffing.

Lykourgos scratched at his stubble of beard, then sat there with his face hidden in his hands for a long while.

"Can you prove that you met with her or paid her?" Switch asked. "Is there any way at all to prove she is involved?"

"No. I paid her in cash."

"Okay, then I can wire you. You invite her back for an icon-related discussion, bring up the theft and her involvement."

"If I never see that cold bitch again it'll be too soon."

"I'm afraid you don't have a choice."

A loud knock at the door made them both jump.

"Not now," Lykourgos shouted.

"It's about Ariadne," a male voice said from the other side.

Lykourgos buzzed him in, and both he and Switch hurried to the door. "What happened?" they asked in unison.

Lambros, Ariadne's bodyguard, was close to tears. "I can't find her. According to a waitress in the hotel restaurant, she and Melina slipped out early this morning after coffee. Neither has contacted the girls or me, and we've tried calling them, all of us, but nothing." The guy was close to hyperventilating, and Switch was sure a lot of it had to do with his fear of Lykourgos's reaction.

"You incompetent fucker!" he shouted. "I want you to find my daughter, *now!*"

"Lambros." Switch stood in front of Lykourgos. "Look at me. Look at me." She repeated her demand to help him focus on her and not his boss's rage. "Has Ariadne done this before?"

Lambros took notice of her presence for the first time and frowned at the change in her appearance. "Alex?"

"Answer me." Switch was running out of patience.

"No," he replied.

"Where did she go last night?"

"To different bars with her friends. They stayed about an hour at each, three bars in total. I took them back to the hotel around two o'clock."

"Did you notice anything unusual at any or all of the bars?"

"Of course not. I would've done something if I had. It was just the usual dancing and flirting."

"Did Ariadne talk with anyone?"

"She spent most of the evening watching the others have fun. She wasn't into it, know what I mean? I kept her company at one of the places until a woman she'd met at the club the day before showed up with her brother. I stayed with them for a while before I returned to my post."

"What woman? What did she look like?"

"Blond, short hair," he replied. "Tall, kinda her type."

Switch doubted this was a coincidence. Her gut was never wrong, and she hadn't liked the blonde from the beginning. "What else?"

"Now that you mention it, her brother kept staring at me," Lambros said. "At first, I thought it was a gay thing, but later I saw him making out with some girl."

"Names?"

"Niki and Phaidon, no last name."

Ariadne struggled to open her eyes. Her mouth was so dry she had difficulty swallowing. She forced her eyes open until she could at least take in what was in front of her. In the dim light, she made out a couch and a large window behind it. The heavy wooden shades were closed, so she couldn't tell whether it was night or day. She tried to move and finally realized she was tied to a chair, her hands bound behind her back and her feet wrapped tightly with more white nylon rope.

"What the fuck happened?" She heard Melina's voice from behind her.

"Are you okay?" Ariadne craned her neck to look at Melina, who sat a few feet behind her, also tied to a chair.

"My head hurts, but we've got bigger problems than my migraine."

"I can't remember what happened. We were on the boat when I felt this sting in my neck, and then nothing."

"Same here, though I do remember smacking the bitch after I felt the pinch and turned to find her behind me."

"And this is why I need Lambros." Ariadne looked around for her purse—her cell phone was in it—but couldn't see it anywhere.

"So, it's my fault we were snatched?"

"I'm just saying."

"It's bad enough I'm here because of you. Now you're going to pin the kidnapping on me?"

"Of course not."

"So, what happens now?" Melina sounded almost bored.

"I don't know. It's not like this is a monthly routine."

"Let me spoil the surprise. They call in with the ransom, your dad delivers, and we go home."

"I don't know. I guess." Ariadne's eyes had started to focus and adjust to the sparsely lit room.

"How long do you think we'll be here?"

"You're the one who memorized *Kidnapping for Dummies,* so you tell me."

"I'm going to guess forty-eight hours," Melina replied.

"Thanks for the update." She went quiet for a long while, and so did Melina.

"Are you afraid?" Melina finally asked.

"Yes."

"Me, too," Melina said.

"I thought you had it all figured out."

"Well, why take us otherwise? I mean, if not for money."

"Because they're serial killers?" Ariadne offered.

"Well, that's just fucking great. I hadn't even considered that until you opened your pessimistic trap."

"I'm being realistic, and I'm so terrified I feel like throwing up."

"So do I, thanks to you."

"We need a plan," Ariadne said.

"Have you not noticed that you're tied to a chair?"

"Oh, is that why I can't move?" Ariadne replied with irritation. "Think with me, will you?"

"Do you have anything sharp on you?"

"I have a Swiss Army knife in my purse, but I can't see it anywhere."

"Mine's gone, too," Melina said.

"Hey, can you scoot over here and see if you can untie me?"

"Wait." Melina started to edge her chair toward Ariadne, an inch or two at a time.

"Seriously? You're making more noise than a church organ."

"My legs are still kind of numb. If you think you can do it better, then—" Melina stopped when a key turned in the lock. "They're coming," she whispered.

The door opened and two men came to stand in front of them, one bald and the other tall and thin. "Good evening, ladies," the bald guy said in English. "I know both of you can understand English, so from here on anything you say will be in English. No talking amongst yourselves in Greek."

"Why are we here?" Melina asked.

"You'll be told what you need to know, so no questions. For now, consider yourselves our guests and show respect for our hospitality. We would hate to have to get violent."

"Are you serial killers?" Melina blurted out.

Both men looked at each other and smiled. "No questions, remember?" the thin guy replied.

"Is this about my father?" Ariadne dared ask.

The bald man walked up to her and smacked her across the face so hard her neck hurt more than her cheek. "No questions. Is that so hard to remember?" With that, both men left.

CHAPTER TWENTY-THREE

"I have to find her." Lykourgos paced his office like an animal. "We have to call the police." He was talking to himself, planning the next move.

"You're not going to call anyone. TQ, or her men, are going to call you soon," Switch said. If sitting and waiting for a phone call was rough for her, she knew it was impossible for Ariadne's father. "If you get the police involved, you're going to end up in jail for conspiracy to steal an artifact. You know what Greece does to those who mess with artifacts."

"I don't care." He fished his cell from his trousers.

"You call the police and TQ is going to panic, and if TQ panics, she's going to bail."

"So, let her fucking bail."

"What do you think she'll do to your daughter if she has to leave without the icon? I don't think you fully grasp the magnitude of this woman's sickness. She will not handle defeat very well. There's no telling what she'll do."

Lykourgos put the phone back in his pocket. "Jesus Christ. All this, because of me."

Switch tried to calm him. She put her hand on his shoulder. "I'm sure if you knew just how twisted this woman is, you would've never gotten involved with her. It's not your fault, Mr. Lykourgos."

He took a seat in his armchair and placed his phone on the coffee table in front of him. "It *is* my fault. My damn greed put my daughter in danger just so…so I could live. What's the point in getting better if… if she's gone?"

"You'll get her back as soon as we get TQ."

"So, what the hell are we going to do?"

"Set her up." Switch tried to remain composed, hoping it would rub off. "Look, she's going to ask for the icon in return for your daughter. We give her the icon, and—"

"And something goes miserably wrong in your attempt to get her, and my daughter becomes the victim of my greed, as well as yours." Lykourgos stood and approached Switch. "All you care about is catching Rothschild. You couldn't give a damn about my daughter." He pushed Switch in the chest. "She dies, it's just collateral damage to you and whatever company you work for." He pushed her again. "I know your country teaches you that everything and everyone can be sacrificed for whatever cause you deem worthy but…we are talking about my daughter!" He shouted the last.

"My country is Greece," Switch replied between clenched teeth.

"Bullshit. No one in Greece has ever heard of Rothschild, let alone wanted her behind bars. You're not getting paid by Greece to catch her. You're getting paid by some American company with a personal vendetta."

"I never said anything about a vendetta."

"You didn't have to. I have plenty of my own contacts. If she were sought by the government, I would have known about it and would've never gotten involved with her in the first place."

"Are you sure about that? Desperate people make desperate decisions and even more desperate alliances."

Lykourgos seemed to consider her words. "You're right," he replied. Seeming resigned, he sat back down. "I want to live."

Truth was, Switch couldn't blame him. If saving her life or that of a loved one meant breaking the rules, she would probably do the same. She glanced at her watch. Allegro's charter flight to Thessaloniki was due to leave soon. "Sit tight. I need to make a call. I'll be right back."

Switch stepped out in the hallway and dialed Allegro. "Where are you?" she asked when Allegro finally answered. "It's been ringing forever."

"At the airport. I was about to get in the helicopter."

"I need you to come back to the yacht with the icon."

"Come back to what, now?" Allegro sounded frustrated.

"Ariadne was kidnapped."

"TQ?"

Switch explained the situation. "So, we need the icon," she finally said.

"Yeah, I get that, but what are you going to do about the monks waiting for it? I mean, you can't just let TQ have it."

"The plan is to catch TQ during the exchange, then return the artifact."

"I get that, too," Allegro said. "But she's never going to show in person."

"She never does. That's why we need to figure something out. I have an idea, so get back here so we can work out the details."

"Have they contacted Lykourgos yet?"

"I suspect she will very soon."

"Okay. I'm on my way."

Switch wanted to be present when TQ called Lykourgos to make sure she heard all instructions for herself, so she went back into his office and took the armchair opposite him. She grabbed a magazine from the table and tried to look relaxed for his sake, but nothing could be further from the truth. Switch wanted to bolt out the door, have the EOO move heaven and earth to find Ariadne, and to hell with the icon and TQ.

❖

Ariadne ran her tongue over the corner of her mouth, tasting blood. The kidnapper had split her lip when he'd struck her, and her cheek and neck still ached from the ferocity of the blow.

"Are you okay?" Melina asked.

"No."

"Do you think they're going to kill us?"

"How should I know?"

"They never answered me," Melina said. "You know—about being serial killers."

"I think if they wanted to torture and kill us for kicks they would've already done it."

"So, we're basically waiting for your father to bail us out."

"I think so."

"That's just fucking great."

"I thought you were all prepared for this scenario," Ariadne said sarcastically. "You seemed to have all the answers earlier."

"I was trying to stay optimistic, which is more than I can say for you."

"I'm being realistic, Mel. It's not like I've done this a million times. And we wouldn't be here if you hadn't insisted on ditching Lambros."

"Yeah, sure, go ahead and blame it all on me."

"I'm not. All I'm saying—"

"Is that it's my fault," Melina said loudly.

"Keep your voice down."

"Don't tell me what to do. I'm not one of your lackeys."

"Where the hell did that come from?"

"Just because you have money doesn't mean you get to tell everyone what to do."

"I'm not even going to answer that."

"Of course not. You don't need to answer to anyone because you're your father's daughter."

"What is wrong with you?" Ariadne craned her neck to look at Melina. "Where is all this coming from?"

"You think that just because you're rich, you get to call the shots, tell everyone what to do and when. Get away with anything. Well, I'm sick and tired of it."

"Are you deranged? I've never told you what to do or how to live."

"Really? Because unless someone took your body over, it was you who insisted I stop smoking, drink less, party only occasionally, and sleep with whoever you deemed appropriate."

"I said all that for your own good. I'm sorry if my opinions interfere with your need to cut your life short."

"I may not live long, but at least I actually lived. It's not all about quantity, you know. Or is that hard to imagine when your life revolves around numbers?"

"Screw you, Mel," Ariadne shot back. "You know that's not true."

"Isn't it? Do you think you have what it takes to live like us simple folk? You know, with a nine-to-five, struggling to put food on the table, and that's if your employer actually pays you? We live in a country that takes everything we earn to make up for its deficit, sweetheart, or did Daddy not tell you?"

"I read the financial papers." Ariadne sounded deliberately callous. Of course she was aware of the unfair and dire situation the politics of the country had created. And, true enough, she'd never had to suffer the consequences, especially since ship owners were exempt from luxury taxes, a fact that created even more bitter feelings from the rest of Greece. But it was not her doing, or her decision. She had agreed to take her father's place on the throne when he stepped down, and that was a position she welcomed and dreaded at the same time. She'd have to devote the rest of her life to an empire, and the sacrifices would be insurmountable.

Alex was right. Any woman who would put up with her and her life would be doing it because of what she could offer and not for her, never for her.

Ariadne's previous relationships had been simple and to the point. Fun, sailing, barhopping, and sex, until she felt the other woman get too close. When they did, Ariadne pulled away, fearing they'd ask for more. She'd never be able to give them the unconditional and full attention they'd eventually ask for, and she'd never be able to remain with someone who settled for her money instead of her time.

"Nothing like newspapers to give you a taste of reality," Melina said. "Do you read the horoscopes for advice on what to do with your lonely existence?"

"Stop it, Melina." Ariadne would never admit to anyone just how lost she really was or how bleak her emotional future. "Enough."

"Oh, God spoke, so I guess I'll just stop now."

"What is this really about?" Ariadne asked quietly.

"It's about you calling the shots regardless of what anyone else thinks or feels."

"I've never disregarded your feelings."

"What do you call what you did with Alex? You knew I liked him. I'd told you I wanted to get to know him and not just in bed. But did that stop you from jumping his bones?"

"A, I did not jump his bones, and B…are you kidding me?" Ariadne replied, exasperated. "We've been kidnapped and you want to talk about Alex. I mean, seriously?"

"Alex is an example."

"No, he's not. You truly mean it and that's shocking, considering we're being held captive by a couple of thugs who didn't hesitate to smack me and are capable of doing God knows what else."

"You knew I liked him, and you had to go and make a point."

"Have you gone nuts? What point?"

"That you can have anyone…anything you want."

"I kissed him to prove to him that…that…" That what?

"I mean, seriously. What were you trying to prove? Because I've witnessed countless guys coming on to you, and you've never felt the urge to prove your lesbianism before."

"I wanted to—"

"Hell, I've seen gorgeous women come on to you and you've never given them the time of day. Why Alex?"

"Because I…I think I've fallen for her," Ariadne blurted out, frustrated more with herself than Melina.

"Her? You have your genders confused, sweetie. Also, what the fuck do you mean you've fallen for him?"

Ariadne stared at the floor for a long while. "I…I'm not sure when it happened, but I think I'm in love with Alex," she finally whispered.

"Holy fuck. That's messed up."

"And Alex wants nothing to do with me, because of who I am and what that means."

"So why in the hell did Alex kiss you?"

"I started it."

Melina exhaled loudly. "I guess the rich and famous aren't for everyone."

"Alex said he's not made for the backseat."

"Is it weird that I know exactly what that means?" Melina asked.

"Not really. You've made very clear how self-absorbed and bossy you think I am."

"Had you considered the fact that he would have eventually wanted to get intimate?"

The mere thought made Ariadne's temperature rise. "Yes."

"And your abhorrence for male parts and lack of boobs?"

"I don't know what I was thinking. I'm not the type of woman who could make someone like Alex happy. He's right. He deserves more than a sideline."

"Don't talk like that," Melina said. "You have so much to offer, and he's an idiot if he can't see that. You're more than a company or an heir. You're a beautiful, smart woman who'd kill for those she loves."

"Would I?"

"You've always stood up, front line, for your friends and family. You never take shit or put up with anyone who insults, either."

"That's not what you said a little while ago."

"Screw what I said. You know I get bitchy when I'm stressed."

"I wish Alex would see it that way," Ariadne said. "See me for who I really am."

"When we get out of here, I'm taking you out in Athens. We're going to find you a nice girl to remedy your misplaced attraction for Alex, and all this will be nothing but the memory of a bad summer fling."

❖

Lykourgos paced the room with a red face, the sweat starting to show on his shirt. "What's taking that bitch so long? Why won't she call?"

"She will," Switch replied calmly from the armchair. "I know you're worried, but trust me. She won't touch your daughter as long as she doesn't have the *Theotokos*."

Lykourgos stopped to look at Switch. "I can't just sit here and wait."

"You don't have a choice."

"I—" The phone rang. Lykourgos stared down at the cell. "Unknown number."

Switch ran over to him. "It's her. Take a deep breath and put her on speaker when you answer."

"Hello?" Lykourgos tried to remain composed.

"This phone can't be tracked, so don't waste my precious time with silly conversation."

"Theodora?"

"Were you expecting someone else?" she asked playfully.

"How can I help you?" He tried to compose himself.

"I have something you want."

"Oh?"

TQ laughed. "Your daughter, namely."

Lykourgos was silent for several seconds. He started to pace again. "What are you telling me, Theodora?" His voice shook.

"That I'm interested in an exchange."

"Where is she?"

"That's a silly question."

❖

Colorado

Cassady kicked her shoes off and dropped on the couch. She'd been rehearsing all day for an upcoming concert, and Jack knew that the long hours and repetitions to get it just right were making her wish she were on an assignment.

"Rough day?" Jack sat next to her.

"My fingers feel numb. I can't even count the amount of times I had to play the same stupid eight-bar pizzicato."

"How about a massage and a glass of wine?"

Cass smiled. "How about a kiss?"

Jack planted a deep one on her and sighed. "How about sex, massage, and then wine?"

"I think I need that wine first."

Jack frowned. "What's wrong?"

"Monty called me earlier today."

"So?"

"He said TQ was in the wind. We don't know if she moved for safety measures, or if she found out she was being followed. Either way, she got past Dilbert."

"And what are they doing about it?"

"They don't expect her to leave until she has the icon. She kidnapped the Greek's daughter and has already set up the exchange."

"She's never going to show up in person for that."

"I know."

"So what's Monty going to do about that?"

"He didn't say. He has Dilbert looking for her."

Jack took a deep breath and sat back. "This is fucked."

"Hey." Cass caressed Jack's arm. "They're doing their best."

"Well, their best isn't good enough, is it?" Jack shot back. "She's going to get away again."

"Think positive."

"Thinking positive is not what makes things happen."

"What's that supposed to mean?"

Jack shrugged. "Nothing." She smiled. "It just sucks that she keeps getting away with everything."

"Well, you know what I believe, don't you?" Cass rested her head on Jack's shoulder.

"Yeah, I know. That she'll get what's coming to her, sooner or later."

Cass nodded and kissed Jack on the neck.

Jack caressed Cass's cheek. *I'm going to make sure it's sooner than later.*

CHAPTER TWENTY-FOUR

Santorini Island, Greece

"I haven't heard anything from out there for a long time," Ariadne said in a low voice. "Do you think they're gone?" She'd struggled to loosen the ropes tying her to the chair until they'd cut painfully into her wrists and ankles, but she was still no closer to getting free.

"Why are you asking me?" Melina replied. "Does it look like I have a crystal ball?"

"Try scooting over here again to see if you can untie me. But for God's sake, try to be a little quieter this time."

"I thought we were just going to wait until Daddy paid up. You know he will."

"Of course. But that's presuming this is all about money, and even if we're right, that doesn't mean these two might not intend to have some fun with us in the interim. The one didn't hesitate to hit me. Who knows what else they might do? Do you want to stick around and find out?"

"Not so much," Melina said. "We'll cover the distance between us in half the time, though, if you try to scoot toward me, too."

They both moved in small increments, just a couple of inches at a time, pausing now and then to see whether the noise they were making was alerting their kidnappers to what they were up to. But there was nothing but silence from the outer room.

After twenty minutes, they'd managed to maneuver their chairs so they were back to back. Ariadne's shoulders and arms ached from the effort and uncomfortable position, and her hands were beginning to go numb from the tight bindings around her wrists. "Can you reach the rope around my hands?" she asked, as she splayed out her fingers and groped around blindly behind her back for Melina's hand.

"I can't—" Melina did the same and stopped when her hands found Ariadne's. "Okay, got it. Now what?"

"Find where the knots are. See if you can unfasten them."

"I'm trying. Not like I can see what I'm doing, and I have a hard enough time just keeping my sneakers tied." Melina pulled and tugged at the cord around Ariadne's wrists until it was digging unbearably into her raw flesh.

"Stop! You're cutting off the circulation."

"This was your idea, not mine."

"Just take it easy. Don't pull on that same cord again. Just try to find the knot."

"Bitch, moan, groan. Okay, wait. I've got it." Melina started working on the bindings, and before long, Ariadne could definitely tell she was making progress. "Got one of them," Melina said, "but there are more."

"You're doing great. I can feel them getting looser." Ten minutes later, Ariadne's hands were free. She quickly untied her feet and the rope binding her to the chair, then did the same for Melina.

Ariadne went quietly to the door and put her ear to it. "Still don't hear anything from out there. Come on, let's see if we can get out that way." She pointed to the only window.

They peered out the heavy wooden blinds.

Ariadne could see they were somewhere in the mountains. The landscape beyond the window was forested and rolling, and rose to a high peak in the near distance. Very close to the building were a few olive trees, a couple of bee hives, and a long-neglected patch of garden, suggesting this had once been someone's home or hunting cabin, but not for a long while.

She could see no other buildings or man-made structures of any sort from their limited perspective: no electric wires, or cars, or roads. But the forest seemed thick enough to easily get lost in, and at least they were on the first floor, close to the ground.

Ariadne tried the window. It wouldn't open, though it wasn't latched. She looked closer and saw that it had been nailed closed. "We're going to have to break this. Once we do, they're sure to hear it if they're anywhere around, so we've got to get out of here fast and into those trees."

Melina looked down at her two-and-a-half inch pumps, then over at Ariadne's sneakers. "Leave it to you to come prepared. If you leave me in the dust with those two, you know I'm never, ever going to forgive you."

Ariadne put her arm around Melina's shoulder. Despite her bluster and false bravado, Melina was just as afraid as she was. "You know I'm not going to leave you. Now, we better get going. No telling when they might come back."

She grabbed the hard, wooden chair she'd been tied to. "Stand back and cover your eyes." Once Melina did, Ariadne got a good grip on the rungs of the chair and used it to break the window. Shards of glass flew everywhere, and the noise was even louder than she expected. If the men hadn't left, they'd be in here in a hurry.

Ariadne used the legs of the chair to clear away the broken pieces of glass still clinging to the frame. "Go! You first!" she told Melina, no longer caring how much noise they made.

Melina crawled through the open space, cursing when she dropped awkwardly onto the ground a few feet below and cut her hand on a piece of glass.

Ariadne followed, dropping safely feet-first in time to help her up. They ran for the trees as fast as they could, Melina hampered by her footwear. Neither looked back until they'd made it there and paused to catch their breath.

The men weren't pursuing them, and she saw no sign of a car or whatever vehicle had brought them here. Ariadne relaxed a little.

"Now what?" Melina asked.

"We get away from here. We'll figure out the rest later. Come on." She led Melina deeper into the woods, climbing higher toward the peak she'd seen from the window.

"Slow down. What are you, part mountain goat?" Melina complained a short time later as they neared the rock outcropping that looked to be a good vantage point to survey their surroundings.

Ariadne didn't reply. She was anxious to see whether they might be able to judge how far they were from help, or at least determine which direction to take to get back to civilization. But when they emerged from the trees, they could see only a better overview of the small house where they'd been held and a half mile or so of the crude two-track road leading up to it. The rest was all trees and rolling terrain.

"Any idea where we are?" Melina asked.

"Not a clue. Obviously we need to get off this mountain, and that little road looks like the only clear way down. But they'll be expecting us to follow it."

"And if we don't, we could wind up lost for days. I'm sure it gets pretty cold up here at night. So, what's the plan?"

"I guess we just try to use it for a general sense of direction but keep out of sight as much as we can." Ariadne pointed to a small ravine off to their left. "I bet we can get down and past the cabin if we take that—" She shushed when Melina suddenly clamped a hand on her arm. "What?"

Then she heard it, too. A distant motor, getting louder. They could hear the car long before they could see it. Both of them immediately shrank back into the trees, crouching behind some low brush.

A dark Jeep soon came into view on the two-track, spewing a cloud of dust into the air as its tires sought purchase on the steep, gravelly lane. Their kidnappers parked outside the cabin and leisurely made their way inside.

Ariadne knew they should start running in the opposite direction, farther up into the mountains to get as far away as possible as fast as they could, but they remained transfixed on the scene below to see what the men would do once they discovered their captives were gone. She was hoping they'd think they'd taken the road and go looking for them there.

Seconds after they'd gone in, both men came running back out again and immediately went to the back window they'd smashed. One crouched down and pointed to something, and then both men looked up in their direction.

"That's not good," Melina muttered under her breath.

They watched as one of the men returned to the car to get a rifle from the trunk, while the other pulled his handgun and started toward them, his gaze fixed to the ground as though he was tracking them.

As one, and without a word, Ariadne and Melina hurried away from the overlook, keeping low until they were sure they couldn't be spotted from below. Then they started running for their lives, Ariadne in the lead and Melina struggling to keep up.

She had no idea where to go, which direction to take. She tried to keep to the densest growth of trees and the most uneven terrain, hoping it would help keep them from being spotted from a distance. When she was nearly out of breath, she saw a massive fallen tree they could hide behind, to rest for a minute. Melina seemed as grateful as she was for a moment's respite.

"Do you think they can track us?" Melina asked once her breathing had calmed.

"Half the men I know are hunters," she replied. "And we're at a big disadvantage if either or both of them are familiar with this area. We could be heading to the edge of a cliff, for all we know. Come on, we have to keep moving."

But just as she started to rise from their hiding place, they heard a distant shout. "Come on, ladies, it's useless to run from us! There's no place to go. Come out before you hurt yourselves."

Ariadne's heartbeat accelerated as she quickly ducked back down, out of sight. Stay put or run? She peered over the top of the log. She couldn't see them, but perhaps they were just waiting somewhere, watching from behind trees for any sign of movement. Maybe the men had lost them and were just trying to get them to reveal themselves.

"Should we—?" Melina started to whisper, but Ariadne waved at her impatiently to be quiet.

She thought she'd heard something off to their left, but she couldn't be certain. The dense undergrowth was too thick to see through. Then she heard it again, the unmistakable sound of a branch being snapped. At least one of the men was close. Too close. And he was working his way around their position to get behind them.

With an increasing sense of panic pervading her senses, Ariadne desperately searched for a way out. One man was to their left, and the other's shouted directive had come from somewhere in front of them. Melina's eyes were wide with fright as Ariadne gestured silently in the direction they needed to take, but she nodded that she understood.

Then they were running again, full out, and this time, they could clearly hear their pursuers chasing them, the nearest crashing through the brush not far behind, the other shouting at them to stop from a bit farther away.

A shot rang out, and almost simultaneously, Melina screamed from behind her and landed hard on the ground, face-first.

Ariadne ran to her. Blood was pouring from a bullet hole in Melina's thigh, and her face was contorted in pain. "Shit, Mel. Stay with me!" In a panic, she put her hands over the wound, applying pressure to stop the bleeding, but it wasn't working well. Blood seeped out from between her fingers.

"That was a stupid move," said a voice from behind her. The tall kidnapper, his handgun still in his hand.

"Give me something to stop this bleeding!" she begged him. "Some cloth. Your shirt. And I need your belt!"

He seemed to consider this request for a couple of seconds before relenting. He pulled off his T-shirt and belt and tossed them to her as his friend caught up and joined them.

"Hurts so bad." Melina moaned. "Am I dying?"

"No chance. Hell isn't ready for you," Ariadne replied as she tightened the belt around her makeshift dressing. It seemed to be working. The blood flow slowed considerably. "We need to get her to a hospital," she told the men. "You're not going to get a euro from my father if anything happens to either of us."

The bald guy laughed and turned to his friend. "Still thinks she can call the shots." Then he looked at Ariadne with a menacing glare. "You got it all wrong, honey. Unless he pays up, and fast, neither one of you is getting off this mountain."

CHAPTER TWENTY-FIVE

Off Santorini Island, Greece
Next day

Lykourgos kept the heavy icon on his lap as he steered the Zodiac away from the *Pegasus*. Switch watched him caress the hard case absentmindedly, as though he wanted one last chance to call upon its healing powers, or perhaps he was asking the Virgin Mother to watch over Ariadne.

Switch checked her scuba tank one final time before donning her fins and mask. She wanted to be ready to slip over the side as soon as they caught first sight of the kidnappers' boat.

TQ had chosen a location far enough from the coast and normal shipping lanes that there was no chance of running into other boat traffic. They were still a good distance from the GPS rendezvous point when she spotted a tiny speck on the horizon.

"Reduce your speed. That may be them," she told Lykourgos, and he slowed enough for her to roll over the side and into the water. Clinging to one of the inflatable's exterior ropes, she kept out of sight behind the dinghy as he towed her, while careful to avoid the outboard's propeller.

"I see them," Lykourgos said ten minutes later. He looked down at her and Switch gave him a thumbs-up.

She pressed the mic that was pinned against her ear by the rubber hood of the wetsuit. She'd planted a listening device under the dashboard and not on Lykourgos, just in case they checked him. Although Switch couldn't fathom TQ might have given orders to kill someone with his high profile and the girls after her goons got the icon, she wanted to make sure everything went as planned.

Switch ducked down farther, leaving only her eyes exposed to view the situation from the rear of the Zodiac. She could see them now, too, in a small but fast-approaching skiff. One man stood on the boat with an automatic rifle pointed at Lykourgos while the other drove. Switch let go of the Zodiac and ducked completely under the water when they were still several yards away.

Lykourgos cut the engine about the same time, and Switch quickly caught up, hiding from view beneath the inflatable.

"Daddy!" she heard Ariadne yell.

Lykourgos didn't reply, but soon afterward, the other boat stopped, too, and pulled up alongside the Zodiac.

"Where is it?" one of the men asked.

"Here," Lykourgos replied.

"Let's have it."

He must've been in the process of handing it over because both boats rocked.

Switch dove deeper until she couldn't be seen from the surface and swam to the other boat.

"I want my daughter, *now!*"

One of the men laughed. "Move, bitches," he said.

Taking advantage of the commotion the girls were causing to get from one boat to the other, Switch stuck a tracker to the bottom of the men's boat and moved back beneath the Zodiac.

"Daddy!" Ariadne shouted.

"My God, what happened? What did they do to you?" Lykourgos sounded worried. "You're bleeding."

Switch's breath caught. Was Ariadne hurt? She'd kill whoever had touched her. She couldn't wait to surface and see what was going on.

Soon afterward, the kidnappers' boat started to move away and quickly accelerated to maximum speed as though they were being chased.

"All clear, Alex," she heard Lykourgos say.

Switch surfaced and found him and the two women looking down at her. She immediately focused in on Ariadne. "Are you hurt?" she asked as she pulled off her mask and threw it into the inflatable.

"N…No. What's going on?" She looked from Switch to her father.

Lykourgos extended his arm to help Switch on board the Zodiac. "Alex is a private contractor," he replied.

Ariadne and Melina gaped at her.

It was then she noticed the bloody bandage around Melina's thigh. "Why don't we talk about all that back on shore," she said. "We need to get Melina to a hospital."

"Privately contracted to do what?" Ariadne asked.

"I was hired to…" Switch unzipped her diving suit. "Why don't you ask your father?"

Instead, both women continued to stare at her. It took a few seconds for Switch to realize they were looking at her chest. She'd unzipped down to her crotch, revealing her swimsuit. She followed their gaze and then looked over at Melina.

"Am I hallucinating, or does he have boobs?" Melina glanced from Switch to Ariadne, then back to Switch's breasts. "Maybe it's the fever. The infection's gone to my head."

"He is a she," Ariadne said.

"You knew?" Melina looked like she'd seen cows fly.

"Yes. Though it's becoming very clear that her gender wasn't the only thing she lied about."

"Now I understand why you're crazy about—"

"Not now, Melina," Ariadne said. "Can we just go?"

Colorado

"Jack's gone," Cassady Monroe said as soon as Monty answered the phone.

"I see." He sat back in his armchair and switched off the news. "Since when?"

"I woke up and she was gone. She left a note saying she'd be back in a few days."

"Didn't say where?"

"Nothing."

"I see."

"What's wrong with you?" Monroe sounded irritated. "What's going on?"

"I don't really know, but I'm sure she's fine. She probably remembered she had to take care of something in New York."

"There's nothing there to take care of." Her frustration was evident. "You don't sound the least bit concerned."

"Whatever she's up to is something important to her. She'd never leave you, otherwise."

"Then why not tell me?"

"Probably because it's not important."

"If I find out you're keeping something from me, I'm going to be really mad."

"Just give her a few days," he said. "She probably needs some space to think."

"Think about what?"

"Listen, I'll try giving her a call. See if I can find out where she is."

"Let me know ASAP."

"Of course."

"You'd better not be hiding something from me."

"Stop worrying," he said calmly. "She knows what she's doing."

"You're freaking me out, Monty. She knows what she's doing about what?"

"She's crazy about you, Cassady. She'd never do anything to jeopardize what you have."

"Just let me know if you hear something."

"Same goes for you," Monty replied before he disconnected.

Joanna walked into the living room with tea and biscuits. "What was that all about?"

"Cassady is looking for Jaclyn," he replied.

"You mean she's disappeared again?" With a worried frown, she set the tray on the table in front of him.

"It would appear so."

Joanna sat in the armchair across from him. "What's going on, Montgomery?" She crossed her arms over her chest like she always did when she demanded an explanation. "You know where she is, don't you?"

"I do, indeed."

"Did she tell you she was leaving? Where she was going?"

"No."

"Oh, for Christ's sake, speak up."

"I told her TQ was in Greece."

Joanna looked shocked. "Why in the world would you do that?"

"Because she will never be truly happy or safe until that woman is dead."

"But we have people on it. Ops perfectly capable of taking her down. They're so close to finding her."

"Jaclyn needs to do it," he replied quietly. "It'll haunt her if she doesn't, and she has enough haunting her as it is."

"But that woman is crazy. You've sent her straight into the lion's den."

"Jaclyn knows what she's doing. I need her to get this last obstacle out of the way so she can concentrate on her future."

"Let me get this straight," Joanna replied, looking at him as though she barely knew him. "You deliberately told her about TQ so that she could go after her and get it out of her system?"

"Like I said..." Monty sipped his tea slowly and set it back on the table. "I need her to be ready. No loose ends, no grudges."

"Ready for what?"

"To face the future." Monty stared at the Rocky Mountains outside the large picture window. "Ready to decide for the future of others."

❖

Fira, Santorini Island, Greece

"And?" Switch asked as she approached Allegro at the harbor's café.

"You just missed them. They tied up and left without the icon." Allegro had been tracking the kidnappers' boat from ashore and so was waiting for them when they pulled into the marina at Fira.

"Are you sure?"

"They took off empty-handed. I was just about to go check the boat. See if they left it there to pick up later."

"They'd never risk that."

"I'm going to check anyway, as soon as they go. They're still hanging out by the car."

Switch sat down and stared out at the sea. "Doesn't make sense."

"Who knows what the hell that crazy bitch has put them up to."

"The girls are fine, by the way. Melina got shot in the leg, but she'll be okay."

"And how's your favorite girl doing?" Allegro asked.

"Who?"

"You know who I'm talking about."

"She's not my girl, and we hardly had a chance to talk. I dropped them off at the hospital and changed in the car, then drove straight here."

"So, I guess you won't be seeing her again. I mean, Lykourgos no longer has the icon, so…"

"Yeah." Alex took a deep breath. With everything that had been going on that day, she hadn't stopped to consider that after the exchange, she'd be out of Ariadne's life for good. "I guess you're right." The realization hurt like hell.

They remained silent, but Switch couldn't let go of the fact that TQ's men would be callous enough to leave the icon on the boat. Unless, of course… "Hand me the transponder," she said impatiently.

"What for?" Allegro opened her rucksack and pulled it out. "What's—"

Switch grabbed it and turned it on. They both watched as the green beam scanned circles on the monitor.

"What are you looking for?" Allegro asked.

"There." Switch pointed to the screen. In addition to the small blip nearby that marked the boat's location, the device was picking up another signal far offshore. "They placed a tracker of their own on the icon and dumped it in the sea."

"To pick up later."

"Just in case Lykourgos hadn't kept his promise and police were waiting for them."

"But why didn't I see it earlier when I was tracking the boat?" Allegro asked. "I never got two signals."

"They activated it after they realized the coast was clear. My guess is, they won't be diving for it until dark."

Allegro consulted her watch. "It's going to be a long wait."

"They're going to lead us straight to TQ."

"Monty's going to shit a rainbow."

CHAPTER TWENTY-SIX

Ariadne was grateful her father's status and influence allowed them to circumvent the usual official inquiries that were required when doctors treated patients with bullet wounds. Melina had been spared police questioning after her father spoke with the hospital administrator, quietly explaining the embarrassment he wanted to avoid over the "unfortunate hunting accident."

He'd taken the further step of having a rental car delivered so he could drive them all himself to the marina, where Manos would be waiting with a Zodiac. And just in case any hospital personnel might have tipped off the press, they exited through a staff-only door that led to the rear employee parking area.

"I've made a career out of avoiding cellulite only to end up with a scar on my thigh," Melina complained as Ariadne helped her from the wheelchair into the big sedan.

"The fact that you almost died doesn't bother you, but a one-inch scar does?" Ariadne smiled.

"Let's go, girls." Lykourgos got in the driver's seat.

"I'm getting there." Melina was moving exceptionally slow because of the drugs they'd given her, but Ariadne got her comfortably situated and then slipped into the front passenger seat beside her father before anyone took notice of them.

"So, what was that all about?" Melina asked after a few moments of silence.

Ariadne knew immediately what Melina was referring to. "You mean the fact that Alex is a woman or that she's a private contractor?"

"You knew?" her father asked, looking over at her in surprise.

"I knew about the first," she replied. "I found out when I walked in on her a few days ago."

"Jesus, why didn't you tell us?" Melina punched her playfully on the shoulder from the backseat.

"She asked me not to, because she desperately needed the job."

Lykourgos shook his head. "She was there to keep an eye on me."

"But why? What's going on, Dad?"

"How did I not see she was a woman?" Melina mumbled from behind them. "No wonder she's so attractive and soft."

Lykourgos lifted an eyebrow and eyed her through the rearview mirror.

"Yeah, she had a crush on him," Ariadne told her father.

"Maybe I still do." Melina laughed. "What do I care if the dude's a woman?" She laughed again. "I guess I'd probably miss—"

"We're not alone, Mel."

Melina sighed. "Not that it matters, anyway. It's obvious she's into you and not me."

They remained silent after that, and within a scant few minutes, Melina started to snore.

"Why was Alex watching you, Dad?" Ariadne asked. "You never answered."

"Because I did something." He glanced up at the rearview mirror, apparently to confirm that Melina was indeed out cold.

"What did you do?"

"I took something that wasn't mine."

"So, you stole something?"

"I had it stolen."

"What is it?"

"It was an icon," he replied. "Alex found it and took it back." He told her the whole story and Ariadne listened without interrupting.

"But why would you steal the *Theotokos*, Dad? Why was it so important to add to your collection? I mean, you already have so much."

Lykourgos didn't answer and Ariadne turned to look out the window. How could her hero, the man she admired and had always considered ethical, both as a family man and a businessman, be a thief? She wanted to understand and was willing to forgive a lot when it came to family, but to steal from a church was just low. "I don't know how to respond," she finally said without looking at him. "You have so much. You need nothing, so why..." Ariadne rubbed her tired eyes. "We were almost killed because of you, Dad."

"I know," her father whispered, his voice tinged with regret. "I know."

"Why did you do it?"

"I can't...I don't want to talk about that."

"Seriously?" Ariadne pounded her fist on the dashboard. "We were abducted, almost killed, and you don't want to talk about it?"

The loud thump woke Melina. "Pink bunnies everywhere," she said groggily before immediately drifting off again.

"And what's going to happen when this hits the news?" Ariadne asked her father in a low voice. "It's going to destroy us."

"It won't. Alex and I have an agreement."

"Dad, tell me why this was important enough to risk so much?"

"I did it for me. For selfish reasons. I can't explain better than that," he replied vaguely. "Not now, anyway."

"That's so fucking ridiculous."

"Your language."

"A thief has no right to criticize me or how I speak, so fuck my language."

Her father pulled over at the harbor, and Ariadne jumped out to assist Melina.

"Let me," Lykourgos said, getting out of the car.

"I don't need your help." She waved him off. "It's because of you she almost got killed in the first place."

Manos drove the Zodiac slowly from the marina to the yacht to minimize Melina getting bounced around in the bottom of the inflatable. She didn't seem to feel any pain at the moment, but God help them all when the drugs wore off. No one spoke. Melina was drifting in and out, the tension between her and her father was palpable, and Manos was smart enough not to ask any questions, though he was clearly curious about what recent events had brought them to this.

All the way to the *Pegasus*, Ariadne questioned what possible motive her father could have had to have risked so much to get this particular treasure, and why he was being so evasive about it all. She decided that if he wasn't going to tell her the truth, she'd get it from Alex.

After Ariadne helped Melina into bed, she caressed her hair until Melina was out cold again. Then she pulled out her phone and dialed Alex's cell. She had no idea if the number still worked, since it belonged to Alex the bosun, but after it rang several times, Alex finally answered.

"Yes?"

"It's Ariadne."

"Are you all right?" Alex sounded concerned.

"I'm fine." Ariadne bit her lip. "I need to talk to you."

"What about?"

"My father."

"I don't think it's my place to discuss him."

"I need to know why he stole from a church."

"Ask him," Alex said.

"He won't tell me."

"I don't think I can."

"Do you know why he did it?" Ariadne asked.

After a very long while Alex answered. "Yes."

"Then tell me why this damn icon was important enough to risk my life."

"That was never the intention. Had he known it would come to that," Alex replied, "he would have never taken it."

"It's still theft."

"He had his reasons." Alex's tone was surprisingly sympathetic.

"And you're okay with that?"

"Not at all, but…" Alex sighed. "He's a good man, Ariadne."

"He's a thief and a liar."

"Maybe some day you'll understand."

"No, I…" She didn't want to do this on the phone. The conversation was getting her nowhere. "I want to see you."

"I'm afraid that's not possible right now."

"Then when?"

"I don't know."

"Are you going to leave?" Ariadne asked.

"Yes. Probably tonight."

"Will you be coming back?"

"I don't think so."

"You were just going to leave without so much as a good-bye?"

Ariadne couldn't catch a break. She was sinking deeper into despair by the minute. "Did you pretend to like me just to get close to my dad?"

"No!" Alex blurted the word out with conviction. "You just happened."

"Just happened? What is this, screw-with-Ariadne's-sanity day?"

"I never expected to…"

"To what?"

"I really can't do this right now." Alex took a deep breath. "I really can't do this at all." She sounded upset. "I'm sorry. I have to hang up."

"Where are you?" Ariadne had to go see her. She had to talk to her and see in person what Alex wanted to but couldn't say.

"I can't talk about that."

"Because you're some kind of big-shot private contractor on a mission?" Ariadne shouted. "Well, screw that, and screw all of you for lying to me!" She hung up.

❖

Fira, Santorini Island, Greece

Switch and Allegro had walked along the coast and around the harbor to stretch their legs and kill time, occasionally checking the transponder to make sure the tracking device on the icon hadn't moved. No one gave them a second glance. They blended in like locals with their dark complexions and dressed in jeans and trendy summer T-shirts. Allegro had talked nonstop about Kris and their relationship and life together. Switch had mostly nodded and offered polite responses when necessary.

Now that the sun was soon going to set, they had resumed their positions at the café/bar that overlooked the marina. Allegro ordered a small array of Greek appetizers since they hadn't really eaten all day, but though she dug in with gusto, Switch had no appetite and stuck to her espresso.

She looked at her watch. "I hope we don't have to wait much longer."

"Especially since sulking seems to be your favorite pastime," Allegro replied as she munched some fried calamari.

"I'm preoccupied."

"You had plenty of time to meet with her. You know that, right?"

"And say what?" Switch replied with irritation. "Do what?"

"Depends. Do you really not want to see her again?"

"Of course I do, but what's the point? The faster I remove myself from her life, the easier it'll be for both of us."

"You're not a Band-Aid. And besides, saying good-bye even if you never want to see her isn't a bad thing."

"It's unnecessary grief."

"Maybe it is for you, but it doesn't work like that for everyone," Allegro pointed out. "Some people need closure."

"We hardly knew each other."

"That apparently doesn't matter to her. And regardless of what you say, I think the same applies to you."

"Yeah, well…" Switch didn't know how to respond. It was true that though they'd spent only a few days together, Ariadne had made a deep and lasting impression on her in a way no woman had before.

"You're being selfish."

"Look, I'm fine without attachments and whatever comes with caring for another. I don't have the time and don't need the distractions."

"But you like her…a *lot*."

"So, what's that got to do with it?"

"Everything." Allegro shrugged and speared a grilled anchovy with her fork. "But hey, you want to spend the rest of your life alone lamenting a previous relationship, then that's fine, too. There's absolutely nothing wrong with being a well-paid, retired op who spends her remaining years with a grudge and what-ifs."

Surprised, Switch turned to look at Allegro. "How do you know about my previous relationship?"

"Because only someone who's been burned bad runs the way you do."

"I gave her my heart, and she…" Switch played with her zipper. "Why does one of the two always love more?"

"I don't know that that's true. I think the difference is, one is willing to repair what's broken, while the other simply wants to buy something new."

"Same thing."

"Kinda, but not really. It could be that the one leaving or giving up doesn't have letting-go issues and prefers to leave before the love turns to hate. Why drag what used to be beautiful through the mud if you can avoid it?"

"She dumped me for someone else," Switch said. "Had been seeing another woman for weeks when I found out."

"That's always tough," Allegro said sympathetically. "But you gotta focus on the fact that cheating is a consequence, never the reason."

"I thought I made her happy. I mean, I know my job isn't easy, and I made mistakes, but I loved her so much."

"She probably needed different things from you."

"She said she needed more of my time," Switch said. "I gave her as much of it as I could. It's just that I was setting up the gallery, meeting with lots of people, and so on. I so wanted the gallery to work, and it does. But regardless of my work and job and long days—weeks, even, I loved her to pieces."

"Quit with the 'I loved her,'" Allegro said. "Love alone is never enough. You wanted different things. It's that simple. So it didn't work out. It's not the end of the world."

"No, it's not," Switch mumbled.

"So, do yourself a favor and give Ariadne—or *any* Ariadne—a chance. Maybe it works out, maybe you crash and burn. But either way, you get to love again, and sure, who knows, maybe feel pain again, too, but at least you get to live. Love is intense stuff. Don't miss out on it because of fear. You need to learn from past relationships, not use them as an excuse to avoid future ones."

"How many did you have, before Kris?" she asked.

"Women? I don't know. Plenty."

"I meant relationships."

"None."

Surprised, Switch turned to Allegro. "So, where do you get off telling me to just get over my hang-ups and give someone else a chance?"

"I don't know. It just sounds right." Allegro smiled.

"You're unbelievable."

"In a good or bad way?"

"Not sure." Switch smirked.

"Finally, a smile." Allegro applauded.

"Whatever."

"But you know I'm right," Allegro said seriously.

"I don't know. I guess."

"Of course I'm right. Because I'm wise, and smart, and good looking, and I have—"

"Shut up, egomaniac. Here they come."

TQ's two men seemed in no hurry as they ambled from the parking lot toward the dock. But the men surprised them when they passed the small skiff they'd previously used in favor of a much larger rental boat, a yacht with two engines and built for rough waters and longer trips.

"They're leaving the island by boat after they get the icon," Switch said.

One of the men started to pull on a diving suit while the other took his place behind the yacht's wheel.

Allegro fished something out of her rucksack. "Be right back." She fluffed her hair and sashayed over to the men. Switch couldn't hear what she was saying, but both men went from looking wary to smiling within a matter of moments. Allegro leaned against the yacht, and Switch saw her discreetly place a tracker under the boat's rim. Then, she giggled loudly like a schoolgirl and sashayed away.

"That was creepy," Switch said as soon as Allegro came back.

"Nah. Piece of cake."

"I meant the cackling and funny walk."

"Scary movie, right? But hey, they bought it."

They watched as the boat took off in the direction of the icon's tracking device.

Allegro and Switch kept watching the radar, and fifteen minutes later, the yacht's tracker stopped right above the icon. After another forty-five minutes, one of the two signals disappeared, which meant they had retrieved the icon. Then the lone, remaining signal started to move again.

"Let's see where they're going," Switch said.

An hour into the men's journey it was clear they were bound for the mainland.

"Athens," Allegro said.

"Let's jet." Switch pulled out her cell as soon as they got in their rental car. "Switch 140369."

"What's going on, Switch?" Pierce asked as soon as he picked up.

"They're headed to Athens by boat with the icon and we're en route to the chopper. They won't reach Pereas before roughly 0500 hours. We'll be there waiting."

"Keep me posted." Pierce hung up.

"I'll bet he's happy," Allegro said.

"He didn't sound as though he was."

Allegro checked her watch. "He couldn't have been sleeping."

"He sounded...I don't know, wheezy."

"Maybe the old fart was getting it on with Grant." Allegro shivered. "Geriatric sex freaks me out."

CHAPTER TWENTY-SEVEN

Pereas, Greece
Next morning

"And there they come," Switch said when the yacht got near enough to see it clearly. One of TQ's men was behind the wheel, and the other was on the bow, ready to tie off as soon as it pulled up to the dock.

She and Allegro had reached the harbor south of Athens hours earlier and had opted to pass the time in their rental car. All the time they'd spent waiting around—both at this marina and the one in Fira— had exhausted them. Empty coffee cups littered the floor of the rental.

"About damn time," Allegro replied. "I think I nodded off at least twenty times."

"Lucky you."

"Hey, I suggested we take turns."

"I can't sleep. Can't stop thinking long enough to rest."

"Ariadne?"

"Yup."

"Well…you know how I feel about it."

"Okay, they're getting in a car," Switch said, happy they could finally move again. She needed to stop thinking about Ariadne. All these hours of waiting, combined with the conversation she'd had with Allegro, had given her cause and time to relive every word and every smile they'd shared. She couldn't take the thoughts and memories any more. She needed to do something before she drove herself crazy.

"They have the case with them," Allegro said.

They waited until the men were well ahead of them before they followed on the still, quiet road. They'd been driving for a quite a while when Switch realized they weren't headed to Athens, but to Thessaloniki, which was another five hours farther by car. She didn't relish the further delay in confronting TQ, but at least it confirmed that the bitch hadn't gone far once she'd checked out of her hotel and lost Dilbert.

"All the fuss over an icon," Allegro said. "I mean, come on."

"Miraculous icon," Switch said.

"You don't really believe that, do you?"

"It doesn't matter what you or I believe," she said. "It's what someone wants to believe that makes it miraculous."

"It's all between the ears."

"And if some people need an icon, crucifix, or statue to help reinforce their hopes, then so be it. Now, the church is a whole different matter."

"I'm with ya. It's all political cover."

"Always has been."

"More wars have been fought in the name of religion and church than for any other reason," Allegro said.

Switch nodded. "So many deaths for political power and gain. What a waste, especially since the world is more fucked up than ever."

Allegro leaned back in her seat. "Hey, want me to drive so you can get some rest?"

"There's no point in getting there before them." Switch liked to kid about Allegro's notorious need for speed.

Three hours before they reached Thessaloniki, however, Switch had given in and let Allegro drive. She needed to close her eyes for a little while before she drove them straight off a cliff.

They reached the city center at noon, where the two men entered an underground parking lot.

Switch waited outside while Allegro followed them in to park in the underground as well. Only a couple of minutes later, the two men exited the lot through a side stairwell, the bald one carrying the case with the icon. Switch stayed with them as they took off down one of the pedestrian-heavy streets near Thessaloniki harbor and phoned Allegro, updating her with their location.

Allegro caught up soon enough. "I called Dilbert. He's coming our way, though I don't really know what help he'll be. He's fine for intel, but the guy simply doesn't have the makings of an op. How did he manage to lose TQ in the first place? All he had to do was sit and watch."

They followed the men on foot, always well enough behind to not get noticed. The one carrying the case with the heavy gold icon kept switching it from one arm to the other.

"They're going in." Switch saw them enter a big café along the seaside boulevard.

Allegro texted the location to Dilbert.

While most people were sitting outside basking in the sun, the two men chose a table inside. Switch and Allegro, not wanting to risk getting too close, selected a table outside where they could keep an eye on them through the open glass doors. Switch studied everyone who entered the bar, just in case the two men had stopped for more than a cup of coffee. A few minutes later, Dilbert showed up and sat with them.

One of the men made a phone call and said something to the other. Ten minutes later, the one holding the box all this time handed it over to his skinny friend, who then headed to the restroom with it.

"Weird," Switch observed.

"You're up, Dilbert," Allegro said.

Dilbert got to his feet. "You do know that that's not my name, right?"

"Whatever." Allegro shrugged. "It suits you."

He made his way to the bathroom.

Not long after, Switch saw both Dilbert and the goon with the case exit the restroom almost simultaneously. Then, a few moments later, a young man with a rucksack came out, too.

"Slick," she said sarcastically of their nerdy associate. "Could he be more obvious?"

"You think they made him?"

"Let's hope they're too stupid or tired to notice."

Dilbert walked back over to his seat, but Switch's attention was still on the icon. The man handed the case to his colleague, who took it with one hand.

"You see that?" Switch shot forward.

"Fuck."

"What?" Dilbert asked, surprised.

"The case. It's empty." Switch got up and looked around. It took her a few seconds to spot the young man who had exited the WC just after the goon. He was casually walking down the street. His rucksack looked heavy and packed full.

"Allegro, you stay here with the goons, just in case I'm wrong, and don't lose them. I'll call you if I'm right."

"How about me?" Dilbert got up, ready for action.

"Have you ever considered gardening?" Switch heard Allegro say before she hustled to catch up to the young man. He blended in well with all the dark-skinned street hustlers in this tourist-rich district: illegal immigrants from North Africa, the Middle East, and East Bloc who roamed the streets hawking knock-off purses, perfume, watches, homemade bracelets, and other cheap trinkets.

She followed him to the seedier part of town, known for its strip joints, sex shops, street girls, pimps, and by-the-hour rooms for rent.

Switch had started to think she'd made a mistake. If this guy was supposed to deliver the icon to TQ, why in the hell would he be in this part of town? She found it unlikely that someone of TQ's caliber would choose this low-rent, high-crime area. Was he going to hand it over to another middleman? Then again, TQ was in the wind, and this would be the last place anyone would look for her.

The guy walked into a less-than-reputable hotel, and Switch waited a minute before following. She surreptitiously scanned the lobby before going in to make sure he wasn't there before she approached the receptionist.

"My friend just came in," she told the woman, who was busy applying bright-red polish to her nails. "Young guy with a rucksack."

"Okay," the young blonde replied with a Russian accent.

"I forgot which room he booked."

"He already has company," she replied.

"I'm aware."

"Oh." The Russian smiled. "The more, the sexier."

Switch smiled back. "You know it."

"Twenty euros. Second floor, room 204."

"Twenty euros?"

"We charge extra for parties." The woman winked. "They cause too much damage to the furnishings."

Switch placed a twenty on the counter and didn't wait for the elevator. She pulled out her cell and dialed Allegro's number as she climbed the stairs. "Atlas Hotel on Egnatia Street, room 204. You can be here in ten if you run."

"Dilbert?" Allegro asked.

"Leave him with the goons," she said, and hung up.

Minutes later, as she waited outside, the door to the room cracked open and the young guy she'd been following started to step outside, but paused in the doorway. He had his back to her as he finished the conversation he was having with whoever was in the room.

Switch pulled out her Sig Sauer and shoved the business end of it between his shoulder blades. "Get back in there," she said.

The boy put his hands up and followed her instructions. "Hey, I'm just the delivery guy."

Switch closed the door behind them. To her left, a petite Asian woman with an eye patch sat on the bed. Next to her was the boy's rucksack.

"Open it," Switch said to the Asian.

The young woman looked so terrified Switch almost felt sorry for her. She kept opening her mouth to speak but nothing came out.

"Open it," Switch repeated, and pushed the youth forward. He fell on the bed next to the Asian girl.

Switch pointed the gun at both of them. "I'm not going to say it a third time."

The woman was shaking now. "I was told not to."

"Open it!" Switch shouted.

The woman jumped in fear but didn't touch the rucksack. Instead, she shut the one eye she still had and calmly folded her hands in her lap, like she had accepted Switch was going to kill her.

Finally, the young man leaned over and opened the rucksack. Switch moved closer and bent over to look.

There it was, the heavy gold icon in all its glory. Though she'd already seen it, Switch couldn't help but marvel again at the artistry and opulence of the ancient treasure.

"Who do you work for?" she asked them.

"I don't know," the young man replied, his hands still in the air.

Just then Allegro came barging in, gun in hand, with the Russian receptionist not far behind her screaming that Allegro owed her twenty euros.

The blonde stopped screaming when she saw both women were holding guns.

Allegro looked from the Russian, to the Asian, to the dark-skinned youth. "It's all nice and ethnic in here, but where's Lady Lizard?"

CHAPTER TWENTY-EIGHT

Thessaloniki, Greece

When her cell phone vibrated against her hip, Jack checked the caller ID, but the number read *not available*. No one knew she was in Greece, and she didn't want to start lying about it if it was Cass calling from an unfamiliar phone, so she stuck the cell back in the pocket of her black cargo pants and continued down the streets of central Thessaloniki. She had no idea how to proceed. She hadn't thought ahead about how she would find TQ once she got here, and the one op she knew who was working the case—Allegro—wasn't going to be in any hurry to help her. Allegro had made it very clear she didn't like her because of Jack's past history with a good friend of hers, agent Domino, during the period she worked for the underworld.

A minute or two later, her phone vibrated once again with the same mysterious lack of identification for the caller, so she continued to ignore it. When it buzzed a third time, she found a text message waiting: *Call me. I have the info you need. Reno.*

"What the...?" Jack whispered. Why the hell would Reno contact her with any intel at all? She dialed the EOO main switchboard.

"How may I help you?" asked the woman who answered.

"This is Jack Harding." She refused to give her old code name and number, which was standard protocol. "Reno has been trying to reach me." She didn't expect the EOO operator to help, but she had nothing to lose.

Jack was surprised when the woman responded. "Just a moment."

After a couple of clicks on the line, in the background, she heard the operator say, "Reno, I have Phantom 100613 on the line."

"Hi, Jack," Reno said politely. "How you been?"

"Fine, and you?" She responded automatically, thinking all the while how surreal this was getting.

"You know how it is around here, I—"

"Yeah, that's great. I was just being polite."

He laughed. "Okay, so I contacted you for an update."

"Concerning?"

"Rothschild's maid is in custody," he said without further preamble. "Agents Switch and Allegro are holding her at the Zaliki Hotel." He rattled off the address. "So far, she's refused to talk to anyone, let alone give us TQ's location. We don't know if Rothschild has skipped the country yet or if she still has hopes the maid will return with the icon. If the latter is true, then I suspect she's not going to risk waiting for her return much longer. She's going to panic and want to disappear again. My advice is that you talk to the maid today and see if you can get her to talk to you. At this point, she's our only hope."

Jack, although shocked, didn't want to show it. "So, you know where I am."

"Of course."

"Who else knows?"

"I can't give you any more information," Reno replied.

"Pierce," Jack said. "Cass told him I was gone and he knew I'd go after TQ."

"Like I said…"

"Did he ask you to contact me?"

"Look, I told you, I can't say much more. And besides, what does it matter? The point is you're there, TQ is there, and well…do what you gotta do. You need the fifth floor, room 501."

"Thanks." Jack hung up.

She flagged down a cab and gave the address to the driver. Ten minutes later, the taxi stopped in front of the hotel.

Jack took the elevator to the fifth floor and knocked on the door.

"Who's there?" a female voice asked from within.

"Jack," she replied. "Reno gave me this address."

An attractive androgynous woman with olive skin opened the door. "I'm agent Switch," she said. "Come in."

"Hey, if it isn't Pierce's pet project." Allegro greeted her from the couch as soon as she got inside.

"Hey," Jack responded.

"Reno called. Said to expect you."

"Well, here I am." Jack looked around the room. They were in a small outer suite with a sitting area and desk. The curtains to the balcony were drawn, and the two doors she saw—presumably leading to the bathroom and bedroom—were both closed. "Where's the girl?"

"In the bedroom." Allegro pointed to the door on the right. "She's terrified. She refuses to talk, eat, drink, and even use the toilet. The woman's biggest organ is clearly her bladder."

Jack walked to the room Allegro had pointed out. "Do not under any circumstances interrupt me."

"Good luck," Switch said.

Jack opened the door and found the petite woman sitting on the edge of the bed, gazing out the window. She didn't turn to look, neither when she heard the door nor when Jack shut it.

Jack approached her slowly and crouched at the woman's feet. "Remember me?" she asked softly.

The woman turned her head slightly and nodded, but never tore her gaze from the window. "I remember you," she replied, her voice barely a whisper.

"Great." Jack smiled. "You don't have to be afraid. We're not going to hurt you."

The woman nodded again in understanding but looked no less terrified by the reassurances.

"I just want you to tell me where your employer is," Jack said.

"But I can't."

"Is it because you don't know, or because you're afraid to say?"

The woman nodded again and unconsciously reached up to adjust her eye patch.

"The second?"

"Yes."

"I see."

"Will you tell me your name?"

"In my country they call me Jasmine," the woman replied. "My lady calls me Yu Suk."

"But that's not your name, is it?"

"No."

"So, screw what she calls you." Jack smirked. "You don't have to worry about her ever again."

"She will find me, you know," the woman said, with resignation. "She will always find me."

"Now, that's not true. I can make sure she never touches or sees you again."

The woman shook her head. "I will be free of her only when I die."

"Not if she dies first."

Jasmine's smile revealed more bitterness than genuine happiness. "People like her have a contract with the devil. She will never die."

"What if I tell you that I hold the deeds to that contract?"

"She almost killed you before," Jasmine reminded Jack. "What do you think you can do to hurt that woman? No one can hurt her."

"The first part's true." Jack hadn't soon forgotten the horrendous torture the bitch had put her through, and neither would Cass. "But she threatened to kill someone I love. That was why I let her do bad things to me. Now, that no longer applies."

"You don't love someone any more?" Jasmine looked at Jack for the first time.

"No," Jack lied. "I have no one in my life she can hurt."

"I wish I could say the same." Her response confirmed Jack's suspicions that TQ was using threats to Jasmine's family to keep her cowed and obedient.

"Let me give you your life back."

Jasmine shook her head. "I can't remember how to live any other way. It has been too many years."

"I'll help you learn. You can't possibly go on living in fear, and besides, there's no way she's going to come back for you. She's too afraid of getting caught. She must realize by now that something has gone wrong, so it's only a matter of time before she gets on her broom."

"Let her go. Let her go to hell."

"Thing is, I want to send her there for good so that she never hurts anyone again."

"But what if you don't?" Jasmine asked. "She will know I told you where to find her. No one knows but me."

"Look." Jack grabbed the woman's hands and held them gently

in hers. "I promise you, I swear to you, that I will not let her get away, because I intend to kill her. So, you don't have to worry about her coming after you."

"But what if you don't succeed?" Jasmine asked again.

"I will. It's that simple. All you have to do is give me her location, and I promise she will be dead before tomorrow. And then you will be free to do what you want. Stay in the States, go back to China, or whatever. We will help you financially. Make sure you have everything you need."

Jack could tell from Jasmine's expression she wanted very much to believe what she was hearing, but her long association with TQ had made her unusually wary of trusting anyone. "How do I know you're not lying?"

Jack stood. "I have made very few promises, and to only one person. You are the second one I am making a promise to." She placed her hand under the woman's chin and lifted her face so that she could see Jack's eyes. "I never make a promise unless I know I can keep it." Jack caressed her cheek. "Do you believe that?"

Jasmine nodded.

"I promise I will get rid of TQ forever, and I promise to take good care of you when this is done."

Jasmine caressed Jack's hand. "I believe you."

Jack smiled. "I'm honored."

Jasmine took a deep breath. "She is on a yacht at the harbor in Porto Carras. She has hired a crew of two and is waiting for me to leave for some island. I don't remember the name. But after that, she is going to take a plane to Madrid, and from there to South America."

Jack bent over and kissed the woman's forehead. "Thank you."

"Thank you," Jasmine replied, and curled up on the bed. "I think I can finally sleep."

❖

Off Santorini Island, Greece

Ariadne did what she'd never done before, and that was barge into her father's office without notice or even knocking. She'd gotten virtually no sleep in the last twenty-four hours, and her usual polite decorum seemed absurd, under the circumstances. She wanted some answers, and her father had been hiding away in either his suite or his office ever since their return to the *Pegasus* the day before.

"We need to talk," she said.

Her father sat reading the newspaper on the couch. "Have a seat."

Ariadne sat across from him and crossed her legs and arms. "I'm waiting."

Her father rubbed his eyes. Although it had been a restless and trying few days for him, Ariadne had to admit she hadn't seen him look this lively and healthy in a long time. Even his ever-present coughing had stopped. He folded the newspaper and placed it on the coffee table.

"It's not exactly what you think," he began in a quiet voice.

"Then enlighten me, because I want to know why you had to have that icon at that extraordinary price."

"I made a deal with Rothschild. She was to get it to me, and I, in return, would pay her a ridiculous amount of money. She, with the help of her people, managed to extract the *Theotokos* and deliver it to me."

"I remember her flying in, the day you said you acquired a new something."

"Yes, well…" He looked down at his feet. "I had no idea I had hired a psychopath."

"Clearly."

Her father went on to explain how Rothschild had never intended to let him keep the icon, and about Alex's role in all of this.

"You mean Alex's sole reason for being here was to find and return the icon?" she asked when he'd finished.

"Yes, and then things got complicated when it turned out Rothschild was involved. All Alex cared about after that was finding her. A lot of people apparently have issues with her."

"I knew she was a crazy bitch the moment I laid eyes on her."

"Your gut is never wrong, I'll give you that," he replied with a hint of pride in his voice.

"And now for the actual reason we got involved in all this in the first place. I want to know *why* you desperately wanted that icon. Isn't everything you already have enough?"

"It wasn't about adding to my collection." Lykourgos cleared his throat. "The *Theotokos* is known for its healing powers. For centuries now, it has been one of the best-kept secrets worldwide."

"Not so much if you know about it," she pointed out.

"I know someone inside, but aside from that, a very small circle of serious collectors know about it as well."

"You, of course, are one of them."

"Of course."

"And now that vicious woman has it."

"Not for long. I hope, anyway. Alex intends to get it back to its rightful place in the monastery after she deals with Rothschild."

"So, if you didn't want it for your collection," she said, "I have to assume you wanted it for its powers."

Her father stood and paced the room. "Yes," he finally answered.

"You don't really believe in all that, do you?"

He turned to face her. "I do." He looked so serious that Ariadne didn't feel she should get into a religious debate.

"What is there to heal?" she asked.

He went to sit back down across from her. "About a year ago, I was diagnosed with terminal lung cancer. Stage three."

"You *what*?" Ariadne shot up, his words resonating through her like a cold chill. "You're joking, right?"

"They gave me a year, and I am now a few months away from that."

"The coughing and weakness..." She flashed back to all the clues she'd failed to see, too absorbed in her own interests and her friends. "You hadn't looked good for a long time."

"I was dying."

"Does Mom know?"

"Of course not. She can't handle stress."

"Why didn't you tell me?"

"Because I didn't want you to look at me the way anyone looks at a dying man," he replied. "I wanted and needed all of you to know I was still the rock you all could count on. I don't handle pity and coddling very well, and it would have killed me even sooner if I had given in to it, acknowledged it."

"But it would have given us the choice to spend time with you."

"I never want you to spend time with me out of fear or pity, honey. I want you to do that only because you truly want it."

"Jesus, Dad, this is crazy. You have a few months to..." Ariadne couldn't keep the tears in any more. Her anger had turned to fear and pain within fifteen minutes. She let the tears fall and ran to her father and held on to him. "You should have told me, Dad. I…I want to spend every moment we have left together. Not because I have to, but because I don't know anyone else I'd rather spend my time with." She cried into his neck. "I love you so much, Dad. I don't know what I'm going to do without you."

"Hey, there." He caressed her hair. "That won't be for a long time."

Ariadne pulled away to look at him. "What do you mean?"

"Haven't you noticed how I've stopped coughing, my color is better, and I have so much more energy?"

Ariadne frowned. "Well, yes. Of course I've noticed, but—"

"I started feeling better almost at once. I prayed to the *Theotokos* day and night for hours and…" He teared up. "And…"

"And you think you're cured?" Ariadne asked softly, not wanting to disillusion him.

"I haven't had any tests done or seen a doctor, but I know I have been spared."

"Dad, don't you think you need to see a specialist before you break out the champagne?"

He shook his head adamantly. "I will show no doubt for what I know is true. That would be blasphemy."

"But Dad—"

"Please, honey, trust me. I know what I feel and I know what is true. Do I look like a dying man?"

It was true that he seemed in perfect health—his color was good, the glint was back in his eyes, and he had regained the vigor she remembered. "You look like a million bucks, but that could mean that your cancer is in some kind of miraculous remission."

"Call it what you want. I know I'm cured."

"Dad—"

"No more talk about cancer, okay? Now, sit down. I want to talk to you about business."

Ariadne didn't plan to drop the subject, but he wasn't open to discussing this any more, right now. She took her seat across from him again, her mind not at all in business mode.

"I'm listening."

"I want to retire."

"Good, it's about damn time. You need to sit back and enjoy." *Especially if you're terminal.*

"For this reason," he said, "I need to hand the company over to the most capable person I know."

"Dimitriades has proven to be a great asset—"

He held up his hand. "Yes, he's a genius, but I'm not going to let him run the company."

"Who do you have in mind?"

"The most talented, most dedicated to the job, and the most hard-working individual I know."

"I—"

"I'm handing it over to you. You will have full run of everything."

Ariadne opened her mouth, but nothing came out. Though he'd been grooming her to be an integral part of his empire, she'd never expected to have complete control, and certainly not any time soon. "Dad, I don't know that I can handle the responsibility," she finally said. "It's a multimillion-euro business."

"I am very well aware of what it is."

"I don't know enough to run it."

"Who are you kidding?" he asked, smiling. "You know more than I do."

"I…I'm not ready."

"You don't need to decide right now. Get back to me in a week," he said. "But no longer than that."

"Why?"

He looked out the window at the sea. "Because I want to go away for a few months, and I need to know who'll be running things."

"Go where?" she asked.

"Mount Athos. I intend to spend six months on my knees thanking God for the gift of life."

CHAPTER TWENTY-NINE

Thessaloniki, Greece

Jack got out of the rental car and opened the back door for Jasmine. Allegro and Switch stayed seated. They'd found an open parking space where they had a good view of the marina with binoculars, but where they were too far away to be recognized by anyone on the numerous anchored boats.

"Hand me the rucksack," Jack said to Switch, who was in the back.

"Okay, Jasmine," Jack said as she took the heavy icon from Switch. "Call your boss, let her know you're here. As soon as she tells you which yacht, you go there and I'll come find you on the boat."

The woman nodded, clearly terrified.

"You have nothing to worry about." Jack squeezed her shoulder. "Tonight's the last time you'll see her."

Jasmine called TQ and Jack could hear the ice bitch screaming at her, asking her why she took so long.

Jasmine replied it was the young deliveryman's fault because he couldn't find the address.

"But you didn't answer when I called you!" TQ shouted.

"Someone stole my phone, madam, when I was out to get coffee. I think it was a gypsy." Jack gave her a thumbs-up.

"Do you have the icon?" Rothschild asked.

"Yes, madam."

"Well, get your retarded ass here, right now. I'm in slot thirty-five."

"Coming, madam."

"You're going to do great," Jack said. "Give her the rucksack and tell her you don't feel well. Sound like you need to throw up. Tell her you had seafood this afternoon and have felt bad since. Go to your room, and don't leave till I come get you."

"Be careful, Jack," Jasmine said. "She's crazy."

"She's about to find out just how crazy I am."

As Jasmine headed toward the pier, Jack got Switch's wetsuit out of the trunk of the rental and wrestled into it in the car. When she was ready to go, Switch handed over her Sig Sauer handgun and a Spyderco switchblade, and Jack tucked both into her wetsuit. She waited fifteen minutes in all, to allow Jasmine sufficient time to complete her part and get safely to her own quarters on the yacht. "What do you see?"

Switch was looking through the binoculars. "A man on deck, and he's packing up. I see another one—the captain. He's at the wheel and it looks like they're taking off soon."

"I'm going in." Jack got out of the rental.

"Hey," Allegro called after her. "Be careful, okay? You don't want to go breaking Monty's heart. For some reason, he's got a thing for you."

"Yeah, it's called guilt," Jack replied, and headed toward the pier.

She slipped into the water without being noticed and swam to the big luxury yacht moored in slip thirty-five. Surfacing close to the starboard side, opposite the dock, she pulled herself up and peered over the side to look around before she climbed on board.

The coast was clear from this side. Both the captain and the other man in view were busy untying lines and preparing to get under way. And close by her was the yacht's covered dinghy in its davits, a perfect hiding place, so she slipped beneath the canvas and waited. Almost immediately, they set out to sea.

Ten minutes later, she heard footsteps. Probably TQ's goon doing the rounds. She peeked from under the canvas, and when he turned the corner, Jack got out. She waited patiently for him to come around again, and just as he did, she stuck the knife in his throat. She held on to him so he wouldn't make noise when he dropped, and when he was lifeless, or close to it, she gingerly placed him on the deck.

In a crouch, she made it to the back of the yacht and peeked through the half-open door to the cockpit. The captain had his back turned. Jack snuck up on him and hit him on the back of the head with the butt of her gun. She killed the engine and used some duct tape she found to seal his mouth and bind him to the cockpit chair.

Jack went down the small flight of stairs to the cabin and ended up in a small hallway with two doors on each side. One of the doors was open and the room empty. She'd have to guess now. She knocked gently on the door at the far end.

"Why have we stopped moving?" TQ replied angrily from within.

Gun in hand, Jack opened the door.

"What are—" Rothschild was seated at her desk, but as soon as she saw Jack, she got up surprisingly fast for her age.

"Sit back down, bitch," Jack said.

"Help!" TQ shouted.

"Scream all you want, crazy fuck. They're all dead. Your maid included."

The shock on her face was priceless. TQ abruptly sat back down.

"I want you here on the sofa," Jack said. "Where I can see your ugly hands."

TQ got up and did as she was told. "So, what now?" she asked, regaining her trademark smirk.

"Oh, I don't know. How about tea and biscuits?"

"I'd love to oblige, but you've killed the help."

"True." Jack frowned. "Got any scotch?"

"Over there." TQ pointed to the bar.

Jack walked over and poured herself a glass. "Care for one?"

TQ sighed. "Please."

Jack poured another and placed one glass in front of TQ, then took her own to the armchair across from her. "So, how's life?"

"About to be cut short, I suppose."

"Yeah, but I mean aside from that." Jack sipped her drink.

"Oh, you know, business as usual."

"Kill anyone lately?"

"A few. You know how it is." TQ crossed her legs.

Jack scratched her head casually. "Yeah, I do."

"Is there any chance we can negotiate this situation?"

"What did you have in mind?"

"More money than you'll ever know what to do with," TQ replied.

"How much?"

"Ten million?"

"That all?" Jack asked. "Is that all your life is worth to you?"

"It's more money than you'll ever see in your pitiful life."

"I don't think you're in any position to be criticizing my life." Jack shrugged. "Because I at least will have one, pitiful or not."

"I'd rather be dead than live…" TQ flapped her hands in disgust.

"Like the rest of us?"

"Yes."

Jack laughed. "Where do you get off feeling so privileged? You're the daughter of two nobodies who gave you to the neighbor to raise. You personally have done nothing to deserve fame or money. It was all your husband. You know, the one you had killed."

TQ sat forward and glared at her. "I took what he had and made it better and bigger," she asserted with an almost religious fanaticism. "*I* made the Rothschild name what it is. Me, not him."

"By stealing, bribing, threatening, and killing."

"You do what you have to, in a man's world." She sat back again.

"And you got away with it."

"Because I own the right people. Not my husband. Me."

"Boy, you've got some chip on your shoulder when it comes to your husband. What's that about?"

"Why are you interested in my life? Why not just do what you came for and get it over with?" Though she was trying hard to appear unaffected by the situation, TQ wasn't entirely successful. Her forehead shone with perspiration and she kept glancing about, as though escape might still be possible.

Jack checked her watch. "I've got time to spare. My flight doesn't leave till tomorrow and there's nothing on TV." She feigned concern. "Unless, of course, you'd rather we get it over with."

"What I'd rather is that you were never born."

"I'm afraid I can't do anything about that."

"So, what's it going to take for you to let me live?"

"You better start rubbing that magic icon, because nothing short of a miracle is going to make that happen."

"Ah, I see. You want to torture me." TQ sipped her scotch.

"A little."

"I'm not afraid to die."

"But it's the anticipation that's killing you, right?"

"Fuck you," TQ said calmly, like she was commenting on the weather.

"Would you? If that meant saving your life?"

"Fuck you?" TQ smiled.

"Uh-huh," Jack said playfully.

"I'd fuck you even if it didn't."

Jack smiled seductively. "I'm speechless. You'd really do that?"

"You are very much my type, Jack."

Jack leaned forward. "And you, Theodora, are the most disgusting excuse for a corpse I've ever met. The thought of you touching me makes me want to hurl."

Rothschild grabbed her glass off the table and tossed the whiskey in Jack's face. "You sorry piece of shit. How dare you sit there and judge me, when you are no better than me?" The veneer of composed indifference she'd mustered evaporated in an instant, replaced by the reptilian narcissism that marked her true character. "You've killed and stolen and done anything and everything for a buck. How dare you judge me? You think you're something special because you got some blonde to love you? Well, guess again, because it's only a matter of time before she finds out just how emotionally inadequate you are. People like you can't be loved, because you're too damaged. Oh, they'll try for a few years, but they'll eventually tire of your moodiness and silence, and the dark secrets that you dare not speak of because you don't want to lose their respect. She'll tire of it, all right, and you'll be left with nothing. And you're no spring chicken anymore, Jack. You're going to end up a drunk in dark, seedy bars, trying to get laid." TQ grabbed Jack's glass and took a sip of whiskey. "You don't deserve happiness, Jack, and you don't deserve her. She is way above your league...*killer.*"

With that, Jack got up and put the gun to TQ's temple.

TQ froze with the whiskey in her hand.

"Maybe you're right," Jack said. "Maybe I don't deserve her, and maybe someday she'll get tired of me." She took the glass from TQ's hand and downed the whiskey. "And maybe I will end up in seedy bars pissing in my jeans. But if that happens, I will have one memory to put a smile on my face." Jack cocked the gun. "The memory of your face, as I count to three."

"Don't do this, Jack."

"One."

"We can work out a deal, any deal." Her words came out in a rush of desperation.

"Two."

"You can have anything!"

"In that case, it's your life I want. Three." Jack pulled the trigger.

❖

Jasmine was waiting for her in the hallway, her expression one of hopeful expectation, no doubt because of the gunshot.

Jack closed TQ's door behind her and nodded. "It's over."

Jasmine broke out in tears and wrapped herself around Jack.

"The captain is out cold," she told the young woman as she hefted the rucksack with the icon over her shoulder. "Wait until I'm far away in the dinghy, then rouse him and tell him you were in your room when you heard a shot but never saw anyone. He never got a look at my face, so he has no idea I was ever here."

"Thank you," Jasmine said.

"Write down my number."

Jasmine ran back to her room and came back with pen and paper. Jack gave her her cell number. "Call me when you're back in the States. We'll take care of you."

Jasmine hugged Jack again. "I can't believe I'm really free."

CHAPTER THIRTY

Mount Athos, Greece
Next day

Switch had only one last task to complete her assignment—returning the icon to the Simonopetra Monastery—and for that she'd transformed into her male persona one final time. Allegro had left that morning for Venice, and Jack would be leaving later in the day for Colorado.

She'd be happy to put Operation Divine Intervention behind her. It definitely hadn't been one of the more dangerous or trying missions she'd been on, but she felt emotionally drained. She had contemplated calling Ariadne at least a million times but could never think of what to say or how to start. Switch had practically told her to get lost when Ariadne wanted to see her, and she didn't know how to take that back.

Even if she *could* think of a way, and even if Ariadne agreed to see her, what could Switch possibly say, aside from *Let me tell you what happened, so I can go back to my life. And...oh, yeah, I want you like crazy, have fallen like a ton of bricks for you, but I'm afraid of commitment and generally not an easy person to be around.*

"I can't believe you found it!" Archbishop Manousis exclaimed when Switch walked into his office with the *Theotokos*. He smiled broadly at the gold icon as she took a seat opposite his desk.

"I'm glad we could help." Switch couldn't muster the excitement she usually felt after accomplishing a job.

"Are you not well?" the archbishop asked. "You seem troubled."

"I don't know anyone without troubles, Father," Switch replied flippantly.

"Of course, of course. We all merely get short breaks in between worries."

"Amen to that."

"Is it something you want to talk about?"

"I don't see how talking about it will help."

"Maybe it won't," he said gently, "but you have nothing to lose and perhaps something to gain. If nothing else, the unburdening of saying something out loud."

Switch studied his face for a long while, then stood and put her hands in her pockets.

"Would you like to talk while we walk?" he asked.

Without a word, Switch went to the door and waited for him. Manousis called another priest, who came at once, and instructed him on what to do with the icon. Once the man disappeared with the *Theotokos*, the archbishop got up and led the way to the gardens that ringed the rear perimeter of the administrative building. Neatly tilled plots of vegetables and flowers were laid out in a semicircles, and beyond were rows of olive trees. "Talk when you're ready," he told Switch. "I have all day."

It took her a few minutes to know how to start. "I'm afraid to love."

"Of course you are," he replied. "Who isn't? There is nothing that exposes us more or makes us exceptionally vulnerable."

"I don't want to hurt again, Father."

"I see."

They walked silently for a while.

"There are no guarantees." The archbishop stopped to pick up an olive. He examined it for a long while, like it was a diamond. "It's very likely that you will hurt again, but that's life. What's important is the journey and the lessons we take while on it. Everything is a passage until we shut our eyes for good. Death is the final destination, and everything else—every memory, every disappointment, every sweet moment—prepares us for our departure."

"How do you figure?" she asked.

"Your fear comes from a previous relationship? A woman you

once loved?"

Switch nodded. "She claimed to have loved and accepted me as well. Only thing is, I never stopped loving her. It took years to get over the pain, and she just moved on with someone else without a care in the world."

"Just because it didn't work out or because she found another does not mean she didn't love you," Manousis said. "Love cannot be measured or compared. Some people give their heart whole, and others give what they think is a whole heart. Some want to stay and fight for what they believe to be true, and others...others." He gestured with his hand. "Others need distractions to end the fight, because it's only then that they feel strong enough to do so."

"But it's not fair," she replied. "Then why utter the words 'I love you' if you can't stick to them? If, when times get rough, they get going?"

"Would you have preferred she'd said that she'd love you as long as it was easy?"

"Well, yeah...I mean, no. I don't know."

"Alex, I'm sure she never intended to hurt you, and that you never intended to hurt her by being...difficult. Sometimes, people are meant to enter and leave our lives and we theirs, but it's never for no reason. Regardless of the result, we take lessons and beautiful memories to strengthen our journey." Manousis put the olive in his pocket. "Don't dwell on the bad. Reminisce about the good and let that give you strength. Let the past be something you remember with sweet nostalgia, not bitterness. And..." He stopped to look at her. "In God's name, do not let cynicism enter your heart or make decisions. It is only the foolish who forsake the future because of a few rough patches."

Switch stood looking at the archbishop, but her mind was hundreds of nautical miles away in Santorini. "I know you're right," she finally said.

"I do not mean to belittle your worries, but think of the child who loses its mother. Or worse, the mother who loses her child. Now, those are grievances that scar lives forever, and still, because we are, after all, instinctual animals that will fight to survive, they find ways to cope and move on in their journey. I'm sure that in your line of work, you have seen much distress and despair."

He was right. There was so much pain in the world—true horrors and loss of hope people had to face every day—that Switch felt almost ridiculous sulking about not having been loved enough.

"I'm so grateful for your time, Father Giorgos." Switch smiled. "I think it's helped me a lot."

"You can come talk to me anytime." He patted Switch on the shoulder.

"I have one more question," she said. "And you are not at all obligated to answer."

He quirked an eyebrow. "Hmm, this sounds interesting."

"It's about the icon."

"Yes?"

"The *Theotokos* was never stolen, was it?" she asked.

"What do you mean?"

"Back at the office, you seemed happy to see the icon, but not relieved."

The archbishop cleared his throat and crossed his hands behind him. "It was important that we get it back."

"I suspect that the real *Theotokos*," she said, "serves as the base of the icon that was taken. That simple, hand-carved, and extremely old piece of wood. You were much more anxious and concerned about me handling that, as I recall."

Manousis looked from Switch to the ground as if contemplating how to answer. "I'm afraid I cannot discuss this." He gazed up at Switch.

"The man who had it stolen did it because he is dying, but in the short time he had it, he's gone from being a very sick man to one who looks perfectly healthy. I know it wasn't the real *Theotokos*, so how did…a placebo, if you will…?"

"Faith is more potent than any icon," the archbishop replied. "More powerful than any church, and more reassuring than any priest."

"So it's all in the mind?"

"It's all in how strong your faith is."

CHAPTER THIRTY-ONE

Next day

Ariadne watched Melina get out of her lounge chair to stand by the rail, shading her eyes against the glare coming off the water. The girls were all in their bikinis. They'd been hanging by the aft pool sipping margaritas and trying to fix Ariadne's mood ever since she'd hung up on Alex in frustration.

"Isn't that Alex, the faux-male secret agent, undercover whatever?" Melina asked as she pointed toward a Zodiac zooming toward them off the starboard bow.

Ariadne and the other two looked in that direction. Alex was driving the inflatable at top speed, but slowed down when she got close to the yacht.

Ariadne wanted to say or do something to stop staring and look busy, but she couldn't come up with anything. Her mind and vision blurred, and all she could focus on was Alex. Her face burned, and it wasn't from the sun.

"She has some nerve showing up here after she lied to us and… and totally avoided giving you any answers," Natasa said.

"Hey, welcome back!" Manos shouted as Alex approached the aft docking area.

Ariadne watched from behind her shades as they talked for a while. Manos was all smiles.

Alex was wearing a pair of old-looking jeans and a white, long-sleeved shirt, unbuttoned enough to expose her cleavage. Her hair was combed differently and, though short, made her appear very feminine.

All in all, she looked simply edible, and Ariadne hated herself for admitting that.

"She cleans up pretty damn well," Jo said as though reading her mind. "She's even sexier as a woman."

"Yeah, she sure does," Ariadne mumbled.

Alex approached them slowly, like she was giving Ariadne and her friends a chance to check her out.

"Stop staring," Ariadne said.

"Look who's talking," Melina replied.

"Yeah, but I'm wearing shades."

"Yeah, but I don't care," Melina said.

Alex stopped in front of them. "Hi."

"Hi to you, too." Melina shaded her eyes with her hand and openly assessed Alex from head to foot. "No sock in your briefs today," she commented.

Jo and Natasa laughed.

"Nope." Alex smiled, that sexy and inviting smile that always twisted Ariadne's stomach into knots. "Not today."

"You make a very convincing man," Jo said.

Ariadne wanted her friends to stop talking so Alex would move on and go see her father or whomever she was there to see. This small talk and casual demeanor were driving her crazy. If Alex thought they could just converse like friends and pretend that kiss never happened, then good for her, but Ariadne was nowhere near ready to play girlfriends and probably never would be as long as she couldn't ignore what happened to her body every time she saw Alex.

"So I've heard," Alex replied. "What can I say? Practice makes perfect." She didn't seem to mind the teasing at all.

"Sure does. You've managed to perfect the male role down to the nasty habit of love 'em and leave 'em," Melina said with open sarcasm.

"Stop it, Mel." Ariadne spoke up for the first time but didn't look at Alex. "Besides, being a jerk is not a male prerogative." She picked up her *Fortune* magazine and pretended to resume reading.

"I'd like to talk to you, Ariadne," Alex said.

Ariadne looked up but didn't reply.

"What about?" Melina asked when she didn't respond.

"It's personal." Alex never took her eyes off Ariadne.

Ariadne finally responded. "Since when?"

"Since we kissed."

Ariadne's stomach fluttered at the mere mention, but she looked back down at her magazine and tried to remain nonchalant. "It was just a kiss. You don't have to explain yourself."

"But I do have to explain what it meant to me." Alex knelt next to Ariadne's chaise. "If, of course, you care to find out."

"Why?" Ariadne hated herself for reacting this way, but her defense mechanism was crumbling under Alex's intense and smoldering gaze.

"Because I can't stop thinking about it…about you."

Ariadne quit the fake-reading bit and finally looked straight at her. Alex was less than a foot away. Her blue eyes penetrated past Ariadne's shades to her heart.

"Because I'm in love with you," Alex whispered.

Ariadne's stomach did a back flip. She thought she was going to lose her mind and her breakfast. "I, uh…I…wh—"

"Can we take this somewhere else?" Alex placed her hand on Ariadne's leg. "Somewhere private?"

"Oh, for Christ's sake, just get a room," Melina said.

"She's right." Alex continued to caress Ariadne's leg. "I'd really like to see you alone."

Ariadne would've shot up if she weren't too breathless to move. Alex's hand on her knee, combined with her sexy smile, was driving her crazy.

"So, what do you say?" Alex asked.

"S…sure," Ariadne muttered. "Is my room okay?"

"Perfect." Alex stood and offered her hand to help her up.

Alex couldn't take her eyes off Ariadne as she led the way through the yacht. She wasn't in the mood for conversation and explanations. They had time for that later. After her talk with the archbishop, she'd resolved to put her heart out there again and open up to Ariadne. But seeing her now, so provocatively enticing in her smoking-hot bikini, all she wanted to do was undress her and do all sorts of—

"This is me." Ariadne stopped in front of her door.

"I know."

Alex noticed Ariadne's hand shake as she slid her card through the lock.

Once inside, Ariadne turned to her. "So, here we are. Alone like you wanted."

Alex stood a foot away from her. "I'm sorry I lied to you."

"You could've told me that on deck."

"Did you not hear that I'm in love with you?"

Ariadne looked away. "I did. What do you want me to do about that?"

"Am I alone in this?"

"You gave me a whole speech about not wanting to take a backseat to my life and family. What changed?"

"I did."

"Oh?" Ariadne raised a curious eyebrow. "Wasn't it you who told me not to trust anyone who was willing to sit on the sidelines?"

"If I remember correctly, you told me that would be the case."

"And you believe me, now?" Ariadne asked sarcastically.

"I want to believe you."

"When did that change?"

"When I realized I was condemning you and forgoing a possible future with you because of a bad experience."

Ariadne bit her lip. "My father asked me to take his place, starting...soon. He also told me about his miraculously cured illness."

"I think he should check with a doctor before—"

"He won't. He wants to retire and spend time on the Holy Mountain."

"Good for him, then."

"That's what I said. I also told him I didn't know if I was ready to take over the company. I love the job, but it means a lot of late hours, trips, huge responsibilities, and the list goes on."

"Sounds a lot like my life. I'm gone a lot, too. I never know where they're going to send me next, and very often, lives depend on how I handle a situation."

Ariadne stared at Alex for a long time before she spoke. "Great. We get to be pen pals, then."

"I want more."

"Like what?"

"Spend every minute I can with you."

"I..." Ariadne moved away and turned to stare out her port window at the sea.

"I asked you if I was alone in this. Alone in love. But you never said."

"I don't know how to answer that." Ariadne kept her back turned to Alex.

"A yes or no is sufficient."

"I don't like being lied to, or fooled, or ignored." Ariadne kept her back turned.

"I get that about you," Alex said to lighten the atmosphere.

"I also don't like—" Ariadne stopped mid-sentence when Alex closed the distance between them and put her arms around her. The scent of her was intoxicating, and Ariadne's sharp intake of breath when they touched made Alex suddenly light-headed.

"You also don't like what?" Alex whispered in her ear.

Ariadne turned around to face her. Her eyes were shining with unmasked desire and need. "Just kiss me." She sounded breathless.

Alex placed her hand around Ariadne's neck and pulled Ariadne up against her. "I can't stop thinking about you." She kissed her softly on the lips. "I can't stop thinking about your mouth." Another kiss, still sweet and gentle. "I've fallen so hard," she said against Ariadne's lips and kissed her thoroughly then, probing and exploring Ariadne's mouth with her tongue, unleashing her pent-up passion.

"Yes," Ariadne mumbled when they came up for air. "Head over heels."

Alex's breath caught at the admission. "I don't know if you have to be somewhere, and I don't care." She thrust one leg between Ariadne's thighs. "I want to show you how much in love I am with you."

"I can't remember if I need to be anywhere, and I don't care to remember."

Alex smiled and led her to the bedroom.

Ariadne started to untie her sarong.

"Let me," Alex said. "I've been wanting to undress you ever since I laid eyes on you."

She pulled Ariadne forward and undid the knot. The sarong pooled around their feet.

"And I've been meaning to tell you how much I want to see that beautiful body of yours." Ariadne unbuttoned Alex's shirt. "I'm so glad you're a woman." She pulled off Alex's shirt and gazed admiringly at the sight of her bare-chested.

Alex was equally mesmerized. She couldn't look away from Ariadne's breasts, barely covered by her bikini top. The material was so sheer she could easily make out her erect nipples, beckoning her. "I want you naked. I've always wanted you naked." She removed Ariadne's top with one move. Her head was telling her not to stare like a schoolgirl, but she couldn't help herself. "I want to feel you against me." That's all she could say.

Ariadne moved in and pressed her body against Alex's. Both sighed, and someone—Alex wasn't sure which of them—said something, but she was in such a haze of desire that words had ceased to matter.

She grabbed Ariadne's ass and pulled her even closer, then buried her head in Ariadne's neck and kissed her there. Trailing her mouth upward to Ariadne's jaw and along her chin, she took her time, a teasing caress of the smooth, fragrant skin with her tongue and her lips, until she finally reached Ariadne's mouth.

She kissed her slowly, deeply, and Ariadne returned the kiss in the same rhythm. Alex was getting so worked up she stopped to catch her breath before she came in her jeans.

She moved her mouth to Ariadne's shoulders, then turned her around and kissed her neck. Her pelvis pressed hard against Ariadne's ass and they moved together, against each other, for each other, creating a delicious friction that drove her higher. When she cupped Ariadne's breasts in her hands, their breaths caught, and when she teased Ariadne's nipples, Ariadne writhed against her.

"Oh, God." Ariadne sighed. "You're driving me crazy."

"I haven't even started." Alex sounded breathless herself. She felt Ariadne slump against her as her knees buckled.

"I don't know how long I can last," Ariadne said.

"Let's find out," Alex whispered in her ear before she licked, then bit her earlobe. She turned Ariadne around and pushed her back onto the bed, then stripped off the bikini bottom, finally revealing all of Ariadne's magnificent body.

"Now yours," Ariadne said, as though in a trance.

Alex removed her jeans and boxers and stretched out on top of Ariadne, so they were flesh to flesh along the entire length of their bodies. She reveled in the sensation of Ariadne moving beneath her, in the invigorating scent of her hair and skin, and in that wonderful, provocative mouth as they kissed again.

Her arousal growing by the second, Alex broke the kiss and moved her mouth to Ariadne's breasts.

"Yes! Suck hard." Ariadne gasped.

Alex took one nipple, then the other, and sucked as hard as Ariadne instructed.

Ariadne put her hand on Alex's head and pushed her deeper, harder, onto her breasts. "I love your mouth," she said.

"I'm glad, because my mouth loves the way you feel." Alex continued to lavish kisses down her body, skimming over the apex of her thighs and down her legs.

Ariadne moaned and mumbled something unintelligible. "Please," she finally said, with a desperate urgency.

"Please, what?" Alex was lost in Ariadne's scent.

"I need you."

Alex slid up Ariadne's body, and just as she reached Ariadne's mouth to claim it with her own, Alex entered her.

The sensation made them moan with pleasure, though they never broke the kiss.

"Yes!" Ariadne gasped against Alex's mouth and arched her back. "Please, don't stop."

Alex penetrated Ariadne with a slow, driving rhythm, taking her time, even when Ariadne pushed against Alex's hand and signaled with her body that she wanted harder and faster strokes.

"Not yet," Alex said. She continued to fuck her at her own pace while she slid down Ariadne's body to lick her center.

"Oh my G—" Ariadne grabbed the sheets.

"Not yet," Alex said again. Fucking Ariadne, driving Ariadne crazy, and Ariadne's intense response were going to make Alex come, but she was enjoying her own painful torture too much to let it end. "Turn around," she ordered, but didn't wait for Ariadne to comply. Alex flipped her over and lay on top of Ariadne. She rubbed herself against Ariadne and pushed her own groin against Ariadne's ass.

"Fuck me," Ariadne begged, and groaned into the pillow.

Alex knelt behind her and lifted Ariadne's pelvis. She caressed Ariadne's breasts as she licked and kissed Ariadne's back.

"Now!" Ariadne said, each successive plea spoken with greater urgency and need.

Alex repositioned herself and lifted Ariadne's pelvis higher. She licked Ariadne's already wet center from behind and entered her again.

"I…I'm…" With a loud groan, Ariadne came in Alex's mouth. Alex continued to fuck her gently until Ariadne came again and dropped onto the bed, facedown.

Alex went to lie beside her and kissed and caressed her shoulders and her neck as Ariadne's breathing calmed.

After a while, Ariadne turned over, onto her back, and looked up at her. "That was amazing." She still sounded breathless.

"You're amazing." Alex smiled as she got on top of her. "And beautiful, and…and making love to you is all I want to do, forever."

"I've fallen so hard," Ariadne whispered.

"Show me." Alex reached down and pushed into her again. "Because I can't wait any longer."

Ariadne writhed beneath her as she licked Alex's throat, her ear, and her lips, before reclaiming her mouth for another deep, passionate kiss.

Her arousal was building so quickly Alex knew she was going to come soon.

Ariadne shifted beneath her and grabbed Alex's ass with both hands. "Kneel on top of me. I want to taste you, now."

Alex knelt above her and guided her throbbing crotch to Ariadne's mouth.

Ariadne looked up at Alex and licked her lips provocatively. The expression of want and need in her eyes drove her crazy with desire.

Alex grabbed Ariadne's head and moved it to her aching clit. "You're so sexy."

Ariadne kissed and licked everywhere but where she needed it most, then entered her slowly with her hand.

Alex almost lost her mind; she let go of Ariadne's hair, afraid she'd hurt her, and grabbed the headboard. "Harder, baby." She groaned in pleasure.

Ariadne sucked Alex, as she pumped harder, faster, deeper.

Alex moved in time with Ariadne, and seconds later, she came so hard her whole body went limp in the aftermath. It took a few moments for Alex to orient herself. Finally, she sagged back down onto the bed on top of Ariadne and buried her head in Ariadne's neck.

"Tired already, stud?" Ariadne laughed.

Alex laughed as well. "Don't you sound smug?"

"What can I say? I love to see you weak in the knees."

"In that case, you should know that just looking at you leaves me breathless."

Ariadne kissed Alex as she caressed her back and ass.

That was all it took.

"Okay, I'm good to go again," Alex said.

CHAPTER THIRTY-TWO

Colorado
Two days later

Joanne Grant prepared Monty's lunch like she had every day since they finally started dating. She had always wanted to take care of the man she'd secretly loved for decades, and now that they could finally love each other without inhibitions and fear, she intended to make up for the lost years in every big and little way she could. Preparing a meal for the person she loved and sharing that time eating together had always been her idea of "home" and "family." Joanne set their salads and a basket of fresh-baked bread on the tray and made her way over to his den.

She knocked on the door with her foot. "Lunch is ready," she sang out. "Open up, my hands are full." When no one answered, she repeated herself. "Monty, open up."

Still no answer. Maybe he was in the bathroom. Joanna set the tray on the floor. "Bending over isn't as easy as it used to be," she mumbled to herself as she opened the door and picked the tray up again.

Monty sat in one of the armchairs, his back to her, facing the large picture window that looked out over their view of the Rocky Mountains. He'd seemed unusually content and relaxed since getting the word that TQ was finally dead and Jaclyn was safely home with Cassady.

"Are you listening to music again?" she asked. Although he was wearing earphones, she could hear the music all the way to the door: a violin solo, no doubt the one Cassady had sent him last month from her performance with the Philadelphia Symphony. "I'm sure Cassady would appreciate you listening to her play without risking your hearing."

He still didn't answer as Joanne walked past him and set the tray on his desk. "Lunchtime!" she loudly announced. She hoped that now that he'd seen her he'd remove the earphones, but when she turned around, she saw that his eyes were shut, his head tilted back. Also, he was still in his robe and pajamas, which wasn't like him, though she'd been nagging him in recent weeks to work less and relax more. "How can you sleep with the music so loud?"

Still no answer. Not wanting to scare him, she nudged him gently on the shoulder. "Time to wake up." She reached down and removed his earphones.

"Monty?" she said when he didn't react. "Sweetheart, wake up!" she called out, much louder, and shook him harder. So hard, his head fell forward, his chin resting on his chest.

But he still didn't move.

A chill ran through her, and her heart started hammering so hard she could hardly breathe. "Oh, my God! Monty, are you okay?" She took his head in both of her hands and only then realized that his face was cold and his skin had started to stiffen.

"No!" Joanna wailed in anguish as reality hit home. "No! No! No! You can't leave me!" She broke down, sobbing, as she pulled him to her chest, absentmindedly caressing his hair. "We just started."

❖

Colorado Springs
One week later

The church parking lot was already full, so David Arthur pulled the sedan into an open spot at the curb, then hurried around to open Joanne's door. He'd been her rock since Monty's death, helping to make all the arrangements and making sure that every op, past and present, had been notified with ample time to make travel arrangements. Ordinarily, their mourning the death of an op was a private affair, conducted within their secret campus and attended only by current staff and students. But Monty's legacy and contribution to the organization deserved a wider tribute, and it was only fitting—in light of his own appreciation for family—that the spouses and children of ops be allowed to attend.

She'd hoped there would be a big turnout, which was why she'd chosen to have the wake in the massive cathedral, and she was gratified to see so many cars. Many of those who'd come were clustered in small groups on the front steps, visiting and catching up with old classmates. Misha and Kris were admiring Luka and Hayley's daughter, Landis and Heather were chatting with Cassady, and Gianna and Zoe were catching up with Harper and Ryden. Alex was there, too, with the new woman in her life, and was introducing her around to the others. As she and David neared, the groups split up, and several came over to offer their condolences.

Luka spoke up first. "I'm sorry for your loss. We're all going to miss him."

Misha stepped in. "I mean, who's going to badger me about my speeding tickets and dysfunctional disposition?"

"I can do that." Cassady patted Misha on the back. "My condolences, Joanne. I can't even begin to imagine what you're going through." Cassady looked like she'd been crying. "I already miss him so much." Her voice cracked.

Thank you, everyone."

"He was a good man," Gianna said. "He was like a father to me."

"A very strict and stubborn father, but the only father we've ever known." Landis hugged Joanne. "Let me know if there's anything I can do for you."

"Thank you, Landis. That's very sweet." Joanne had promised herself she wouldn't have a meltdown in front of everyone, but they were all being so supportive she was finding it hard to hold back the tears. She looked past the group in front of her and saw Jack, standing off to the side, dressed in a black suit, as were many of the others. She was wearing shades and staring up at the sky.

"Excuse me, guys." Joanne walked past them and went to stand next to Jack. "How are you?" she asked.

"I should be asking you."

"I'm trying not to have a breakdown."

"Yeah, I bet." Jack continued to stare up at the sky.

"He loved you so much."

"Yeah, I know."

"Do you really?"

"He told me where to find TQ," Jack replied after a long while, still without looking at her. "He never said so, but he wanted me to... take care of her."

"That's right," Joanne admitted.

"He knew I wouldn't rest if I didn't."

"I guess he realized his time was up, and he didn't want to leave you living in fear and anger."

"Uh-huh." Jack ran her hand through her hair and continued to stare up at the sky.

"He made sure you had plenty of backup."

"Uh-huh."

"You were his biggest regret and love."

Jack turned to look at her finally.

"Up until the end," Joanne said, "he regretted not telling you he was your father. And he never forgave himself for not pulling you out of Israel."

Jack looked away. "No one's perfect. He did what he thought was right. Like the rest of us, he was limited by rules and screwed-up laws. He was just another EOO victim."

Joanne saw a tiny tear escape to Jack's cheek.

"He was a good man trapped in a bad situation," Jack said.

Joanne could see how hard she was trying to maintain her composure. She took Jack's hand. "Maybe it's time for new rules."

Jack looked down at their entwined hands. "Yeah, well...I hope you change things for the new generation."

"It's going to take more than me and David to do that. We're going to need someone with a lot more strength than we possess. Someone younger and more potent."

Jack smiled. "Good luck with that."

"It's time." David appeared by her side and took Joanne's arm. "Shall we go in?"

Joanne took a deep breath to steel herself and nodded.

"Join me?" She extended her other arm to Jack.

"It would be my honor."

The church was packed, and as they came down the aisle, familiar faces reached out to her or offered a few words of sympathy. Many she hadn't seen in decades and barely recognized; others had several children in tow, some taller than their parents. They'd come from all over the world to acknowledge the man who'd been their first and only father figure, despite the often horrific missions he'd sent them on, which spoke volumes about their respect for him and the ever-loyal unity of the organization.

As they passed the flag-draped coffin, Joanne paused to lay her hand on the side. "Your family is all here, darling," she whispered. "As I knew they would be."

Beside her, David swiped away a tear as he escorted her to the podium before taking a seat in the front row.

Joanne looked out over the gathering as the cathedral went silent. She took out the piece of paper she'd found in his desk and laid it on the podium. "Montgomery spent his life living in the shadows," she said, "but I want his death to reflect his heart, full of openness and generous light." Her voice trembled. "I know Montgomery was not the easiest man, nor was he the type to wear his heart on his sleeve, but he was a man capable of so much love and respect for the family he created. Not a day went by that he didn't ask how each and every one of you was doing or performing, including those of you who have long gone from the academy and are living your lives all over the planet or retired."

She looked down at the casket. "I have loved Monty from the day I first saw him, but that was back in the day when ops were forbidden to express or give in to their feelings. We didn't express and let our love for each other live and grow until time had started to run out."

Grief took over as she imagined going on without him in the cozy home they'd built together, and Joanne sobbed aloud. It took her several seconds to compose herself enough to continue, but still, not a sound could be heard in the church. "Our time together as a couple was brief, but our love has existed for decades and will only grow stronger in preparation for when I see him again." She broke down again and dropped her head, letting the tears fall freely.

Jack jumped up and ran to her side. "What can I do?" She sounded almost desperate.

"I need to finish this," Joanne replied.

"You sure?"

She nodded. "That's what he wanted."

Jack hugged her reassuringly and took her seat again in the front row.

"Please forgive me," Joanne said to everyone. "I…I." She looked around the room. "He wanted me to read this."

She unfolded the paper and reached into her pocket for her reading glasses. "I know this is not the time or the place for professional announcements, but since I'm already dead, I don't give a damn about what any of you may think."

Low laughter was heard throughout the church.

Joanne's hands shook but she didn't care. "The reading of my formal will, with specifics about my possessions and the future of the EOO, will be conducted by my attorney with only a select few present. That includes the official announcement of who my chosen replacement as chief of the EOO will be. But until that happens, and since I would like to think that most of you made it to my funeral, I want it to be known that I, Montgomery Pierce, hand the position over to my daughter, Jaclyn Harding."

The collective gasp was so loud Joanne looked up from the paper in front of her. Jack had bolted to her feet in shock at the announcement, and all eyes were on her.

"Please, sit down. There's more," Joanne said to Jack, looking over her spectacles.

Everyone immediately hushed, and she waited until Jack had taken her seat. Joanne cleared her throat and continued. "Should Jaclyn refuse the position, I leave it up to Joanne and David to elect a new third for the Governing Trio. I, however, think that there is only one person who can carry my position forward with openness, fairness, and dedication, and that is my daughter. She has been, is, and will always be a much stronger, more capable, and better leader than I could be. I expect everyone to show nothing but respect for her decisions and do everything in their power to make this transition smooth and welcoming."

Joanne paused to look down at Jack before she read the final paragraph. Cassady had her arm around her protectively. "Jaclyn, I'm sorry for keeping you in the shadows and the biggest secret of my life. I wish I could've started over and done better, acted wiser, but…I can't. But please know, I have never loved, worried about, and respected anyone more than I have you. I realize the feelings are not mutual, and rightfully so, but I hope that with time, you can come to forgive me. I have and always will love you. Your father, Montgomery."

EPILOGUE

EOO Campus, Colorado
One month later

Jack walked into the auditorium with Joanne to her right and David Arthur to her left. Everyone fell silent and turned to look at them. Young and old were all there, except for a handful of ops who couldn't be pulled off missions.

The three walked to the front of the auditorium and took their places, with Jack in the middle.

Joanne stepped up to the microphone. "Ladies and gentlemen, Jaclyn Harding has accepted the position of Chief of the Governing Trio. From here on, you will consider her your superior and leader. This new management will decide any and all decisions regarding your life here and your work out there, with Ms. Harding acting as president and therefore having the ability to veto any decision. Ladies and gentlemen, girls and boys, please welcome your new EOO President, Jaclyn Harding."

Everyone got up to applaud, and Cass, who stood in the front row, even whistled.

Jack moved forward to the mic. "Thanks, everyone, for the warm welcome." She smiled, overwhelmed by the warm reception. "Please, take a seat so we can get this over with. I hate public speeches."

The crowd laughed and sat back down.

"Let me start by saying this was not an easy decision. I once ran from this place because I felt unappreciated. Felt I was putting my life on the line for three people who didn't give a damn about me. It took years of hiding and faking my death, doing things I'm not proud of, to realize what I had run from. Sure, this organization gives no guarantees of longevity or happiness, but it does promise a family that will stick together, fight and die for one another, and for the betterment of the screwed-up world we live in. I promise to do everything in my power to be fair. For this reason, I have made certain changes in the EOO policies. First of all, anyone over forty-five can retire with full and generous benefits."

Some in the audience whistled and clapped with enthusiasm.

"Secondly, should you choose to know about your past—where you came from, who your biological parents are, etcetera—you are welcome to that information. I personally know what it's like to crave the truth and sense of past…roots."

"Yes!" some shouted.

"And one last thing. Screw this rule about not being able to get involved or marry within the organization. Love should know no restrictions." She looked at Cass. "I found the love of my life in this place, and so did my father."

❖

Somewhere in Russia
One month later

Jack talked at length to the staff of the orphanage, and nearly every one of them gave the same name when asked whether any of their charges stood out as having exceptional learning skills. Despite her tender age and meager schooling, the little girl could already read and write, and she was rapidly picking up English just from watching American sitcoms and movies. She was also very athletic and hyper, and was always getting into trouble. Jack picked out the six-year-old from across the park. The dark-haired girl was darting around like she'd caught fire, fearlessly chasing four boys.

She approached the girl and waved at her. The girl ran over immediately.

"Hello," the girl said in Russian.

"Hi, I'm Jack," Jack replied in Russian.

"I'm Ksenia."

"Nice to meet you."

"Are you here to decide if you want to adopt me?"

Jack was surprised by her openness and perceptiveness. "I think I already know."

"So, are you or not?" She looked Jack straight in the face.

"Yeah. Yeah, I want to adopt you."

"I think I'd like that," the girl said shyly.

"Why?"

"First of all, because I want to get away from here. And I like your eyes."

"My eyes?"

The little girl nodded. "They make you look like a good person."

"I'm glad you think so."

"So, what are we going to do when you take me away?"

"I'm going to teach you a bunch of new stuff."

"Like what? I'm just asking because I already know a lot."

Jack smiled. "Like what?"

"I can write and read and draw."

"That all?"

The girl shook her head. "I'm good at sports."

"That's great. What else you got?"

"I'm stronger than all the boys here."

"Are you?"

"I can beat them all up."

"Cool."

"So, you see? You don't have to teach me anything."

"I think I do." Jack laughed. "I'm sure I can offer you a few more things."

"Like what?"

"Languages. Math. Manners." Jack ruffled the girl's hair. She had the most amazing blue eyes. "Teach you how to control your strength and temper, all sorts of sports and—"

"How about how to use a sword?" She jumped up and down. "I love swords. The knights have swords."

Jack looked down at the little bundle of wiseass. If she'd been blond, instead of brunette, she could easily have been Cass a couple of decades earlier. "I know just the person who can teach you how to handle a sword like a ninja."

"Ninja!" the girl screamed gleefully. "I want that, but..." She looked at her feet. "I want to be a knight when I grow up."

"That's great, because my friends and I are going to teach you how to protect yourself as well as other innocent people."

"When can we leave?"

"You sure you want to?"

The girl nodded enthusiastically. "If I can be with you and learn all the cool stuff."

"You can be with me as much as you like."

"Okay. Let me get my teddy bear, first." She grabbed the sleeve of Jack's shirt and tugged her toward the dormitory.

"Okay." Perplexed at the girl's fearlessness, Jack followed.

"Where will you take me?" Ksenia asked as she skipped along a few steps ahead.

"To America."

"Okay!" She looked even more excited. "I can speak English, you know."

"Really?" Jack sounded surprised.

"I learned from the TV."

"You're a special little girl, you know."

Ksenia stopped and turned to look at her. "Can I hold your hand?" She extended her skinny arm.

Jack extended hers as well, and the girl placed her tiny hand in Jack's. "We studied America. On the map, it looks very, very big."

"It is."

"So, where are we going to live there?"

"Colorado, with a bunch of other kids."

"That's in the Southwest," she said proudly. "How many kids do you have?"

"Lots." Jack kept being surprised every time the tyke opened her mouth.

"Do you love them?"

"Yeah, I guess I do." Jack surprised herself again with the realization.

"Are they as nice as me?"

"No one is as nice as you," Jack replied.

Jack let the little girl lead her into the building to get her teddy bear. She didn't know how it had been for her father to have to go through this process of choosing children, but now, as Jack walked with this tiny hand in hers, she knew she was making a difference. Not only in the girl's life, but also in lives of the others whom this little girl would one day have to protect and defend. "Welcome to the EOO," she told Ksenia.

"The what?" the girl asked.

"Welcome to my family."

About the Authors

KIM BALDWIN (kimbaldwin.com), a former network news executive, has made her living as a writer for more than three decades. In addition to the Elite Operatives Series, co-authored with Xenia Alexiou, she has published eight solo romantic adventure novels: *Hunter's Pursuit, Force of Nature, Whitewater Rendezvous, Flight Risk, Focus of Desire, Breaking the Ice, High Impact,* and *Taken by Storm.* She's also had several short stories published in BSB anthologies. A 2012 Lambda Literary Award winner and 2011 Lambda finalist, she is also the recipient of a 2011 Rainbow Award For Excellence, a 2010 Independent Publisher Book Award, four Golden Crown Literary Society Awards, eight Lesbian Fiction Readers' Choice Awards, and an Alice B. Readers Appreciation Award for her body of work. She has recorded audiobooks of her own novel *Breaking the Ice,* and the Rose Beecham mystery *Grave Silence.* Kim lives in Michigan but keeps her laptop, camera, and passport handy to travel whenever possible. She can be reached at baldwinkim@gmail.com.

XENIA ALEXIOU (xeniaalexiou.com) lives in Greece. An avid reader and knowledge junkie, she likes to travel all over the globe and take pictures of the wonderful and interesting people that represent different cultures. Trying to see the world through their eyes has been her most challenging yet rewarding pursuit so far. These travels have inspired countless stories, and it's these stories that she has decided to write about. *One Last Thing* is her seventh novel, following *The Gemini Deception, Demons are Forever, Dying to Live, Missing Lynx, Thief of Always,* and *Lethal Affairs.* She is a 2012 Lambda Literary winner, 2011 Lambda finalist, and the recipient of four Golden Crown Literary Society Awards and six Lesbian Fiction Readers' Choice Awards. Contact her at xeniaalexiou007@gmail.com.

Lethal Affairs, Thief of Always, and *Missing Lynx* have been translated into Dutch, and the first two books are also available in Russian. In 2010, *Dubbel Doelwit* (*Lethal Affairs*) won second place among Dutch readers in their vote for best all-time Lesbian International (translated) book.

Visit us at www.boldstrokesbooks.com

Books Available From Bold Strokes Books

One Last Thing by Kim Baldwin & Xenia Alexiou. Blood is thicker than pride. The final book in the Elite Operative Series brings together foes, family, and friends to start a new order. (978-1-62639-230-4)

Songs Unfinished by Holly Stratimore. Two aspiring rock stars learn that falling in love while pursuing their dreams can be harmonious—if they can only keep their pasts from throwing them out of tune. (978-1-62639-231-1)

Beyond the Ridge by L.T. Marie. Will a contractor and a horse rancher overcome their family differences and find common ground to build a life together? (978-1-62639-232-8)

Swordfish by Andrea Bramhall. Four women battle the demons from their pasts. Will they learn to let go, or will happiness be forever beyond their grasp? (978-1-62639-233-5)

The Fiend Queen by Barbara Ann Wright. Princess Katya and her consort Starbride must turn evil against evil in order to banish Fiendish power from their kingdom, and only love will pull them back from the brink. (978-1-62639-234-2)

Up the Ante by PJ Trebelhorn. When Jordan Stryker and Ashley Noble meet again fifteen years after a short-lived affair, is either of them prepared to gamble on a chance at love? (978-1-62639-237-3)

Speakeasy by MJ Williamz. When mob leader Helen Byrne sets her sights on the girlfriend of Al Capone's right-hand man, passion and tempers flare on the streets of Chicago. (978-1-62639-238-0)

Myth and Magic: Queer Fairy Tales, edited by Radclyffe and Stacia Seaman. Myth, magic, and monsters—the stuff of childhood dreams (or nightmares) and adult fantasies. (978-1-62639-225-0)

Venus in Love by Tina Michele. Morgan Blake can't afford any distractions and Ainsley Dencourt can't afford to lose control—but the beauty of life and art usually lies in the unpredictable strokes of the artist's brush. (978-1-62639-220-5)

Rules of Revenge by AJ Quinn. When a lethal operative on a collision course with her past agrees to help a CIA analyst on a critical assignment, the encounter proves explosive in ways neither woman anticipated. (978-1-62639-221-2)

The Romance Vote by Ali Vali. Chili Alexander is a sought-after campaign consultant who isn't prepared when her boss's daughter, Samantha Pellegrin, comes to work at the firm and shakes up Chili's life from the first day. (978-1-62639-222-9)

The Muse by Meghan O'Brien. Erotica author Kate McMannis struggles with writer's block until a gorgeous muse entices her into a world of fantasy sex and inadvertent romance. (978-1-62639-223-6)

Advance by Gun Brooke. Admiral Dael Caydoc's mission to find a new homeworld for the Oconodian people is hazardous, but working with the infuriating Commander Aniwyn "Spinner" Seclan endangers her heart and soul. (978-1-62639-224-3)

UnCatholic Conduct by Stevie Mikayne. Jil Kidd goes undercover to investigate fraud at St. Marguerite's Catholic School, but life gets complicated when her student is killed—and she begins to fall for her prime target. (978-1-62639-304-2)

Season's Meetings by Amy Dunne. Catherine Birch reluctantly ventures on the festive road trip from hell with beautiful stranger Holly Daniels only to discover the road to true love has its own obstacles to maneuver. (978-1-62639-227-4)

Courtship by Carsen Taite. Love and Justice—a lethal mix or a perfect match? (978-1-62639-210-6)

Against Doctor's Orders by Radclyffe. Corporate financier Presley Worth wants to shut down Argyle Community Hospital, but Dr. Harper Rivers will fight her every step of the way, if she can also fight their growing attraction. (978-1-62639-211-3)

A Spark of Heavenly Fire by Kathleen Knowles. Kerry and Beth are building their life together, but unexpected circumstances could destroy their happiness. (978-1-62639-212-0)

Never Too Late by Julie Blair. When Dr. Jamie Hammond is forced to hire a new office manager, she's shocked to come face-to-face with Carla Grant and memories from her past. (978-1-62639-213-7)

Widow by Martha Miller. Judge Bertha Brannon must solve the murder of her lover, a policewoman she thought she'd grow old with. As more bodies pile up, the murdered start coming for her. (978-1-62639-214-4)

Twisted Echoes by Sheri Lewis Wohl. What's a woman to do when she realizes the voices in her head are real? (978-1-62639-215-1)

Criminal Gold by Ann Aptaker. Through a dangerous night in New York in 1949, Cantor Gold, dapper dyke-about-town, smuggler of fine art, is forced by a crime lord to be his instrument of vengeance. (978-1-62639-216-8)

Because of You by Julie Cannon. What would you do for the woman you were forced to leave behind? (978-1-62639-199-4)

The Job by Jove Belle. Sera always dreamed that she would one day reunite with Tor. She just didn't think it would involve terrorists, firearms, and hostages. (978-1-62639-200-7)

Making Time by C.J. Harte. Two women going in different directions meet after fifteen years and struggle to reconnect in spite of the past that separated them. (978-1-62639-201-4)

Once The Clouds Have Gone by KE Payne. Overwhelmed by the dark clouds of her past, Tag Grainger is lost until the intriguing and spirited Freddie Metcalfe unexpectedly forces her to reevaluate her life. (978-1-62639-202-1)

The Acquittal by Anne Laughlin. Chicago private investigator Josie Harper searches for the real killer of a woman whose lover has been acquitted of the crime. (978-1-62639-203-8)

An American Queer: The Amazon Trail by Lee Lynch. Lee Lynch's heartening and heart-rending history of gay life from the turbulence of the late 1900s to the triumphs of the early 2000s are recorded in this selection of her columns. (978-1-62639-204-5)

Stick McLaughlin by CF Frizzell. Corruption in 1918 cost Stick her lover, her freedom, and her identity, but a very special flapper and the family bond of her own gang could help win them back—even if it means outwitting the Boston Mob. (978-1-62639-205-2)

Rest Home Runaways by Clifford Henderson. Baby boomer Morgan Ronzio's troubled marriage is the least of her worries when she gets the call that her addled, eighty-six-year-old, half-blind dad has escaped the rest home. (978-1-62639-169-7)

Charm City by Mason Dixon. Raq Overstreet's loyalty to her drug kingpin boss is put to the test when she begins to fall for Bathsheba Morris, the undercover cop assigned to bring him down. (978-1-62639-198-7)

Edge of Awareness by C.A. Popovich. When Maria, a woman in the middle of her third divorce, meets Dana, an out lesbian, awareness of her feelings brings up reservations about the teachings of her church. (978-1-62639-188-8)

Taken by Storm by Kim Baldwin. Lives depend on two women when a train derails high in the remote Alps, but an unforgiving mountain, avalanches, crevasses, and other perils stand between them and safety. (978-1-62639-189-5)

The Common Thread by Jaime Maddox. Dr. Nicole Coussart's life is falling apart, but fortunately, DEA Attorney Rae Rhodes is there to pick up the pieces and help Nic put them back together. (978-1-62639-190-1)

Searching For Forever by Emily Smith. Dr. Natalie Jenner's life has always been about saving others, until young paramedic Charlie Thompson comes along and shows her maybe she's the one who needs saving. (978-1-62639-186-4)